"When I get married, it's going to be to a man who loves me

and is willing to be a full-time father to my child. I need those things. *Especially* now."

"I can't give you that," Cam said flatly.

"And I'll never settle for anything less," she said quietly.

He shot off the couch and turned away, his hands clenched into tight fists at his side. "I have a right to fatherhood, Pippa. You can't take that from me. I won't allow it. I'll fight you with every breath I have."

Some of her frustration fled. She took a step forward and put her hand gently on his arm. He flinched underneath her touch.

"I'd never take that from you, Cam," she said softly. "I'm merely giving you reasons why I won't settle for a relationship like the one you're offering."

"I want my child safe," he gritted out.

"So do I."

"Then let me take care of you both."

She wondered if he even knew that he was nearly pleading with her.

Dear Reader,

Undone by Her Tender Touch brings with it the end of the PREGNANCY & PASSION miniseries involving four men who are friends and business partners. This was such a fun series to write. I grew to love the characters and regarded them as friends. I wanted them to be happy and to triumph over adversity.

Cam and Pippa have perhaps the most difficult path to their happily-ever-after. Cam has lost it all and has no desire to ever experience that kind of pain again. Pippa challenges him on every level and dares him to give life—and love—a second chance.

Of all the heroines in this series, Pippa occupies a special place in my heart for her resiliency and her determination not to settle for anything less than the absolute best for herself and her child. And the message I leave for you, the reader, is to be exactly as Pippa is. Never settle for less and don't be afraid to go after what you want.

Love as always,

Maya

UNDONE BY HER TENDER TOUCH

BY
MAYA BANKS

Published in Great Britain 2012
by Mills & Boon, an imprint of Harlequin (UK) Limited,
Eton House, 18-24 Paradise Road, Richmond, Surrey TW9 1SR

© Maya Banks 2012

ISBN: 978 0 263 89339 7
ebook ISBN: 978 1 408 97202 1

51-1012

Harlequin (UK) policy is to use papers that are natural, renewable and recyclable products and made from wood grown in sustainable forests. The logging and manufacturing processes conform to the legal environmental regulations of the country of origin.

Printed and bound in Spain
by Blackprint CPI, Barcelona

Maya Banks has loved romance novels from a very (very) early age, and almost from the start, she dreamed of writing them, as well. In her teens she filled countless notebooks with overdramatic stories of love and passion. Today her stories are only slightly less dramatic, but no less romantic.

She lives in Texas with her husband and three children and wouldn't contemplate living anywhere other than the South. When she's not writing, she's usually hunting, fishing or playing poker. She loves to hear from her readers, and she can be found on Facebook or you can follow her on Twitter (@maya_banks). Her website, www.mayabanks.com, is where you can find up-to-date information on all of Maya's current and upcoming releases.

For Huggy Bear

One

She shouldn't be so nervous about catering for a bunch of muckety-mucks, but Pippa Laingley wanted everything to be perfect for her friend Ashley Carter's housewarming.

And really, why should she be nervous? Just because the net worth of the assembled guests was more than the national debt shouldn't be cause for her to sweat. Okay, and there was the fact that Pippa was on the verge of opening her own storefront café and catering business and she needed this to go off without a hitch so there would be good word of mouth and maybe a few referrals.

She spun around in Ashley's huge kitchen, mentally taking stock of what was ready to go out. Where were the damn waiters?

On cue, the door swung open, and a guy who couldn't be more than twenty hustled through. Pippa took one look and groaned.

"Where's your uniform?"

He gave her a blank look.

She sighed and closed her eyes. "White shirt? Black slacks? Nice polished shoes? Preferably well-groomed hair?"

His mouth worked and then he snapped it shut. "I'm sorry, ma'am. I'm the emergency fill-in. I just assumed whatever I needed would be here."

Pippa blew out her breath. "First day on the job?"

"Yeah," he mumbled. "A friend told me about part-time gigs that paid good money. I'm sort of filling in for him."

Her gaze narrowed. Great. She wasn't even getting an official employee. Some moron had decided to skip and had worked a deal with his buddy to split the proceeds for a night's work. No way he was going to handle a room full of people. Which meant she was going to have to wade in and help.

So much for having a nice glass of wine with the girls and gushing about Ashley's new house.

Grabbing the kid by the arm, she pulled him toward the stairs. "Come on. You have to get into something better than that."

He blinked but allowed her to drag him all the way to Ashley and Devon's bedroom. She barreled into Devon's closet and hurriedly riffled through his clothing until she found something appropriate.

"Strip," she ordered crisply.

A dull flush rose up the kid's neck.

The sound of a clearing throat was Pippa's first warning that she and the kid weren't alone.

"Perhaps I should come back later."

The low drawl shivered over Pippa's nape and she squeezed her eyes shut in mortification. Now she and the kid both were blushing fools. She turned to see Cam Hollingsworth leaning lazily against the door, his eyes flashing with amusement.

"Why, Pippa, you cradle robber."

She could never understand why the man always caught her at a disadvantage. She was an intelligent, well-put-together, very articulate career woman. She owned her own business, never took any crap off anyone and people rarely intimidated her. And yet, every single time she crossed paths with Devon's friend, she always made an ass of herself.

No way she was going to let this spiral into a mire of humiliation. She glared at Cam and then stalked over, tossing him the shirt and slacks.

"Get him into this. I need him downstairs in two minutes."

To her utter delight, Cam blinked in surprise. She'd caught him off guard. Then he frowned and looked beyond her to where the kid still stood.

"What the hell? Aren't these Dev's clothes?"

"I need a waiter or no one is going to get food or drink," she gritted out. "He's all I've got. I'm not letting Ashley down tonight and neither are you. So get your ass in gear."

She stomped past him and hurried down the stairs, not waiting to see Cam's reaction to her dictate.

When she got back into the kitchen, she quickly lined up the trays, set wine and champagne glasses out and then grumbled under her breath about having to help ferry food and drinks to Ashley's guests.

She'd asked for three servers. She'd gotten some college kid in need of beer money. Just great.

A moment later, college kid presented himself, and to Pippa's surprise, he'd cleaned up well. The pants and shirt were a bit too large for his lanky frame, but he looked neat and presentable. His hair had been combed back until he looked almost polished.

She gestured him over, shoved a tray of lobster tarts into his hands and then pushed him out of the door toward the living room, where Ashley and Devon were entertaining their guests.

Then she returned to the island and began pouring wine into half the glasses. She filled the rest with champagne.

"Would you like some help?"

She whirled around, still holding the bottle, and darn near tossed the contents onto the floor.

"Help?"

Cam nodded slowly. "Assistance? You look as though you could use it. How on earth did you think you'd manage this on your own? Ashley was nuts for allowing you to cater the event."

Pippa was horrified by the offer and then, as she processed the rest of the statement, she was just irritated as hell.

"I'd hate for you to sully those pretty hands," she snapped. "And for your information, I've got this under control. The help didn't show. Not my fault. The food is impeccable if I do say so myself. I just need a way to deliver it into the hands of the precious guests."

"I believe I just offered my assistance and you insulted me," Cam said dryly.

Her eyebrows drew together. Oh, why did the man have to be so damn delicious looking? Why couldn't he be a toad? Or be bald? Although on the right guy, bald was totally hot. Why could she never perform the simplest functions around him?

"You're Ashley's guest," Pippa said firmly. "Not to mention this isn't your thing. You're used to being served, not serving others."

"How do you know what my thing is?" he asked as he reached for one of the trays.

She had absolutely nothing to say to that and watched in bewilderment as he hefted the tray up and walked out of the kitchen.

She sagged against the sink, her pulse racing hard enough to make her dizzy.

Cameron Hollingsworth was gorgeous, unpolished in a totally sexy way, arrogant and so wrong for her in so many ways, but there was something about the man that just did it for her.

She'd seen him often enough ever since Ashley had become involved with Devon Carter. Cameron and Devon were close friends and business partners in a consortium of luxury hotels and resorts. As Ashley's best friend, Pippa had been to many of the same social events as Cameron. He'd been paired with her at Ashley's wedding, and that had been ten sorts of hell, being close enough to smell him, and him so perfectly indifferent to her.

She sighed. That could be what irritated her the most. He

was a luscious specimen of a male and he couldn't be any less interested in her.

Maybe she just wasn't his type. The problem was, she didn't know what his type was. She never saw him with other women. He was either intensely private or he didn't have much of a social life.

She was itching to shake his world up just a little.

Realizing she was spending far too much time mooning over Cam, she grabbed another tray, took a deep breath to compose herself and then headed toward the living room.

Pippa smiled brightly, hoping her lipstick at least was still visible. The rest of her makeup had probably melted off by now. She made her way through the room, relieved to see that many of the guests now held wineglasses. Cameron had indeed delivered the goods.

"Pip, what are you doing?" Ashley hissed.

Pippa jerked around to see her friend staring aghast at her.

"Hey, Ash, how is everything going? All your guests arrived?"

"Stop acting like the hired help," Ashley said with a frown. "Why are you and Cam walking around serving drinks and hors d'oeuvres? And who's the kid wearing Devon's clothes!"

"Don't get worked up, Ash. It's not good for the baby," Pippa said cautiously.

Ashley folded her arms over the noticeable baby bump—really, it was so adorable—and pinned Pippa with her most ferocious stare. Not that anything Ashley ever did could exactly be called ferocious. Could puppies or kittens be ferocious? "Pip, I asked you to do this because I wanted to help. Maybe get the word out about you, but I didn't want you working yourself silly at my housewarming party. I need my best friend beside me, not serving me!"

Pippa sighed and handed Ashley one of the yummy snacks off her tray. "Look, the help didn't show. All you got is me, the kid wearing your husband's clothes and Mr. Mouthwateringly Gorgeous over there."

Ashley's eyes widened. "Cam? You're talking about Cam?"

Pippa gave her an exasperated look. "I'm damn sure not talking about the infant wearing Dev's clothes!"

"Whoa," Ashley breathed. "I had no idea. I mean, yeah, Cam is hot in a broody kind of way, but I had no idea that was your thing."

Pippa couldn't even look over at him without getting a betraying flutter in her belly. "I'd like to lick those brooding lips," she muttered.

Ashley giggled and then clapped a hand over her mouth. Her eyes sparkled merrily.

"Stop staring at him!" Pippa hissed. "You may as well be holding a sign up announcing we're talking about him."

Ashley turned her back to Cam, a grin still flirting with her mouth. "So how'd you get him to help out? Did you bat those gorgeous green eyes?"

"I don't even know," Pippa said in bewilderment. "He offered. I was kind of rude to him."

Ashley snickered. "You? Rude?"

Pippa glowered at her. "Shut it."

Ashley put her hand on Pippa's arm and rose up on tiptoe to look over her shoulder. "I think I'm being summoned. Seriously, though, Pip. I'm not worried about the food so much that I want my best friend to be the serving wench for the evening. Go put the tray up and join us for a drink."

Pippa switched the platter from one hand to the other as she surveyed the room. There were too many important potential clients to just shrug off such an opportunity. Ashley had given her the chance and she wasn't going to squander it.

"I'll check with you later, Ash. I have mingling to do. Your guests look hungry."

Before Ashley could respond, Pippa was off, wading into the crowd, a bright smile on her face.

"Are you out of your mind?"

Cameron turned to see Devon staring at him as if he was

nuts. Cameron set the empty tray onto the sideboard and grinned at the look of absolute *what-the-hell?* on his friend's face.

"Wouldn't be the first time I've been asked that."

"You're playing waiter tonight?"

Cameron shrugged. "Pippa needed help. She looked like she was close to melting down. I figured that wouldn't make Ash very happy."

Devon frowned as he studied Cameron for a long moment. "I think you're full of crap."

But Cameron ignored Devon as his gaze caught Pippa melting into the crowd. She moved with effortless grace. She was mesmerizing to watch. He tracked her progress across the room as she smiled and greeted many of the guests. She laughed, and irritation sparked that he hadn't been able to hear what it sounded like.

He'd been watching Pippa for months. She'd drawn his notice the very first time he'd seen her. He hadn't actually met her then. They hadn't been officially introduced until the third time they were at the same event. Even then he'd treated her as he treated most people. Cordial politeness. Faint disinterest. But he'd been anything but disinterested.

She hadn't realized it, but he'd marked her from that very first moment. Like a predator marking prey. He watched and waited for that perfect moment. Working up to when he'd take her to bed and lose himself in that satiny skin and silky mane of glossy dark hair.

He could just feel the strands brushing through his fingers and falling down around them both. Her astride him, head thrown back as he pulled her down onto him again and again.

He muttered a foul curse when his body reacted fully to the erotic fantasy. He was at a housewarming, for God's sake. The focus was supposed to be on babies, happy homes, puppies and rainbows. Not how fast he could get Pippa to his house a half mile down the road so they could indulge in a night of hot sex.

He was certain she was as attracted to him as he was to her. Often when she thought he wasn't looking, her eyes glowed warm with lust as she fixed her gaze on him. He enjoyed those stolen glances because that was when he could see the honesty in her eyes.

The rest of the time she hid behind that brassy facade, the take-no-crap-off-anyone exterior. But inside? He was absolutely sure she was warm and gooey and all feminine purr. He couldn't wait to run his fingers over her body and elicit that throaty sound of pleasure.

"Cam, what the hell, man? Hello? Anyone home?"

He blinked and turned to see that Devon was still standing there. He scowled. "Don't you have a wife to tend to?"

Devon shook his head. "Do you have any idea how pathetic you look mooning over her from across the room?"

Cameron's nostrils flared. "I don't know what the hell you're talking about."

"Keep telling yourself that," Devon said with a snort. "Good God. Just go over there and get it done with. And then get a room, for Pete's sake."

"Oh, I'll get a room," he said softly. "She's going to be locked in mine the entire night."

Devon made a strangled sound of annoyance and then turned as if he couldn't get away fast enough. Cam was too busy watching Pippa to care, though. He could see that her tray was empty. Her gaze was searching the rest of the room, a slight frown on her face. She was looking for the kid, and she didn't look happy.

Her brow creased in annoyance, she left in the direction of the kitchen. Cameron picked up the empty tray he'd discarded moments ago and hurried after her.

He found her in the kitchen muttering swear words that would make a sailor wince. He grinned when she threatened to kick the asses of every single waiter who'd stood her up tonight.

"Where's the kid?" Cameron asked.

She jumped, nearly sending the platter she was filling flying in the opposite direction. She whirled around, a ferocious scowl on her face. "Would you stop doing that?"

He held up his hands and took a cautious step back.

"He skipped out," she growled. "He didn't even give Devon's clothes back! How am I going to afford to replace them? The shirt cost more than an entire catering job nets."

Cameron laid his hand on her arm and she went completely still. The slender muscles in her arm rippled and he could hear the quick intake of her breath. He was right. She was satiny soft and yet firm. She either worked out or she was particularly blessed with excellent body tone. He'd lay odds that she worked out. She seemed rather disciplined.

"I'm sure Devon won't miss a white shirt and black slacks," he drawled. "He likely has two dozen more outfits just like it. He's a well-ordered bastard. Not into too much variety, if you know what I mean."

"That's not true," she defended staunchly. "He has a very laid-back wardrobe. Casual. Expensive casual, but still very casual."

Cameron shrugged. "Can't say I've ever made it into his closet."

She suddenly giggled and then stopped herself, but her eyes were full of mirth.

"Glad you find me so amusing."

"It's not you as much as the idea of you poking around in Devon's closet. You have to admit, it's pretty funny."

He rubbed the pad of his thumb in a slow up-and-down pattern above her elbow, and she went quiet again.

"Would you like me to take food out this time or would you prefer I make another round with wine and champagne? Hell, it's Dev's tab. I vote we take some bottles out and let everyone pour up what they like. You and I can circulate with food and watch everyone get wasted."

She studied him a moment, cocking her head to the side. "I never realized you actually had a sense of humor."

He lifted an eyebrow, taken aback by her candor.

Then she blushed and briefly closed her eyes. Just when he thought she'd stammer out an apology, she reopened her eyes and stared evenly at him.

He couldn't help it. He laughed. This time it was her eyebrow that went up.

He pushed in close to her, until their bodies were nearly touching. So close that her scent and soft warmth enveloped him and held him captive.

He brushed his hand over her cheek, pushing back that velvet cascade of hair. And it was every bit as silky as he'd imagined. He wrapped one finger in it, tugging experimentally.

"Here's what I propose," he murmured. "Let's make another pass. Load everyone up on food and drink. Set out a few trays within easy reach and then we ditch this place and go to mine."

Her lips parted and her eyes went glossy, the pale green mesmerizing. "Is that a proposition?"

"Bet your sweet little ass it is."

"Surely you can do better than that."

Both his brows went up.

She narrowed her gaze. "You'll do better or I'm taking my sweet little ass home. Alone."

Ah, but he did love it when she got all sassy.

He leaned in, touched his lips to hers. He cupped the side of her neck, sliding his fingers around the slim column to delve into her hair. He pulled her close, molding his body to hers as he took full possession of her mouth.

Heat slicked through his veins like rapidly flowing lava. He wanted her. To the point of desperation.

When he finally pulled away, they both breathed heavily and her eyes took on a sleepy, drugged look.

"How about I take you home with me and we make love all night long?" he murmured.

She licked those delectably swollen lips. "Now that's better."

Her husky voice shot straight to his gut and he realized he was a short fuse away from taking her right here in his friend's kitchen and damn anyone who saw.

"You get the food," he said in a strained voice. "I'll get the wine."

Two

Cameron pulled Pippa out the back door and the brisk chill of the winter air blew over her ears. She tugged her hand from Cameron's long enough to pull her coat tighter around her, but he quickly reclaimed her wrist, hauling her ever closer to his car.

He stopped abruptly when they got to a midnight-black Escalade. He turned with a frown, still holding tightly to her hand.

"How did you arrive? Did you drive?"

Drive? She didn't even own a car. Nor did she have a license, which was problematic given that she needed a delivery van to cater events.

She shook her head. "Ashley sent a car for me."

He paused, arching one eyebrow. "And how did you get all that stuff here from New York?"

She flushed, feeling as though he were judging her and her abilities.

"I shopped here. Had the wine delivered. Ashley has an excellent kitchen." Pippa should know since she was the one who'd stocked it from floor to ceiling. Ashley was clueless when it came to cooking, but Pippa was working to rectify that.

Cameron opened the passenger door to the Escalade and all

but pushed her inside. "Good enough. It works out perfectly. I'll have a car drive you back to the city in the morning."

With that, he shut the door, leaving her a little disgruntled at how eager he seemed to be to get rid of her before they even had sex.

He stalked around the front, yanked open his door and climbed in, keying the ignition before he'd even settled onto the seat.

Then again, her feminine pride was stroked just a bit over how desperate he acted to get her to his house so the sexing could commence.

She knew he didn't live far. Ashley had commented on the fact that they were now neighbors with Devon's purchase of the new house.

Cameron tore down the driveway, his hands tight around the steering wheel as he navigated onto the paved lane. He drove about a quarter mile before turning into a gated drive. The gate swung open and Cameron accelerated up the winding path to the house.

Pippa couldn't make much out about it in the dark. There weren't any lights on. The mansion loomed in the shadows. It looked unwelcoming. She wondered if it was a hulking monstrosity built from stone like a medieval dwelling. She'd heard Devon tease Cameron about his "cave" and now she was curious.

Just before they got to the house, lights began to flicker on. Pippa realized that Cameron was turning them on remotely from the SUV. She leaned forward, trying to get a glimpse but was prevented as Cam pulled into the garage.

Determined that she wasn't going to succumb to nerves or be caught at any disadvantage, she slid out of the passenger's side and walked around to meet him by the door. He ushered her inside, one hand pressed to the small of her back.

They walked into a sprawling kitchen that made her drool with envy. It was nirvana to someone like her, who'd rather be hard at work over a stove than anywhere else. It was like a showroom, so immaculate that she wondered if anyone ever used it.

He didn't pause or allow her to, either. He pressed ahead, running a gauntlet through a huge living room to the wooden staircase that opened into the foyer where the front entrance was. Tugging her behind him, he mounted the steps. She nearly had to run to keep up.

By the time they made it into the spacious master bedroom, she was slightly winded. But before she could think to catch up, he yanked her to him, molding her body against his. His lips found hers in a ravenous kiss that muddled her senses.

"You are so damn beautiful," he muttered as his mouth skimmed down her jaw to her ear. "You drive me crazy. Across the room. If I even know you're near."

She smiled a tiny smile of satisfaction. What woman wouldn't love to hear this?

He set her apart from him, his hands almost rough on her shoulders. He stood breathing hard, his fingers curled into her flesh.

"We need to discuss a few things before we get carried away."

Though his words came out calm, his eyes blazed with a wildness that made her shiver. He wanted her. There was no question. She'd never been quite so devoured by something so simple as a man's gaze.

"There are things you should know. Things I need to make clear so there is no misunderstanding."

Her curiosity piqued, she lifted an eyebrow and gently shook away his hands. She eased onto the edge of the bed and then crossed one leg primly over her knee.

"Do go on. I'm listening."

He frowned a moment, as if he couldn't quite ascertain whether she was teasing him. Okay, she totally was, but what could be so important that he'd put a screeching halt to some pretty hot foreplay? Not that they'd really gotten that far into anything yet, but the way he kissed made her feel like they were already having sex.

He wiped a hand over his mouth, cupping his chin for a brief moment before he pinned her once more with that glittering gaze.

"I don't do commitment. I need you to understand that if we go to bed together, this is a one-night stand. I won't call you in a few days. I won't call you, period. I'll expect you to leave in the morning. I'll provide a car for your transport back into the city."

She blinked and then she laughed. It was clear it was the very last thing he'd expected her to do. Had he maybe expected her to stomp out of his bedroom in a huff?

Still smiling, she rose and sauntered toward him. When she was in his space, she let her fingers trail up the buttons of his shirt and then to his neck and jaw.

"You're way too serious, Cam," she drawled. "I was hardly anticipating a marriage proposal. If you expect me to cling to you and beg for more when this night's over, you're destined to disappointment. What I want is hot sex. Can you give me that?"

Relief flared in those gorgeous blue eyes and his nostrils quivered as his breaths came in harsh spurts. He was reaching for her when she put a hand to his chest.

"Not so fast, hotshot. I have a few things I'd like to get out of the way, too."

He looked caught off guard and his brows furrowed in quick reaction.

"I assume you've got condoms. Or rather, I'm not assuming anything. No condoms? No sex. I'm clean, in case you're wondering. It's none of your business when the last time I had sex was or who with, but it's been long enough that I've had blood work done since. And I never have unprotected sex."

"I've got them," he growled. "I'm clean. I don't give a f—" He cleared his throat. "I don't care who you had sex with last or when. Been a while for me, too. I'm clean and I always use condoms."

She reached for him, bunching his shirt into her fist, and then she yanked him forward. "Then we have nothing else to talk about," she said just before she dragged him down to meet her kiss.

Lust gripped Cameron by the throat and squeezed until he was light-headed. She was everything he'd imagined and a whole hell of a lot more. She was sweet, spicy, feisty as hell and she was seducing him in his own bedroom.

He loved how impatient she was, yanking at his shirt, pulling it from his pants. He was used to being the aggressor in bed, but it was a huge turn-on to have Pippa boldly staking her claim.

When her fingers slipped into the waistband of his slacks and began undoing the fly, he nearly lost it. He took in deep breaths, trying to calm the adrenaline boiling through his veins.

But then, as soon as the fly was loosened, she reached down and cupped his erection.

Oh, hell.

She leaned up on tiptoe to kiss him, all the while caressing his length with soft, silky fingers. "You know, I'd love nothing more than to drop to my knees and give you the best experience of your entire life, but not the first time. I'm a little more demanding the first time with a new guy. I expect him to rock my world first."

If that wasn't a challenge, he didn't know what was. He pulled her away from him enough that he could walk her back to the bed. He pulled just as impatiently at her clothing until she was wearing nothing more than the sexiest damn lingerie he'd ever seen up close and personal.

She was an absolute siren in black. Black hair and wicked black lacy panties and bra that barely covered her nipples. Her hair was delectably mussed, giving her that just-out-of-bed look. And her eyes. So sultry with liquid eroticism. She wasn't just beautiful. She was bloody amazing.

He tumbled her onto the mattress, enjoying the way she sprawled, laid out for him, a feast for his senses. And he wanted to indulge them all. Touch, sight, smell… He wanted to hear her whisper his name and her throaty sounds of passion. But most of all he wanted to taste every inch of her skin.

Knowing if he didn't take care of the condoms now, he'd never stop in the heat of the moment, he fumbled in the nightstand, pulled out the entire box and tossed it on the bed.

Then he came down over her, captured her mouth and molded her soft body to his.

It was like being struck by lightning. An electrical charge surged through his body, tightening every one of his muscles. She returned his kiss every bit as passionately as he kissed her. Her hands roamed over his back, exploring every inch of his flesh.

Remembering the vivid fantasy he'd had earlier that night, he rolled, taking her with him until she was positioned astride him.

The reality far surpassed the weak fantasy he'd spun in his head. Nothing compared to having her here, in his arms, her thighs pressed to his sides.

"Undress for me," he said hoarsely. "Right here where I can watch."

A wicked smile glimmered on full, kiss-swollen lips. Slowly she reached behind her and began to unclasp her bra. Instead of letting it fall immediately, she held the tiny lace confection to her chest and then allowed the straps to slide down her arms inch by inch.

He was barely capable of breath. The anticipation was killing him. And then finally she pulled the bra away, baring her full breasts to his avid gaze.

And they were perfect breasts. Perfectly shaped. Perfect size. Just the right amount of bounce. Firm. High. Delectable nipples that just begged for his mouth.

"I'll need your help with the panties," she murmured, her eyes flashing mischievously.

He couldn't even stammer out a reply. He nodded, but then right now he'd agree to damn near anything.

She leaned forward, pushing her gorgeous breasts mere inches from his mouth. Then she slid one leg over him so she was no longer straddling his hips. She turned then and began working her panties slowly down her buttocks.

He wasn't at all sure what he was supposed to help with, but he was game. He turned over on one elbow and reached to steady her waist with his free hand, letting his fingers wander down the small of her back, enjoying the feel of so much silky flesh.

When the underwear was down to her knees, trapped there by the mattress, she turned on her back and stretched her legs over his chest.

More than happy to accommodate, he took over, pulling the panties the rest of the way until they came free of her feet. He tossed them across the room and went after her like a starving predator.

He slid over her body, the sensation of skin on skin nearly undoing him. He kissed her neck, nibbled, tasted and teased and then worked down, wanting nothing more than to have her breasts underneath his tongue and lips.

She was utter perfection. Curvy, sweet, not too slim, not too heavy. Just…perfect.

A sigh escaped her when his lips closed over one straining nipple. It was an intoxicating combination of hardness and velvet. Luscious. So very soft. He sucked gently at it, rolling it between his lips. He flicked his tongue repeatedly over the point, bringing it to an even harder bud.

Then he slid his mouth over the hollow between her breasts to the other nipple. For several seconds he played, idly toying with it. She twisted restlessly beneath him, her breaths coming more rapidly now.

"You are so damn perfect," he murmured. "I can't get

enough of you. You taste better than anything you could possibly cook."

He looked up to see her lips form a pout. "You haven't tried my cooking, then," she said. "I'm a wonderful cook."

He laughed. "It was a compliment, or at least it was meant to be."

"I think you're doing just fine without the compliments," she said in breathy delight.

He cupped her breast in his palm, shaping it, watching as the nipple hardened again. "You like this. What else do you like, Pippa? Tell me how to please you."

"Oh, you're doing fine. No complaints here. I love it when a guy takes his time and doesn't just think about his own pleasure."

"Oh, but this is my pleasure," he murmured. "I love touching you. I love tasting you. Love watching you respond. How your eyes go a darker green when you're really turned on. And that little vixen smile that tells me I'm in for one hell of a good time."

"On second thought, keep on with the compliments. I'm liking this very much," she purred.

"Where do you like to be touched?" he whispered.

Her eyes darkened again. She reached for his hand and slid it down her belly to the juncture of her legs. She guided his fingers over her softness to the tiny bundle of nerves at the apex and gently stroked the tip over it.

Then she moaned when he took over himself. Oh, yeah, she liked that. A lot.

He could be just as wicked as she could. Still stroking through the soft, velvet folds of her femininity, he lowered his head and sucked her nipple into his mouth.

She let out a cry and arched upward, her hands tangling in his hair. She was forceful. Nothing dainty about her. She knew what she liked and demanded it. He loved that about her.

He stroked his thumb over her clitoris one last time and

then he pulled his hand away long enough to snag a condom. He leaned down to kiss her as he parted her legs. He wanted it to last, too, but he also knew this wouldn't be the only time tonight. There was no way he'd get enough and he planned to use every single minute she was here to his advantage. Neither of them would be able to walk the next day but he was more than okay with that.

He nibbled at the corner of her mouth. "Are you ready for me?"

She responded by wrapping her legs around his waist and arching upward. He smiled at her impatience.

He planted his forearms on either side of her shoulders. "Guide me in, Pippa. Show me how you want it."

Her pupils flared and then she reached down, circling him with her fingers. She positioned him against her opening and arched just enough that he slid in the barest inch.

They both let out an anguished sound and he could hold back no longer. Flexing his hips, he drove deep. At first he thought he'd hurt her, but then she dug her fingers into his shoulders and all but roared at him not to stop.

He grinned, kissed that ferocious mouth and then began to move in a frantic rhythm. There was no style, no grace. Their lovemaking couldn't be described as polished or smooth. Far from it.

It was animalistic, with Pippa taking every bit as much as she gave. She demanded everything he had and more. He'd never made love to a woman more fierce than her, and he loved every minute of it.

She fused her mouth to his. Then she nibbled at his jaw and moved her mouth lower to sink her teeth into his neck. He'd wear her marks for days and it stroked his male pride to think of someone else being able to see the marks of her possession.

But she wouldn't be without marks of her own. Oh, hell, no.

"Are you with me, Pippa?" he panted out. "I need you with me. I'm close."

"Sooo there," she said from behind clenched teeth. "Go hard, Cam. Don't let up. Please just don't let up."

As if he could.

He let out a roar of his own and began driving into her with powerful, quick strokes. He wasn't aware of anything but her. Only her. Writhing beneath him. Surrounding him with her sweetness. He smelled her, heard her, could still taste her on his tongue. And, oh, man, he felt her all the way to his bones.

"Cam!" she cried out.

Her fingers gripped his shoulders and she shuddered violently beneath him. He gathered her in his arms and let out a shout of his own as his body seemed to fracture and break into about a million pieces.

The next thing he knew he was flush against her, all his weight atop her body. It felt so damn good even though he had to be crushing her. But she wasn't complaining. In fact, she was wrapped so tightly around him that he couldn't have moved if he wanted to.

He lay there several long seconds while he caught his breath, and then with a groan, he rolled to the side so he could dispose of the condom.

When he looked back, Pippa was sprawled rather indelicately on her back, her expression dazed.

"I think you killed me," she murmured. "When can we do it again?"

Three

Pippa dragged her eyes open and stared dumbly at the white cloud enveloping her head. Her body felt as though it had been hit by a freight train, but, oh, man, was it a wonderful feeling.

It took her a moment to realize she was facedown on the pillow. She lifted her head, her hair falling like a curtain over her eyes. Impatiently, she shoved it back and propped herself up on her elbow.

The bed was empty. Well, almost. At the end, her clothing was neatly folded, a nice subtle reminder that she was to depart as soon as she awakened. She wrinkled her nose. Cam certainly hadn't stuck around. She couldn't even tell he'd been in bed with her. No indention in the pillow. No lingering scent. No warmth. Nothing at all to indicate that they'd spent the entire night tearing up those wonderfully luxurious sheets.

With a sigh, she pushed herself up farther, holding the sheet over her breasts. Then she snorted over the realization that she was being unreasonably modest. He'd made himself clear. He wanted no awkward next-morning encounters. She didn't have to worry about him barging in unannounced. And even if he did, it wasn't as if he hadn't seen her boobs already.

Not only had he seen them but he'd licked them, kissed them, nibbled at them and worshipped them over and over.

A shiver stole over her and her skin prickled, her nipples hardening at the memory of just how hard and often they'd made love through the night. She'd be lucky if she could manage to dress herself and get down those damn stairs.

She was tempted to take a really long hot shower. Her last attempt at a shower had been interrupted, and, well, she'd just gotten sweaty all over again. Many times again after that shower with Cam. But he wanted her out and she wasn't going to delay things.

She checked her watch and groaned. It was past nine. She should have been up and out a lot earlier but she hadn't drifted to sleep until well into the morning.

Nothing like wearing out her welcome.

She scrambled out of bed, wincing as all of her muscles protested the movement. Hell, she hurt in places she'd never even used before.

After pulling on her underwear, she slipped the dress over her head and put on her shoes, beating a hasty path to the bathroom to try to do something with her hair. She had makeup in her purse but she wasn't going to bother. She had no one to impress and the car would drop her outside her apartment.

After brushing the tangles from her hair, she twisted it into a loose knot and fixed it in place with a large clip she'd pulled from her purse. She perched her sunglasses on her nose, satisfied that she didn't look like such a fright.

Taking a deep breath, she exited the bedroom and quietly walked toward the stairs. She had no idea if Cam was even here, but the last thing she wanted to do was draw attention to her late exit from his bed.

She tiptoed down the stairs and when she reached the bottom, she was greeted by a tall, somber-looking man who was an indeterminate age somewhere between forty and seventy.

"Miss Laingley, the car is out front waiting to take you into the city."

She winced. "I'm sorry. Has it been waiting long? I'm afraid I overslept."

The older man smiled kindly at her. "Not at all. There's no need to offer an apology. Come, I'll see you out."

He offered his arm, but that was awkward so she pretended not to see and walked ahead of him toward the massive double front doors. She paused when she got there, suddenly realizing she hadn't gotten her coat. With a frown, she turned, only to see the man holding it open for her.

"Thank you," she murmured.

No matter what Cam had said about it being a while, it was obvious she wasn't the first woman he'd given such a spiel to. His butler or whatever the hell this guy was had the whole process way too down pat.

She slid her arms into the sleeves and then pulled the coat closed as the man opened the door. Cold air billowed in and Pippa blinked at the sudden white. Then she smiled. "It snowed!"

"Indeed it did. At least six inches according to the weather."

This time when he offered his arm, Pippa took it to descend the steps. She still had on those toothpick heels she'd worn the night before, and while they were sexy beasts for shoes, they weren't appropriate for icy conditions.

He was solicitous of her the entire way, ushering her into the back of the sleek black sedan that was already warm and toasty. He hung there a moment, staring into the backseat as he held on to the door.

"Have a safe trip, miss."

"Thank you," she murmured.

He closed the door and the driver pulled down the drive that had already been cleared of snow. She turned in her seat, staring back at the house she hadn't gotten a good look at the night before.

It was a hulking piece of construction, but it wasn't as looming or intimidating as she thought it might have appeared. It looked entirely normal. In keeping with the other mansions that dotted this area.

It was, however, extremely private and surrounded by thick

woods on all sides. There was no way to tell the total acreage, but she guessed it was a lot. She couldn't see another house or even the road as they wound their way down the drive.

Yes, it did appear that Cam was Mr. Reclusive as Devon had suggested. Now that she'd had a taste of all that dark, broody passion, it made her wonder just how often Cam ventured out to lure a woman back to his cave.

She nearly laughed. She made it sound like he was the Beast, sulking in his lair while he waited for Beauty. But if anything, Cam was Beauty. The man was sinfully gorgeous and forbiddingly perfect.

And he could make love like a dream. She'd wear and feel the effects of his lovemaking for a week. A sharp tingle snaked down her back, invading her limbs, bringing awareness and arousal all over again.

She gave one last look to the imposing structure as the car turned the final bend of the driveway. Then with a sigh, she leaned her head back and closed her eyes.

Cam stared through the slat in the blinds of his upstairs office as the car bearing Pippa back to the city drove away. For several long seconds, he continued to stare, even when it disappeared from view.

He turned away and stood for a long moment, hands thrust into his pockets. It annoyed and bewildered him that he had no idea what he was going to do next. He experienced a sudden surge of restlessness, an urge to go do something, although what, he had no idea. He only knew that being here, alone, in his too-quiet house was suddenly…unbearable.

He scowled. It was the damn woman. He'd been caught off guard by everything about her. Maybe he'd expected someone more like Ashley. Sweet, shy, innocent, naive, a bit vulnerable, in need of protection. Maybe his ego had been stroked by offering Pippa a night in his bed. Maybe he thought he'd been granting her a favor while indulging in what he'd wanted to do from the moment he'd met her.

Instead, she'd rocked his world. This was a confident, self-assured woman who wasn't afraid to reach out and take what she wanted, and she'd wanted *him*. His ego should be assuaged by that. But he found himself disgruntled because…the damn roles had been reversed.

It was almost as if she had been the one to say, *Hey, I want you but I don't want any strings.* She'd taken control.

He'd acted like an out-of-control, desperate, raging sex fiend. Nothing like the composed, commanding man he liked to present to the rest of the world.

And that…well, that bothered him. A lot.

Shaking his head, he walked down the hall back to his bedroom. He entered hesitantly, which *was* stupid given that he'd seen her drive away, but somehow her presence was still firmly imprinted. He could smell her.

His gaze traveled over the rumpled bed linens, the mussed pillows. One of the sheets was barely clinging to the bed. Most of it was on the floor.

He should have taken her to one of the guest rooms. He didn't bring women to his bedroom. Ever. If he'd actually been thinking the night before, he would have remained downstairs where she wouldn't have breached the areas private to him at all. But the only prevailing thought he'd had was to get her into bed, however fast he could do it.

Lust was a bitch.

A controlling, fickle mistress from which there was no escape. At least not when it came to Pippa Laingley. Maybe now that he'd had her six ways to Sunday, his blood would cool and he wouldn't lose his damn mind every time she came within a hundred feet.

His gut told him this was in no way true, but for his peace of mind, he was going with it.

He walked into the bathroom, wincing at the mess facing his cleaning lady. The shower door was still open. Towels had been discarded on the floor. The countertop was a mess thanks to his impatience. He'd swept the surface bare with a quick hand right before lifting Pippa onto the edge so he could have her again.

There were at least two discarded condoms on the floor.

He gingerly leaned down to toss the one by the sink into the nearby trash can and then went for the one on the floor by the shower. He used a tissue to pick it up and started for the trash can when he noticed something that sent panic knifing through his stomach.

He froze, unable to even process the evidence before him. Then a string of obscenities blistered the air. His stomach balled into a knot. Sweat broke out on his forehead and his mouth went completely dry.

He closed his eyes, willing it not to be so, but when he re-opened them, he saw irrefutable proof in his shaking hand.

The condom had torn.

Four

Pippa was tempted to throw her cell across the street, but only the knowledge that she'd have to replace it kept her from giving in to the urge. What else could possibly go wrong today?

She'd found the perfect place for her bakery and catering business. It was in a nice area. The terms were satisfactory. It had already been outfitted with the necessary facilities. All she'd need was a little remodeling to the front to accommodate eat-in customers and she'd be set.

After so long doing word-of-mouth events, she was ready for a more solid step. One that would give her a steady income versus never knowing when she'd land her next gig. Her meager savings had kept her in her current apartment, but if she didn't start bringing in a regular income, it would be gone in a year.

She was certain she could qualify for a small-business loan, but in order to get the necessary funds, she needed a signed lease. Which she had, at least until her Realtor had called her to inform her that there was a problem.

Suddenly her dreams of cute cupcakes, yummy little pastries, intricately decorated bonbons and delicious-smelling breads evaporated.

She blew out her breath in a cold fog and mounted the steps to her apartment. She fumbled with the lock just as her cell phone went off, which only renewed her desire to toss it into oncoming traffic.

She managed to push inside to where it was a great deal warmer, and after kicking the door shut with her foot, she glanced down at her phone. It wasn't a number she recognized, but given that she'd handed her number out to potential clients, she couldn't afford not to answer the phone.

With a sigh, she punched the receive button and put it to her ear. "Pippa Laingley."

She was in the midst of trying to shrug out of her coat when she heard Cam's voice over the line.

"Pippa, it's Cam."

She paused and then chuckled, leaving her coat dangling from the arm that was bent to her ear. "Well, hello, Cam. What a surprise. I distinctly remember you saying you wouldn't call. To what do I owe this honor?"

"One of the condoms broke," he said tersely.

She quickly switched the phone to her other hand so she could shake away the coat. She left it there in the doorway and walked toward her living room, sure she hadn't heard him correctly.

"Say that again," she said shakily.

She sank onto the couch, clutching the phone tightly to her ear.

There was an indistinguishable sigh and then he said, "The condom we used in the shower. It broke. I didn't discover it until after you'd left. Since we were in the shower, there would have been no…evidence…at the time. I didn't notice."

Her heart lodged solidly in her throat and she closed her eyes. No, she wouldn't have noticed, either.

He'd been insatiable, but then so had she. The very last thing she'd considered at the time was whether the condom had performed as expected. Obviously if it would have happened at any other point, they would have known. But in a shower?

"Pippa, are you there?"

The strident demand shook her from her thoughts.

"I'm here," she said faintly.

"There are things we have to discuss."

She frowned. "Why are you only just now calling me? When did you discover this?"

There was a pause. "I found it yesterday after you left."

"And you're only just now telling me?" she shrieked. "This would have been good to know yesterday when there was something I could have done."

Even as she was furious at him, she wasn't sure what she would have done. A morning-after pill? It would have been a bit late for that, but what did she know about such things? She could have at least done some research and made an informed decision.

"Calm down, Pippa."

The condescension in his tone just pissed her off even more.

"Don't tell me to calm down," she seethed. "You aren't the one who has to live with the consequences of that broken condom."

"Don't I?" he snapped. "If you think an unplanned pregnancy doesn't affect me every bit as much as it does you, then you're delusional. Now quit shouting at me so we can discuss our options like adults."

She bit hard into her lip to prevent the outburst straining to break free.

"Now, I assume from your reaction that you aren't on any sort of birth control."

"No one can ever accuse you of being stupid."

"Cut the crap, Pippa. I get that you're scared and caught off guard. This isn't a picnic for me, either. You taking this out on me helps neither of us."

Realizing she was doing exactly as he'd accused, she went silent, her grip still tight around the phone. She should have thrown it when she'd had the urge. If she had, she wouldn't be having this harrowing conversation right now.

"I think you should move in with me, at least until we know if you're pregnant."

Her mouth fell open and her brow creased in disbelief. "What?"

He sighed again. "Perhaps this isn't a conversation we should be having over the phone. I can pick you up in an hour."

She got her wits back in time to utter a hoarse, "No."

"Then what's your preference?" he asked impatiently.

She put her hand to her temple and dug her fingers into it, massaging the increasing ache.

"Look, Cam, I'm not moving in with you. That's about the most absurd suggestion I've heard. We don't need to talk face-to-face. Right now, I have no desire to see you. I'm in shock. I need time to figure out my options. I don't need you breathing down my neck. If it turns out I'm pregnant, I know where to find you, and believe me, you'll be hearing from me then. Until that point, I'd appreciate it if you just backed off."

"Damn it, that's not what I want. Look, Pippa, I need to know that you and the…baby…are safe. If there is a baby, I mean. The best way to do that is for you to be close where I know you're taken care of."

There was quiet desperation in his voice and an odd detached tone that suggested to her he wasn't even focusing on the real issue at hand. His head seemed to be somewhere else and that annoyed her all the more.

He was worrying about her and a theoretical baby's safety, and at this point she was just worried that there *was* a theoretical baby.

"I don't care what *you* want," she said evenly.

She pulled the phone away from her ear and punched the end button. Then realizing that Cam was the persistent sort, she turned it off and thrust it away.

She sat there for several long minutes, staring into nothing as she tried to absorb the implications of that broken condom. She wasn't stupid enough to laugh it off and say something absurd like, *Who gets pregnant from that one time?* There were any number of pregnant women who'd naively asserted the same thing. She wasn't one of them.

She shot to her feet, needing to do something. Information. Probabilities. She knew the timing was probably good, but she hurried to her bedroom to dig out her diary where she kept information on her menstrual cycle.

Any single, sexually active woman was a moron if she didn't keep track of such things.

She slipped to the page where her last entry had been written and then calculated the days in her head. Then she let out a harsh groan. Could the timing have been any better? Not that she could possibly predict when she was ovulating, but if she went with averages, there was a good possibility that this weekend had been her prime baby-making window.

Okay, so it was entirely possible. The next thing she needed to do was figure out her options, if she had any.

She went back to that damnable phone, turned it on and ignored the cacophony of sounds signaling missed calls, voice mails and text messages. They were probably all from Cam. The man was likely on his way here.

She punched in Carly's number and hoped like hell her friends were available.

A moment later, Carly's sunny voice spilled over the line and Pippa sagged in relief.

"Pip! How's it going? Have your lease all straightened out? I have to tell you I'm so excited for you! How did Ashley's housewarming go? I was so sorry to miss it. I hope she wasn't too disappointed."

Pippa flinched from the onslaught and waited to get a word in edgewise. "Carly, are you free? I need the girls. This is an emergency."

There was a brief silence and then Carly said, "Pip, are you all right? What's happened?"

"I'll tell you when we're all together," Pippa croaked. "Can you call the others?"

"You bet. Oscar's?"

Pippa hesitated. "Yeah, but make sure we get a private table."

"Do you want me to call Ashley?" Carly asked. "Is she still in Greenwich?"

As much as Pippa wanted and needed Ashley there, she wasn't sure if it was a good idea. But she was just selfish enough to see if Ashley would make the trip in for her.

"See if she can make it," Pippa said in a low voice. "But make sure... Tell her I want her to be careful."

"If she knows you need her, she'll be there," Carly said in a comforting voice. "We'll all be there, Pip. You know that."

"Yes, I do, and I love you all for it."

"Give me some time to get everything ironed out and then I'll text you with a time everyone can meet. In the meantime you know you can come over. I only have one appointment this afternoon. You can always hang out here at the salon. I'll even do your nails."

Pippa smiled. "Thanks, Carly, but I'll just meet you guys later. I need to figure some stuff out."

Pippa could practically see her friend's frown.

"I'm worried about you, Pip. Be careful, okay? I'll see you as soon as possible."

Pippa hung up the phone, relief so great she was shaky with it. She had the best friends in the world. Smart friends. They'd be able to help her figure this out.

In the meantime, she wasn't sticking around the apartment in case Mr. Broken Condom decided to make an appearance. The very last thing she wanted right now was to face the potential father of her potential child.

Five

Pippa lengthened her stride as she neared Oscar's. There was a mix of snow flurries and tiny pellets of sleet in the air, stinging her cheeks as she walked.

She'd hoped the cold would bring her around. Make some of the shock wear off. But she was still reeling from Cam's phone call and all that was going to help her right now was an emergency session of the girlfriends' round table.

She opened the door to Oscar's and unwound the scarf she'd hastily thrown around her neck. She scanned the room, relief easing some of the awful tension when she saw her friends already seated in a corner booth way in the back. It was perfect.

As she made her way through the maze of tables, Tabitha looked up and waved fiercely. Sylvia, Carly and Ashley quickly turned. Carly rose as Pippa approached.

She got hugs from everyone and finally she squeezed into the booth beside Ashley, who looked at her with concern.

"What's wrong, Pip? Carly called us all but she wouldn't say what was the matter."

"I haven't told her yet," Pippa said ruefully. "I may be jumping the gun here, girls. But I'm freaking out and need your help sorting through my options."

"Oh, my God, what is it?" Tabitha exclaimed.

Sylvia frowned. She was the older and more serious-minded of the group. Not to mention ultrapractical. She'd have solid advice. Pippa would bet any amount of money on it.

Pippa drew in a deep breath. "I could be... Well, there's at least a slim possibility that I'm pregnant."

"What?"

Pippa winced as all four of her friends exclaimed at the same time.

Ashley's eyes rounded and she stared at Pippa in question. "Oh, Pip, how sure are you?"

"I had a one-night stand the other night." She glanced up at Ashley and grimaced. "With Cam. We left Ashley's party together. He took me to his house and we had sex. *Lots* of sex."

Ashley looked robbed of speech. Sylvia just kept wearing that frown. That damn disapproving frown that reminded Pippa way too much of how a mother would look. Well, Pippa's mother wouldn't look that way. She'd congratulate her daughter on snaring a wealthy baby daddy and then tell her to milk him for all he was worth. Not exactly mother-of-the-year material.

Oh, Miranda wasn't evil. She wasn't even a bad mother. She was just superficial and very mercenary. Pippa supposed she could even admire her mother for being so shrewd when it came to relationships. Miranda Laingley was out for number one and number one only. And she refused to apologize to anyone for it.

"I'm not following," Tabitha said slowly. "Maybe I'm dense here. If you *just* had sex with him, why on earth are you worried about pregnancy?"

"Because one of the condoms broke and the timing is perfect in my cycle," Pippa replied.

"Cam?" Ashley squeaked. "Okay, I knew you were kind of crushing on him, but you and him? Really?"

"You needn't look so flabbergasted," Pippa muttered. "The attraction was mutual, I assure you."

Ashley looked immediately contrite and threw her arms

around Pippa, hugging her tightly. "Of course it was, sweetie. Oh, my gosh, poor you!"

"I'm so unbalanced by all of this. The timing couldn't be worse. Oh, my God, you guys don't even know this yet. With the pregnancy scare, I just blanked it out, but the lease on the building space fell through. I don't have a place for my shop. And now this. I'm trying to get my business off the ground. I have no health insurance and I'm in no way prepared to be a mother. I just want to cry, but I know that solves nothing."

"You cry, honey," Carly said fiercely. "We'll figure this out."

"You know we'd do anything for you," Ashley said. "You all helped me so much when I was going through such an awful time with Devon. I can never repay you for that."

Pippa sniffled, trying to hold back the tears that threatened. "You never have to repay me, Ash. I love you. We all do. I love all of you guys."

"When exactly did you have sex?" Sylvia interjected.

"Saturday night. All of Saturday night. Well into Sunday morning."

Sylvia reached for Pippa's hand. "You can go to your doctor and have him advise you of the alternatives."

"I'll pay for you to go to the doctor, Pip," Ashley said. "I'll take you myself."

An uneasy flutter settled into Pippa's chest. She rubbed absently at the discomfort. It was the way she felt when she imagined taking measures to prevent a pregnancy that could already have begun.

"Pippa?" Sylvia asked gently.

"Oh, God, I feel so stupid," Pippa whispered. "I can't make that kind of decision in an instant. How can anyone?"

"Okay, what is your gut telling you?" Carly asked. "What are you afraid of? Is it the pregnancy itself that scares you? Or is it the idea of being an unwed mother and not being able to support yourself and a baby?"

"You aren't making any of it sound appealing," Pippa muttered.

"You don't have to make a decision right this minute," Tabitha broke in. "Taking a morning-after pill or getting a shot aren't your only options. You could totally wait and see if you even are pregnant and then pursue your options then. Women have many choices these days, Pippa."

Ashley squeezed Pippa's hand and stared urgently at her friend. "If you want this baby, if there is a baby, you have to know we'd help. All of us. You wouldn't be alone. I just want you to make the best choice for you. But whatever that is, you have our absolute support."

Pippa could no longer hold back the tears. They streamed down her face as she stared at her best friends in the world. "I don't know what I'd do without you guys."

"You forget one important part of the equation," Sylvia pointed out.

Everyone looked at Sylvia.

"The father. Obviously you'll have us, but is he going to take responsibility in this matter?"

Pippa nodded. "He would. I have no doubt he would. I told him I'd let him know if I was pregnant and until then to back off. I just had to process all this, you know?"

"Yes, honey, we know," Carly said sympathetically.

"This probably sounds crazy to all of you, but from the moment I realized there was a possibility, everything changed for me. I began to imagine this tiny life inside me and even though I could take a pill and it would all go away…" She took a deep breath. "I'm not sure that's what I want."

She looked up at each friend in turn, but she saw no judgment or condemnation in their eyes. All she saw was unwavering love and support. Determination. Loyalty.

"If… If there's a baby. I think I want it." She swallowed the knot in her throat and then spoke with more conviction. "I know I want it."

"Take some time to get used to the idea," Sylvia advised.

"There's no hurry. You don't have to make up your mind today or even tomorrow."

But Pippa knew the more the initial shock wore off, the more firmly she'd be entrenched in the idea of having and keeping her baby.

Her baby.

Already she felt fiercely protective of it.

Out of the wreckage of her shock and confusion came the very firm realization that she'd never do anything to end the pregnancy. Nor would she ever give up a child she gave birth to. Her possessiveness and the strong surge of love she already felt were shocking in their intensity, especially because she didn't even know if she was pregnant.

If she was, whatever happened, she would keep the child. She'd go to Cam and together they'd work out an amicable solution.

Maybe she was being stupidly naive, but until he showed her differently, she was going to believe wholeheartedly in his sense of responsibility.

Her hands shook as she raised a glass of water to her mouth. After taking a long drink, she put it back down and then leveled a stare at her friends.

"Okay, girls, how long do I have to wait before I can take a pregnancy test?"

Six

Pippa paced the floor of her living room, trying not to stare at the little stick lying on the coffee table just a few feet away.

"It isn't time yet," Ashley said when Pippa stopped and hesitated.

"Why does it have to take so long?" Pippa exploded.

She couldn't take not knowing another minute. The past weeks had been ones of unimaginable stress with Cam breathing down her neck, asking her every few days if she knew anything yet. The last time he'd asked, she'd all but screamed at him to back off. Maybe he'd finally gotten the hint or maybe she'd just sounded that desperate because he hadn't been in contact for the past couple of days.

The hell of it was, he acted concerned. It almost seemed as though he was acting on the assumption that she *was* pregnant and had made it his mission to "check on" her frequently.

He was making her insane.

"It's only been two minutes," Ashley soothed. "It doesn't do any good to sit and stare at it. It won't make things go any faster."

Pippa sank onto the couch. "You're right. It's driving me crazy, though. I just feel it. In my gut. I'm pregnant. And don't tell me it's some psychological crap and that I'm imagining all the symptoms. I'm just telling you that I feel different. My boobs are sore. I'm queasy. My smell is off. Weird stuff gets to me. Like the smell of cupcakes. Who the hell gets sick smelling a cupcake?"

Ashley smiled. "I don't think you're imagining anything, sweetie. Let's wait for the results and then we'll tackle the solution together. Okay?"

Pippa groaned and closed her eyes. The past three weeks had been a form of torture she never wanted to repeat. She changed her mind from day to day. One day she thought having a baby would be great. She and Ashley would have little playmates. On other days she thought she was solidly out of her mind and was terrified by the prospect.

And, well, she felt a little stupid. An unwanted pregnancy at her age? She wasn't some stupid teenager playing around with unprotected sex. She'd always been so damn careful. Always!

She'd never considered herself terribly old-fashioned, but still, she'd preferred to have children within the boundaries of a loving, committed relationship.

"Okay, you can look now."

They both stared at the stick on the coffee table like it was an ugly bug neither of them wanted to get close enough to squash.

Pippa's stomach curled into a vicious knot. "You look. I don't think I can."

Ashley reached over and took Pippa's hand, squeezing hard. "Just remember, that no matter what the outcome, it'll be okay. I promise."

Pippa nodded, then slammed her eyes shut as Ashley reached for the stick. She didn't even want to see Ashley's reaction. Her heart thundered until she could feel it jumping into her throat.

"Pippa," Ashley said gently. "Open your eyes."

Pippa cracked open her eyes to see Ashley's solemn expression. Ashley laid the stick back onto the table, her gaze still centered on Pippa.

"What?" Pippa demanded, unable to stand it any longer.

Ashley's expression told her nothing. Nothing at all! "Am I pregnant?"

"According to the test you are," Ashley said slowly.

Pippa deflated in a whoosh, sagging forward as she reached for the test, wanting to see the confirmation herself. It was a bit blurry and she blinked rapidly to bring it into focus.

And there it was. A big, glaring plus sign that pretty much said, *Yes, you're pregnant.*

"Oh, my God," she whispered.

Ashley looked uneasily at her. "You aren't going to do something crazy like faint on me, are you?"

Pippa managed to close her mouth, but she was numb from head to toe. It was as if Ashley was talking from a mile away and Pippa was having this surreal out-of-body experience. The entire room seemed to slow down and become a big void of white noise.

Pregnant.

With Cam's baby.

Mr. I Don't Do Relationships.

Mr. I Won't Call You.

As screwups went, this one was epic.

She closed her eyes again and groaned. "What am I going to do, Ash? Cam is going to freak. He gave me this long speech about how he didn't do commitment, it was just sex, blah, blah, blah. A baby is definitely a commitment."

"Take a few days. Let yourself come to terms with the shock. Then talk to Cam," Ashley advised.

"I need to talk to him now."

Ashley frowned. "Pip, you're upset. You aren't thinking rationally. The last thing you need is to go up against Cam. He can be… He's intense, okay? He'll bulldoze over you."

"No one's going to bulldoze me. I need to talk to him now. Other than me, this affects him the most. He deserves to know so he can start planning accordingly. It's not like I'm going to wait a week and then suddenly decide not to tell him. The result will be the same no matter when I talk to him, so why wait? Besides, he's been blowing up my phone for weeks now. No sense holding off any longer."

Ashley sighed. "I just don't want you to make any impulsive decisions. He can be persuasive. That's a nice term for it. He can be ruthless."

"I can hold my own with him. I'm not afraid. This is as much his problem as it is mine. I'll be damned if I spend the next week agonizing over my future alone. If I suffer, so can he."

A laugh escaped Ashley and her eyes danced merrily. "Okay, you just convinced me that he won't rip you to shreds and have you for dinner."

"Damn right he won't," Pippa muttered. "If he even tries, he won't ever have to worry about fathering another child."

Ashley laughed again and then impulsively leaned over to hug Pippa. "You know, this is going to be just fine, Pip. We'll be pregnant together for a little while at least. Devon and I will do anything we can to help, and you have Tabitha, Carly and Sylvia. Oh, and my mother. She views you as another daughter, and when she finds out you're pregnant, look out. She'll have you packed in so much bubble wrap you won't be able to breathe."

Pippa grinned. "I love your mama."

"And she loves you."

Pippa sighed and then rose from the couch. "Not to be rude, Ash, but I need to do this before I end up losing my nerve. I just want to get it over with so I don't have to live with unnecessary stress."

"Get your coat, then. We'll ride together over to Cam's office and then I'll have the driver take me home."

"Thanks, Ash. For everything. For holding my hand and being with me so I didn't have to do this alone."

Ashley hugged her again. "I seem to remember a time when you held my hand a lot longer."

"Okay, let's do this," Pippa said as she went for her coat.

* * *

Cam sat staring out his office window. There was a mixture of rain, sleet and snow, although soon the temperatures would drop enough that it would turn entirely to snow. His mood was as foul as the weather.

He'd largely ignored work even though he'd been a steady presence in the office. He sat in on meetings with Devon and their other two business partners and friends, Rafael de Luca and Ryan Beardsley. Their newest hotel, the flagship resort for the newly formed merger between Tricorp and Copeland Hotels, was coming along at a rapid pace. Things were on the upswing. He should be on top of the world.

But the past weeks had been the worst sort of hell as he tortured himself with the thought of Pippa being pregnant. The thought that she wasn't taking care of herself, that something would happen.

Worry, guilt and anxiety had taken over his every waking moment and his dreams, as well. And he only had himself to blame. He should have never given in to such temptation. He damn sure should have been more careful with the birth control. He should have just left Pippa the hell alone.

Then he wouldn't be sitting here feeling gutted with worry over losing something precious for the second time in his life.

The fact that he hadn't heard from her should have reassured him. Because if she was pregnant, he would have heard. She'd promised to let him know, and he trusted her to do that. Nothing about her had led him to believe otherwise.

But the longer he went hearing nothing, the crazier he got.

It had become a regular habit since their night together for him to reach into his desk drawer—the only one he locked—and pull out a small folding picture frame.

It contained two photos. One of Elise and one of Colton.

He stood staring at them now, his fingers tracing the lines of Elise's smiling face. Colton was merely a day old in his picture. Tiny. Wrinkled. Still red and he had a misshapen cone head, but Cam had never seen such a beautiful sight in his life.

All these years later, just looking at the two people he'd loved and lost had the power to stop him breathing.

He couldn't do it again. He couldn't bear it. He didn't want to set himself up for that kind of agony. He'd never wished for anything as hard as he wished for Pippa not to be pregnant.

With each day that passed without him hearing from her, some of his tension eased. He could breathe a little easier.

She wasn't pregnant. He had to believe that.

His secretary buzzed him, interrupting his thoughts.

"Mr. Hollingsworth, there is a young woman here to see you. She doesn't have an appointment."

"Did you get her name?" Cam asked impatiently.

His secretary put him on hold to inquire. Why the hell hadn't she asked already? He was about to tell her he wasn't to be disturbed when she came back on.

"Pippa Laingley. She seems sure you'll agree to see her."

There was a disdainful sniff in Mrs. Milton's voice that told Cam she'd probably already tried to get rid of Pippa.

"She would be right. Send her in at once."

Cam shot to his feet, his gut in knots as he fixed his gaze on the door. A moment later, Pippa showed herself in, pausing at the threshold as she searched the room for him.

He watched her closely, examining her every nuance, searching for a sign that she was in some way…different. His hands knotted into tight fists but he kept them behind his desk, not wanting her to see how on edge he was. His instinct was to go to her. He wanted to haul her into his arms and hold on tight. Promise her that things would be all right. But he'd learned long ago that nobody could make those promises.

He had to play this cool if he had a prayer of making it through this encounter.

"Pippa," he greeted. "Sit down. Please. Would you like something to drink?"

As she drew closer, he could see the paleness of her features. The shadows under her eyes. She even looked as though she'd lost weight. With sudden guilt, he realized the past weeks had been far more stressful for her than they had been for him.

"I hope I'm not interrupting something important," she said quietly. "I had to come and see you right away."

The knot grew larger in his stomach and he swallowed hard so his voice wouldn't crack.

"Not at all. I'm all yours. What would you like to discuss?"

He cringed at the obliviousness in his tone. No one was that stupid. Denial didn't make everything go away. Dread mounted with every breath until he wanted to just yell at her to say what it was she wanted to say.

"I'm pregnant," she said baldly.

Something inside him withered and died. Dismay weighed down on him like the heaviest of burdens. Grief welled deep in his chest and he stood there, motionless, because if he so much as twitched, he'd crack and crumble right there in front of her.

Finally managing to find his voice and his composure, he asked, "Are you certain?" But he knew she was. There was no denying the truth in her eyes. If only he could go back.

She nodded grimly, then hesitated. "As certain as I can be without a doctor's confirmation. I took a drugstore test. They're supposed to be ninety-nine percent accurate, or something like that."

He cleared his throat. "I'm sure it's right. We knew it was a distinct possibility."

She stood there, her hands shoved into her coat, her uneasiness obvious.

"Are you all right? Have you been well?"

He hated the distance in his voice even as he embraced it, wanted it. He didn't want the intimacy that two people who'd created a child should have and enjoy. He hated that she'd already adamantly turned down his offer—or rather, his demand—that she move in with him. Not that he could blame her. He was certain he came across as some unbalanced freak. Pushing her away, then yanking her back.

But as badly as he didn't want to allow himself any sort of closeness with her, he had to be certain she was provided for. That she had everything she needed, the best medical care, emotional and physical support. He couldn't have anything happen to her...their...*his* child. Never again.

Maybe it was the coldness of the arrangement that had put her off. Maybe she wanted...more. He cringed even as he thought it, but marriage? Maybe it was the best solution. A practical solution. She'd certainly benefit and he'd get what he most wanted. Peace of mind.

"I'm just tired. And worried," she admitted. "It will be better now, regardless. It's just a relief to finally know so that decisions can be made."

Alarm skittered up his neck, prickling every one of the hairs. "Decisions? What kind of decisions?"

She lifted one shoulder in a shrug. He really wished she'd take that damn coat off but he wasn't certain he wanted her to stay. He damn sure knew he didn't want her to leave. What a mess this entire situation was.

Deciding to take charge, he took a step back from his desk and turned sideways, keeping her in sight. "We have a lot to work out. I will have a lawyer draw up papers. We should think about living arrangements."

She held up a hand to stop the flow of conversation. Her other hand went to her temple and rubbed even as she shook her head.

"I refuse to have any sort of a conversation about my future or your future or the baby's future in some damn office where who knows what can be overheard. I'm still struggling to come to terms with this. I just thought you should know, so that maybe you'd have time to come to grips with this, as well. I thought we could talk later. After we've both had time to think. I just... I just needed to tell you. I couldn't wait."

"I don't think—"

She raised her gaze to meet his and her eyes sparked with quick anger. "I don't care what you think. I'm going now. If you'd like to discuss this later, you can come to my apartment. Right now I'm going to have lunch. Alone. I'll be home by six."

If she'd just been snappish and churlish he probably would have wanted to wring her neck. But what he saw was a woman valiantly trying to maintain control. She was rattled—every bit as rattled as he was—and it looked as if she would shatter at any moment.

He couldn't push her. It would be unconscionable. Even as the thought of allowing her to walk out without having anything settled made his stomach knot. It was all he could do to slowly nod his agreement.

"All right," he said quietly. "I'll be at your apartment at six. Don't worry about dinner. I'll bring something."

Seven

It shouldn't have surprised Pippa to find Cam waiting for her on the stoop of her apartment, but when she looked up and saw him there, her eyes widened in shock. Then she checked her watch, wondering if she'd lost more time than she'd thought on the walk home. But nope, he was just really damn early.

He was wearing a long coat, but no hat or scarf, and his hair was damp from the drizzle that still couldn't decide on whether it wanted to be snow or not. His mouth was drawn into a grim line, but his expression softened when he saw her. She could swear she saw relief glimmering in his eyes.

She quickly dug into her pocket for her keys and mounted the steps. He moved to the side, frowning as she fumbled with the lock.

"Did you walk all this way?"

She pushed open the door, welcoming the instant warmth. Cam came in behind her and helped her with her coat before removing his. She started to take them, but he shook his head and asked, "Where do you want them?"

She gestured toward the closet door. "There is fine."

She waited until he'd finished and then led him into the living room.

"You didn't answer my question. Did you walk all the way home in the rain? It's frigid out there."

"Just the last ten blocks. I rode with Ashley to your office and then hopped a cab to the restaurant where I had lunch. There was little sense in getting one home since it's so close."

His frown didn't go away but he eased his large frame into one of her too-small chairs. He looked enormous in her tiny living room. His presence overpowered everything else and she had the instant sensation of not being able to breathe.

He seemed nervous and on edge. Guilt for her earlier unreasonableness ate at her. She'd been a bitch with the way she'd dumped the news on him at his office and then left in a snit.

He dragged a hand through his hair, then glanced her way again. "I know I'm here early, but perhaps you'll understand my impatience to get this matter settled."

"Settled?" she echoed. She eased down onto the edge of the couch. She should be offering him a drink or…something… but somehow it seemed silly because neither of them cared for observing social niceties at the moment. "I don't see that this will ever quite be settled. It's not something to *be* settled."

He sat forward, his body language tense and impatient. He dragged a hand through his hair several more times as he seemed to be trying to figure out what to say next.

"I'd like to know your plans."

She gave a jerky laugh, then closed her eyes because she was teetering on full-on bitch mode again. "You and me both. You have to give me a break, Cam. I only just found out this morning."

"Do you want the baby?"

"Yes!" she said fiercely. "Yes," she said again, calmer this time. "I've battled that question constantly over the past weeks, and no matter how stressed, worried, panicky or dismayed I may currently be, I do want this baby."

Was it relief that flashed in his eyes? It was hard to tell because the rest of him was so intense.

She rose, unable to sit still another moment. She paced

away, keeping her back to him for a long second before finally turning to face him once more.

"I don't have a plan, Cam. Does anyone ever plan for something like this? Obviously I'm going to need your help. I don't have health insurance."

"You'll have the best available care," he cut in.

Her shoulders sagged forward. "Thank you. I've been trying to get my business started and health insurance is one of those pesky little details I haven't sorted out yet."

His expression was somber, his eyes serious. "You won't have to worry there. I'll want you and our child to be well taken care of."

Okay, maybe this wouldn't be so bad. He seemed to be taking it all very well, and moreover he was being exceedingly accommodating.

"I don't expect you to support me," she said quickly. "The health care is more than generous. I have some savings. It's enough until I get my business up and running."

She paced back and forth as she assimilated her thoughts. The very last thing she wanted was for him to think she expected a gravy train since she was having his child. There'd be too many damn strings attached anyway.

"Surely we can work out a suitable arrangement between us." She looked up then to find him staring at her. "Will you want to be…involved? With the pregnancy, I mean. Some men aren't interested. Well, Devon is with Ashley, but I know some have no desire to go to things like doctor's appointments and stuff like that, and it's okay, really."

She was babbling endlessly and the strange thing was, the more she talked, the angrier he seemed to get. His brows drew together until his face resembled a thundercloud.

"Just wait a damn minute. I *will* be involved. I have the *right* to be involved in this pregnancy."

She blinked. "Well, okay. I wasn't saying you couldn't be. Just that I thought maybe you wouldn't want to be."

His expression grew fiercer. "You thought wrong."

"Cam, look. I'm not too sure what I'm doing here. I'm trying to be civilized and cooperative, but you've got to help me. You're sitting there glaring at me and I have to tell you I'm this close to completely losing my mind."

The words rushed out in shaky succession and her hands trembled as she clasped them in front of her.

Cam cursed softly and rose to stand in front of her. "Sit down. Please."

She hesitated only a moment before allowing him to guide her back to the couch. He curled his hand around hers and gave it a gentle squeeze.

"Now, here's what I think we should do. First we'll get you to a doctor so that we can make sure you're in good health and everything is okay with your pregnancy."

She nodded. That much she could deal with. Going to the doctor was a logical first step. At least one of them was capable of rational thought.

"Then I think we should get married."

So much for rational thought.

Before she could ask him if he'd lost his mind he put a finger to her lips. Then he heaved in a deep breath almost as if he was having to convince himself every bit as much as her.

"Just hear me out. We can get married, have separate living arrangements—or rather, quarters. My house is large enough for us to share without tripping over each other. You'd have your space. You'd be provided for. But most important, I could be assured that you and the baby were safe."

She gaped incredulously at him. "Are you insane?"

His eyes narrowed.

She yanked her hand away from his and pushed upward to her feet. The room was too small. She felt caged and like her world was spiraling out of control.

"Don't be unreasonable, Pippa."

She swung around. "Unreasonable? Cam, three weeks ago you told me in no uncertain terms that you wouldn't call me, that this was just sex and you didn't do commitment. Well, guess what. Marriage is a big freaking commitment!"

"I wasn't suggesting we have a relationship," he said tightly.

Oh, this was just going from bad to worse.

"What are you suggesting, then?"

"A mutually beneficial partnership. You and our child will be well provided for and I'll have peace of mind."

Her brow furrowed. "Peace of mind for what, Cam? I feel like there's something huge I'm missing here. You keep harping on wanting to be sure me and the baby are safe. That we're provided for. Look, I appreciate that. More than you could possibly know. It touches me that you aren't turning the other way. I just don't understand your adamancy here. What are you so afraid of?"

Silence fell. So pronounced that she could hear them both breathing. Pain flashed in his eyes and his lips tightened. Then as if someone had flipped a switch, his face became impassive. His expression gave nothing away.

"Isn't that enough?" he finally asked. "That I'm willing to step up here? That I want you and our child to have the protection of my name and everything else that goes with it?"

Slowly she shook her head. "No. It's not enough."

"It was damn well good enough for you three weeks ago," he growled. "You didn't want anything but a night of sex, either, so don't make me out to be the bastard here."

"This isn't about you!"

It came out as a near shriek and she put both hands to the sides of her head in frustration. For a moment she stood there, eyes closed, her nostrils flaring as her breaths blew out in angry puffs.

When she reopened her eyes, Cam was staring at her, concern etched into his brow. "Pippa..." he began.

"No, just listen to me for a minute. Please," she begged. "You made yourself clear before we went to bed together. You were honest. I was honest. But things have changed in a huge,

huge way. What I wanted then isn't what I want *now*. And no, I'm not asking you for anything. I need you to understand that. *I've* changed. My *priorities* have changed.

"You were right. That night I wanted sex. With you. I was attracted to you. I wasn't looking for more. A relationship isn't what I want or need at this stage of my life. But I'm pregnant now. And there is no way I'm going to shortchange myself or my child by entering into a cold, loveless relationship for the purpose of convenience. When I get married, it's going to be to a man who loves me and is willing to be a full-time father to my child. I need those things. *Especially* now."

"I can't give you that," Cam said flatly.

"And I'll never settle for anything less," she said quietly.

He shot off the couch and turned away, his hands clenched into tight fists at his side. "I'll be damned if I watch you marry another man when you're pregnant with my child." He turned back around, raw anger lighting his eyes. "I have a right to fatherhood, Pippa. You can't take that from me. I won't allow it. I'll fight you with every breath I have."

Some of her frustration fled. She took a step forward and put her hand gently on his arm. He flinched underneath her touch but she curled her fingers tightly into his skin. There was something terrible and painful in his eyes. Something that knotted her stomach and made her want to soothe some of the torment she sensed within him.

"I'd never take that from you, Cam," she said softly. "I'm merely giving you reasons why I won't settle for a relationship like the one you're offering."

"I want my child safe," he gritted out.

"So do I. I love this baby already. I've lain awake at night imagining its future. I'd never do anything that wasn't in his or her best interests."

"Then let me take care of you both. I don't want anything to happen to you. Move in with me. If you won't marry me so my child has my name, then at least move in with me so you're both provided for."

She wondered if he even knew that he was nearly pleading with her. As vehement as he was that he could never give her what she wanted or needed from a relationship, he seemed just as determined to tie her to him.

She let her hand slide down his arm until she caught his fingers and laced them with hers. "If I agreed to this, I could never respect myself. If I have a daughter, I want her to know she never has to settle for second best or nothing at all. If I'm going to teach her to be strong and resilient and self-reliant, I can hardly have settled in my own life."

He tensed again as if to argue, but she squeezed his hand. "No, listen to me, Cam. Neither of us wanted this. We sure didn't plan it. Think about what you're doing here. Our emotions are heated. Neither of us are thinking straight. Don't do something we'll both regret. That speech you gave me three weeks ago speaks to the heart of you. That's what you want. Not marriage. Not the inconvenience of a wife underfoot when the last thing you want is commitment. Because you know what? Sooner or later I'll resent you for not being able to give me what I want. And it'll eat away at me until I hate you for it. What kind of environment is that for our child?"

His lips thinned. He looked as though he wanted to argue further. But he remained silent, his hand in hers as they stared intently at each other.

"I'm willing to let it go for now," he said grudgingly. "But there are things that I will want to do to ensure your safety and you're just going to have to deal with it."

She lifted an eyebrow in question. "What on earth is your obsession with safety? I can't live in a bubble. You can't hover over me for the next eight months."

"The hell I can't."

"What are you so afraid of?"

It was the second time she asked the question and for a moment she thought he might actually respond.

But he went silent again, his eyes darkening.

"Will you at least let me move you into a more secure apartment?" he asked.

She shot him an incredulous look. "What's wrong with the apartment I have?"

"It opens to the street. There's no security. The steps are dangerous, particularly in winter."

She blew out a frustrated breath and shook her head. "There's nothing wrong with this apartment. And by the time I'm bigger, winter will be long gone. I like my apartment. I like the location. This is the area where I want to try to start my café. Besides, I can't afford more than what I have right now."

"I don't give a damn what you can afford."

"Well, I do. I can't just halt my life and allow you to sweep in and take care of me until the baby's born. What would I do afterward?"

"I wouldn't just quit because the child was here," he said in outrage.

"Please just stop," she begged. "We're getting nowhere. I'm tired. I'm stressed. I honest to God want to go to bed and cry."

He looked horrified by the possibility. Instant regret flashed across his face, and she knew, she knew deep down, that they weren't really the two people who stood here so volatile and on edge. They had been pushed beyond their endurance. The past weeks had put enormous strain on them both. They just needed time. And distance. A better perspective. Anything but standing here in her apartment arguing endlessly.

"I think you should just go now," she said gently. "We both have a lot to process and we're both too raw to have a sane, intelligent conversation. We're going to have a long eight months together. Let's not start it off by arguing endlessly over details."

"I'm sorry," he said gruffly.

To her surprise he pulled her into his arms. She rested her forehead against the hollow of his throat and closed her eyes.

"I didn't intend this to happen," he said in a quiet voice. "I would have given anything at all for it not to. But it's a reality and it's something we must both come to terms with. Like you, I want this child very much. I have to know you're both safe. Grant me that at least."

She nodded against him before pulling away.

He grimaced and checked his watch. "I didn't bring dinner as I said I would. I was in too big a hurry to get here. I know you're tired and upset, but perhaps we could order in and have a quiet dinner together."

"Would it offend you if I only wanted to crawl into bed and go to sleep? Fatigue is killing me so far."

He looked as though he might argue and then he simply nodded, touching her cheek before he walked past her to the door.

Eight

"So when exactly were you going to tell me the news?" Devon asked in an irritable voice.

Cam turned to find his friend leaning against the door frame of his office.

Even though they shared a suite of offices, Cam hadn't seen his friend in quite some time. With his other partners, it was understandable—ever since they'd gotten married, Rafe and Ryan spent most of their time overseeing projects on their respective islands where they'd settled with their wives. But Cam had to admit that he'd avoided Devon ever since the night he and Pippa had left Ashley's housewarming. Pippa was very good friends with Ashley, and Ashley was nothing if not intensely loyal. She'd probably already filled Devon's head with all the ways in which Cam was a first-rate jerk.

Cam sighed and motioned Devon in with a wave of his hand. Devon ambled forward and dropped into one of the chairs in front of Cam's desk.

"Well?"

Cam swore under his breath and took a seat in his leather executive's chair. "Well, what? I'm sure you know the whole bloody story by now. With the way Pippa's avoiding me, you probably know more than I do at this point."

Devon raised an eyebrow. "Avoiding you? Don't tell me that fatalistic charm of yours is an epic fail?"

"Charm has nothing to do with it," Cam bit out.

"Evidently."

Cam sighed. "Did you just come to put the screws to me or do you actually need something?"

"More like I was wondering why my best friend doesn't bother to tell me he knocked up my wife's best friend."

Cam winced and closed his eyes. "Christ, Dev, you think I set out to do it on purpose? You of all people should know this is the very last thing I'd ever want."

Devon slowly nodded. "Yes, I do know. Which is why I found this all a bit strange."

"It was supposed to be a one-night thing. I was attracted to her. She was attracted to me. Things kind of came to a head the night of your housewarming and we went to my place."

"You brought a woman back to your cave? I knew you had the hots for her but didn't think you were serious about taking her back to your place."

The utter disbelief in Devon's voice annoyed Cam. It wasn't as though the decision was earth-shattering.

"It made no sense to drive back into the city and get a hotel or go back to her place when my house was a quarter mile away."

"Of course," Devon said mockingly.

"Whatever," Cam muttered. "The point is, this was not planned. In fact, the effort was made to prevent it. Unfortunately, the damn condom broke and here we are, both about to be parents. She isn't any more thrilled about it than I am. I mean, with the way it happened. Hell, I'm making it sound like neither of us wants this baby. We do. We just don't agree... Well, we don't agree on anything so far."

"I'm sorry to hear that," Devon said sincerely.

Cam waved the sympathy away. It did him no good at this point. "Have you seen her? Has Ashley said anything about her at all? She's avoiding me and it's starting to piss me the hell off."

Devon cleared his throat. "Pippa was out at the house the other night. She's pretty upset at the moment."

Cam sat forward. "Upset about the pregnancy? Has she changed her mind about having the baby?"

Devon held up his hand. "Slow down. Nothing like that. As far as I know, she's taking the pregnancy very well. Things aren't going so well for her business plans, though. Apparently the lease she'd signed for her shop fell through and she's not having any luck finding anything else suitable. She's on a pretty tight budget, and now with a baby on the way, she's starting to panic."

Cam swore long and hard. "Damn fool, stubborn, mule-headed female. All she had to do was agree to marry me. Or move in with me. She had options. A hell of a lot of options."

Devon stared at him like he'd lost his mind. "Marry you? Move in with you?"

"I know what you're thinking, and yes, I'm obviously out of my mind. But damn it, Dev, all I can think about is what if something happens? Something I could prevent? I just need…"

"I know, man," Devon said softly. "So what are you going to do?"

"Hell if I know," Cam muttered. "What is there to do? She doesn't seem to want anything to do with me. At least, not yet. And I've tried—really tried—to give her the space she seems to want and need, but I'm getting impatient here. I've tried to call her. Arrange dinner. She always has something else to do. She was supposed to tell me when her next doctor's appointment is but so far I've heard nothing. I need to know she's safe and is taking care of herself and the baby. How can I do any of that when she won't agree to see me?"

"Try letting go of the past and stop allowing it to over-shadow every single thought and decision. You can't change the past, but you can sure screw up your future."

Red-hot rage clouded Cam's vision. His fingers curled into tight fists and he sat there, refusing to even look at his friend because he knew Devon meant well but he also knew he'd do or say something he'd regret if he wasn't careful.

How the hell could Devon possibly understand? He wanted to tell Devon that he wouldn't be so quick to give advice if something happened to Ashley and their child, but he couldn't be so cruel as to even make Devon contemplate such a future. He wouldn't do it to his worst enemy.

"I'm sorry," Devon said, regret heavy in his voice. "No one expects you to ever forget. I just think at some point you have to be willing to move forward and take a chance again."

Cam nodded curtly, still refusing to look Devon's way.

"Look, if it's any consolation, Pippa is mostly devoting her time to trying to get her business started. Ashley's been helping her come up with ideas. I doubt her avoidance is personal. She's stressing because now that she's pregnant, she feels even more pressure to get her business off the ground so she can provide for her child."

"She wouldn't have to stress if she'd just accept help from me," Cam growled.

"Have you offered? And I mean in a no-strings kind of way?"

"Maybe my mistake is in asking her. It occurs to me that when given the opportunity to say no, women will, if for no other reason than to be contrary."

His mood brightened considerably as he warmed to the idea that had just taken root.

"The trick is not to ask but just do. Wouldn't you agree, Dev?"

Devon gave him an uneasy look. "You're on your own, man. Don't ask me to get involved. I'm not going to help pave the way for you to have your nuts painfully removed."

"Chicken," Cam drawled.

"Hell, yeah. I'm chicken. I know what side my bread is buttered on. I've discovered in a very short time that Ashley's happiness or sadness has a direct bearing on my own."

For a moment pain sliced through Cam's chest, robbing

him of breath. He envied Devon with a ferocity that left him bereft. Devon was happy. He'd discovered the joys of marriage and the love of a woman. He was looking forward to fatherhood with the innocence of a man who didn't realize that happiness was fleeting. That everything could change in a moment's time. And that you could go from being on top of the world to hell in the blink of an eye.

Cam knew. And if he had any say in the matter, he'd *never* know that kind of pain again.

"But I'll wish you luck," Devon said cheerfully. "If nothing else, you'll provide me with entertainment."

Cam sat back in his chair. "You underestimate me."

Devon studied him for a long moment and then pushed forward in his chair. "What exactly do you want here, Cam? You say you don't want a relationship. Don't want commitment. Don't want anything resembling a permanent situation. And yet you're pursuing Pippa relentlessly and are frustrated by the fact that she's giving you precisely what you want, which is a pass on all of the above-mentioned things."

Cam's eyes narrowed. It was a damn good question and one he didn't have a ready answer to. Nor did he really want to examine all the reasons why he was pulling marriage proposals out of his ass. "I want to do everything in my power to make sure she and my child are safe and taken care of."

Devon sighed. "You can't protect them from everything. Bad things happen. You can't live your whole life expecting disaster."

For Cam, the conversation was over. He ignored Devon's remarks and steered the conversation to business. But Pippa was very much on his mind, and even as he discussed the latest progress on the resort in St. Angelo, he was already formulating his idea on how to rein Pippa in.

The sooner he was certain of her safety and well-being, the faster his own life would get back to normal. And he'd keep telling himself that until he damn well believed it.

Nine

Pippa dug her hands deeper into the pockets of her coat and hunched her shoulders forward as she hurried down the sidewalk toward her apartment. Snow flurries blew furiously around her and the wind cut ribbons across her body, chilling her to the bone.

She clamped her elbow down on her purse when the wind blew it up and then readjusted the strap over her shoulder so it was crossways over her body.

It had been a dismal day in a long line of dismal days, and to make matters worse she was battling morning sickness and overwhelming fatigue. It disgusted her how much she needed to sleep in order to feel human.

She rounded the corner and breathed a sigh of relief. Just two more blocks and she'd be home. As soon as she got inside her apartment, she was going to put on her jammies, curl up with a cup of hot chocolate and then sleep for about twelve hours.

What a party animal she was. She was one happening chick. From having endless energy and being able to function on just a few hours of sleep a night to not being able to hold up her head unless she got about fourteen hours in. Pregnancy had turned her into a pathetic, boring lump.

She was so deep into her thoughts that she wasn't immediately aware of the car pulling to a stop on the street beside her. When she did notice, her heart lurched and she stepped hastily back. Just as a hand curled around her elbow.

She let out a startled cry and then quieted when she saw who it was who held her.

"Cam, you scared the life out of me!"

"Get in," he said tersely. "It's freezing out here."

"It's just a block and a half to my apartment!"

Ignoring her, he steered her toward the open car door and she sighed as a wave of warm air hit her square in the face. Okay, so maybe riding the rest of the way wouldn't hurt. She slid across the seat, Cam getting in after her. He shut the door and gestured for the driver to pull away.

"You haven't returned my calls," he said in a clipped voice. "You have an uncanny knack of never being at home when I come by. Your friends, amazingly enough, have no idea where you are at any given time."

The sarcasm made her flinch, but guilt made her wince even more.

When the car didn't slow as they passed her apartment, she leaned forward. "Right here! My apartment is right here."

"We aren't going to your apartment."

She sank back against the seat and sighed wearily. "Look, I know I've been avoiding you. I'm not offering any excuses. But, Cam, please, I cannot deal with you tonight. I'm tired. I'm in a terrible mood. I'll only make you crazy."

To her surprise, he cracked a smile. "At least you're honest."

The sudden change in his demeanor unbalanced her. He was so damn…appealing…when he smiled.

"Where are we going?" she asked irritably.

"Somewhere I think your mood will be much improved."

"Cryptic bastard," she muttered.

To her annoyance, his grin widened. But just as quickly, his brows drew together and he turned to face her fully. There was no anger in his eyes, but there was most definitely determination. Oh, yes, he was clearly telling her that he'd finally cornered her cowardly butt and he wasn't going to let her go this time.

"What gives, Pippa? Why won't you return my calls? I thought we had an agreement. I don't even know when your doctor's appointment is. Or have you already been?"

She frowned. "Of course I haven't. I told you that I'd let you know so you could come with me."

"You said a lot of things that haven't exactly come to fruition," he said darkly.

"I've been busy," she burst out in frustration. "I've got a lot on my mind, including how the hell I'm going to support a baby. Much less myself. I'm stressed beyond your imagination, Cam. Cut me some slack here. Your life may not change so much but mine sure as hell will."

His eyes grew stormy and his lips tightened into a fine line. She knew she'd gone too far. She knew she'd been careless with her words. She wanted to bite at someone and he was the unfortunate victim because he just happened to be in the wrong place at the wrong time. Not that it was entirely her fault. She could be at home where she wouldn't annoy anyone but herself. But he'd played Mr. Kidnapper and Mr. One Thousand Questions, so in her mind he deserved what he got.

Only he didn't deserve it and she knew it. He'd made the effort. He was doing and saying all the right things. Sort of. But it had been hard for her to come to terms with her pregnancy and what it meant for her. How did anyone do a complete one-eighty in their life and just keep on trucking? Maybe some people managed it, but Pippa wasn't one of them.

"You think you're the only one struggling with this, Pippa? Let me tell you, it sucks not knowing what the hell is going on with you. It sucks not to know if you're okay, if the baby's okay, if there still *is* a baby. Would you like living with that kind of uncertainty?"

Guilt gnawed at Pippa like a hungry beast. He hadn't deserved her avoidance, and maybe, just maybe, if she had been more willing to include him, they could have tackled this whole thing together instead of her worrying incessantly about how she was going to manage alone.

"I'm sorry, Cam."

She leaned forward and then threw her arms around his broad shoulders, hugging him tightly. He stiffened at first as if he had no idea how to take the impulsive gesture. Then he gradually relaxed and put his arms around her, as well.

She hugged him fiercely, burying her face in his neck. It felt good to just hold on to someone stronger than herself because she needed that support.

"I'm sorry," she said again. "I'm no good at this. You don't deserve the way I've treated you, Cam. I'm so sorry."

He gently pulled away and put a finger to her lips. His eyes were soft and so focused on her that she shivered. "How about we just make a pact going forward," he said gruffly. "Don't leave me out of the loop and stop avoiding me."

She nodded, and settled back into his arms.

He stroked her shoulders in a soothing pattern and then said close to her ear, "I've got a surprise for you that I think will alleviate some of this stress you've placed yourself under."

She pulled away, hating to leave that comforting haven, but she wanted to know what the heck he was talking about. He must have seen the obvious question in her eyes because he shook his head.

"We'll be there soon. It isn't far from your apartment."

With that cryptic remark, he closed his mouth and settled back against the seat. He pulled her into his side and directed his gaze out his window as they navigated through traffic.

Just a few more blocks up, the driver slowed and pulled to the curb in front of an upscale cluster of retail businesses. Cam opened his door, stepped into the cold and then reached back for Pippa's hand to help her out.

As soon as she stepped onto the pavement, her gaze went

to the shop on the corner of the busy intersection. Her mouth fell open as she saw the sassy storefront sign.

Pippa's Place. Catering Done Your Way.

It was sort of perfect. Hot pink. Flashy. Contemporary. And girlie! It fit her to a T.

She dropped his hand and surged forward to stare into the window. The inside was immaculate. Already set up with a seating area to the left and a large counter with a display for all the yummy things she'd fill it with. There were two registers at each end of the counter.

"Holy crap, Cam, what have you *done?*"

She whirled around to see him standing there, a smug smile of satisfaction on his face.

"Would you like to go in and see if the rest meets with your approval?"

He held up the keys, dangling them in front of her like the proverbial carrot before the donkey.

"Oh, my God, yes!"

She snatched the keys from him and hurried to unlock the door. She nearly squeaked her delight when a bell above the door jingled, signaling her entrance.

The inside was beautiful. The walls had even been decorated with pictures of cupcakes. Cupcakes everywhere. How could he have possibly known what suited her so well?

"Ashley helped," Cam said, as if reading her mind.

"I can't believe you did this," she whispered.

He gestured toward the doorway to the back. "Better go check out your kitchen and see if it passes inspection."

She let her hand slide along the countertop as she rounded the end. She could *so* see herself inside this place. Could practically smell the mouthwatering delicacies she'd prepare.

She burst into the kitchen and came to an abrupt halt as she took in the perfection before her.

Lining the surfaces of the countertops were rows and rows of top-of-the-line appliances. There were multiple stainless-steel ovens, two huge refrigerators and a huge freezer in the back.

Everything she could possibly want or need was right here. In her kitchen. In her shop.

Her knees wobbled. The practical part of her knew she should refuse all of it. She couldn't afford any of it. She shuddered to even think of what the lease cost. She hadn't even inquired about this property because she knew it was out of her reach.

The other part of her chafed at refusing such a generous gift. Cam had put a lot of time and effort into giving her the perfect place to work. She would be the biggest bitch in the world if she threw it back in his face.

"Do you like it?"

Her chest caved in at the thread of insecurity in his voice. There was no way she was refusing his gesture. No way she'd put them solidly back to square one again. If he was so willing to try, then she'd damn well do the same.

"Like it?" she choked out. "Oh, my God, Cam, I love it!"

For the second time, she threw herself into his arms and hugged him with all her strength. He took a step back to steady himself and laughed as she wrapped herself around him.

She closed her eyes as relief poured through her. This was the answer to all her problems. She could start work immediately, or at least as soon as she got all the red tape taken care of. But permits and the like were the easy part.

"I'll make this a success," she said fiercely. "I won't let your investment go to waste."

Carefully, he extricated himself from her hold and then palmed her shoulders as he stared into her eyes.

"This isn't a damn investment. It's a gift. I've prepaid the rent for two years. Plenty of time for you to get on your feet and start realizing a profit."

"I can't believe you did this for me," she said quietly. "After the way I've been acting. I don't know how to thank you. You can't possibly know how much stress this takes off me."

He sent her an admonishing look. "This gift does come with strings. You'll give me two promises. One, you'll stop avoiding me so we can work together on the issue of your pregnancy. Two, you'll hire enough employees that you won't be spreading yourself too thin."

A helpless smile worked over her mouth. He was too cute when he was all stern and forbidding. "I promise." With the money she wouldn't be spending on a lease, she'd be able to afford to hire actual employees!

He hesitated a moment, his hands sliding down her arms in the gentlest of caresses. "I may not be able to give you what you want or deserve, Pippa, but what I *can* give you is yours without reservation. You carry my child and I'll do anything at all to keep the both of you safe and happy."

How easy it would be to love this man who swore he had no love to give. He seemed so determined to keep her at arm's length and yet he exhibited caring at every turn.

Unable to resist, she moved into the circle of his arms, leaned up and pressed a kiss to those firm lips. His breath caught and held, his body going tense against hers. No matter what he said, he wanted her. But she refused to use that attraction against him.

"Thank you," she said again, before slipping away.

He made a grab for her hand, catching only her fingertips as she stepped back. "Let's go eat dinner. We have a lot to catch up on and I'd love to hear your plans for the shop."

It was an offer of friendship, one that warmed her even as it left her bereft on the inside. They could have so much more. She ached for more. But it was something at least.

Maybe all she'd ever have from him at all.

She smiled up at him and squeezed his hand, lacing her fingers more tightly with his. "I'd like that."

Ten

The next morning when Pippa left her apartment, she noticed a car parked directly in front of her walkway and a driver leaning against the passenger door. As soon as he saw her, he straightened and reached to open the door to the backseat.

"Miss Laingley?" the driver queried. "Mr. Hollingsworth wishes me to drive you to your shop and anywhere else you need to go during the day."

Pippa blew out her breath in a sigh. Okay, this was taking things a bit too far. She'd allowed him to give her the shop. She hadn't wanted to be ungrateful. But providing her a car and driver when she had only a few blocks to go?

As if sensing her hesitation, the driver dug his cell phone out of his pocket and hastily punched a button. Then he thrust it in her direction. She stared back in puzzlement as he closed the distance between them, holding the phone out to her.

"He said to call him if it looked as though you'd refuse," the driver explained.

As she took the phone, she heard Cam's deep voice over the line. She put it to her ear.

"Take the car, Pippa. It's cold, the sidewalks are slippery and it's supposed to snow later today."

She smiled in spite of herself. There was something about his gruff concern that was endearing. "Cam, you can't keep doing things like this."

"Can't I? I thought we came to an agreement last night. Are you already calling off our truce?"

Oh, the man was slick. How neatly he turned this back on her. By refusing, she was the bad guy and he was only trying to provide for the mother of his child.

"Oh, all right," she muttered. "But, Cam, quit it. No more. You've already done way too much."

His amusement was readily evident as he replied, "I believe that's for me to decide."

He rang off and she was left standing there holding the phone while the driver waited expectantly for her to get in.

Grumbling about hardheaded males, she ducked inside the car and waited for the driver to walk back around to his side. When he got in, he thrust a business card over the seat.

"This is my cell number," he said. "Any time you need to go anywhere at all, no matter the distance, you're to call me. Mr. Hollingsworth's orders were quite explicit. He doesn't want you out in the cold on the sidewalks. Weather's supposed to get nasty."

She glanced at the card and saw that the driver's name was John. She shook her head but leaned back as they pulled away. "Okay, John. I'll be a good girl. Somehow I also think you have orders to rat me out if I don't use your services."

He had the grace to blush as he glanced in the rearview mirror. "Yes, ma'am, I do. Sorry, but Mr. Hollingsworth pays my wages so I answer to him."

She chuckled. "Far be it for me to be responsible for you losing your job. I promise to call when I need a ride."

He nodded his approval, then refocused his attention on the traffic.

It had begun to sleet, and she was suddenly really glad she wasn't out in it.

A few minutes later, he stopped in front of her shop and hurried out to open her door for her.

"Remember to call when you're ready to leave," he urged as he handed her onto the sidewalk.

She waved and made a dash to the door. To her surprise, it was unlocked. Had she been a complete idiot the day before and not locked back up when she and Cam had left? She groaned, wondering if she even had any of those lovely appliances left.

She pushed open the door, hit the light switch and then jumped two feet into the air when all her girlfriends popped up from behind the counter and shouted, "Surprise!"

She let out a shriek, dropped her keys and then staggered sideways, her hand flying to her chest to calm the rapid uptick in her pulse.

"Oh, my God, you guys scared me!"

Ashley, Tabitha, Carly and Sylvia hurried around the counter and immediately surrounded her, hugging and fussing over her.

Carly squeezed her in a huge hug. "We're sorry. We just wanted to help you celebrate the new place!"

Pippa stepped back and stared into her friends' excited faces. "How did you even know? And how on earth did you get in?"

Ashley smiled. "Cam called me. He thought you might like a surprise. He dropped a key by the house early this morning."

"The place is awesome, Pip!" Tabitha exclaimed. "I can so totally see your customers out here sitting and enjoying your yummy treats."

An insistent honk interrupted the women's celebration. At first Pippa wrote it off as normal street traffic, but the horn kept blaring and the women turned, frowns on their faces.

A young man, who couldn't be more than twenty, stood outside the door waving frantically to them.

"What the heck?" Pippa murmured.

"Be careful, Pip!" Sylvia cautioned when Pippa went toward the door.

The women crowded around as she opened the door to stare out.

The guy grinned, then gestured toward the street.

"Oh, my God," Carly breathed.

Pippa stared in shock at the brightly decorated delivery van parked in front of her shop.

It was perfect. Absolutely perfect. How on earth could Cam have pulled this off?

Just as with her store sign, Pippa's Place was splashed in hot pink across the side of the white van. There were lavender, yellow and orange flowers surrounding the lime-green tagline: Catering Done Your Way.

"Here are the keys," the guy said with a grin as he held them out to her.

She held out her palm, tears filling her eyes as she stared in astonishment at her delivery van. It was too much.

Her friends crowded in behind her, hugging and squeezing her as they squealed in excitement.

"Let's go for a ride!" Tabitha suggested.

Sylvia's eyes lit up. "Ohhh, let's do it!"

"Don't you have to have a commercial license or something?" Pippa asked. "Or any license at all?" she added with a laugh.

Ashley chuckled. "How would I know? I think you're supposed to hire someone to drive it for you, but hey, we should totally try it out."

Pippa grinned, excitement overtaking her. "Okay, let's do it. Last one in is a rotten egg."

Laughing like hyenas, the women ran to the van, oohing and aahing as they jumped in.

Pippa climbed into the driver's seat and inserted the key into the ignition. Before she cranked the engine, she turned and shot them all pointed glances. "If any of you rats me out to Cam, I'll murder you. That means you, Ash. He'd have a cow if he knew I was driving around the city without a license. I'd have to endure endless lectures on safety and God only knows what else."

Ash blinked innocently. "Who's Cam?"

"Let's go, Pip!" Sylvia said from the seat next to Pippa.

Pippa started the van and then carefully pulled into traffic.

"Turn on the radio," Carly called from the back. "Put something good on."

"I'll do the radio. You drive," Sylvia said as she leaned forward.

Soon the van streaked along the streets of the city, the radio blaring as the women laughed and sang along. Okay, so this was the most fun Pippa'd had in longer than she could remember. This pregnancy thing wasn't so bad. Nothing had changed. Except for the fact she was going to be a mother.

But she still had good friends. Her career was finally going places. And some of the worry was gone.

She had Cam to thank.

Cam, who swore he couldn't give her a damn thing. Cam, who swore he didn't do commitment, wouldn't call and only wanted sex. She nearly snorted. He sure didn't act like a man who wanted to distance himself.

"Let's drive to Oscar's for lunch," Tabitha said. "My treat today. Then we can head back to your shop after and make cupcakes."

Pippa grinned. It sounded like a perfectly wonderful plan to her.

She LOVED it. You did good, Cam.

Cam read the text from Ashley and smiled despite himself before sliding his phone back into his pocket. He felt a pang as he imagined Pippa's eyes lighting up when she saw the van. He could well picture how beautiful her smile was and how radiant she looked now that she was pregnant.

He curled his hand into a tight fist, then rubbed it over his chest in an attempt to dispel the uncomfortable sensation.

But it wasn't something he could wipe away any more than he could wipe Pippa from his thoughts. He was consumed with her every waking moment and there wasn't a damn thing he could do about it.

Eleven

Pippa stood on her stoop until she saw Cam's car coming down the street. Then she hurried to the curb to wait as it came to a stop.

She slid into the passenger seat, cupping the sundress she wore firmly to her rounded abdomen so the ends wouldn't billow up. The city was on the cusp of spring. Still raw and windy, prone to chilly rains and the occasional snow flurry, but today the temps had soared into the sixties and the sun shone brightly, a promise of what was to come.

The past few months had been…nice. It seemed too tepid a word, but it fit. Accepting friendship from Cam had been hard—it was still hard. There were times when she could so see them together long-term. Then it was almost as if Cam realized how close they were getting, and he would back off and erect the wall between them once more.

Today, though? Today was special, and in her heart of hearts, she hoped their relationship would move forward just a bit. How could it not? Today they'd "meet" their child and for the first time see the tiny little life inside her.

"Are you nervous?" Cam asked as he drove toward the clinic where Pippa had her regular checkups.

Pippa took a deep breath. "Maybe?"

Cam smiled indulgently and reached over to squeeze her hand. "Still want to find out what we're having?"

She nodded. "I do. I have to know. I want to be able to establish that bond early. Figure out a name. I can start buying clothes and decide how I want to decorate."

She didn't even realize she had drifted off into a dreamy smile until she became aware of Cam watching her.

"Have you given thought to what you'd like? Are you hoping for a boy or a girl?"

She grinned ruefully. "Depends on what day you catch me on. Yesterday I was sure I wanted a boy. Today I'm leaning toward a girl. What about you?"

His eyes went bleak for a moment. She watched his Adam's apple bob up and down as he swallowed. Then he attempted a smile, but it was lame at best.

"I think I'd like a daughter."

"Really? I thought guys always wanted sons."

His eyes grew dimmer. "No. I think a daughter would be great. A little miniature Pippa. All that dark hair and green eyes."

Her cheeks grew warm and she smiled at how pleased he seemed over the idea of having a daughter who looked like her.

A moment later, they pulled into the clinic's parking garage and Pippa's stomach burst into nervous flurries.

"Oh, my God," she breathed. "We're going to find out in just a little while."

Cam smiled faintly, then reached over to squeeze her hand again. "Let's go do it."

Maybe it was her nerves, but Cam looked like he'd rather be anywhere but sitting in the tiny room where the sonogram tech was about to perform the scan. He looked...tormented. There was raw emotion in his eyes and he kept glancing toward the door like he was seriously contemplating bolting for it.

She bit her lip and controlled the urge to reach for his hand. He wasn't even paying her any attention. He kept eyeing the tech and growing more uneasy by the minute. Instead, she took several calming breaths as the tech rolled her gown up and tucked it just over the slight swell of her belly.

She flinched when the cool gel smoothed over her skin and then the young man smiled at her as he placed the wand over her belly.

She strained closer as the blob took shape on the screen. Tears burned her eyelids when the tech explained that she was seeing the beating heart. She glanced over at Cam to see him equally awestruck. But there was such deep sadness in his eyes that she wondered what he could possibly be thinking.

Several long minutes later, the tech moved the wand again. "Ready to see what flavor of baby you're having?"

"Oh, yes," she whispered.

"Let's take a look here. Hopefully we won't have a shy one. Oh, hello! No shyness here. Look at the little guy."

Pippa sat forward as she stared in amazement at the tiny appendage that clearly signaled the baby's sex. "Oh, my God, it's a boy! Cam, we're having a son!"

Her excitement dimmed when she caught sight of Cam's expression. And then to her shock, he simply got up and walked out of the room, leaving her on the table with the image of their son still vivid on the monitor.

Cam walked straight out of the building. He shoved at the door, needing freedom, needing air. Tears burned his eyes and he was desperate to get as far away from anyone as possible.

The sunlight assaulted his senses. A cool breeze blew over his face, freezing the unshed tears in place. The knot in his throat was so big he didn't have a prayer of taking a breath. So he stood there, chest burning, throat so raw that it felt like he'd swallowed a razor.

A son. Another son.

Why couldn't it have been a daughter? No threat to the memory of Colton. And it wouldn't seem so damn much like he was replacing his first son with another. How could he even bear to look at this child, knowing he'd lost one before?

He fumbled for his cell, punched in his driver's number and then gave a terse order for him to collect Pippa from the clinic. He was being the worst sort of ass. He was walking away from her when she needed him the most. But he couldn't pretend. He couldn't smile and be excited when he felt like he was dying all over again. He wouldn't stand there and suck the joy from her.

After making sure John would take Pippa home, he turned and walked back to where his car was parked. In the past couple of months, he'd been staying more in the city so he could be closer to Pippa, but right now he wanted more than anything to retreat behind the iron gates of his Connecticut estate.

"He just left?" Pippa asked in bewilderment.

John looked discomfited as he led Pippa to where he'd parked the car. "I believe something urgent came up, Miss Laingley."

"Like what?" she demanded. "What could possibly be more important than this? And he couldn't simply tell me he had to leave?"

The more she pondered the matter, the more pissed she got. She was working herself into a righteous fury as John ushered her into the waiting car. All the way home, she fumed. This should have been special. They should even now be celebrating. Instead, she was on her way home alone not knowing what the hell kind of bug was up Cam's ass.

The past couple of months had been terrific. Cam had lightened up. He had seemed to relax his guard around her and didn't act so freaking stiff and uptight all the time anymore. They'd had fun together. If nothing else, they had become friends and for the first time Pippa hadn't looked to the future with gnawing uncertainty that somehow Cam wouldn't be in it for the long haul.

So much for that assumption.

What the hell was wrong with him?

John pulled up to her apartment but Pippa sat in the back-seat for a long moment. Frowning, she leaned forward. "John, where did Cam say he was going? Do you know where he is now?"

"I believe he's returned to Greenwich."

Home? *Home?* What the ever-loving hell? This big emergency brought him home? Oh, hell, no. She'd had about enough of his volatile moods.

She sat back with a bounce. "Take me to Greenwich, John."

John did a double take in the rearview mirror. "Pardon?"

"You heard me. Take me to his damn cave."

"Perhaps it would be better if you called first. Mr. Hollingsworth doesn't like to be disturbed when he's in residence."

"I don't give a damn what Mr. Hollingsworth likes," she said sweetly. "Either you drive me or I'm taking a cab the entire way."

With a resigned sigh, John pulled back into traffic.

She stewed for another hour, and by the time they rolled up the long winding driveway of Cam's home, she was in a foul mood. He'd messed up everything and she was going to hear what his excuse was or else.

When John stopped in front of the house, Pippa was out before he could open his own door. She marched up the steps, considered knocking, but then decided if she came all this way she wasn't going to chance that he wouldn't answer.

She shoved the door open and went inside.

"Cam?" she yelled belligerently. "Where the hell are you?"

She stood a moment, waiting for him to appear, but she was met by resounding silence.

"Cam!" she yelled louder. "Get your ass down here!"

A moment later she heard footsteps and then he appeared at the top of the stairs, his brows furrowed.

"What the hell are you doing here, Pippa? Is something wrong?"

If it wouldn't take so much effort, she'd march up the stairs and punch him. He had the nerve to act like he'd done nothing?

She shook her head, her fingers curling into a tight fist. She was already fantasizing about decking him.

"You ruined the most exciting thing that's ever happened to me and you have the nerve to ask if anything's wrong?"

He descended the stairs in a slow, methodical manner, his footsteps sounding ominous in the quiet. When he reached the bottom, he took a few more steps until he was a short distance away and then he stared coldly at her.

She shivered under his scrutiny. There was no warmth in his eyes. None of the friendship and caring he'd demonstrated over the past weeks.

"What on earth is your problem?"

"You came all this way to ask that?"

She refused to be put off by the censure in his tone. She closed the distance between them, poking her finger into his chest.

"I thought we were friends. I thought you cared a little about me or at least about our child. Friends don't pull what you pulled today. What were you thinking? You left me alone in that exam room and then had your driver come for me? I want to know what the hell your problem is."

"Not everything is about you, Pippa."

The ice in his voice just served to piss her off more because she knew he was holding back. Knew that something was wrong and he didn't trust her enough to tell her what it was. But what right did she have to pursue it? They were "friends." Nothing more. He didn't owe her anything. It hurt to remind herself of that little fact.

"I thought we were *at least* friends," she whispered, her voice cracking with emotion.

She turned away, realizing just how stupid she'd been to

come here at all. It was the one place she wasn't welcome. Had never been welcome since that night when they'd first slept together. He hadn't been able to get rid of her fast enough the next morning and he'd never, ever brought her back here. They met in the city. Never here.

She *needed* this reminder because she'd come dangerously close to building larger expectations. Creating a fantasyland where she actually had a chance at a future with this man.

"Don't bother coming to the next appointment," she said stiffly, her back still to him. She began walking to the door and had almost reached it when he caught her hand. She hadn't even heard him come up behind her.

"Pippa."

The single word conveyed a wealth of emotion. Regret. Sorrow.

She paused, her hand trembling in his.

"I'm sorry," he said quietly. "Please don't leave like this."

She yanked around, fighting to keep angry, frustrated tears at bay. "Why, Cam? Give me one good reason. You don't want me here. I don't even know why we're pretending to have any sort of a relationship at all. Let's just cut our losses and get it over with now."

"I don't like anyone to come here," he said harshly. "It's not personal to you. But… Just stay. I'm sorry for the way the appointment went. I was an ass. I ruined your moment."

"Our moment," she corrected. "It was *our* moment, Cam. It was our child's moment when he was revealed to his parents. It was a moment that neither of us should have ever been able to forget, but in all honesty, I now don't want to remember. Because how will I ever explain to my child that his father walked out the moment it was told to us we were having a son?"

Cam flinched and went pale and those vivid blue eyes stared back at her, flashing with so much dark emotion.

The tears she'd tried so hard to hold back slid down her cheeks as she stood shaking before him. And then she was in his arms. He hugged her tightly. So tightly she couldn't breathe. His body shook against her. She could feel his rapid pulse jumping against his skin.

"Don't cry," he whispered. "I'm so sorry, Pippa. Please just stay. I'm sorry. You didn't deserve this. Forgive me, please."

And then he was kissing her. Hot, breathless, almost desperate. He touched her, frantically, as if his need for her was the most important single thing in the world. Like she was the single most important thing in his world.

She felt his sorrow, his uncertainty. It rolled off him in waves. His despair and grief. His regret. There was so much emotion churning inside him that it was tangible and thick in the air.

And then his touch became gentler, became more beseeching, almost as if he was begging her not to deny him. To touch him back. To offer him the comfort he seemed to crave.

She was unable to remain cold and distant when he was crumbling before her. She kissed him back, her breath hiccuping softly over his lips. And then she slid her palm across the slight bristle of his jaw, cupping his cheek in a simple gesture of acceptance and understanding. Of forgiveness.

He swept her into his arms as if she weighed nothing and carried her into one of the downstairs bedrooms. Leaving the door open, he moved to the bed and eased her down onto the mattress.

He hung over her, his eyes fierce and hungry. Her breath caught when he came down over her, hard and unrelenting. His mouth claimed hers once more and it was several long seconds before she could breathe again.

Impatiently he pulled at her sundress, tugging it free of her body before tossing it aside. He quickly divested her of her underwear until finally she was naked beneath him.

Then his expression changed. Some of the darkness faded and he stared down in wonder. Carefully his palms slid over her slim form to the gentle swell of her belly. He cupped it, and then to her shock, he lowered his head and kissed the firm bump.

"I'm sorry," he whispered again.

Emotion knotted his throat, making the words almost indistinguishable, but the harsh apology hit her right in the heart. Nobody who heard it could possibly think he didn't regret his actions with all his heart. He was essentially stripped and bare, standing before her starkly vulnerable.

She gently wrapped her arms around him to pull him close. "It's all right, Cam."

She pulled him higher to fuse his mouth with hers. Their tongues flirted and played and then he plunged deeper, overwhelming her with his essence. His body moved possessively over hers, though he was careful not to put his weight on her abdomen.

He kissed her neck, in turns gentle and then rougher until she was sure she'd wear marks the next day. He licked and nibbled at her skin, sucking lightly as he made his way lower.

When he got to her breasts, he hovered just over one of the tips and then tilted his head up so he could meet her gaze.

"Are they more sensitive now?" he asked huskily.

He ran his thumb over one crest as he awaited her response. A shudder worked over her body.

"Yes, definitely."

"Then I'll be extra careful."

With infinite tenderness, he slowly ran his tongue over one rigid peak before sucking it into his mouth. She came off the bed, arching helplessly into him as wave upon wave rolled over her.

It had been a long time since that careless night between them. She wanted him desperately. The past weeks had been a form of torture. He'd been so attentive and caring, yet there was an almost tangible barrier between them.

She was pretty sure this solved nothing, but she longed for physical contact. She needed it.

With a blissful sigh, she surrendered to those skilled lips of his.

But then he moved down, cupping her belly between his large hands and he proceeded to kiss every inch of the taut flesh until tears burned her eyelids.

He moved lower still, spreading her thighs as he settled down on the bed. His mouth found her heat and she nearly came apart on the spot.

He cupped her buttocks, holding her in place for his seeking tongue. He took long, sensuous swipes, the roughness of his tongue a contrast to his gentle sucking.

Her fingers dug into his hair, and she became more restless, nearly wild as she moved in rhythm with his intimate caresses.

"Cam, please," she begged. "I need you."

His feet were off the bed, and he stood, his hands curled around her legs. He pulled her forward so that her behind rested on the edge of the mattress.

"Wrap your legs around me," he said roughly.

As soon as she did, he slid into her.

The shock of his hardness made her gasp. Skin on skin. No barriers this time.

His groan was a harsh exhalation in the silence.

His fingers dug into her hips, pulling her closer to him. Then he released her and smoothed his hands over her belly, his fingers suddenly a lot gentler than they'd been just moments before.

"Don't let me hurt you."

She reached for him, pulling him down so their bodies met and his heat enveloped her. "I know you won't hurt me, Cam," she whispered. "Love me."

It was the closest she'd come to spilling what was in her heart. She'd held back because she knew he wouldn't welcome her feelings.

He claimed her mouth. His movements were urgent, a layer of desperation buried deep. His hands were everywhere, caressing, stroking, touching, as if he couldn't get enough of what he wanted. As if he wanted her closer still.

She wrapped her body around him, holding him as he drove deeper inside her. Release wasn't as important as the intimacy of the moment. The connection between them that was being established.

This wasn't…sex. It was so much more.

She kissed the side of his neck and then bit her lip to keep the words she so wanted to say from escaping. Instead, she inhaled his scent and molded her body more fiercely to his.

Pleasure was warm and sweet as it slid through her veins. Her release was a slow rise, no sharp edges or tumultuous explosions. Higher and higher she crept until every muscle in her body tensed in expectation.

"Cam!"

It was a cry of need. It was a plea for help.

She felt him in every part of her body. Hard, so very powerful. His muscles bunched and he tensed above her. He whispered her name and she felt him let go.

For a long moment he held himself just above her before finally lowering his body to hers.

He was like a warm blanket, the very best kind. He pressed his forehead to hers, kissing her with light smooching sounds as their lips met again and again.

"Pippa," he whispered.

It conveyed a wealth of things, that single word.

Twelve

For a moment after Pippa awoke she was disoriented. It took her a few seconds to realize where she was and that she'd fallen asleep. She rolled, searching for a clock, and then breathed a sigh of relief. She'd napped for only an hour.

She sat up, glancing around the dark room. Cam was nowhere to be found, but she was starting to suspect he didn't stick around after sex.

With a sigh, she got up to look for her clothing, but then she saw that a robe had been laid out on the bed. Apparently he wasn't completely thoughtless.

She pulled on the robe and headed for the bathroom to shower and change. Okay, so maybe she shouldn't have had sex with him. It certainly didn't solve anything, but then again, it hadn't made things any more complicated than they already were. She wasn't going to spend any time beating herself up over it because the simple truth was she wanted it.

Her problem was quite a bit more complicated because she'd been stupid enough to fall in love with a man who had no desire to return that love. Worse, she was pregnant with his child so she'd be tied to him forever. Even when he eventually married someone else.

Her stomach churned and she closed her eyes as she completed her quick shower. She didn't think she could handle another woman participating in the care of her child. A step-mother for her son.

Okay, she had to stop this because she'd just make herself crazy. For now, there were answers she wanted from Cam.

Her lips firmed and she sucked in a deep breath. No one could ever accuse her of taking the path of least resistance. What did she have to lose, anyway? It wasn't as if she had to worry about him telling her to take a hike.

Laughter bubbled in her throat as she walked out of the bedroom a few minutes later, her stride determined. Maybe that crap worked with other women, but it wasn't going to work with her.

She found him in the downstairs office. His back was to the door and he was staring sightlessly into the night. For a moment she studied his profile, reluctant to intrude even if she was determined to force a confrontation.

His hands were shoved into the pockets of his slacks and there was a bleakness to his expression that made her breath catch in her throat. Then he turned fully and saw her standing in the doorway.

"Are you hungry?" he asked.

She was, but that wasn't what she wanted to discuss.

"I'd like to talk first," she said in an even voice.

He blew out his breath as if he knew there was no getting around the inevitable.

She started forward, determined she wouldn't let him shrug this off. "Cam, I need to know why the idea of our son haunts you so. You were perfectly happy at the idea of a daughter, and the moment it was revealed that this baby is a boy, you couldn't get away fast enough."

He went completely pale, and his eyes became dull, dead orbs.

Then he closed his eyes and his lips tightened. For a long moment he seemed to do battle with himself. At one point she was sure he'd throw her out. He looked furious and devastated by turns.

What had happened to make him this way?

And then finally he opened his eyes and stared lifelessly back at her. She knew she'd won, but why didn't she feel like this was a victory?

"All right. We'll talk. After dinner."

She very nearly forced the confrontation here and now, but something held her back. Maybe he needed the time to prepare himself. She could give him that.

He herded her toward the kitchen, seated her at the island that doubled as a bar and then went to the refrigerator. He grimaced as he glanced back at her.

"I'm afraid our choices are somewhat limited. My housekeeper freezes meals for me and stocks the pantry, but I don't do much cooking. I eat out a lot."

She slipped off the bar stool and rounded the corner of the island. She waved him off with her hand. "Let me. I can whip us up something with what you have on hand."

"And have you think my hospitality sucks?"

She leveled a stare at him. "Your hospitality *does* suck. Sit and I'll make us something to eat. Then you're going to talk."

He winced at her bluntness but took the stool she'd vacated while she surveyed the contents of the pantry. She wanted something quick because she wasn't going to wait all damn night for this come-to-Jesus moment with Cam. Nor was she going to give him enough time to think better of his promise and toss her out without explaining himself.

She found fresh croissants and decided on melted ham and cheese. There was an array of fruit so she made a quick fruit salad while waiting for the croissants to toast up in the oven.

She set the table with honey mustard, mayo and the fruit salad and then went back for glasses.

"What would you like to drink?" she asked after checking on the croissants again.

Cam got up and hurried around to the wine cabinet. Then he paused and turned back around. "I guess wine is out. What do you usually drink?"

She smiled. "Water. Decaf tea. Fruit juice sometimes, but it gives me awful indigestion. Mostly water."

"I'll have water, too, then."

She set glasses out and filled them with water from the fridge. Then she went to take the cookie sheet from the oven. After depositing the toasted croissants onto their plates, she took a seat next to Cam.

"This is good," he said after finishing the first croissant. "Seemed easy, too. I wouldn't have thought of doing something like this."

Pippa smiled. "I'm the queen of improvising in the kitchen. Growing up, we didn't have very many family meals together, so I learned early to make do with what we had."

He cocked his head to the side. "You don't talk about your family much."

She nearly snorted. It was on the tip of her tongue to tell him he didn't, either, but she didn't want to shut that particular door before it was ever opened.

"Not much to talk about," she said lightly.

His eyes narrowed. "Why do I think otherwise?"

She shrugged. "No idea."

"Oh, come on. Give me a bone here. Do you see your family?"

She sighed. "Yeah, I see my mother when she doesn't give me enough advance warning so I'm sure not to be around."

He winced. "Ouch. That doesn't sound very healthy."

"Oh, it's a lot healthier when we don't see each other."

"What about your dad?"

Pippa sagged, putting down her half-eaten croissant. "He split when I was younger. Not that I can entirely blame him. My mother was difficult to say the least. He died a few years ago and left me the money I'm currently surviving on until I get my business up and running."

Cam frowned. "You're obviously not close to your family."

"Give the man a cigar," she drawled. "Did anyone ever tell you how observant you are?"

"Cut the sarcasm, Pippa. Talk to me here."

"You know, your gall astonishes me. We're supposed to be talking about you. That was the deal."

His jaw tightened and bulged. "It solves nothing."

"Oh, yeah? Maybe not for you. But see, here's the thing. I'm having your baby, and I kind of need to know if I can expect more outbursts like today. Like maybe you run out on his birthday party because you suddenly can't deal. We're going to talk about it, Cam, because if we don't, I'm out of here and I won't be back."

"Is that a threat, Pippa?"

She met his gaze without blinking. "I'm not threatening you. I'm making you a promise."

He shoved his plate aside and got up, nearly knocking the stool over. He stalked out of the kitchen and into the living room, his hands shoved tightly into his pants pockets.

Undaunted, she followed, coming to a stop a few feet behind him. For a long moment, Cam faced away from her, anger radiating in waves. Then he jerked around, his eyes ablaze.

"I had another son. Colton. And a wife. Elise."

Pippa's eyes widened in surprise. She hadn't expected this. She opened her mouth, then snapped it shut again.

"Nothing to say?" he snapped.

She ignored the anger that emanated from him, knew it was how he was maintaining control when he was barely hanging on. Suddenly she understood a lot of things. She wouldn't prod the wounded lion and she wouldn't get angry and defensive over his terseness.

"What happened?" she asked softly.

"I lost them. I lost them both. He was just a baby. The most beautiful, sweet baby in the world. Elise was… She was wonderful. Young. Vibrant. So full of life. She was a wonderful mother."

Pain vibrated in his voice and her heart clenched at the grief still evident in his eyes.

"I could bear the thought of a daughter," he choked out. "I even looked forward to it. But not a son. It feels too much like I'm replacing Colton."

Her mouth fell open in shock. She wanted to immediately deny that by having another son he was somehow replacing his first child, but she remained silent. It may make no sense to her, but it was evident by the torment in Cam's eyes that he absolutely believed it.

How could she argue with something so deeply ingrained?

She stood there a long moment, trying to make sense of it. She looked down at the tiny swell of her belly and was overwhelmed by a fierce need to protect her baby. She glanced back up at Cam, her jaw as tight as his had been.

Anger and sorrow warred inside her. Sorrow for him. For such a horrific loss. But anger that her child would pay the price.

"So you'd deny this child your love because he had the misfortune to be born the wrong sex?"

Cam's nostrils flared and his eyes flashed with anger. He advanced toward her, bristling with outrage. "I never said that."

"But nothing you've said or done so far tells me any different."

He dragged a hand through his hair, rumpling it even more than it already was. "I'm trying here, Pippa. I'm trying really damn hard. You know I didn't want this."

"I get that! Okay? I understand. Believe me, you've made yourself more than clear on the matter. You didn't want me. You didn't want our child. But you know what? He didn't have a choice in the matter. It's not his fault his parents are brainless twits who didn't do enough to prevent his conception. But you know what else? I'm not sorry."

She broke off, her chest heaving.

"I'm not sorry," she said again, more fiercely this time. "I'll never be sorry that the condom broke. I want this child. I want our son. If you want to wallow in the past and deny yourself the miracle that this child is, that's your problem. But I don't have to put up with your stupid crap."

She turned around and stomped toward the front door, yanking up the purse she'd dropped when she'd stormed in earlier. She really had no idea if John was around. At this point, she didn't care. She'd walk to Ashley's if she had to.

"Pippa!"

She yanked open the front door, walked out into the night and then slammed it behind her.

Oh, boy, was she an idiot. She'd fallen into bed with him. Even after he'd ditched her at the doctor's office. He'd been clear from the start, and yet she kept agreeing to see him. Like she had some desperate hope that she was going to be the one to heal him.

She stalked down the driveway, determined to put as much distance between herself and the source of her stupidity as possible.

"Pippa! Damn it! What the hell do you think you're doing?"

She flinched as Cam roared at her from the doorway. She pulled out her cell, hoping like hell that Ashley was home tonight. If not, it was going to be a long-ass walk to public transportation.

When she reached the end of the driveway and turned toward Ashley's house, the beam of headlights flashed over her and the growl of an engine sounded. Cam pulled up beside her and rolled his window down.

"Get into the damn truck, Pippa. This is insane."

She turned to look at him, never breaking stride. "What's insane is me staying at your house another minute. I'm going to Ashley's. I'll be fine."

He swore a streak that scorched her ears. Then he pulled the SUV in front of her and stopped on the shoulder. He got out and strode back to meet her.

"Look, at least let me give you a ride to Ashley's. You don't need to be out walking around in the dark alone."

"As long as you promise to drive straight to Ashley's."

"Get in," he growled.

She walked around to the passenger's side, got in and slammed the door shut. She didn't even look his way when he got back in and put the SUV in Drive.

When he started to speak, she jerked around and put her hand out to silence him. "Just save it, Cam. I don't want to hear it."

He fell silent again and turned into Devon and Ashley's driveway. He pulled to the front and she slipped out almost before he came to a full stop. She slammed the door shut and walked toward the front door, never once looking back.

Ashley opened the door before she got there and only then did Cam pull away.

"Pippa? What on earth is going on?"

Tears filled Pippa's eyes as she stopped in front of her friend. "I need a place to stay tonight, Ash. Is it okay if I crash here?"

Thirteen

"Look, Dev, I know he's your friend, but he makes me crazy," Pippa said.

Devon handed her a glass of juice with a look of sympathy.

"He's a hard-ass, honey. Always has been."

Ashley wrapped her arms around Pippa, or at least as much as she could with a bulging, ginormous belly. The two of them looked like poster children for fertility. Only, Ashley had a loving husband—at least Devon was over the moon about the impending birth of his child.

Pippa sniffled and swallowed some of the juice even knowing she'd suffer for it later.

"I can't believe he's so freaked because we're having a boy."

Devon glanced uneasily at both women, and who could blame him? One pregnant hormonal woman was enough, but two? He was probably ready to either start drinking or run screaming into the night. Maybe both.

"I get that it's hard to lose people you love. I suppose some part of me should be all, 'Awww, you poor thing,' and fawn all over him, pat him on the back and be understanding, but damn it, I can't do that!"

Pippa wiped angrily at her face and leaned forward on the couch to put her glass on the coffee table.

Devon slowly shook his head. "No, Pippa, I think you did

right. Sympathy is the last thing he needs. Cam is my oldest friend, but it's time for him to move on with his life and stop rehashing and living in the past."

She nodded miserably. "It makes me seem heartless and I'm not. Really. It breaks my heart to see him so tortured but how does he think it'll make *our* child feel to know he was rejected because his father didn't want to make it look like he was replacing his first son with his second?"

"You're protecting your baby," Ashley said in a fierce voice. "You should never apologize for that. Cam's an idiot."

Pippa cringed. "It doesn't make you an idiot to mourn people you love. I get that. I do. What makes him an idiot is not being able to look past something horrific and see that he's being given a second chance. This baby won't replace Colton. No one could ever do that. I don't know how to make Cam see that. At this point, I don't even know if I want to try. I'm tired. Tired of this stupid game we're playing where we both pretend that we don't want more and that we're happy having this superficial relationship. I'm not happy. I'll never be happy with a man who gives me only a part of himself. I'm a selfish bitch. I want it all."

Devon cracked a grin and Ashley hugged her all over again. Pippa remained in her friend's arms for a long moment, soaking up every bit of comfort she could.

"You may not see this now, Pippa, but I think you're the best thing that ever happened to Cam," Devon said.

Pippa sighed. "Oh, I agree. I'm not some martyr who refuses to see her own value."

"Atta girl," Devon said.

Ashley squeezed her.

Pippa crumpled into Ashley's arms again, her misery overwhelming her. "God, Ash, I slept with him again. Tonight. After he ditched me at the clinic. After that spectacular demonstration of support, I still slept with him. Someone needs to lock me in my apartment for my own good."

Devon cleared his throat. "I, um, think I'll leave you two alone now. If you need anything, holler."

Pippa watched in amusement as Devon all but ran from the room. Then she sighed and leaned her head on Ashley's shoulder.

"I'm stupid, Ash. He's stupid. We're both stupid and I still love him."

Ashley laughed softly. "Not stupid. Sometimes you can't help who you love. God knows there were times I wished not to love Devon with everything I had."

"He was a bonehead there for a while," Pippa acknowledged. "I guess that was what gave me hope with Cam. I thought maybe he'd come around. I'm an idiot. You can say it."

"You're not an idiot! You're smart and brave and I love you."

Pippa smiled. "I love you, too, Ash. Sorry for getting you all wet and disturbing your evening with Dev."

"Oh, like I didn't crash at your place for days and sob and weep all over you like a dishrag."

"Yeah, you did, but it all worked out in the end." Her lips turned down into an unhappy frown. "I don't see that being the case here. Cam seems too comfortable in his misery."

"He's really not so bad, Pip," Ashley said softly.

"You're not in love with him," Pippa pointed out. "You're not facing an impossible future tied to him but relegated to being a nobody in his life. Not that I would have ever acted this way, but I'm beginning to see why some women don't tell the father of their baby that they're pregnant."

"You're hurting now, but you did the right thing. You'll see. It'll work out, Pip. You have to believe it. Cam will come around. He'll take one look at his child and be a complete goner."

Pippa raised her head from Ashley's shoulder. "I hope you're right."

* * *

The next day, Pippa rode into the city with Devon and had him drop her off at her café. She was getting so close to the grand-opening date, and as a result, her nerves were near to exploding.

All the paperwork was in order. Her first supplies had been delivered and her kitchen was set up with everything she could possibly need to start baking. All she had to do was… start.

She had a list of items she intended to have out on opening day. She'd already placed ads for the employees she wanted to hire. She needed at least one person to help man the front and an assistant in the kitchen as well as a delivery driver for when she began taking catering jobs.

She was finally, *finally* realizing her dream of opening her own business and she'd never been so scared in her life.

After making a few calls to set up interviews, she unpacked the delivery and put everything away. The more she thought about her grand-opening date, the more she wanted to hyperventilate into a paper bag.

But this is what she'd been working for. Cam had certainly made it a lot easier for her, but she would have accomplished it on her own. It might have taken her a few more months, but she would have done it. He'd only facilitated the matter.

Her cell phone rang and she went completely still. Then she pulled it out of her pocket and stared at the screen for confirmation of what she already knew. Her mother had her own ringtone. It was as unmistakable as Miranda herself.

"Boy, do you have rotten timing," Pippa muttered.

She briefly contemplated letting it go to voice mail, but that would be cowardly of her and then she'd have to listen to Miranda complain that her daughter was avoiding her. Okay, it was absolutely true, but if Pippa didn't answer, Miranda would simply persist. Better to have done with it now.

Besides, Miranda was harmless. Clueless, but utterly harmless.

With a resigned sigh, she punched the answer button and then put the phone to her ear.

"Hello, Mom."

"Pippa, darling! Hello! Long time no talk. How are you?"

Pippa smiled despite herself. She always felt guilty about avoiding her mom. She knew in her heart of hearts that Miranda did love her. It wasn't her fault she was… Well, Pippa wasn't entirely certain how to describe her mother. *Harmless* worked well enough because Pippa truly didn't believe her mother ever *tried* to be malicious.

"I'm good, Mom. How are you? How is Paris?"

"Oh, Paris was wonderful, but we're on to Greece now. It's so warm and sunshiny. I'm sure it's much better than spring in the city. Don't you think?"

"How is Doug?"

Pippa held her breath, hoping that she hadn't just stuck her foot in her mouth. Was her mother still with Doug? She'd left the country with him, but one never knew with Miranda. She was just as likely to fall in love in Paris and go off with someone else. Miranda fell in love like most people changed underwear.

"He's having a wonderful time. We both are. He sends you his love."

That amused Pippa given that she'd never actually met the man. She was sure he was perfectly nice. But she doubted she'd ever know firsthand because it would be a miracle if her mother actually made it back home with the same guy.

In a lot of ways, Miranda reminded Pippa of a child who'd been given more Christmas presents than she knew what to do with. She'd pick one up, ooh and ahh, and then promptly drop it and move on to the next one.

That was Miranda's love life in a nutshell.

"When do you think you'll be back?" Pippa asked casually.

She hadn't talked to her mom in months. Miranda didn't know that Pippa was pregnant and she was racked with indecision over whether to break the news to her. It would likely devastate her mother, who considered herself far too young and beautiful to be called a grandmother.

While some part of Pippa did long to share the news, she couldn't bring herself to ruin Miranda's trip. And it would ruin it. She'd spend the rest of her time wailing that she was too young and asking Doug or whatever guy was her current lover for reassurance that she didn't *look* like a grandmother.

"Oh, I don't know. We're having such fun. There's no hurry, you know? Life's too short. Unless you need me? Is there something wrong, Pippa, darling?"

The hope in Miranda's voice decided the matter for Pippa.

"No, Mom. Have a good time, okay? We'll talk more later."

"Love you, dear Pippa."

"Love you, too," Pippa murmured as she rang off.

After shoving the phone back into her pocket, Pippa stood in her kitchen for a long moment, feeling the weight of emotion settle over her shoulders. It was always like this after she spoke to her mother. Regret that she couldn't have a normal relationship with her own mom. She wanted a mom like Ashley's.

Gloria Copeland fiercely loved her children. She was a rock, always there, offering unconditional love and support. If Ashley needed her mom, she was there. No questions asked.

While Miranda might have the best of intentions, and she really did love her daughter, she just didn't have it in her to be…maternal. The concept was as alien to Miranda as settling down with one man for more than a few months.

Pippa had always considered her mother to be very much like a butterfly. Flitting from one thing to the next, never staying in one place for very long.

Pippa herself preferred being a homebody. The idea of deviating from her routine gave her hives. She liked the city. Loved her circle of friends. Loved doing the same things every day. Maybe that made her a coward. Maybe she'd never go out into the world and take it on bare-handed. But she knew what she liked. Knew what she wanted. And she simply wouldn't settle for less.

After putting the last of her things away, she went out the front and locked up. When she turned toward the street, she saw Cam's driver standing there waiting beside the car. She shook her head. She should have known.

John looked pointedly at her and then opened the door and gestured her over. With a sigh, she climbed into the backseat.

Her pride wasn't such that she'd turn down even the short ride to her apartment. She didn't mind walking, but now that her belly was protruding more every day, her feet were paying the price.

John dropped her off in front of her apartment and admonished her to apprise him of her schedule for the next day. After arranging a pickup time, she mounted the steps to her front door only to find a basket with a large blue bow on the stoop.

She unlocked her door, pushed it open and then reached down for the basket to take it inside. After dropping her keys and sweater on the table in the foyer, she went into the living room and deposited the basket on the coffee table.

There was a card attached just below the bow and she opened it.

Forgive me.

Cam.

She hastily reached into the basket and pulled out a tiny Yankees uniform in a newborn size. She broke out in a smile as her vision blurred with unshed tears. It was adorable. The very first outfit for her baby boy.

There was a teddy bear. A baseball and tiny catcher's mitt. And two tickets to the next home game at Yankee Stadium.

If Cam had been there she would have thrown her arms around him and all would have been forgiven. Which was why she was glad he was nowhere near her.

It was a fault of hers. She was too forgiving. She couldn't

let herself be a doormat while Cam waffled back and forth like some sick version of Jekyll and Hyde.

But the idea of him hurting, even as much as he'd hurt her, made her heart squeeze. He had five more months to get over this notion that their son was somehow replacing the child he'd lost. Surely that was enough time. Wasn't it?

"Oh, Cam," she whispered. "What am I going to do about you? About us?"

All she could do was take it one day at a time and hope and pray that Cam came around. Because if he didn't? She and their son would lose, and she'd do anything at all to spare her son the pain of a father who didn't want him.

Fourteen

It was the big day and it felt like Pippa had swallowed a giant rock. She'd been up the entire night before—baking, cleaning, arranging and stressing. Being the wonderful friend she was, Carly had hung out with Pippa until dawn. Pippa had shooed Ashley home much earlier. The poor woman was due to pop any day now and she was miserable.

But everyone had promised to return for the 9:00 a.m. grand opening of Pippa's Place.

"Your displays are gorgeous, Pip," Carly said. "What time are your employees coming in?"

Pippa wiped her forehead with the back of her hand. "Any moment now. I could have had them in overnight to help, but to be honest, I'm too much of a control freak. I want everything just so for the first day. After this I can leave the shop in capable hands when needed."

Carly laughed. Then she impulsively hugged Pippa. "You need some rest, hon. You look exhausted."

"No rest for the weary today," she said with a crooked grin. "I don't close until this afternoon and I'm hoping to draw a large crowd. Cam might have gone a little overboard advertising the big event. Let's just hope he didn't oversell me and nobody likes my cooking."

"Not going to happen," Carly said firmly.

The front bell jangled and Pippa stuck her head through the

kitchen door dividing the kitchen from the rest of the space. She waved her employee back and gave her instructions for stocking the displays with the remaining cupcakes and cookies.

She busied herself with cleaning the kitchen while Carly greeted the second employee and put her to work. Pippa thought about the delivery van, which was parked in front of the shop today. It provided great advertising with its cheerful color and the shop name displayed predominately on the side.

After her illegal drive through the city, she'd spent the next few weeks getting her driver's license even though she hoped she never had to actually drive the thing herself.

Satisfied that her kitchen was in order, she went into the bathroom to repair her appearance. What she really needed was a shower, but she didn't have time to go home.

"Pippa, you in there?"

She cracked open the bathroom door to see Carly and Tabitha both standing there. They started to crowd in, both carrying cosmetic bags.

"We're here to do your hair and makeup," Tabitha announced.

Pippa smiled, put the seat of the toilet down and sat so her friends could fuss over her. Peace replaced the overwhelming sense of panic. This was it. Her dream was coming true today. It hadn't gone exactly as she planned, but she wouldn't change a single thing.

Already she loved her son with a fierceness that surprised her. She hadn't imagined being so connected to another life in quite this way. She talked to him every day. Sang to him at night. Read him stories while she lounged on the sofa after a long day of dealing with business stuff.

Her child had given her a purpose. She was even more determined to succeed. To be a mom her son would be proud of. She never wanted her kid to feel about her the way she felt about her own mother.

Where Miranda was more concerned for her own happiness than that of her child, Pippa was never going to go that route. Her son would be the single most important person in her life.

For the next half hour, Tabitha and Carly kept up a lively stream of chatter as they applied makeup and touched up her hair. Pippa's heart was full of love for her friends. They were working hard to keep her mind off the impending grand opening and to allay her nervousness.

Just as they finished the last brush of the mascara wand, the door burst open and Ashley and Sylvia tried to shove inside.

"Pippa, you have to come see!" Ashley exclaimed.

She grabbed Pippa's hand and hauled her toward the front. As they stumbled into the eating area, Pippa's eyes rounded in shock.

People. Lots and lots of people!

All crowded outside the entrance to her shop. Waiting for her to open. And her employees, bless their hearts, were outside circulating with cups of hot coffee and samples of her baked goods.

Tears gathered and Carly whispered fiercely in her ear. "Don't you dare mess up that mascara!"

Pippa laughed and then excitedly hugged all her friends.

Half an hour later, the doors opened and the customers surged in. There was much laughter as all of Pippa's friends helped serve the crush of people.

For two hours there was no end to the line of people. As fast as they could ring customers up, others came in droves.

It was past noon when Pippa looked up and saw Cam stride through the front door, shoving his way past a line of customers. He sought her out and then fixed his stare on her as he moved toward the counter.

"Go on," Ashley whispered. "I'll take the register for a while."

"You sure?" Pippa looked doubtfully at her friend. "You've

been on your feet for a long time, Ash. Maybe you should take a break. Devon's going to kill me for wearing you out."

Ashley smiled. "I'm having fun and I get to eat all the cupcakes I want. Total win!"

Pippa grinned back and then stepped away from the counter to meet Cam around the side.

"Looks like you've drawn a huge crowd," Cam said when she got close enough for her to hear him.

"It's fantastic! I can't believe it. We've been hopping all morning."

Cam smiled. "Can I get a cup of coffee and a few minutes of your time?"

She glanced over at her friends, who were waving her on and giving her the okay signal that they were fine handling the customers. She waved back and said to Cam, "Okay, you've got me for a few minutes."

She poured him a cup of coffee, grabbed a pastry, a croissant and a cupcake and then motioned him into the kitchen.

They walked through to the office at the very rear of the shop. She closed the door behind them and then took a seat at the small desk. Or rather she sagged into it.

"Oh, my God, I may never get back up." She groaned.

His eyes narrowed in concern. "When was the last time you slept? Have you been here all night?"

"It's been a while," she said ruefully. "And yeah, I was here all night getting ready."

"You should rest. That can't be good for you or the baby."

"I won't argue that point. I plan to go straight home and sleep about twelve hours before I get up tomorrow and do it all over again."

He was silent a long moment. He looked for the world like he wanted to argue. His lips were set in a line and his jaw ticked. He ran a hand through his hair. To her surprise, he seemed unsure of himself.

"I wanted to come by to see how it was going. But mostly I wanted to say once more that I'm sorry for what happened at the clinic. I'm trying, Pippa. I know you probably don't believe that, but I am trying to deal with this."

She pushed the coffee and the plate of yummies at him, her heart melting just a little at the vulnerability she saw in those troubled eyes of his.

"Tell me how awesome I am," she teased as she held up the cupcake.

He looked suspiciously at the cupcake piled high with fluffy pink icing. Unable to resist the opening, she swiped a finger full and then smeared it over his lips.

He reared back in surprise but his tongue automatically came out to lick away the sticky frosting. Then he took the cupcake from her and carefully peeled away the wrapper. He took a cautious bite and then stared down at it as if trying to figure out the mysteries of the universe.

"Okay, you're awesome."

"I know," she said smugly. "Damn good, isn't it?"

He took another bite and then smiled. "Yeah. Does this mean I'm forgiven?"

She cocked her head to the side and decided to let down her guard. "That depends on where you take me to dinner tonight. I'm starving and I want a steak. I'm sugared out from eating my own goodies. Me and baby want red meat."

She waited for the flinch. The inevitable reaction when he was reminded of the son she carried. But he didn't react. He actually seemed hugely relieved that she'd taken the matter in hand and barged forward. Well, that was typical Pippa. Bull in a china closet and all that.

"I'd like that," he said in a somber voice. "I'll make early reservations for us so you can get home and rest. I have a meeting in a little while but I'll swing back by at closing time, run you by your apartment if you want to change and then we'll go eat."

"That sounds awesome," she said with a sigh.

He rose from his seat and then held a hand out to help her up. "You've done a great job making this place your own,

Pippa. By the looks of that crowd, I'd say they agree with me. You have a solid success on your hands."

She squeezed his hand as she came around the desk. "I owe a lot of it to you. If you hadn't gotten me this great place, I'd probably still be looking for space to lease."

"I was glad to do it. You've worked hard for this."

Part of her was saddened by the slight awkwardness between them and the almost formal way they danced around each other. She longed for the easy friendship that she'd come to rely on over the past few months. If she couldn't have a more intimate relationship with him, she'd at least take friendship. Anything but this unease between them.

She gave him a quick hug to convey that she was seemingly unaffected by all that had transpired and then herded him back through the kitchen and out the front, where there was still a steady stream of customers spilling into the shop.

He hesitated a moment as they stood at the counter and then he leaned in to brush his lips across her cheek. "I'll see you in a few hours. Try to take it easy, okay?"

As he walked away, she raised trembling fingers to the place he'd kissed her.

Hot and cold. She could never figure out where she stood with him and it pissed her off. One thing she knew for certain—she wasn't going to wait around forever while he got his act together.

Fifteen

Cam drove past Pippa's café to see the open sign go out and lights start to flicker off inside. He gave the voice command to dial Pippa's cell and then turned to circle the block.

After a few rings, she answered, her breathless voice doing odd things to his insides.

"I'll just be a minute," she said by way of greeting.

"No hurry. I'm circling the block. I'll pull up so you can just come out."

He maneuvered the SUV through traffic and waited for the light to turn so he could turn back onto her street. He tapped his thumbs impatiently on the steering wheel and he realized that he was anxious to see her again.

It didn't compute. He had this sick love-hate relationship going on. He wanted to be as far from her as possible. She made him nervous. She looked at him like she could see right past the front he put on.

At the same time, when he was away even a short period of time, he got anxious. He needed to know she was okay, that she had everything she needed. That she was safe. And hell, if he was honest, he just wanted to see her again.

He had to let go of his pain. He had to move on. But how did one ever just decide that sort of thing? At what point did the hurting stop? At what point did one stop being gripped by paralyzing fear over the thought of losing someone you cared about?

He didn't have the answers, and until he did, this thing between him and Pippa would never work. He didn't want it to work.

Which didn't explain why he was circling the block, anxious to see her again. It made no sense. He should be at home. He should have never apologized, though he certainly owed her the apology and more. But he should have let it go, allowed her to remain angry with him. In the end it was kinder to both of them. A clean break. No remorse. No recriminations. No dragging it out only to rehash it all again later.

But he wanted to see her. He wanted… He wanted her. On his own terms. He recognized the selfishness of it and yet he couldn't stop himself from craving her. In or out of bed. It mattered little to him. He just wanted to be near her because, God help him, he felt more alive whenever she walked into a room.

He slowed as he approached her shop and leaned forward to see if she was waiting. She was at her door, locking up, the wind blowing through her dark hair. Then she turned and he was struck by the picture she presented. Young, vibrant, beautiful.

She saw him and waved, her face lighting up with a gorgeous smile. She hurried forward, one hand cupped to her belly and the other hanging on to her purse. He stopped and leaned over to push open the door for her. She climbed in, melted into the seat with a sweet sigh and then turned that dazzling smile on him.

It was like being kicked in the stomach.

"It is sooo nice to be off my feet," she said.

Blinking, he realized he was sitting still while angry horns beeped behind him. He eased off the brake and drove away, listening as she talked in animated fashion about her day and how amazing the turnout had been.

His blood hummed with desire. With need. He wanted her. He didn't want to want her.

He couldn't process a single rational thought.

Suddenly the thought of spending so much time in a restaurant didn't appeal. She looked tired. He was impatient. He needed to have her to himself.

"Change in plans," he said gruffly as he turned left so he could circle back to her apartment.

She roused from her semistupor and shot him an inquisitive glance. "What's up? You standing me up?"

He smiled at the growl in her voice. "Oh, no, far from it. What I'm doing is taking you back to your place so you can put your feet up on the couch while I order us the best damn steak money can buy. Then I'm going to take you to bed, give you an all-over body massage and make love to you until you pass out."

Her eyes widened and then she blinked, momentarily speechless. "Well, okay," she finally said.

He smiled in satisfaction at her acceptance. It was more than okay.

When Pippa let them into her apartment, the air was electric and heavy with anticipation. She wouldn't even meet his gaze because she was sure she was an open book, and hey, a woman had to have some mystery, right?

Only it wasn't a mystery that she wanted him. Or that from the moment he'd laid out his plans for the evening she'd become a quivering ball of anticipation.

She walked ahead of him into the living room, her step lighter than it had been all day. Her fatigue had fled and she felt energized. Ready.

Her skin prickled with tiny goose bumps every time he so much as looked her way. It felt like her very first date. Her very first kiss. The first time she'd ever gotten naked in front of a man. She wasn't sure whether she liked it or not.

"Why don't you sit and relax," he said. "I can find my way

around your apartment. I'll phone in our order and get things started. Would you like something to drink?"

This suddenly very solicitous side of Cam was confusing the hell out of her. She liked this new Cam very, very much and she could get used to it.

It wasn't as if he was never generous with her. Quite the opposite. He went to great lengths to take care of her needs but he did so as impersonally as possible.

But now his caring seemed very personal. She didn't know if this was a further attempt to make up for walking out of the sonogram or if he was genuinely softening toward her. Who the hell knew with him?

"I'll take a bottled water. There's one in the fridge," she said as she settled on the couch.

She propped her feet on the ottoman and groaned in sheer pleasure. She leaned her head against the back of the couch and closed her eyes while she listened to him putter around the kitchen. Then she heard the rumble of his voice as he placed their dinner order. A moment later, he returned to the living room and handed her the drink.

"Thank you."

"Your grand opening was quite the success," he said.

He took a seat in her armchair and propped his feet just inches from hers.

"I owe a lot of my opening day success to you. Maybe all of it."

He shook his head. "I gave you a place but it was your talent and hard work that made it happen."

"Thank you for saying that. It means a lot. I've been working toward this for a very long time."

He put his hands behind his head and cupped his nape. "Have you thought about what you'll do after the baby is born?"

She cocked her head to the side and glanced questioningly at him. "What do you mean?"

"Will you keep your current schedule or will you employ

others to run the shop so that you have more time with our son?"

For a moment she couldn't respond. She was too struck by the reference to their son. And she was reminded that she and Cam weren't a couple. Of course he would wonder what arrangements she'd made because he wasn't going to be there on a 24/7 basis.

It shocked her how much that hurt. How much she wanted it to be different.

"I haven't decided yet," she said slowly. "A lot will depend on how the café is doing and if I can afford to hire more help. I have to train my assistant so that she can duplicate my recipes while I'm out on maternity leave. But I can't close down. That's not even an option."

"Of course not. If you'll allow me to help, I can certainly put some feelers out. We have a number of pastry chefs that work in our various hotels. I'm sure we could loan one to you for a few weeks."

She stared back at him, mouth open. "Cam, you guys own five-star resorts. There is no way I could afford to pay even three weeks' wages to a world-class pastry chef like the ones you guys employ."

"He or she would of course remain on our payroll."

She sighed. "I can't keep relying on you, Cam. I'm only setting myself up to fail miserably. What you've done is so wonderful and so helpful but it also skews the results. When all your support goes away, I'll be left in a lurch."

He frowned. "No one says it's going away."

"I say it's going away," she said gently. "I have to make a go of this myself, Cam."

He didn't argue, although she had the distinct feeling that he hadn't dropped the subject for good. Then a completely unrelated thought struck her.

"I didn't frame my first dollar."

He blinked in surprise and then seemed puzzled by her dismay.

Her lips turned down into a frown. "You're supposed to frame the first dollar you make. You know, when you start a business. You didn't do that with yours?"

"Hell, Pippa, your first sale was probably a debit card purchase. Nobody carries cash anymore. You could always frame the credit card receipt."

She pulled a face. "You're such a party pooper. You don't have your first dollar?"

He shrugged. "I still have my first million."

She rolled her eyes at him. "Somehow that doesn't surprise me. Does money mean anything at all to you or has it lost its value?"

"Of course it means something." He scowled, making her almost want to giggle. "It means I can support our child and you. It means I can live comfortably and not worry about where my next meal is coming from. It means you don't have to worry about your lack of health insurance."

She held up her hands in surrender. "Okay, okay, I was being a snot. It was an unfair jab. I'm sorry."

"I'm not out blowing my cash if that's what you were wondering."

Her cheeks warmed and she glanced away. "No, I was just stereotyping you and being flip. I really didn't mean anything by it. People who don't have a lot of money tend to not really understand people who do have money. Or their attitude toward money."

He lifted one eyebrow. "I hope you're not implying I'm a snob."

"No," she said truthfully. "I truly don't think you're a snob. You can be a first-class jerk, but not a snob."

He shot her a glare and she snickered.

The doorbell interrupted and Cam quickly rose to go answer. A moment later, he came back, followed by a delivery person who set up the food on the coffee table. The young man smiled at Pippa and then he and Cam disappeared from the living room once more.

She waited, sniffing appreciatively at the mouthwatering aroma floating from the covered plates. She'd leaned over to take a quick peek when Cam admonished her from the doorway.

"Not so fast."

She yanked back guiltily.

"Want to eat in here or the kitchen? Are you okay on just the coffee table?"

"Oh, yeah. I'm comfortable. I'll just lean forward and shovel it all in."

He chuckled. "Not a pretty image."

She sniffed disdainfully. "Watching a pregnant woman inhale her food isn't for sissies."

He went forward and uncovered the dishes. He poured her a glass of cold water and then shoved the plate across the table so that it was directly in front of her. Then he handed her a steak knife and a fork. "Dig in."

He didn't have to tell her twice. He'd ordered a filet and it was fork tender. As soon as she took the first bite, she closed her eyes and sighed in sheer pleasure.

"Good?" Cam asked.

"I don't have words. Best steak I've ever put in my mouth."

He nodded his satisfaction and then sat down to eat his own steak.

They ate in silence, only the clink of forks and knives disturbing the peace. Pippa had been only half kidding about inhaling her food. These days it didn't seem she could put away enough to eat. Which was just as well because she'd read that in the last trimester, eating was a lot more difficult with a baby's head lodged in your lungs.

Cam finished his steak before she'd gotten halfway through hers. He went to put away his dishes. When he came back, he sat forward in the armchair and grabbed her plate.

She frowned her protest but he gestured for her to sit back. Then he put the pillows from the end of the couch on her lap and plunked the plate down on it so she could continue eating.

Just when she had no idea what he was up to, he lifted her feet and propped them back on the ottoman.

He closed his hands around her left foot and pressed his palm into her instep. She sagged precariously and let out a glorious sigh as pleasure seeped into her muscles.

"How can I eat with you doing that?" she complained.

He smiled. "Easy. Just pick up your fork. You were on your feet all day. They have to be sore."

She shoved a bite of steak into her mouth and nodded vigorously.

"Well, then, relax and let me take care of the matter for you."

Oh, hell, yes. She wouldn't say another word. She'd just sit here and eat her scrumptious steak while the most gorgeous man on earth gave her a foot massage.

"Remember what I promised you?" he murmured.

She stopped chewing and damn near choked as she struggled to swallow the bite. Then she nodded because she couldn't seem to find her tongue.

As he gripped her heel with one hand, the other stroked over the top of her foot and up her leg, heat from his touch warming her skin.

"As soon as you're done, I'm taking you to bed, Pippa. How much sleep you get is entirely up to you."

Oh, hell...

She put aside the plate, unconcerned with whether it tipped over on the couch. He stared at her for a moment as if gauging whether she was ready. If she was any more ready she'd be stripped down and holding a sign saying Take Me.

Sixteen

As soon as Cam pulled Pippa to her feet, adrenaline surged like an electric charge through her veins. For a moment he pulled her close, their bodies touching. His warmth leaped to her and surrounded her. Then he dragged a gentle hand through her hair and leaned down to kiss her.

It was brief, just a brush, but she felt it to her toes. He drew away, his breath harsh in the quiet.

"Your bed," he said.

Swallowing hard, she started to drop his hand to go past him toward her bedroom, but he tightened his hold and rubbed his thumb over her wrist.

She went ahead of him, pulling him behind her as she crossed the short distance to the steps leading up to the small loft where her bed was. Her legs trembled as she climbed and then came to a halt, the bed in front of her, unsure of what he wanted next.

He moved past her, this time taking her with him. He eased her into a sitting position on the edge of the bed and then unbuttoned her top.

He went down on his knees as he pushed her shirt over her shoulders, baring her lacy bra. His gaze dropped to the swell of her belly and he went still. She held her breath, wondering if the moment was lost, but to her utter shock, he laid his cheek over the bump and turned his mouth just enough to press a kiss to her taut skin.

She inhaled sharply, the bite of emotion harsh in her throat. She slid her fingers through his unruly hair, her touch gentle and loving.

Slowly he pulled away and then he lifted her just enough that he could ease her pants off.

"I promised you a massage," he said in a husky voice. "I think I'm going to enjoy it more than you will."

She cast him a doubtful look, but okay, if that's what he wanted to think. Right now his hands on her body was about as good as it got.

He curled his arms underneath her and lifted so he could position her on her side. Then he unhooked her bra and carefully pulled her panties down her legs so she was naked, facing away from him.

During a long pause, she glanced over her shoulder to see him disrobing a short distance away. He had a gorgeous, lean body. He wasn't pretty or polished. There was just enough edge to his appearance to send her girlie senses into overdrive.

He strode back to the bed and got on his knees behind her. When his hand slid over her hip, then wandered to her back and shoulder, she closed her eyes and sighed in contentment.

His mouth followed, pressing hot against her neck and then gliding over the curve to her shoulder. When he pulled away, he put both hands to her back and gently began to stroke and caress until her eyes rolled back in her head.

He worked methodically, leaving no part of her flesh untouched. He stroked down to her buttocks, molding the plump globes with his palms before working lower to her thighs.

Nudging her over onto her back, he lifted one leg and began working the muscles with those to-die-for hands. He worked all the way down to her ankle and then began massaging her foot.

She floated somewhere else, hovering on a cloud of sensory overload. Then he lifted her foot and kissed her instep.

She nearly lost it right there. It was the most erotic sensation she'd ever experienced and it was just her foot! But the man made every single touch so damn sexy.

He moved to her other leg but she was only dimly aware. She let out a blissful sigh and surrendered to the euphoric sensation of having a sinfully handsome man cater to her every pleasure.

Each caress sent warmth all the way to her soul. She opened her eyes and watched in fascination as he rose over her, gently parting her thighs before settling his upper body between them.

For a brief moment he glanced up and those sizzling blue eyes connected with hers. His mouth crooked up into a half smile and then he lowered his head to her most intimate flesh.

She couldn't call back the moan. She twisted restlessly but he kept her firmly in place with those hands at her hips. He kissed, licked and made love to her with that delectable mouth. He had such a talented tongue and he was driving her crazy.

She reached for his hair, twisting her fingers with almost desperate strength as she arched into him. He delved deeper with his tongue, loving her with long, lazy strokes. Then he moved one hand from her hip and slid his fingers deep into her warmth.

It was more than she could withstand. She bowed beneath him, tightening to the point of near pain and then she reached her peak in a quick, tumultuous burst.

He tenderly kissed the quivering bundle of nerves, eliciting another shudder from her before he moved his mouth up to her belly to lavish gentle attention on it. His hands molded to the swell and there was such reverence in his touch that she had to swallow back the knot forming in her throat.

She wanted to believe so very much that he was coming around. That maybe he was beginning to let go of his past, but she was afraid to broach the subject. Afraid of his rejection. And she couldn't be patient and understanding. She wasn't going to wait around forever for him to decide he wanted to fight for their future.

"Tell me if I hurt you."

He shifted upward, positioning himself between her thighs. He held his weight off her with one palm pressed to the mattress while he used his other hand to guide his erection to her opening.

Tentatively he pressed forward, his gaze never leaving her face as he probed deeper. She pulsed around him, still hypersensitive after her orgasm. As he pushed even deeper, she closed her eyes and dug her fingers into his muscled shoulders.

"Too much?" he asked.

She opened her eyes to see him eyeing her with concern.

"Oh, no," she whispered. "Not enough."

His pupils dilated. His jaw tightened and bulged and he drew in a deep breath as if he were trying valiantly to maintain control.

She lifted her hands to frame his face, caressing his jaw as she stared up at him.

"Make love to me, Cam. Don't hold back. You won't hurt me."

He closed his eyes and emitted a harsh groan. Then he turned his face into her hand and kissed her palm. Carefully he lowered himself until her belly pressed into his. He rested his forearms on either side of her shoulders and then pushed deeper.

His mouth found hers. Hungry. Hot. Demanding even as he was exceedingly gentle.

He found a slow, sensual rhythm, rocking against her as he filled her again and again. He was patient, working her up that slow rise all over again.

It was less urgent this time. Mellow. A lazy climb upward as pleasure filled her. She felt weightless, surrounded by him. She felt...*loved*.

Even as she knew it was foolish to allow herself the fantasy that he wanted and needed her, she couldn't help but immerse herself in this one moment where everything in her world was utter perfection.

His mouth skimmed down her jaw to her neck where his teeth grazed the sensitive skin underneath her ear. Then he raised his body just enough to send himself even deeper inside her.

She gasped, then clutched at his shoulders, digging her nails into his flesh. She arched upward, wanting, needing more.

"That's it, baby," he murmured. "I love how you respond. Always with me one hundred percent."

Oh, if he only knew just how with him she was and wanted to be. She bit her lip to prevent the words, those damnable words, from slipping out in the heat of the moment. He wouldn't welcome them.

I love you.

She closed her eyes and wrapped her arms around his neck, pulling him down so they were close. So close that his warmth bled into her body and she had no sense of where he began and she ended.

He shuddered against her. Let out a hoarse cry. She moaned softly and then whispered his name as the world crashed around her. Arching. Sighing. Undulating. Their bodies moved in quiet unison until they were wrapped tighter than braided rope.

She melted back onto the mattress, so sated that she couldn't even contemplate moving. For a moment he rested above her, his weight only barely pressed to hers, and then he rolled to the side, taking her with him.

He pulled her in close, anchoring her head in the hollow of his neck. His heart tripped frantically against her cheek and she inhaled deeply, wanting to capture his essence and imprint it in her memory.

He didn't speak but neither did she. Anything she'd say

would only ruin the moment and anything he'd likely say she wouldn't want to hear. So she was content to let things lie.

She closed her eyes, knowing that when she woke again, he'd be gone. Just like the other times. She'd wake to an empty bed and an even emptier heart.

She threw her arm and a leg over him, knowing it was pointless but unable to resist the urge to keep him close for as long as she could. Then she snuggled deeper into his embrace and allowed the veil of sleep to overcome her.

Cam woke in a cold sweat, the horror of his dream still alive and vivid in his mind. For a moment he stared into the darkness, still reliving every moment.

The accident that had taken Elise and Colton from him had been replayed in slow motion. He'd experienced the horrific, numbing helplessness of knowing he couldn't save them. But still, he'd run toward the wreckage, his heart in his throat, praying with everything he had that this time would be different. That this time he'd find them alive.

Only when he'd gotten there, it had been Pippa's bloodied face he'd seen, the last, pained cry of their newborn son he'd heard.

Desperate to get away and to make the awful vision disappear, he shoved hastily out of the bed, Pippa's sleepy murmur of protest dim in his ears.

He yanked on his clothing, nearly tripping in his haste to be gone. He stumbled through her apartment to the front door and lunged into the night, gulping huge, steadying breaths into burning lungs.

He palmed his forehead as he made his way to his car and fumbled with the lock. He got in and slumped against the seat and sat there several long minutes, staring through the windshield, trying to bring to mind Elise's features.

But it wasn't his beloved wife he saw every time he closed his eyes. It was Pippa.

Seventeen

Pippa struggled out of bed the next morning. She should be euphoric. She'd had a terrific turnout for her grand opening. She'd spent a wonderful evening with Cam and an even better night in bed. But as she'd known, even though she'd awakened before dawn to get to her café, Cam had been gone.

She trudged into her shop, feeling thoroughly down. The two people she'd hired to help her bake in the mornings arrived shortly after she did and they worked in silence, Pippa shunning any attempt at conversation.

She needed time to think. Or rather time to berate herself for being such a weak ninny. Cam was...well, he was manic and it was driving her insane. She couldn't continue like this.

Oh, who was she kidding. All the man had to do was smile at her, offer an apology and take her to bed. She'd never envisioned herself as one of those gullible women she and her friends liked to rag on. But apparently Pippa was smart in every aspect except men and relationships.

It was just a few minutes to opening when Pippa's cell phone rang. It was Ashley's ringtone and Pippa felt some of her tension ease. Ashley always made her feel better.

"You're up early this morning. Baby keeping you awake?" Pippa asked as she put the phone to her ear.

"Pippa, it's Devon."

He sounded harried and there was a terse quality to his voice that immediately put her on edge.

"Where's Ashley?" Pippa demanded.

"We're at the hospital. She's in labor and wanted me to call you. I can't reach her mother and she's in a panic. I think she just wants some female company. I'm driving her crazy."

Pippa smiled. "It's all right, Dev. I'm on my way. Hang in there."

Devon's relief was palpable. "Thanks, Pippa."

She rang off and then gave her employees instructions for running the shop in her absence. Leaving her business on its second day wasn't at all what she wanted but she wasn't about to leave Ashley when she needed her most.

After making sure they'd call her if any issues arose, Pippa hurried out the door to hail a cab. She could call John, but she didn't want to wait even that long to get to the hospital. She was nervous and excited to be with Ashley on the big day, but if she were honest, she'd admit that the whole delivery thing scared the bejebus out of her.

She wasn't yet prepared for that aspect of her pregnancy; she'd been existing in ignorant bliss. Childbirth itself was the part of all the pregnancy books she skipped over. She knew all about the nine months leading up to it. She knew all about what happened after the delivery. But she'd blocked out any information about the actual delivery of the baby.

Not smart, but hey, a girl did what she had to just to get through.

Once at the hospital she stopped by the information desk to find out Ashley's room number and then headed up to the maternity ward. She tapped on Ashley's door, half-afraid of what she'd see on the other side.

Devon opened the door and looked relieved to see her there. Pippa hesitantly peeked around Devon, happy when she saw Ashley propped in the bed looking none the worse for wear. Ashley's face brightened when she saw Pippa.

"Pippa! I'm so glad you're here."

Pippa smiled and went over to the bed to enfold Ashley in a hug. "Hey, you. How's it going? When's that baby going to get here?"

Ashley pulled a face. "Not soon enough. It could be hours yet. I'm only dilated to four."

Pippa blinked. "Four what?"

Ashley's brow furrowed. "Centimeters."

"Oh."

Pippa really didn't want to know what exactly that meant. It sounded painful. These were things she avoided. She'd much rather read about the baby's first movements and all the development stages after birth.

"Can I get you anything, Ash?"

Ashley shook her head. "No, just stay with me. I'm driving poor Dev nuts. He wants to make it all better and I'm grumpy."

Pippa laughed. "You grumpy?"

"Here, have a seat, Pippa," Devon offered as he pushed a chair behind her. "You don't need to be on your feet, and like Ash said, it's going to be a while."

Pippa settled in the chair beside Ashley's bed while Devon continued to pace in a small area behind them. She reached for Ashley's hand and offered a comforting squeeze.

"Are you excited?"

Ashley took a deep breath. "Excited. Scared out of my mind. I just want to know how soon I can get my epidural."

Pippa shuddered.

"I kind of wish now that I'd found out what we're having," Ashley said mournfully. "I thought it would be exciting to be all surprised when the doctor said 'it's a boy' or 'it's a girl,' but now I'm thinking no surprises is a good thing."

Pippa nodded her agreement. Of course if she'd opted not to find out, maybe Cam wouldn't have wigged out, but then it probably wouldn't have been good for him to find out on delivery day. The more time he had to come to terms with the fact he was having another son, the better. Or at least that was her way of thinking.

Devon moved to the other side of Ashley's bed and leaned down to kiss her temple. "It'll be all right, Ash. You're going to do great."

Ashley looked up with such love in her eyes, love that was openly reflected in Devon's tender gaze. Pippa had to look away and swallow against the knot forming in her throat. She wanted this. What they had. She and Cam hadn't even discussed if he'd be here when the baby came. She assumed he would, but she was learning it was dangerous to assume anything when it came to him.

She stood abruptly, tears burning the lids of her eyes. "I'll be right back. I need to make a phone call. Check on the store."

She all but fled from Ashley's hospital room, shutting the door behind her and leaning heavily on it as she tried to clear her blurry vision. She pushed off the door and hurried down the hall to the waiting room where hopefully she could regain her composure. Ashley needed her to be strong today.

Throughout the day, visitors came and went. Ashley's mother barged into the room a few hours after Pippa arrived, mortified that she couldn't be reached the minute Ashley went into labor. Pippa was glad to see Mrs. Copeland. She just had a way of making everything better. She'd already hugged Pippa no less than a dozen times and Pippa gloried in each one.

Tabitha, Carly and Sylvia came by but didn't stay long since the room was growing more crowded with Ashley's family. Pippa herself had already decided she'd retire down the hall to the waiting area so she wouldn't be in the way.

She crept out, snagged a cup of water from the cooler and sat in a comfortable chair to wait the arrival of the baby. As the day wore on, more people filtered into the waiting room and it was alive with conversation and excitement.

Ashley had a large family and it seemed that every single one of them was going to be present for the birth of Ashley's child.

Pippa's heart squeezed because she couldn't imagine such a wonderful fuss when it came time for her baby to be born. How marvelous it must be to have a huge, loving family who gathered for special occasions and celebrated with such vibrancy.

Here in a room full of warm, friendly people, she'd never felt so alone in her life.

"Have you eaten anything today?"

She jumped, pulled suddenly from her thoughts by the sound of Cam's voice coming from behind her. She turned around and shook her head, watching as he frowned his disapproval.

"Let's go down to the cafeteria," Cam said.

He started to take her elbow but she pulled away. "I'm not leaving now. Ashley is going to deliver at any minute. No way am I missing this."

Cam seemed to take in the expectant air that permeated the room. He drew his lips into a thin line and then said, "I'll go get you something. You need to eat."

She shrugged—which seemed to irritate him—but she wasn't exactly concerned with him at the moment.

With another inquisitive look in her direction, Cam turned and walked out of the waiting room. Pippa blew out her breath and settled back in her seat. Yeah, he probably was confused as to why she was snippy. In his mind, he'd probably already blown off the fact that he'd hightailed it after sex again. And he had no way of knowing just how muddled Pippa's own feelings were and how close to her breaking point she was.

Fifteen minutes later, Cam returned with a foam carry-out container and handed it to her with plastic utensils.

"I wasn't sure what to get you to drink, so I got you a bottle of water."

"That's fine," she said, retrieving it from his grasp. "You aren't eating?"

"I ate before I came."

He parked himself in the chair next to her, extending his long legs as she opened the container. The spaghetti and garlic bread looked good, but she had absolutely no desire to eat. Her stomach was too churned up.

She managed a few bites and pushed the food around so it would look like she was eating. The only problem was, she could feel Cam's stare on her and knew he wasn't fooled.

She was saved when Ashley's father, William Copeland, burst into the waiting room, grinning from ear to ear. "It's a girl! I have a granddaughter!"

The room erupted with excitement. Pippa put her plate down and rose with the others to converge on Mr. Copeland. The smiles were huge. Lots of hugging. It was everything Pippa wanted for her own delivery.

A few minutes later, Devon appeared holding a tiny bundle in his arms. He was smiling so big that his face had to hurt. But then Pippa watched as Cam converged on his friend, his own smile a match to Devon's.

Her mouth drooped as Cam peered over the blanket at the baby, his eyes glowing as he and Devon exchanged comments. Worse, Devon readily handed the baby over to Cam and they stood together cooing and talking baby nonsense.

Pippa hadn't thought it possible to hurt more than she had the day of her sonogram. She stood locked in stone as she watched the same man who'd walked away from her and her baby make a total moron of himself over that tiny little girl.

Cam handed the baby back, slapped Devon on the back and heartily congratulated him. The room was a buzz of excited chatter, congratulations and oohs and aahs. But Pippa was focused on Cam. Cam, who was smiling. Cam, who was happy. Cam, who clearly had it in him to love.

So why couldn't he love her and their child?

Eighteen

Pippa was no longer able to stand there and pretend that everything was fine when she was dying on the inside.

In the excitement, she was able to slip away unnoticed. As she headed toward the elevator, she bumped into one of Ashley's cousins and asked her if she'd make Pippa's excuses to the new mother. She walked into the elevator, turning to stare at the jubilation at the opposite end of the corridor. Tears pricked her eyelids as she punched the button for the first floor.

Just as the doors started to slide closed, Cam looked up and their gazes connected. His brow furrowed and he started forward, but the gap closed and the elevator began its descent.

Realizing that Cam would likely come down after her, she headed out and crossed the street, deciding to walk a few blocks before hailing a cab.

The night air was chilly despite the earlier sunshine and warmth. And what a perfect day it had been for Ashley's baby girl to be born. Spring. The beginning of new life. A fresh start. Life after a long winter.

So symbolic, and yet for her, spring meant death.

Okay, so she was being a little dramatic, but sadness had a firm grip on her throat and it wasn't letting go.

She loved Cam. Despite his many flaws.

But she wanted him to smile at her and their child the way he'd looked down and smiled at Devon and Ashley's daughter. She wanted to see him light up and look…happy. Had he ever seemed so carefree when he was with her?

It had been like looking at an entirely different person. Was this the way he was around people he cared about? Ashley had said he was always gentle and even tender with her.

So it wasn't that he didn't care about people or that he was incapable of love. It was just as he'd said. He didn't want to love her. Or their son.

A sob escaped as she raised her hand to hail an oncoming cab. It never slowed and she dropped her hand, staring down the street in search of the next one.

Tears streaked down her cheeks, but she made no effort to wipe them away. What was the point?

She leaned out when she saw another cab approach and slow down. She climbed in, barely managing to tell the driver her cross street. He gave her an odd look in his rearview mirror as he pulled into traffic.

Her cell phone rang but she didn't bother to dig it out of her purse. It was Cam. She'd known he'd call. After a moment, the phone went silent and then a ping sounded, signaling a text message.

She was nearing her apartment, when her phone rang again. It was Ashley's ringtone. Pippa dug into her purse, fumbling for the phone.

"Ash?" she said as she put the phone to her ear.

"No, it's Devon."

Pippa went silent for a moment. "Is everything okay with Ashley and the baby?"

"I'm more concerned with whether you're all right," Devon said in a low voice.

"I'm f-fine," she said in a shaky voice. "Really. I hope I didn't hurt Ashley's feelings by not hanging around. I just figured she'd be exhausted and with all her family there I'd just be in the way."

"You're never in the way, Pippa," Devon said gently. It was as if he knew precisely how upset Pippa was. As if he was standing in front of her, watching her cry. "I just wanted to make sure everything was okay with you. I know…I know it had to be hard for you to see that. Cam, I mean."

It was then Pippa realized that Devon had indeed picked up on the very thing she had. She closed her eyes, a fresh resurgence of tears sliding hotly down her cheeks.

"I appreciate your concern, Dev. Truly. But I'm okay. You should be focusing on Ashley and that beautiful baby girl. Tell Ash that I'll come see her tomorrow when things are a little less crazy, I promise. But you're right. I couldn't stay there tonight. I…I just had to go."

"I understand," Devon said. "Chin up, Pippa. If killing him would help, I'd give serious consideration to it. Only the knowledge that I was once the same sort of bastard and that I eventually saw the light is saving me from tossing him off a bridge."

Pippa smiled as her cab pulled to a stop. "Thanks, Dev. I'm home now so I'll let you get back to your family. Give Ash my love and I'll see her tomorrow."

"Take care, Pippa," Devon said. "If you need us, you know we're here."

"I do know," she said softly.

She thrust money at the driver and then ducked out and hurried down the sidewalk toward her apartment. She glanced down at her phone to see she had several text messages. All from Cam.

The last?

Damn it, Pippa. Pick up the phone. What happened? Are you all right?

She slid the phone back into her purse and grabbed her keys as she mounted the steps to her door.

No, she wasn't all right. She'd never been so *not* all right in her life.

The next day was a test of her endurance. She woke early after having not slept well at all and went into the café to get a start on the baking.

She enjoyed a steady stream of customers, many effusive in their praise of her goodies. She should be on top of the freaking world but it was all she could do to keep her head up for the duration of the day.

The only thing that made it bearable was the fact that Cam didn't show up. She was half-afraid he would after she refused to answer his calls or texts the night before.

After locking up, she went home and took a long nap. Or at least she tried. She lay down and went through the motions of napping, but her mind wouldn't shut down and all she could do was replay Cam's smile and his joy from the night before.

She was wrung out, disillusioned, and she knew it was time for her to make a decision. She could no longer afford to hang around hoping that one day Cam woke up, pulled his head out of his ass and realized his life wasn't over.

She pushed herself from the bed, made a halfhearted attempt to straighten her appearance and then trudged to her kitchen to get a drink and try to shake the cobwebs from her brain.

First she'd go visit Ashley and make up for the fact that she'd bailed on her the day before. Her friends came first.

Not bothering with a coat—it was her hope that the chilly evening air would give her a much-needed wake up—she left her apartment and walked to the end of the block to hail a cab. She just didn't have it in her to walk the extra few blocks to the subway.

When she got to the hospital, visitor hours were almost over but she headed up to the maternity ward, anyway. The worst they could do was kick her out.

She knocked quietly on Ashley's door, hoping her friend wasn't asleep. A moment later, the door opened and Devon appeared.

"Come on in," Devon said with apparent relief. His gaze sharpened as he took in Pippa's appearance, and without a further word, he simply pulled her into his arms and gave her a huge hug.

She hadn't known just how badly she needed that until his arms surrounded her. She bit into her lip to keep from bursting into tears on the spot. She was here to see Ashley and the baby, not blubber all over her and her husband.

"Thank you," Pippa whispered against Devon's chest. "How is Ash?"

"Go see for yourself," he said as he pulled away. "She's holding Katelynn now."

Pippa hurried past the private bathroom and approached the bed. She stopped and stared at the beautiful sight of Ashley with her daughter cradled in her arms.

Ashley smiled broadly. "Hey, Pip. Come on over and see her. She's so beautiful."

"You're breast-feeding her?" Pippa whispered as she went to Ashley's bedside and stared down at the tiny infant. "Is it hard?"

Ashley smiled. "A little at first but the nurses here are so great. They helped a lot and then Katelynn did the rest. She's a real champ at it now."

Devon pushed a chair to the side of the bed and motioned for Pippa to sit.

"So Dev said Cam was a real butthead last night," Ashley said in a low voice.

Pippa sighed. "Let's not talk about him, Ash. This is your time to be happy and enjoy your beautiful baby without listening to your friend complain."

Ashley gently broke suction and pulled her gown back to cover her breast. Then she looked toward Devon. "Want to see if she'll burp for you?"

Devon reached over Pippa to take the bundle and went to sit in the recliner by the window.

"Now," Ashley said, crossing her arms over her chest. "Spill. You look terrible, Pip. You're clearly unhappy."

The knot grew larger in Pippa's throat and her eyes clouded with tears once again.

"I'm miserable, but it's my own fault. I totally set myself

up for this. I walked into this knowing the score. I'm just frustrated and heartsick. I'm going to confront him, Ash. It's stupid but it's something I have to do."

Ashley reached over to take her hand and squeeze. "What are you going to say to him?"

Pippa emitted a harsh laugh that grated on her own ears. "I'm going to tell him I love him."

Ashley blew out her breath. "You're so much braver than I am. You always were."

"Yeah, but you're smarter, so we're even," Pippa muttered.

"Not true. Okay, so after you tell him you love him, what then?"

Pippa sighed. "Then nothing. He'll do what he always does and I'll walk away but this time it'll be for good. I just feel like I have to give him this last chance. Or maybe it's just me and I want one last chance. Either way, I need it to be final. I can't continue this hot-and-cold thing we have going. My eyes were opened last night. I realized that he's happy around other people. Just not *me*. And that hurt."

"Oh, Pip," Ashley said, her whole face a mask of sympathy. "I wish…"

"I do, too," Pippa said. "But wishes aren't real. Wishing is for fairy tales. Cam is no Prince Charming and I'm no princess living happily ever after."

Ashley seemed to be on the verge of tears and the very last thing Pippa wanted was to further upset her friend. Not when she should be on top of the world. So she forced cheer into her voice and a smile onto her lips as she rose to hug Ashley.

"I'm going to steal that baby from Devon for a minute and then I'm going to get out of here and let you rest."

She turned toward Devon, who slowly lifted his daughter away from his shoulder and placed her in Pippa's arms.

She held the baby close, studying every inch of her softness. She touched the tuft of hair on top of Katelynn's head, feeling the silky, delicate strands. Someone had affixed a tiny little bow just in front of her soft spot. Pink and girlie. So much like Ashley.

She ran her finger over the tiny fingertips and watched in fascination as they curled around Pippa's own finger and made a tight fist.

She was instantly and completely won over, heart and soul. She was absolutely in love with this little girl. Who wouldn't be? But then it had been the same when she'd seen her son on the sonogram monitor for the first time. Instant love. Unconditional. A bond that couldn't be broken.

It hadn't been the same for Cam. He hadn't been able to leave fast enough.

She briefly closed her eyes and then lowered her head so she could brush her lips across Katelynn's forehead. She inhaled the sweet baby scent and then brought the baby back over to where Ashley lay.

"She's absolutely perfect, Ash. You did good."

Ashley beamed and held out her arms to collect her daughter. Then she looked back up at Pippa.

"It's going to be okay, Pippa."

Pippa nodded because there was nothing else to do. She turned to offer Devon a wave. "I'll see you guys later."

"Call me if you need anything," Devon said.

Pippa nodded and then walked out of the room, closing the door softly behind her. She checked her watch and stood there a long moment, simply leaning against the wall in the hallway.

There was no way she would sleep tonight. Not until she settled things with Cam. She had to get this over with before it ate her alive.

It would be a long trip on an already late night, and it meant dragging Cam out of his bed, but at the moment she didn't care. One way or another, it would be settled tonight.

Nineteen

Convincing a cab driver to take her all the way to Greenwich had been next to impossible, and it was going to cost her a fortune to boot. The ride seemed interminable and traffic was heavy even at the late hour. By the time she reached Cam's gate, it was past midnight. He might not even be there for all she knew, but she suspected he was. He'd retreated to Greenwich with increasing frequency lately.

They waited at the gate while the driver spoke through the intercom. It wasn't Cam who answered. She was pretty certain it was John. A moment later, the gate swung open and the cab pulled up the driveway. He parked in front and she paid him and got out after telling him not to wait.

John opened the front door and came out to greet her, worry on his face.

"Is Cam home?" she asked quietly.

"He is. He retired an hour ago," John replied as he ushered her inside.

"I need to see him. I'll wait in his office."

She didn't give John a chance to argue. She simply turned and walked across the living room to the office. She didn't bother turning on the lights. There was something soothing about the darkness.

She stopped by the window, staring out into the night, at

the bright, star-filled sky. Fairy dust. A million wishes. She only needed one. Just one.

The door opened behind her. She closed her eyes for a brief moment and then turned to see Cam standing there in the dark.

"Pippa?"

There was concern and bewilderment in his voice. He took another step forward and then reached down to turn on a lamp that rested on the table by one of the armchairs.

She flinched at the sudden burst of light and turned away, not wanting him to see what she was sure was obvious on her face. But how could she hide it? How could she hide how devastated she was?

"What's wrong, Pippa? What are you doing all the way out here at this time of night?"

She swallowed, squared her shoulders and then took a deep breath. She turned to face him fully, uncaring of what he'd see.

"Are we done, Cam?" she asked bluntly.

He blinked in surprise. He opened his mouth and then snapped it shut again and frowned. "I'm not sure what to say here."

She took a step forward. "Let me make this easy for you, Cam. I love you."

He went pale and flinched. His reaction spoke volumes. It told her everything she needed to know but some demon inside her persisted. She'd gone this far and she'd see it to the bitter end even if it humiliated her in the process.

"I need to know where I stand," she said in an even voice. "One minute you seem to want me and we act like—we *are*—lovers. The next you can't get away from me fast enough and you're cold, like I'm some random stranger."

Cam's lips tightened. "I was honest with you from the onset."

She nodded. "Yes, you were. No doubt about that. But

you're sending mixed signals. Your actions contradict your words. I need to know if I have a chance here, Cam."

He started to turn away and it infuriated her.

"Don't turn your back on me," she bit out. "At least give me that. Face me and tell me why you can't give me commitment, why you can't love me. I understand you lost people you loved. I get it. But it's time to move on. You have a child, a son, who needs you. *I* need you," she finished in an aching voice.

Cam whirled back around, his eyes flashing furiously. "Move on? You *get* it? How the hell do you get it, Pippa? You think that by spouting some clichéd armchair psychology crap at me that I'm supposed to say, oh, you're right, and then live happily ever after?"

"What I think is that it's ridiculous to believe you can't love anyone else."

He closed his eyes and his jaw tightened. When he re-opened them, he stared directly at her, his tone even. "It's not that I can't love again. I'm not one of these people who believes you only get one shot, that there's only one soul mate out there and if you screw that up you're out of luck for the rest of your life."

Her mouth fell open because, of all things, this was not what she'd expected to hear. "Then *why*?" she whispered. "Why can't you love me and our baby?"

He slapped his hands down on his desk and glared at her with eyes so dark and haunted that she flinched.

"It's not that I can't love you, Pippa. *I don't want to.* Do you understand? I don't *want* to love you."

She recoiled, so stunned that she couldn't even respond. She wrapped her arms around her belly and stood back, hurt spreading to every corner of her soul.

His words when they came were angry and frustrated, as though he hated having to explain himself, as if he hated admitting what he'd just blurted out.

"If I don't love you, then it won't hurt me if something happens to you. If I don't love you, then nothing you do will touch me. I don't ever want to feel the way I did when I watched Elise and Colton die in front of me. You can't possibly understand that. I hope you never have to."

Her arms crept tighter around herself, as if to ward off the unbearable pain of his rejection.

"You would shut out me and your own child because you're too afraid to take that risk?" she asked hoarsely. "What kind of an unfeeling monster are you?"

He jabbed a finger in her direction. "You've got that right. Unfeeling. It's exactly the way I want to be. I don't want to feel a damn thing."

Anger hummed through her veins, replacing the ice that had rapidly formed. "You bastard. You callous, manipulative bastard. What the hell have you been doing for the past months? If you were so determined not to have a relationship, then why did you continue to make love to me?"

His gaze dropped and guilt shadowed his face.

"Am I supposed to feel sorry for you? Am I supposed to be all sympathetic and pet your poor damaged heart just because something horrible happened to you in the past? I've got news for you, Cam. Life sucks. It isn't perfect for anyone and you aren't special. Bad things happen to people all the time but they don't become heartless jerks and piss on everyone around them. They get up, dust themselves off and keep on living. Maybe you never got that memo."

"That's enough," he said tightly.

"Oh, hell, no, it isn't. I'm just getting warmed up and you're going to listen to everything I have to say. You *owe* me that much. One day you'll regret this. You'll regret that you turned your back on me and our baby. You'll find someone you want to marry and you'll think about the fact that you have a son out there who never had a father because you were a coward."

"Somehow I don't think my future wife would care for the fact that my mistress and our love child were in such close proximity," he snapped.

The blood left her face and she took another step back as if he'd physically hit her. His face went gray and he started toward her as if he knew he'd gone too far.

She held up her hand to halt him. She was barely holding on to her composure and only her pride was keeping her upright at this point. This was pointless. They were two snapping dogs trying to hurt each other with quick, angry words. It solved nothing. It never would.

"We're done," she said in a cold voice. "I want nothing from you, Cam. Not your support. Not your money. Definitely not your presence. I don't want you anywhere near me or my child. *My* child. Not yours. You don't want us and quite frankly we don't need you."

"Pippa…"

She shook her head. "I don't want to hear it. But know this, Cam. One day you're going to wake up and realize you've made a horrible, horrible mistake. I won't be there." She cupped her hands over her belly. "*We* won't be there. I deserve more. I deserve a man who'll give me *everything* and not just throw money or convenience at me. More than that, my child deserves more. He deserves a father who'll love him unconditionally. Who'll go to the wall for him every damn day. Not a father incapable of loving anyone but himself."

She turned to walk out but paused at the door. She faced him one last time, ignoring the utter bleakness in his eyes.

"I loved you, Cam. I never asked you for anything. That's true. And yes, you were up front from the beginning, so shame on me for changing the rules. I have equal responsibility for this debacle, but just because I made a mistake doesn't mean that I'm going to punish myself for the rest of my life and I'm damn sure not going to make my child suffer for my stupidity. I'd tell you to have a nice life, but somehow I don't think that's going to be possible because you're far too content to wallow in your misery."

She yanked open the door and walked out, slamming it behind her. It wasn't until she got outside the front entrance that she remembered she hadn't asked the cabbie to wait and now she was stranded at this damn monstrosity of a house.

"Miss Laingley, will you allow me to drive you home?"

She turned to see John standing there, his eyes soft with sympathy. It was the last straw. She burst into tears and then allowed him to guide her toward the waiting car.

Twenty

Cam sank into the chair behind his desk and buried his face in his hands.

He'd followed Pippa out the door and seen that John was giving her a ride home. He'd watched as the car drove down the lane, the lights disappearing in the distance.

For how long he stood there, numb, he didn't know. He realized the door was still open and the wind had picked up. A chill had stolen over him but he knew it wasn't the temperature. He was cold on the inside. Dead. Still breathing and yet dead. He had been for a long time.

Now, sitting at his desk, his gut clenched. His chest ached. It shouldn't. He should be relieved. It was done. There was no possible way for Pippa to misunderstand.

Clean break. He'd done exactly what he should have done from the very beginning.

So why didn't he feel vindicated? Relieved, even? He should be glad. He could go back to his unemotional existence where he didn't have to feel pain.

Only none of that was true. He hurt *now*. He hurt so damn much that he couldn't breathe around the knot in his throat.

He'd lost Pippa.

The very thing he'd tried to protect himself from was the pain of loss. The despair and frustration of not being able to keep a loved one safe was his reality. Right here, right now.

He'd lost Pippa. He'd lost his son.

His *son*.

An innocent, precious life.

A child who deserved to have the world at his feet. Two parents who loved him. A father who'd protect him from all the hurts and disappointments life had to offer.

Oh, God, he was a bastard. He was such an unfeeling monster, just what Pippa had accused him of being. Only he wasn't unfeeling. Right now he'd give anything not to be able to feel this agony.

Seeing Pippa tonight and the evidence of just how low he'd brought her down made him want to die. She'd stood before him, pain in her eyes, and yet she'd still put herself out there. She'd taken a chance. Laid it all out.

And he'd slapped her down because he was afraid.

It was humbling to realize just what a coward he was. What a coward he had been for so long.

He'd been given something many people never got. Something others wished for, would kill for, would live every single day of their life in gratitude for.

A second chance.

Another chance at something so special and wonderful.

Pippa was a breath of fresh air into a life he'd quit living. He went through the motions. He performed. But he'd stopped truly living a long time ago.

Pippa had changed all that. From the moment he'd first seen her walk into a room, she'd been like a bolt of lightning to his senses.

Her smile, her laughter, her take-no-prisoners attitude. Her confidence. Her inner beauty. And her courage.

When he really stopped to consider just how much she'd had to shoulder alone these past few months it made him physically ill. She was young, had plans. She could have anyone and yet she'd chosen him. He'd made her pregnant and yet she soldiered on, making the best of a difficult situation.

She'd fought fiercely, was still fighting fiercely for his son.

He was so damn proud of her and so damn ashamed of himself that he couldn't bear to think about it.

He didn't deserve her. She was right about that.

But he wanted her. Oh, God, he wanted her.

It was laughable that he'd actually thought that he could spare himself the pain of loss by shutting himself off and away, by closing the door on a relationship with Pippa.

He'd been so worried about losing her that the very thing he feared the most had happened. At his instigation!

Stupid didn't even begin to cover it.

He pushed upward from his chair, suddenly agitated and more determined than he'd ever been in his life.

He loved her, damn it.

He'd lied to himself and to her. He'd spouted all kinds of crap about not wanting to love her. Yeah, he hadn't wanted to but he did and that wasn't going to change.

And now he had to crawl on hands and knees and beg her to give him yet another chance.

He hurried out of his office and through the kitchen to the garage. He yanked the keys from the hook, and not giving any consideration to how he looked or how he was dressed, he climbed into the Escalade.

He was driving back to the damn city and he was going to her apartment and he didn't care if it was four in the morning. This couldn't wait. He couldn't wait.

Some things needed to be done immediately, and this was one of them. He'd made her wait all this time. He wasn't waiting another damn moment.

It had taken immeasurable courage for her to come to his house and face him down, tell him she loved him and wait with her heart on her sleeve.

How could he not do the same for her?

It would be the hardest thing and yet the easiest thing he'd ever do. Because when faced with the alternative of living his life without her and their son? Crawling didn't seem so bad.

* * *

Pippa trudged into her apartment, weariness overtaking her. Her head ached from trying to hold off the tears. Her eyes were swollen and scratchy. She was heartsick and numb from head to toe.

She felt…lost. Like she wasn't sure what came next. There was such finality to her confrontation with Cam. What was she supposed to do?

She sank onto the couch, tossed her purse onto the coffee table and closed her eyes. Her head throbbed. She needed sleep. At least there, she could escape for a while and not feel so horrible.

She arranged one of the cushions against the arm of the couch and pulled her feet up, curling up on her side. Exhaustion beat at her, making her remember that between her grand opening, Ashley giving birth and all the angst over Cam, she hadn't had a good night's sleep in longer than she could remember.

She pulled out her phone, looked at the time and winced. She'd need to be up in just a couple of hours. She set the alarm on her phone so she'd be sure to wake and then she reached over to set it on top of the coffee table next to her purse.

Then she closed her eyes and let the comforting blanket of sleep slide over her.

The smell of smoke woke Pippa from a dead sleep. She opened her eyes, confused by the darkness and the acrid smell of something burning. She blinked away the cloud of disorientation and then shoved herself up from the couch in horror.

Flames surrounded her and the scorching heat singed her skin. Everywhere there was a wall of orange fire and smoke billowing heavily. It was so dense she had no idea where she was or which way was out or if there even was a way out.

She breathed in and then coughed as her lungs burned. Panic slammed into her as she realized the horrific danger she was in.

Clutching her belly, she lunged from the couch, trying to see through the flames and smoke to know if she could make it to the door.

Then she remembered that in a fire, the safest place to be was as close to the floor as possible. She dropped down, as low as she could with her burgeoning belly, and pulled her shirt up to cover her nose and mouth.

Her phone. Where was her phone?

She turned back but lost sight of the couch in the haze of smoke. She was fast becoming so disoriented that if she didn't do something now she was going to die.

She closed her eyes and pictured the layout of the room and forced her panic down so she could focus. She knew every inch of her apartment and she wasn't going to let her hysteria make her do something stupid.

She had to save her baby. She had to save herself.

Still holding her shirt over her face, she began to crawl in the direction of the front door. Above her, flames licked over the ceiling and smoke billowed from every corner. It was becoming harder and harder to breathe and she was sick with worry of what this was doing to her baby.

Thoughts of her child renewed her determination to get out no matter what. She scrambled over hot, smoldering rubble and made it to the foyer. Just a little farther. There didn't appear to be as much smoke close to the door and she put on a burst of speed, ignoring the cuts and burns to her palms and knees.

She was a few feet away when the door splintered and cracked and caved in. Smoke began drawing through the opening, pulling around her and enveloping her. She heard a shout and then strong hands gripped her, pulling her upward.

The fireman cradled her in his arms and barged out the front door into the cool night air. Around her, the world was a sea of flashing lights, smoke and flames shooting toward the star-filled sky.

"Is there anyone else in your apartment?" the fireman yelled to her.

She shook her head. "No," she replied, dismayed by the fact the denial came out in a barely audible croak.

He carried her to a waiting ambulance where she was handed over to another man who promptly put her on a stretcher.

"The baby," she rasped out. "I'm pregnant."

An oxygen mask covered her face, blocking out anything further she'd say. The next thing she knew, she was laid flat, pushed into the back of the ambulance and two paramedics hovered anxiously over.

There was a prick in her arm. They shouted down questions to her. She tried to tell them she was okay, but she couldn't say anything through the mask and her throat hurt too badly, anyway.

Numbly she lay there, trying to process what had just happened. Darkness grew around the edges of her sight and then one of the medics leaned down close, shouting at her to stay awake and with them.

"There's nothing wrong with me," she tried to say, but she couldn't get her mouth to work.

She blinked twice and then the world went black around her.

Twenty-one

As soon as Cam turned onto Pippa's street, his stomach dropped and his mouth went dry. He gripped the steering wheel with white knuckles as he accelerated.

The entire world was ablaze with flashing lights. Police cars, ambulances, fire trucks. The smell of smoke was heavy, and the sky was colored orange with the glow of flames.

He screeched to a halt in front of a police barricade and he was out of his SUV like a shot, running toward Pippa's apartment. The entire row of buildings was ablaze and firemen directed a steady stream of water from multiple directions.

"Hey! You can't go in there!"

He ignored the shout, his only thought to get to Pippa. Oh, God. Not again. Anything but this. He couldn't lose her! A sob tore from his throat.

He'd just reached the front line of fire trucks and ambulances when he was hit by a flying tackle. He hit the ground hard and came up swinging. A police officer hovered over him, shouting something Cam couldn't hear or understand.

Another officer joined in, helping wrestle Cam to the ground.

"Get off me!" he yelled hoarsely. "I have to get to her. Pippa! She's pregnant! I have to save her."

"You aren't going anywhere," the officer growled as he exerted more pressure over Cam's neck. "Get it together, son. The entire block is on fire. You'll just get yourself killed."

"Don't make us arrest you," the other officer threatened. "I get that you're worried, but they're doing everything they can to make sure everyone gets out. Let them do their job. The last thing they need is to have to go in to save your stupid ass."

"Let me up," Cam demanded. "I have to know if she's okay. Did they get her out?"

Slowly the first officer eased up on the arm across Cam's throat. He glanced warily at Cam as he and the other officer hauled Cam to his feet.

"Don't make any sudden moves," the officer warned.

Cam put his hands up, his heart pounding with dread as he eyed the carnage around him. This was his worst nightmare playing out in real time.

Fate was dealing him yet another blow, one he may never recover from. But no, this wasn't fate. He could have prevented this. If only he'd reached out as she had done. If he'd only been willing to take the chance that she had taken by coming to him.

He alone was at fault. If something happened to Pippa and their child, his life was over.

"Pippa," he said hoarsely. "Pippa Laingley. She lived there." He pointed at her apartment, his hand shaking, his voice cracking under the weight of his terror. "She would have just gotten home not so long ago. She was tired and upset. Please, can you just tell me if they found her?"

The officer pointed at Cam, his expression stern. "You stay here. I'll go see what I can find out." He gestured for the other officer to stay with Cam.

He watched the officer wade through the firefighters and other EMS workers. It was all he could do to stand there while his heart was dying with each breath. The officer standing beside him eyed him with sympathy.

"They got several out already," he said in a low voice.

"Many have already been taken to the hospital. I'm sure if she was in there that they got her."

A few moments later, the first officer returned, a grim expression on his face. Cam lunged forward, getting so close he was almost pressing up against the policeman's chest.

"They took her away in an ambulance maybe a half hour ago. She was one of the first they got out. I don't have any further details. It's crazy right now, but they said she was conscious and appeared to be unharmed."

Cam's knees buckled and he nearly went down. All his breath rushed out in a violent explosion of relief.

"Whoa, steady there. Maybe you should take a seat."

Cam shook his head. "No. I have to go. Where did they take her?"

He was already turning to run to his SUV when the officer called after him with the name of the hospital. Cam sprinted from the scene, got into his truck and pulled away from the chaos.

He had to force himself not to drive recklessly when all he could think was to get to Pippa as fast as he could. He had to see her. Had to know she was all right. Had to hold her again and tell her everything that was in his heart. Everything he'd been too stubborn and too stupid to tell her before.

He only hoped to hell she would listen.

Pippa lay on the uncomfortable bed in the small cubicle in the emergency room as nurses came and went. Her horrific panic had settled somewhat with the news from the doctor that the baby was okay. She hadn't been subjected to the smoke long enough to do any lasting damage to her or the baby.

But she kept imagining what could have happened.

What if she hadn't awakened when she had? What if she hadn't gotten out as soon as she did?

The images wouldn't go away.

She rubbed her belly in a soothing circle, reassured by the baby's movements. The past hour had been a blur as she'd been poked, prodded, stuck, checked over. A sonogram had been ordered and she'd gotten to see for herself that her baby was still there, still alive and didn't seem in any distress.

She reeked of smoke. She looked like hell. But she didn't care. All that mattered was that her baby was okay.

Her door opened and to her surprise Devon poked his head in. To her further surprise, Ashley came in behind him and all but ran to Pippa's bedside.

"Pippa! Oh, my God," Ashley choked out.

Ashley threw her arms around Pippa, who lay there, stunned and unable to find her voice.

"What on earth?" she finally managed to sputter. "Ashley, what are you doing here? You just had a baby! You should be in bed."

Devon came around to the other side of Pippa's bed and leaned down to kiss her forehead. "We were worried, Pippa. When we heard, Ashley had to come right down. I couldn't very well tell her no."

Pippa frowned. "You should have. Where's Katelynn? Ash, are you okay?"

Ashley hugged Pippa fiercely and then pulled away, her eyes flashing. "I'm fine! The question is how are you? I had a baby, Pip. Normal delivery. I've been up walking around all day. And Katelynn is in the nursery for now. Tell me what on earth happened!"

Ashley slid onto the edge of the bed beside Pippa and grasped her hand, squeezing tightly. It was the last straw. Tears streaked down Pippa's cheeks and she hiccuped back a sob.

Devon gently stroked Pippa's hair. Ashley gathered Pippa's hands in hers and leaned forward, concern etched on her brow.

"Oh, Ashley," Pippa whispered. "It's been such an awful night."

"Wait, did you go see Cam?" Her eyes widened as she seemed to realize something. "Oh, no. What happened?"

"It's over," Pippa said, her voice cracking under the emotional strain and the rawness from the smoke. "I went to his house, told him I loved him and now it's over."

Ashley held on to her tightly, rubbing her hand up and down Pippa's back.

"I'm going to step outside," Devon murmured. "Give you girls some time alone. If you need anything, I'll be right outside the door."

He gave her one last affectionate touch on the arm and then left.

Ashley pulled away and gently pushed Pippa's bedraggled hair from her face. "Tell me everything, starting with what the doctor said. You scared me to death. I want to know you're okay first and then I want to know everything that happened at Cam's."

"The doctor says I'm fine. The baby is fine. I went to sleep on the couch and when I woke up, the whole apartment was on fire. But I got out before I inhaled too much smoke. I was lucky. I'm a bit scraped up from crawling, but I'll be fine. The doctor even says that I can go home by tomorrow afternoon.…"

She trailed off, realizing that she no longer had a home.

Fresh tears surged, spilling down her cheeks.

"It'll be okay, Pip," Ashley soothed. "I promise you. I don't want you to worry. Mama will be here later in the morning. You know she loves you just like a daughter. She's already making plans to bring you home with her and take care of you."

Pippa smiled shakily. "You have no idea how much I need her right now." She broke off and sighed. "I should be happy. I made a decision. I told Cam off. Rightfully so. But I'm so miserable. I love that jerk and I'm mad that I can't make it stop."

"Tell me," Ashley said quietly.

Pippa looked down at her hands, humiliation and devastation pummeling her all over again. "He told me he didn't *want* to love me or our baby. Not that he couldn't or that he didn't believe he'd ever find another soul mate. Just that he didn't want to love us. He was so…cold."

Ashley scowled. "I hate him. I don't care if he's Dev's best friend. I swear the man fell out of the stupid tree and hit every damn branch on the way down."

Pippa tried to laugh but she dissolved into a coughing fit instead.

"Easy," Ashley murmured. "Catch your breath. You've been through a lot tonight."

"Oh, God. It all feels so unreal."

Ashley squeezed her hands again. "I don't want you to stress about this. I know that sounds absurd. You've had the rug pulled out from underneath you and right now you likely think your entire world is falling apart. But it's going to be okay. You have me. You have Mama. You have Sylvia, Carly and Tabitha to help. Devon will do whatever he can, you know that. Please don't make yourself sick worrying. Right now you just need to focus on you and the baby and making sure you're both healthy."

Pippa gave her a watery smile. "Thank you. I love you, Ash. I don't know what I'd ever do without you."

"I want you to get some rest now, okay? It's almost time for Katelynn's next feeding so I'm going to go back up, but I'll have Dev check in on you. Mama will bring you something to wear home. I want to know the minute you're released. I'm supposed to go home today, too, so maybe we can blow this joint together."

Pippa squeezed Ashley's hand. "Thanks, Ash. You're the best. Kiss that baby for me."

Ashley fussed with the pillow and tucked the sheet more firmly around Pippa before she finally backed away from the bed and started for the door.

As soon as Ashley disappeared from view, Pippa closed her eyes and melted into the bed. Exhaustion beat at her. She'd reached her absolute limit. She was physically and emotionally spent. There was nothing left except vast emptiness and an unnerving ache in her heart.

Twenty-two

Cam strode through the doors of the E.R. and went to the desk to inquire about Pippa. He blatantly lied, saying he was her husband and then demanding to see her. One of the nurses motioned him through a series of doors and then pointed down the hall and told him she was in room seven.

As he rushed forward, he realized that Devon was standing out in the hall. He was about to call out when the door to Pippa's room opened and Ashley came out.

Devon put his arm around his wife and started to lead her down the hall when he and Ashley both looked up and saw Cam.

He hadn't expected there to be much love for him from Ashley at the moment, but the anger in Devon's tight expression surprised him.

"How is she?" he demanded.

He would have just shoved by and gone into her room, but Devon blocked him. Then Ashley put her hand on Cam's arm, which halted him immediately. He had no desire to risk hurting her. She shouldn't even be running around the hospital after just having had a baby.

"Cam, please," Ashley said softly. "Leave her be."

He backed away and shoved his hand through his hair.

"Leave her be? I need to see her. I need to see for myself that she's okay. You can't possibly understand what it was like to drive up to her apartment and imagine that she was trapped inside that inferno."

It made him sick all over again just thinking about it. It was an image that would live with him for a long time to come.

"She's exhausted. She needs rest. Cam, she's so…fragile right now."

Her hesitant description only made him more determined to get into that room.

Ashley gripped his arm once more and it was only then he realized he'd moved forward.

"Let her rest. You've done enough tonight. You can't barge in there and upset her. She's been through hell. She doesn't know you were the one who called us. She didn't even ask us how we knew she was here."

He closed his eyes as bleakness settled over him. "She hates me."

"No, she loves you," Ashley said softly. "And that's the problem. It's why you can't go in there and take advantage of how distraught and run-down she is. I'll never forgive you if you don't give her some space and let her at least sleep a few hours. She looks terrible, Cam. Part of that is your fault."

"Don't upset her," Devon said, speaking up for the first time. "Ashley's right. She's extremely fragile right now. Barging in there to assuage your guilt won't make that any better. For once think of someone other than yourself."

The angry censure in Devon's voice made Cam flinch.

"This has nothing to do with guilt," he said in frustration. "Damn it, I love her. I have to tell her. I can't let things go the way they ended between us."

Devon put his hand on Cam's shoulder. "If you love her, then it'll wait. You can wait. Don't push right now, Cam. I promise you, the result won't be good. She's past her breaking point."

"I'm not leaving," Cam said fiercely.

"Nobody says you have to."

Cam closed his eyes, his shoulders sagging. "All right. I won't go in now."

The idea that she was exhausted, weak and emotionally spent tore at him. He wanted nothing more than to hold her. To cradle her in his arms, whisper that he loved her and that everything would be all right.

He hadn't been there for her before but he'd be damned if he'd desert her now.

Ashley's gaze found his and her big blue eyes stared imploringly at him. But they also held a warning.

"Make this right with her, Cam. And don't you ever hurt her again."

"I'll spend the rest of my life loving and protecting her if she'll have me."

Devon blew out his breath. "Yeah, that's the big question, man. You're not going to have an easy time of this."

Cam knew it but his heart still sank at the conviction in Devon's voice.

"I'll be down later to check in on her," Devon said.

It was a warning to Cam that Devon would be back and that he better not find her upset. Cam acknowledged him with a nod and then watched as Devon and Ashley slowly walked down the hall.

Cam glanced at the closed door, wishing for the world that he could just see her. Just touch her. He walked to the end of the corridor and grabbed a chair. He set it across from Pippa's door and sat down to begin his vigil.

He wasn't leaving.

And so he sat, staring broodingly at her door. At one point a nurse went in, giving him an apprehensive glance. A moment later, she came back out and Cam surged to his feet.

"How is she?" he asked, his voice almost a croak.

The nurse stared at him a moment, her brow furrowed. "I'm sorry but I'm not allowed to give out that information."

"I'm her husband," he said, and then realized how stupid it seemed for him to be sitting in the hall if he were married to her. "I…I just wanted her to rest and I've been so worried. I didn't want to put additional stress on her."

Her expression softened. "She's sleeping. Quite soundly. She never even moved when I checked her vitals."

Cam nodded and murmured his thanks. He wiped nervous palms down his pant legs as the nurse hurried away and then he tentatively opened the door, careful to not make a sound.

If she was asleep, then she'd never know he was here. He could watch her for a while and know that she was safe. He eased the door open farther and stepped inside, his gaze immediately seeking her out in the semidarkened room.

She was lying on a narrow bed with her back elevated. She was sleeping as the nurse had said, but she didn't look at all comfortable. She was sagging to one side and seemed precariously close to sliding off the bed.

He took another step closer and for a moment he couldn't breathe. Fragile had been a good word to describe her. She looked so small against the bed. Her hair was in disarray. He could smell the faint scent of smoke.

She was pale and her face seemed thinner. There were dark smudges underneath her eyes. His gaze dropped to her hands and he frowned to see scrapes on her palms.

She looked worn through. As Devon had said, past her limits. Cam had pushed her there.

Unable to resist, he lowered his fingers, simply wanting to touch her. He traced the lines of her face, gently pushing back a tendril of hair that rested close to her mouth.

Then he bent and gently kissed her forehead, closing his eyes and allowing his mouth to rest there for the briefest of moments.

"I love you," he whispered.

Pippa awoke with the nagging sense that she'd missed something. Her dreams had been odd, occupied by Cam and infinite tenderness instead of flames, smoke and fear. They had been nice but bizarre.

There was no clock in the room and if it weren't for the bright sunlight streaming through the small window, she'd have no idea it was daytime.

She automatically smoothed her hands over the bulge of her belly and smiled when the baby kicked. Relief was sweet. She and the baby were going to be all right.

Just then, her door opened and Gloria Copeland bustled through, looking determined and agitated. But the moment their eyes met, her gaze softened and she rushed over to the bed to enfold Pippa in her arms.

"My poor baby," she crooned. "Are you all right? Devon told me what the doctor said but I've been so worried about you."

To Pippa's never-ending shame, she started crying again. It was becoming ridiculous how easily she became a watering pot.

"Oh honey," Gloria said. "Don't cry. You know you're coming to stay with me. I have a bedroom all ready for you. I'm putting you next to Ashley's old room. I'm hoping she and Katelynn will stay a few days and it'll be just like old times. Having my girls around will be such a delight. I can fuss over all of you."

"I love you, Mrs. C." Pippa sniffled.

Gloria smoothed Pippa's bedraggled hair from her face and then kissed her forehead. "I love you too, baby. It's going to be all right. I promise. It may look bad right now but we're going to get you back on your feet in no time."

Pippa squeezed Gloria's hand. "I'm so lucky to have you and Ashley. You're the only family I have."

And Pippa knew it was true. Blood didn't count for much at all. Miranda may have given her life, but family wasn't necessarily about blood. It was about uncompromising love and support. About always being there no matter how hard things were.

This was what she wanted for her son. And she'd give it to him no matter what she had to do.

Gloria hugged her again, and really, Pippa was perfectly happy to be hugged all day. Each time, a little more of her melancholy drifted away.

"Tell you what we're going to do. I'm going to take you home and put you to bed. As soon as you're up to it, we're going to have a spa day. If that doesn't put the pep back into your step, I don't know what will. We'll bring Ashley, too."

Pippa smiled. A girlie day with Ashley and her mom sounded…wonderful.

"There now, see? You're smiling already," Gloria said. "Seriously, honey, I don't want you worrying about a thing. I'll have William sort out your hospital bill. You'll stay with us until the baby's born. There's no sense you shouldering the stress of trying to find a new apartment when you should be focusing on your baby. We'll have great fun. You'll see."

Pippa wouldn't refuse Gloria Copeland's hospitality even if she wanted to. Nobody ever stood a chance against her. She was a force of nature and Pippa loved her for it.

Then she frowned as reality crashed in. "What about my bakery? I can't just leave it."

"Of course not," Gloria soothed. "We'll manage. You have employees who can handle things for a few days while you rest and recover. After that, we'll work out a way for you to get to work each morning. William will be more than happy to provide a driver for you."

Pippa smiled again. "Thank you. Seriously. I don't know what I'd do without you and Mr. C. and Ashley."

Gloria beamed. "William will be glad to hear that. You know he loves you just as much as I do even if he can be an old goat sometimes."

Pippa snickered.

"Now, let me find out when they're going to let you out of this place," Gloria said. "The sooner we get you home, the better. We'll have our physician check in on you daily just to make sure all is well."

Pippa leaned back against the pillows and sighed. Things

were already looking up. She'd get beyond this with the help of the people she loved.

A few moments later, Gloria returned. Once again she had that odd look on her face as she came through the door.

"What did the doctor say?" Pippa asked.

Gloria blinked. "Oh, I didn't talk to him. I spoke to the nurse. She says you'll be ready to go home in just a couple of hours."

An uneasy feeling crept over Pippa. Something was up with Mrs. C. "Is anything wrong?"

Gloria looked up at the sharpness in Pippa's tone. She glanced back toward the door and then she sighed. "You'll know soon enough, anyway. Cam's outside the door. Looks like he's been there all night. He refuses to budge. Just sits there in that chair and broods. He wanted to come in, but I told him not to. I didn't want to upset you."

Pippa's heart thudded painfully. Her fingers automatically curled into fists and she went quiet. Her breathing was loud in the silent room and she stared at the wall as if she could see through it to Cam sitting on the other side.

"I don't want to see him," she whispered.

Gloria put her arm around Pippa's shoulders and squeezed. "You don't have to, baby. I just didn't want you to get a shock when you left and he was there in front of you."

"No, it's okay. Thank you for the heads-up. It's just that we have nothing left to say to each other."

Gloria kissed her temple and squeezed her a little harder. "Ashley's being discharged today and is bringing Katelynn home. We'll all just go to my apartment together once you're released."

Pippa nodded numbly, her mind still on Cam. She wasn't a coward, but the very last thing she wanted right now was another confrontation. His words had cut her to the core and it was a wound she wouldn't recover from in a day or even a week.

One day at a time. Things would get better. She had to believe that.

Twenty-three

Cam paced the hallway outside of Pippa's door, wondering at one point why he didn't just walk in and force a confrontation. Then he shook his head. It wasn't the time or the place. Devon and Ashley were right. Pippa was holding on by a thread. This wasn't about him.

He glanced up when he saw Devon coming down the hallway.

"Have you been in to see her?" Devon asked as he stopped in front of Pippa's door.

Cam shook his head. "Ashley's mom is in with her. She didn't want me anywhere near Pippa. I don't blame her. Where's Ashley and Katelynn?"

"They're in the car. I pulled it around to the exit. Ashley's father is out with her. He's going to drive Pippa and Gloria home."

Cam grimaced and rubbed a hand through his hair. Pippa had no home to return to. But she should. It was with him. Always with him. She should have never been anywhere else all these months.

He blew out his breath, not knowing what to do. It was a feeling he wasn't accustomed to. He was always decisive even when he was dead wrong. He never had a problem knowing what to say even when he was putting his foot in his mouth. Right now he lacked for words.

And then Pippa's door opened and there she stood, Gloria hovering just behind her. His gaze zeroed in on Pippa. She was pale and wan, deep shadows under her eyes. Her hair was pulled back into a rough ponytail and her cheekbones were more pronounced than ever. Her arms even seemed more slender. The only part of her that seemed normal was the bulge in front where their son rested.

"Pippa," he said in a low, unsteady voice. "Thank God you're okay."

He reached out, wanting to touch her, to somehow confirm that she was really standing before him, but she flinched away. He withdrew his hand, curling his fingers into a tight fist at his side.

She started to move past him and he closed his eyes knowing he couldn't let her walk away. Not again. Not like this.

"Pippa, wait, please."

She halted in midstep and stood there a long moment, her back still to him. Then she slowly turned, her eyes dull and lifeless as she stared back at him. Then her chin came up and she squared her shoulders.

"Wait outside for me," she said to Devon and Gloria. "I'll just be a minute."

Gloria Copeland looked very much like she wanted to argue but she kept her mouth tightly shut.

"I'll wait down the hall so I can walk you out," Devon said.

Pippa nodded and then turned back to Cam as Devon and Gloria walked away.

No longer able to keep from touching her, Cam reached out to capture Pippa's hand. He pulled her close so he could feel the steady reassurance of her heartbeat against his chest. She sagged against him, her sigh hitting him right in the gut. It was a forlorn, tired sigh that told him she was at the end of her rope physically and emotionally.

She closed her eyes and turned her face into his neck for just a moment before she pulled away, her expression locked in stone once more.

"I need to go. They're waiting for me."

Cam's protest was automatic. "You can come home with me, Pippa. I'll take care of you. We have a lot to talk about. There's a lot I need to say to you. But my first priority is you."

"No."

He expected more. An argument. Something he could counter. But all she uttered was a clipped *no* and stared woodenly back at him.

His heart lurched. This was so much worse than he'd imagined. All the emotion he'd held back since the night before came rushing forward, bulging in his throat.

He put his hand to her face. "My God, Pippa, I thought I'd lost you when I saw the fire and the smoke and all those fire trucks and ambulances."

The cold, lifeless eyes that stared back at him sent chills down his spine. This wasn't the Pippa he knew. This was someone else entirely. Someone he'd made with his indifference and his determination not to get emotionally involved with her.

"I knew this would happen. I knew something would happen and I'd lose you both, and that fear controlled me. It made me do and say horrible things. Things I didn't mean, Pippa."

"You're a moron," she bit out. "You already lost me. The only difference was I didn't die in the fire. But for all practical purposes I'm dead to you. You lost both of us long before this happened. You spend so much time trying to shield yourself from hurt and you don't give a damn who you hurt in the process. How's that working out for you, Cam? Because from where I stand it sucks. Now if you'll excuse me, I want to go home and go to bed."

You already lost me.

It was a crippling blow even as he knew it was the truth.

As she pushed by him, he caught her hand, allowing his fingers to trail over it. Then the connection was lost and she turned away.

Cam watched her go, numbness creeping through his body with insidious speed. Her words had penetrated the wall around his heart, the one he'd erected after losing Elise and Colton.

Tears burned his eyes until he blinked to ease the discomfort. She'd stormed right past that supposed barrier the first time he'd ever seen her across a crowded room. There had been no defense no matter how hard he'd tried. No keeping her out. No lying to himself.

He loved her. Had loved her from the start. He'd never really believed in love at first sight until Pippa. His dumb ass had known even then that she was a threat. And so he'd pushed her away. Tried everything in his power to tell himself he didn't love her, that he didn't want to love her.

But he did. He wanted to love her more than he wanted to live.

And now it was too damn late.

A hand came down on his shoulder. Startled, he looked to the side to see that Devon had come back to get him.

"I think it's time you and I had the same talk that I had with Rafe right after I screwed things up so badly with Ashley that I feared I'd never get her back."

Cam shoved his hands into his pockets, despair and hopelessness weighing down on him from all sides.

Devon pulled him along, herding him toward the doors. When they got to the parking lot, he shoved Cam inside the car and then walked around to get into the driver's seat. When they were on their way, Devon glanced over at Cam.

"Go big or go home."

Cam rubbed a hand over his eyes. "Stop talking in riddles. Just say it, man."

"I'm saying it. You gotta go big or go home. This is it, Cam. You're playing for all the marbles. For your future. For your son's future. This is your last chance. You won't ever get another. It's time to pull your head out of your ass and start living again. You're going to have to crawl to Pippa on your hands and knees and lick her shoes if that's what it takes."

"I said some unforgivable things."

Devon shrugged. "Define unforgivable. It's only unforgivable if *she* refuses to forgive you. And you don't know if she will because you haven't begged for it."

"I wouldn't blame her if she never spoke to me again."

"Neither would I, but are you going to throw in the towel just because you're a huge ass and don't deserve another chance with her? Hell, man, we've all screwed up. Rafe, Ryan, me and now you. We seem to have a common thread of being the biggest bastards on the face of the earth when it comes to the women we love. But you know what? Bryony forgave Rafe. Kelly forgave Ryan. Ashley forgave me and Pippa will forgive you. You just have to give her the opportunity and the right motivation."

"I love her."

"I know you do. I think you're the only idiot who didn't know it until now."

"I can't believe what I almost did," Cam said painfully. "I tried to deny her. I tried to deny my own son. How do you ever get over something like that?"

"The key word is *almost,*" Devon said. "Tell her you're a dumb ass and then swear you'll wise up and never be a dumb ass again."

Cam sighed. "I just hope she'll listen."

"You make her listen. If she means enough to you, then you won't give up so easily."

Mean enough? She was his damn world. Her and their son. It was time to take a chance. The biggest chance of his life. It could end badly. They could be taken from him just like Elise and Colton had been.

But it could also end wonderfully. A long life filled with love and laughter. More children. Pippa's love and her smile. Wasn't that worth the risk?

Twenty-four

"Pippa, darling, Cam is here to see you, and I should warn you that he's vowed to sleep outside our door until you agree to talk with him."

Pippa stared back at Gloria Copeland, her mouth dropping open in astonishment.

"Are you serious?"

Gloria nodded. "I'm afraid so. He does seem quite determined. I would have thought it an empty threat but he's carrying an overnight bag with him."

"He doesn't give up," Pippa muttered.

In the past two days, Cam had haunted Pippa's existence. He'd called. He'd come by the Copelands' apartment. He'd gone by her bakery. He'd made it a point to show up in every conceivable place she could possibly be.

When none of that appeared to work, he'd resorted to text messages. I love you. Flowers. Tons of flowers. Every card signed *I love you.* The few times she'd actually come face-to-face with him, he's just stood there, looking so haunted and determined, his eyes never leaving her face.

She felt hunted but not threatened. She was baffled by his persistence, confused by the messages.

After hanging on to desperate hope for so long, she'd made the painful, difficult decision to sever her ties to Cam. And now he was storming back, demanding her attention. Wanting things he'd vowed he'd never want from her.

It made no sense and she was at her wits' end.

She nibbled at her bottom lip and stared nervously over the back of the couch toward the door. She had no doubt he'd be stubborn. The past two days had proven that much.

"What should I do?" she asked anxiously. The very last thing she wanted was to cause trouble for the Copelands when they'd been nothing but kind and generous to her.

Gloria smiled indulgently and then came to sit beside her on the couch. She pulled her into a tight hug and patted her comfortingly on the back.

"My dear, you do whatever you wish. If you want to talk to him, I'll be happy to show him in and give you some privacy. Or if you don't want to be alone I'll stand guard like a mama lion. If you prefer not to see him, I'll simply have security remove him from the premises."

"I do love you, Mrs. C. If only…"

She broke off with a sigh and looked down.

"If only what, dear?"

Pippa raised her gaze and smiled. "If only my mother was like you."

Gloria smiled back and then leaned forward to enfold her in another of her glorious hugs. "You know you're like a daughter to me, and Miranda loves you as much as Miranda is capable of loving anyone."

Pippa sucked in a breath. "You know what? I'm not ready to see him. Not yet. He'd just run over me. When or if I decide to talk to him, it'll be on my terms. Not his."

"That's my girl. Okay, let me go make a call to the building security. Now don't go looking like that. It'll be quiet and discreet."

Pippa frowned unhappily all the same and hunched her knees toward her chest as Gloria got off the couch to go make the call.

She wasn't being vindictive. She wasn't being anything at all. She'd said what she'd wanted to say to Cam. There was nothing else.

But even as she reassured herself, doubt nagged at her, because somehow she knew this time Cam wouldn't walk away as he'd done in the past.

Go big or go home.

The past few days had been the most frustrating days of his life. Hell, he'd tried everything he knew to get Pippa to talk to him. Or just acknowledge him in some way. Getting thrown out of the apartment building where the Copelands lived had certainly capped off an already crappy day and earned him a warning from Devon.

Yet Pippa's continued resistance just strengthened his resolve. He wasn't going to give up no matter how long it took.

Which is how he found himself standing in the reception area of an exclusive salon. A very *girlie* salon filled with women of all shapes, sizes and ages waiting to be pampered.

Somewhere in one of those back rooms was *his* woman, and come hell or high water, today was the day she was going to listen to reason. If he had to lay bare his soul in front of countless strangers, then so be it. But Pippa *was* going to listen this time.

But first he had to get past the dour-faced dragon lady who stood guard over the doorway leading from the reception area.

He'd simply be honest. Weren't all women softies when it came to groveling men and the grand gestures they made for the women they love? If that didn't work, he'd get on his knees and he damn well knew no woman would turn down that kind of an opportunity.

He started toward Dragon Lady only to see her cross her arms and scowl directly at him. He sighed. This was so going to suck.

* * *

Pippa was covered in some sort of muddy goo—or at least her face and belly were—but she couldn't find it in herself to complain. Besides, it felt good. She was relaxed.

Somewhere down there someone was massaging her feet. She closed her eyes in bliss just as someone else put nice, cool cucumber circles over her eyes.

She almost laughed at how ridiculous she must look, but then it occurred to her that she was in heaven, and really, did it matter if she looked like a cream puff in a bikini with cucumber eyes?

The hands left her insteps and she grumbled her protest but then a new set of hands—firmer, larger, not nearly as smooth as the others—closed around her heel and began massaging.

Warmth spread up her legs and her lips parted as a sigh escaped where moments before she'd protested.

She liked these hands better. They weren't as practiced or smooth. But they hit all the right spots.

The hands moved up her leg, tenderly applying just enough pressure. Rubbing, kneading, leaving no spot untouched as they ventured higher.

It occurred to her to be alarmed at the familiarity of this person's touch, but it felt too wonderful to end just yet.

The hands left for the briefest of moments and then a warm cloth wiped gently at her belly, cleaning away the fluffy mixture of God only knew what.

Then those wonderful hands palmed the bulge of her belly and she sighed again. But when lips pressed to her firm abdomen, she reared up, cucumber slices flying from her eyes.

To her complete surprise it was Cam who stood there, his hands molded to her belly. And it was his lips that had pressed to her skin.

She tried to scramble up, but it was difficult and Cam put a hand to her shoulder, gently pressing her back down to a lying position.

"Why are you here?" she squeaked. "And what are you doing? Where's my attendant? How long have you been here?"

Cam spread his hands out, palms up. "I'm it. I'm yours. Completely and utterly at your service to fulfill your every whim and desire."

Her eyes rounded and her mouth flapped open and shut like she was a senseless twit.

He looked...broken. Hopeful and yet hopeless all at the same time. He looked tired. Worn. Worried. But more than anything he looked determined. There was a glint in his eyes that told her he wasn't backing down this time.

"I'm not having a conversation with you with all this crap on my face and wearing nothing more than a bikini," she muttered.

He bent down, captured her face in his hands and proceeded to kiss her breathless. When he finally released her, there was as much fluffy goo on his face as there was on hers. He looked...ridiculous.

She couldn't help but smile. Then she laughed.

"I don't care what you look like," he said hoarsely. "You're still the most beautiful woman I've ever known in my life."

She sighed, ignoring the flutter in her chest. "What are you doing here, Cam? I mean, really. What is it you want? We've said all that needs to be said. There's nothing left to do but get upset all over again."

His eyes became fierce blue orbs that burned a trail over her face. "No. Not even close. I have plenty to say and I want you to listen, Pippa. Really listen to me."

She blinked at his vehemence. Well, she wasn't having this conversation lying down. The very last thing she wanted was to feel at a disadvantage.

She struggled for a moment and finally reached her hand out to Cam. "Help me, please. If we're going to talk, I don't want to do it with us both looking like cream puffs."

He clasped her hand and helped her forward until she swung her legs over the side of the reclining chair. She slid off and went to the sink to wash the remainder of the cream from her face. Then she dampened a cloth and returned to dab at Cam's face.

He stood, completely still, while she wiped at his cheek. His eyes never left her, though. When the last bit of goo was gone, she took a step back, suddenly feeling the need to cover herself so she didn't feel quite so vulnerable.

She grabbed a robe off one of the hooks and wrapped it around herself, tying the ends tightly over her swollen belly.

And still Cam was staring at her, unshakable. She was sure there was a message in his unshakable gaze, but it wasn't one she could discern.

Then it was as if he couldn't stand it a moment longer. He crossed the distance, dragged her into his arms and kissed her like there was no tomorrow.

He wrapped his arms tightly around her body, holding her so close to him that she couldn't breathe. He shuddered against her. His lips moved over hers, devouring, hungry, *desperate*.

When he finally pulled away, she was shocked by the emotion so prevalent in his gaze. He had the look of a tortured man, someone who'd lost everything.

"I can't live without you, Pippa," he said in a low voice. "Don't make me live without you and our son. I love you both so damn much. It's eating me alive. I wake up thinking about you. I worry for you all day. I go to bed at night aching to hold you. Being without you is gnawing away at my soul. You are everything to me. *Everything.*"

She swallowed, her nostrils flaring as she tried to control her own emotions. She wanted to lash out but knew it solved nothing. But his words—words he couldn't take back—still hurt. They cut deeply, a wound that was still open and raw.

"It's awfully cliché to realize you can't live without me and that you've seen the light after something life-threatening happens," she said in a low voice.

"You're wrong," he said fiercely. "I already knew it. I

fought it. But I knew. I already loved you. I never said I didn't love you, Pippa. Never. What I said was that I didn't *want* to love you. I didn't just figure this out because of some damn fire. Did that scare me? Hell, yes. I haven't been able to sleep at night for imagining you in that apartment and the unbelievable fear you must have experienced. I was coming for you that night. Ask me how I knew you were in the hospital, Pippa. *Ask* me, damn it!"

Her fingers trembled as she stared back at him. "H-how?"

"Because I drove like a bat out of hell to get to you after you left. I knew I'd just made the biggest mistake of my life letting you walk away. I was gutted. But I knew if I could just get to you that I could make everything all right. And then when I got to your street, all I saw were those lights and the flames and smoke and I wanted to die because I thought it had happened all over again but this time I could have prevented it. Just by telling you what was in my heart. Just by not being so damn afraid."

Her eyes widened and her mouth popped open in shock at the vehemence in his voice.

"Hell yes I was terrified that I'd lost you. But that's not why I'm here. It's not why I'm putting myself at your feet and hoping to hell you'll give me another chance. I love you, Pippa. I've loved you for so damn long and I didn't want to. I fought it. But some things just are and one of those things is my love for you and our son."

She opened her mouth to respond, but he came in close again and put a gentle finger to her lips.

"Don't talk. Just listen to me. Please. I have so much to say. So much to make up for."

Mutely she nodded.

He framed her face in his hands and stared down at her with such torment in his eyes that it made her chest ache.

"I'm tired of fighting myself. I want a life with you and our son. I'm tired of always expecting the worst, of trying to forget the pain of losing someone and protecting myself from the worst sort of agony. If I only have a year with you, I'd take it and treasure it for the rest of my life and I'd die a happy man having that time with you even if it meant living the rest of my life alone."

The words, so heartfelt, so bleak and raw and powerful, shook her to the core. There was no mistaking the sincerity. The truth was there in his eyes to see.

His thumbs caressed a line over her cheeks. His hands were gentle on her face, and he stared down at her with so much love that her throat knotted and tears burned her eyelids.

"I've been such a bastard to you, Pippa," he said hoarsely. "I've done everything possible to alienate you. I don't deserve another chance with you or my son, but I'm begging. I'll get down on my knees. I'll do whatever it takes to convince you that I'm not that man. I'm better than that. I want to be better than that. I'll spend the rest of whatever time I have with you proving to you that you can count on me."

Her heart surged with love. So much her chest ached. "Oh, Cam, what you can do for me is stop expecting the absolute worst. I'll never leave you if I can possibly help it. Me and our child will love you and stay with you."

She reached up to stroke her hand over his jaw. "I'm so sorry for what happened before. But you've been given another chance. What you do with that gift is up to you."

He caught her hand, turned his face into it and kissed her palm. "You *are* a gift, Pippa. I never imagined having someone like you. And now our son." He choked off, caught his breath and for several long moments just breathed into her hand. "I love you. Please forgive me."

Her heart nearly bursting, she pressed into his arms and wrapped herself tightly around him, squeezing hard until he had no choice but to feel her love from every angle.

"I do forgive you," she whispered. "I love you, Cam. I love you so much."

He stroked her hair and kissed the top of her head as they simply held each other.

Then from behind came the sound of applause. They both whirled around, Pippa tucked protectively into Cam's side, to see Gloria, Ashley and several other women standing in the doorway of the room.

There were smiles and tears on the other women's faces.

"Well done, my boy," Gloria said, giving him a thumbs-up.

Cam smiled back and squeezed Pippa a little closer to him. He was shaking against her. She glanced up, shocked to see just how close he seemed to breaking down.

She reached for his hand, twining her fingers with his and then pulled him toward the door that led out to the little tranquility garden. She waved to the others to let them know she was all right and then tugged Cam the rest of the way from the room.

The only sound in the lush open garden was water cascading over a fountain. The air was heavily scented with blooming flowers, their splash of color dominating the small area.

It was as if a hole had been cut out of the center of the building, leaving an isolated slice of peace for whoever ventured out.

"Sit," she ordered Cam.

He sagged onto the bench by the fountain but he wouldn't relinquish her hand. He tugged her toward him as if afraid she'd leave.

"I love you," he said raggedly. "Say it again, Pippa. Tell me you love me and that you forgive me for being such a bastard to you. I need to hear you say it."

She smiled, then leaned forward between his legs. He wrapped his arms around her and rested his cheek on the bulge of her abdomen. She ran her fingers through his mussed hair.

"I love you, Cam. And I forgive you. I do."

He let out a groan and his hold tightened on her. Then he raised his head so their gazes met.

"Come home with me, Pippa. Stay with me. I don't want to

spend another hour without you. Marry me. Love me. Spend your life with me. I swear I'll make you happy."

Her chest caved in a little more and she smiled until her cheeks ached. "Oh, yes. I don't want to spend another hour away from you, either."

"And you'll marry me? I know it wasn't the best proposal. I'll get it right, I promise. I'll get the ring and get on my knees. Whatever it is that makes you happy."

She touched the lines of his forehead, easing them with her fingertips. "What makes me happy is you loving me."

"Then you're going to be one happy lady," he vowed. "Because I'm going to love you with every breath I breathe, every minute of every day for the rest of our lives."

Epilogue

The living room was alive with conversation and laughter. Cam's house no longer resembled a somber cave; instead, it was light and airy. It was a house filled with love and happiness.

She settled onto the couch and hoisted her feet onto the ottoman, watching fondly as Cam and his friends oohed and aahed over a whole passel of babies.

Rafael de Luca and his wife, Bryony, had arrived two days ago with their daughter, Amy. Ryan Beardsley and his wife, Kelly, had been the last to get here and they'd flown in today from St. Angelo where they lived permanently. Their daughter, Emma, was nearly the same age as Amy. The two were born mere weeks apart.

Though it had been touted as a time for everyone to get together and visit, Pippa knew that Cam had arranged it to give her the kind of delivery surrounded by friends and family that she'd so wistfully dreamed of.

In addition to the love and attention he lavished on her

at every opportunity, he'd set it up for her café to be staffed
for the last month of her pregnancy and for a period of three
months after the baby was born until she decided to return to
it full time or not.

Finally, she was living the ultimate fairy tale. One she'd
thought she'd be forever denied. It was the most wonderful
feeling in the world.

Pippa liked Cam's friends. They hadn't been exactly as
she'd expected. She'd thought they would be more like Cam
had been in the beginning. Reserved. Standoffish. But they
were warm, outgoing and exuberant people. She'd first met
them when they all came in for Cam and Pippa's wedding. It
hadn't been a huge affair. They'd both opted for a quiet gathering of close friends and family only.

Kelly was probably the quietest woman in the group, but
Pippa liked her a lot. She had a sweet smile and she clearly
adored her daughter. Her husband, Ryan, never strayed far
from their sides.

Pippa smiled and then promptly grimaced when she was
seized by another contraction. She recovered quickly, pasted
back on her serene smile and glanced at Cam.

He was standing next to Ryan, holding Emma in his arms
while the men talked and laughed. The interesting thing was
that they weren't discussing business. No, they were all trad-
ing baby stories and boasting about how their daughter was
smarter, prettier and more clever than any other baby in the
world.

Bryony rolled her eyes and flopped onto the couch beside
Pippa. Ashley settled on the other side while Kelly sat in an
armchair right beside the couch.

"I'm amazed by the change in Cam," Bryony said quietly.
"He seems so…happy. He's not as dark and brooding as I remember. I don't ever remember hearing him laugh. He rarely
even smiled. You've performed a miracle, Pippa."

"He's great. He's still way overprotective and he can get
worked up when he thinks about something happening to me

or the baby, but he's really learned to let go and not dwell so much on the negative."

Ashley reached for her hand and squeezed. "He loves you, Pip. You've been so good for him. You saved him."

Another contraction tightened her belly, and she nearly groaned aloud. Kelly frowned and leaned forward in her seat.

"Pippa, what's wrong?"

"Shhh!" Pippa hissed. "Don't let Cam hear. He'll freak."

"Then tell us what's wrong," Ashley said in a quiet voice. "I saw that look, too. Are you having contractions?"

Pippa blew out her breath. "Yeah, for a while now."

"What?" Bryony demanded. "Why didn't you say anything?"

"Because I didn't want Cam to freak out and be stressed for longer than necessary. I'm not supposed to go into the hospital until they're two minutes apart, anyway."

"Uh, Pip, I'm pretty sure you're supposed to be there before they're that close together," Ashley said.

"My doctor told me that I should come in when my contractions were five minutes apart, regular and lasting at least a minute," Kelly offered.

Bryony's brow wrinkled in concentration. "I think mine told me five to seven minutes apart and regular."

Pippa swallowed uncomfortably and then put a hand on her belly.

"Another one?" Ashley demanded. "Pippa, how far apart are they coming?"

"Closer than five to seven minutes," she grumbled. "I know I read somewhere that I should wait to go in until they were two minutes apart."

Ashley gave her a look of exasperation. "Where would you have read that? You refused to even look at the chapter in the childbirth book that dealt with the ninth month or any part of labor and delivery."

Bryony was on her feet, pulling at Pippa's arm. "Cam," she called. "Pippa needs to go to the hospital."

All four men whirled around and Cam's brow immediately furrowed. Then when he seemed to realize the significance, he went pale and concern burned bright in his eyes.

He handed Emma back to Ryan and hurried over to Pippa. "Honey, is it time?"

"Hell, it's *been* time," Ashley said in exasperation. "She should have gone hours ago."

Cam's gaze flicked from Ashley to Pippa. "What is she talking about?"

"I may have misunderstood when I was supposed to go to the hospital," Pippa muttered.

She grimaced and closed her eyes as another contraction started low in her back. By the time she opened her eyes again, she was panting lightly and the entire room was looking worried.

Cam reached down, plucked her into his arms. "Let's go," he said as he strode across the room.

She laughed but settled against his chest as he made his way to the garage. Behind them there was chaos as everyone juggled babies and diaper bags and hurried to get to their vehicles.

Cam placed her in the passenger seat, then carefully put the seat belt around her and buckled her in. As he was about to pull away, she put her hand on his cheek and cupped it lovingly.

"Hey," she said softly. "It's going to be okay. We're going to be okay."

He kissed her fiercely, then let his fingers linger on her face as she'd done to him. "I know. Now let's get you to the hospital so we can meet our son."

"Push, Pippa! That's it. Now breathe. Okay, one more time, breathe in deep. Hold it! Now push and count to ten."

Dear God but this baby delivery stuff was for the birds. Pippa puffed and strained and she really did try to hold her breath but it all came rushing out by the time she got to five.

If it wasn't for epidurals, she would have given this up already and begged for someone to knock her out.

"You're doing great, sweetheart."

Cam's voice, low and reassuring, gave her a much-needed jolt of energy. He had his arm behind her back, holding her tightly as he breathed through each contraction with her. His hand was tightly curled around hers and he murmured words of encouragement in her ear in between kisses.

"When is he going to be here?" Pippa wailed.

The nurse on her right smiled and then the doctor looked up from between her legs. "One more push and we'll have the head. Concentrate hard and bear down with this next contraction."

That sounded better. She was almost finished with this.

As the contraction began, she felt the mounting urgency to push, almost as if her body took control and she no longer had any say in the matter.

She sucked in her breath, closed her eyes and put her chin to her chest.

"Push, baby. Push," Cam whispered over and over. "You can do this. We're almost there."

"The head's out. Okay, Pippa, relax for a moment while I suction. We'll get him all the way out on the next push but the hard part's over."

"So says you," she grumbled.

The nurse laughed and the doctor just smiled.

A moment later, the doctor told her to push again and suddenly it was as if her belly caved in. The enormous pressure was gone as the baby slid from her body.

She gasped, overwhelmed by the sensation, and a baby's cry echoed across the room.

"Oh, my God," she whispered.

"Ready to meet your son, Pippa?" the doctor asked.

It took just a moment to finish suctioning and to wrap the baby in a blanket before the nurse laid him in Pippa's arms.

Tears burned her eyelids as she stared down at the red-faced squalling baby.

Then she looked up at Cam and slowly held the bundle out to him.

Cam took the baby gingerly, his expression one of complete and utter awe. He stared down in fascination and then he smiled.

It was the most beautiful, honest smile Pippa had ever seen. There was so much joy in his expression that it choked her up and she had to swallow away her tears.

"He's beautiful," Cam whispered.

And then to Pippa's complete surprise, a tear slid down Cam's cheek, followed by another and then another. His hands shook as he cradled the baby closer to his chest.

Then he leaned forward, touching his forehead to hers as he held the baby between them.

"I love you," he choked out. "Thank you for this, Pippa. Thank you for my son. Dear God, he looks so much like you. He's so perfect. Every part of him."

Pippa closed her eyes as tears of her own trickled down her cheeks. There was never a more perfect moment than this. Never would she forget this time in their lives.

"What are we going to name him?" she whispered.

Cam carefully put his son back into Pippa's arms but leaned forward on the bed so he could watch every movement.

"What about Maverick?" Cam suggested. "Maverick Hollingsworth."

"Our little Mav," Pippa said with a smile. "I like it."

Cam found her lips again as the baby settled to sleep against his mother. As he drew away, he caressed her face with trembling hands.

"I'm going to love you and Maverick every single day, with every single breath I have, for the rest of my life. I'll glory in every single memory we make."

Despite her fatigue, Pippa's smile was so big that her cheeks ached.

"I know you will, Cam. But you know what? I'm going to love you every single minute of every single day of my life and I plan to live a damn long time. When you're eighty I'm going to be the biggest pain in your ass you ever had and I swear you're going to love every single minute of it."

Cam threw back his head and laughed. His eyes twinkled merrily. "I absolutely believe every bit of it. I have no doubt that when I'm old and gray you'll still be telling me to straighten up and fly right."

The nurse interrupted to give Pippa instructions and get her ready to move to a regular room.

"Why don't you take Mav out to see his family?" Pippa suggested. By now the Copelands would be here and all of Cam's friends had followed them to the hospital and had kept vigil the entire time Pippa was in labor.

Cam rose and once again took Maverick from Pippa's arms. He stared down at his wife—he'd never grow tired of that word—and thought she'd never looked as beautiful as she did right now.

Tired, beautiful, so very courageous. He leaned down, kissed her brow and then stood to his full height again.

"We'll be back before you know it."

She smiled tiredly and gave him a look so full of love that it was like a fist to his stomach. She still did that to him. Every damn time.

He turned and walked to the door, his arms cradling his new son protectively. The knot grew in his throat as he walked down the corridor to where the others waited.

His son. His miracle. His second chance at life and happiness. At being a father.

His eyes burned and he blinked to keep his vision clear.

The others looked up and then surged to their feet when Cam entered the waiting room. Cam stopped and then smiled.

Smiled so big that it was like stepping into the sun after living in the dark his entire life.

"I want you all to meet my son."

* * * * *

"There's one part of this job we haven't discussed."

"Which is?"

"Sex."

"Ah," Lucius said. An expression came into his eyes, one that had her throat going dry and a hot pool of want forming in her belly. Waves of it lapped outward, roiling and seething in endless demand. "How could I have neglected something so vital?"

"I gather that's a yes."

"No."

She stiffened, shocked by his answer. Had she miscalculated? Had he considered their kiss a mild and forgettable flirtation, easily forgotten and dismissed, while she'd built it up into something far more serious and memorable?

"Not a yes?" she asked faintly.

"Not a yes," he responded gravely, "but rather a *hell* yes."

Dear Reader,

More Than Perfect brings together two people who have experienced betrayal and must learn to trust again. Add to the mix a baby in desperate need of a mother and father, and you end up with one of my favorite types of books to write—one that is emotional, has a touch of humor and deals with issues from the past that must be overcome.

Trust is one of my favorite themes to explore because so many of us have trust issues. We've all been let down by those we love and must decide to either keep our hearts tucked safely away, or take that leap of faith. I've always chosen to try one more time, to take the risk and hope that somehow, someway everything will work out. So, it never fails to delight me when love overcomes the scars and pain from the past.

For those of you with scars, I wish healing. For those wondering whether or not to take the plunge again, I hope you'll go for it. And for those of you who've risked everything, I wish you the ultimate success …love.

Warmly,

Day Leclaire

MORE THAN PERFECT

BY
DAY LECLAIRE

Published in Great Britain 2012
by Mills & Boon, an imprint of Harlequin (UK) Limited,
Eton House, 18-24 Paradise Road, Richmond, Surrey TW9 1SR

© Day Totton Smith 2012

ISBN: 978 0 263 89339 7
ebook ISBN: 978 1 408 97203 8

51-1012

Harlequin (UK) policy is to use papers that are natural, renewable and recyclable products and made from wood grown in sustainable forests. The logging and manufacturing processes conform to the legal environmental regulations of the country of origin.

Printed and bound in Spain
by Blackprint CPI, Barcelona

USA TODAY bestselling author **Day Leclaire** is described by Mills & Boon® as "one of our most popular writers ever!" Day's tremendous worldwide popularity has made her a member of the "Five Star Club," with sales of well over five million books. She is a three-time winner of both a Colorado Award of Excellence and a Golden Quill Award. She's won *RT Book Reviews* Career Achievement and Love and Laughter Awards, a Holt Medallion and a Booksellers' Best Award. She has also received an impressive ten nominations for the prestigious Romance Writers of America's RITA® Award.

Day's romances touch the heart and make you care about her characters as much as she does. In Day's own words, "I adore writing romances, and can't think of a better way to spend each day." For more information, visit Day at her website, www.dayleclaire.com.

To friends and family
who have been with me from the beginning.
My thanks and my love.

Prologue

He awoke to soft morning light and an empty bed.

Lucius Devlin turned his head toward the subtle indent where Lisa should have been…and wasn't. In the distance, he caught the soft murmur of her voice and couldn't quite decide if he felt relief or regret that she hadn't left.

Last night had been a mistake. A bad one.

He rolled off the mattress and crossed to his dresser. In the bottom drawer he found an old pair of drawstring sweatpants and yanked them on before heading to the kitchen. Lisa was there and at his appearance, she ended her call and flipped her cell phone closed. She sat at the table, wearing her red power suit from the day before, a cup of freshly made coffee resting at her elbow. Thank God she'd made coffee. Right now he needed it almost as desperately as he needed air to breathe.

She regarded him with eyes every bit as dark as his own while he filled a sturdy mug to the brim. "You're dressed," he said, stating the obvious. He took a swift, settling hit of caffeine, his eyes narrowing at her through the haze of steam. "I gather you're leaving?"

"Yes." She played with her cell phone with long, supple fingers and actually allowed a slight frown to crease the space between her winged brows. Damn. If she were risking wrinkles, that meant it was serious. "I am leaving, this time for good."

"Or until you and Geoff have another fight?" He gestured toward her phone. "I'm guessing he called."

Her mouth tightened a fraction. "You always were too smart for your own good."

"That makes two of us."

Lisa sighed. Leaning back in her chair, she crossed her spectacular legs and eyed him with reluctant amusement. "Why couldn't you have been a stupid billionaire and made the incredible mistake of marrying me when we were first together?"

He took her question at face value. "Probably because *stupid* and *billionaire* are incongruous since I wouldn't be a billionaire for long if I were stupid."

"That's true in your case." She tilted her head to one side, her gaze watchful. "I'm not sure you can say the same about Geoff."

Great. Now she'd forced him into the bizarre position of defending his best friend to the woman who'd slept with them both—first with him, then when he wouldn't stick a ring on her finger, she'd moved on to Geoff, the head of his PR department at Diablo, Inc. Lucius suspected it was a foolish attempt to force a proposal out of him, one that had proved a spectacular failure.

"Geoff is neither a billionaire, nor stupid," Lucius informed her. "Naive, perhaps, especially when it comes to women like you. But he's solid gold."

"Unlike us?" She didn't need his silence to confirm her question. She already knew the answer. She picked up her cup and took a dainty sip. "He's an angel with two devils sitting on his shoulders, poor boy. Would you care to place a small wager on which devil he'll listen to, Lucius? Which devil he'll obey?"

He refused to participate in whatever game Lisa seemed intent on playing. "What do you want?"

"From you? Nothing."

"And from Geoff?"

She offered a catlike smile, full of sly confidence. "I have what I want from him, as well."

Lucius stiffened, something in her tone warning of incoming mortar fire and he braced himself for the hit. "Which is?"

"A marriage proposal." Her smile grew. "That was Geoff on the phone. He's seen the error of his ways and asked me to hop on the next plane to Vegas with him. We'll be married this afternoon and on our honeymoon by tonight."

The words pounding through Lucius's brain were coarse and crude enough that he refused to speak them aloud, even in front of Lisa. "Fast work. You roll out of one man's bed one night and into another's the next, then back again on the third." He tilted his head to one side in consideration. "I think there's a name for that...."

Her smile died and her dark eyes swam with accusation and fury. "At least when I roll back into Geoff's bed I'll be wearing a wedding ring. That's more than you ever offered."

"And if I call and tell him where you were last night?"

"He already knows. Why do you think he proposed?"

For the first time he caught a crack in her legendary

control. "I'm sure you'll be relieved to hear he forgives me. Forgives us both."

This time Lucius did swear aloud. "Don't do this, Lisa. He won't survive marriage to you. You'll eat him alive."

And maybe that's why he'd allowed her to talk him into a final fling last night, in the hopes that Geoff would hear about it and finally see Lisa for what she was. An opportunist. An amoral cat who'd bed down with anyone who could afford her price. Instead, all he'd managed to do was guarantee his best friend a marriage made in hell. Great. Just great.

"If you didn't want me with Geoff, then you should have been the one to offer marriage. But you're just too damn clever for your own good, too intent on manipulating your world and everyone in it." She shoved her porcelain cup and saucer aside with a quick little jerk. The coffee sloshed over the rim and stained the virginal white saucer in bitter darkness. "I'm marrying Geoff and that's the end of it. I can make him happy and I fully intend to."

"What do they say about the road to hell?" He snapped his fingers. "Oh, right. That smear of pavement is one long, filthy tarmac of good intentions."

"In that case, I'm going to hell, though I doubt I'm going there alone. You'll be right there beside me." She shoved back her chair and stood. To his surprise tears glittered in her eyes. "Would you like to know what's funniest of all? Geoff wants to start a family right away. It's the one thing we both agree on. I may be a gold digger, but I'm a maternal one."

A fierce wave of cynicism swept through him. "Not to mention that when your marriage bombs, that little tyke you pop out ensures nice, fat child support payments to go along with that nice, fat alimony check."

Instead of his words sending her up in flames as he expected, it cooled her. "You're a total son of a bitch, Lucius. Thanks for reminding me of that fact." She snatched up her phone, shoved it into her purse and faced him with a pride he could only admire. "And one of these days I plan to make you eat those words. I may not want Geoff the way I want you, but he's a good man. A decent man. I haven't had many of those in my life. I plan to make him very happy. Delirious, in fact. And I hope you're stuck watching us enjoy that happiness for the next fifty years. That way you can choke on it."

And with that, she swept out the door.

One

"You aren't just a devil, you're a total son of a bitch!"

Angie Colter's head jerked up at the unmistakable sound of a hand striking flesh and she swiveled to stare at the closed door of her boss's office—Lucius Devlin, owner and CEO of the Seattle based company, Diablo, Inc., a multibillion dollar business that specialized in buying and rehabbing commercial real estate. The next instant the door slammed open and Ella, the gorgeous redhead Angie had ushered in not ten minutes earlier, emerged. The woman had been Devlin's latest in a long string, lasting a full two weeks. A record breaker among the spate of women her boss had seen over the past three months.

"I don't know how you could possibly think I'd be interested in your insane proposal." With that, she swept across the plush expanse of carpet on impossibly high heels, her backside twitching out her profound irritation as she headed for the private elevators.

Okay. That was interesting and added to Angie's growing suspicion that something was up with Lucius. She hadn't figured out what, but suspected the six-month-old baby he'd received guardianship of a short three months earlier was somehow responsible. The baby, Mikey, was the son of the former head of PR for Diablo, Geoff Ridgeway. He and his wife, Lisa, had died in a train wreck in Europe shortly before Christmas, appointing Lucius the guardian of their infant son. From the moment Angie had first taken Mikey into her arms, she'd fallen in love with the little guy. Maybe it was due in part to the faint ticking of her biological clock. More likely it was those huge dark eyes staring so gravely into hers. Whatever the cause, an emotion unlike any she'd ever experienced before had fisted around her heart and refused to let go.

Angie glanced toward Lucius's office in open speculation. Initially, she'd thought her boss was searching for the perfect nanny, someone to replace the sweet-natured woman who'd accepted the job in a temporary capacity. But lately… Unable to contain her curiosity, she snatched up her electronic tablet and stylus. Crossing to the open doorway, she gave a brisk knock.

Her boss stood in profile, drowning a handful of ice cubes in scotch. Through the floor-to-ceiling windows behind him sprawled the city of Seattle, modestly veiling its beauty behind a misty, gray morning. At six foot two Lucius "The Devil" Devlin possessed a powerful physique at odds with a job that required endless hours behind a desk. No doubt he'd spent some of his billions on a home gym, filled with the best equipment money could buy. And used it with the same ruthless efficiency that characterized everything else he did in his life. He was a gorgeous man with hair the color of soot and eyes as dark and mysterious as a moonless night. A man who could steal a woman's breath without even trying. And the first time he'd tossed his devil-may-care smile in her direction, he'd stolen her heart…and quite possibly her soul.

Maybe that was why she'd committed the ultimate folly and fallen in love with him.

He glanced over his shoulder at her and frowned. "This isn't a good time."

The scowl snapped her back into focus. Ignoring his order, she stepped into the office. "Try using some of that ice on your jaw," she instructed crisply. "It'll help with the swelling."

"She packs quite a punch for a woman."

"I don't doubt it. Ella can bench-press a hundred and a quarter."

He swiveled to fully face her. "Get out. Seriously?"

"Dead serious. We go to the same gym. You're even more lucky she didn't use those Christian Louboutin heels on you. I've seen what she can do in our kickboxing class. She'd have skewered you like a shish kebab."

"She never mentioned she knew you."

Angie didn't doubt it. That would involve connecting with someone of the female sex. Ella only had eyes for men. "I doubt she noticed me. I don't exactly stand out."

Lucius tossed back the scotch, then took her suggestion and pressed the iced glass against the red mark darkening his jaw. His gaze swept over her. Even though he stripped her with that swift look, it was in a—sadly—asexual manner. Not that it surprised her. She knew what he saw. She'd come to the conclusion long ago that she had a head for business and a bod for…well, business.

At five foot eight, she was as slender as a reed, her curves best classified as subtle. Granted, she possessed an attractive enough face and great hair, even if she did keep it confined in an elegant twist, the color containing every shade of brown known to man. But her most attractive feature were her eyes, a brilliant aquamarine that her former lover had called "unnerving." Of course, that was right before he'd dumped her for her five-foot-two, blonde and buxom—*former*—best friend, whom he'd promptly married. Nine months later they produced the baby she'd dreamed of having with him, and that he'd claimed he not only didn't want, but would never want. Maybe that was why Angie had chosen to throw every scrap of her time and energy into her career. While Britt was giving birth to Ryan's baby, Angie secured the prime job as Lucius Devlin's PA. She hadn't quite decided who got the better deal, which told her that maybe her feelings for Ryan hadn't run as deep as she'd thought.

"Ella didn't notice you because you're female," Lucius stated, echoing her earlier thoughts. "Not because you don't stand out. The right clothes, the right hairstyle—"

She stiffened, pricked by his careless dissection. The hazards of loving a man who saw you as a piece of equipment rather than a human being. Damn him. Her chin shot up and she pinned him with her "unnerving" gaze, pleased to have found some use for it. "Oh, wow. Advice from Lucius 'The Devil' Devlin on how to transform myself into the perfect woman. Wait now. Let me take notes." She flipped her electronic tablet over and allowed the stylus to hover above it. "Please, Lucius. Don't keep me waiting. Other than the right clothes and hairstyle, how else am I lacking?"

"Hell, woman."

She narrowed her eyes at his use of the word *woman,* pleased to see him wince. Huh. Maybe she'd patent the look. It was certainly coming in handy. "You should know all about hell, Lucius."

A grim expression closed over his face and he snatched

up the cut glass decanter, splashing more scotch into his glass. "I should and I do."

Despite the threatening storm clouds, Angie refused to back down. "I don't doubt it." She lifted an eyebrow in open challenge. "Anything else you'd care to add about my appearance?"

He took a long swallow, regarding her over the rim of his tumbler with intense black eyes. "Not a chance."

"I didn't think so." She gestured toward his glass. "Put the ice back on your face or you'll have to explain that bruise to your clients. I shudder to think what sort of nose-dive your reputation will take when you're forced to admit you were coldcocked by a woman."

"That's not how I'm going to tell the story." Still, she couldn't help but notice that he rested the glass against his jaw—an aching jaw if she didn't miss her guess.

She offered an angelic smile. "No, but it's how I plan to tell it."

"How the hell could I have thought you'd make the perfect PA?" he snarled. "I must have been out of my mind."

"Agreed." Unable to contain her curiosity, she asked, "What in the world did you say to Ella that made her so mad?"

His annoyance intensified. "You would think it was my fault."

"Do I owe you an apology?"

She could see the internal debate rage, before he settled on admitting the truth. "No, it was my fault. I made the mistake of proposing to her."

Angie struggled to breathe. He couldn't have hit her any harder if he'd been the one doing the kickboxing. "What?"

He glanced her way and blew out a sigh. "Oh, get over it, Colter. This isn't high school. We're not talking about some grand romance. Hell, I've only known the woman for two weeks. I made a business proposition that involved marriage and for some reason that ticked her off. Go figure."

Her world righted itself and she found she could breathe again. It took a second longer to settle her face into something that passed for mild interest. Another few seconds to gain control over her vocal cords so she didn't sound as shrill as a steam whistle. Until that moment, she hadn't realized just how bad she had it, just how desperately she'd fallen for him. His brilliance. His innate kindness, a kindness he worked so hard to encase in a cold, tough exterior. The wealth of inexplicable pain buried in his eyes, and no doubt his heart. In the year and a half she'd worked for him, she'd gotten to know the man behind the reputation. And with that knowing had come the sort of love she'd only played at with Ryan, skating across the surface of the emotion without embracing the true depths and scope.

Gathering her control, she allowed a cool smile to drift across her mouth. "You're right, Lucius. I can't imagine why any woman in her right mind would find a marriage proposal phrased as a business proposition in the least offensive," she commented drily. "Go figure."

Lucius set his glass down with a decisive click that caused the ice to shiver in warning. He took a step in her direction and fixed her with a dark, impenetrable gaze. "You have an opinion to offer on the subject?"

She didn't answer the question directly, didn't dare. "Is this about Mikey?" She couldn't help the softening that came into her voice when she said the name, any more than she could help the softening that invaded her whole being when she held the baby in her arms and imagined what it would be like to have something so precious come from her own body.

He hesitated and she could tell that he wanted to rip her

apart in order to release some of his fury toward Ella. But he wasn't the type to take his aggression out on an innocent. He gathered himself, banked the fire, then nodded. "Yes," he admitted. "This is about Mikey."

"You're attempting to find someone who would make a suitable wife for you and a good mother for the baby?"

"Again, yes."

"And you expected Ella to jump at the opportunity after a two-week courtship?"

His teeth came together with a snap. "I had my reasons for believing it a distinct possibility. Are you done with the cross-examination?"

He'd reached the end of his rope and she responded accordingly. "Absolutely."

"Then may I suggest we get some work done? We still have to finalize the schedule for my meeting with Gabe Moretti."

She touched the screen of her tablet and called up the pertinent information. "He's agreed to go in on the Richter building with you?"

"Only if I give him majority interest."

"No doubt," Angie replied. "But if he remodels it the way he did Diamondt Towers, it'll be well worth the investment, even with only a minority stake."

"That's not good enough."

"No, it never is." He was a man who needed to hold the reins. Unfortunately, so was Gabe Moretti. "Will Moretti concede the point?"

"We plan to meet and discuss terms."

Meaning…no. Moretti had no intention of giving up majority interest, which suggested a showdown between titans. What she wouldn't give to see that! She touched an app on the screen that accessed Lucius's calendar. "Would you prefer a lunch meeting or dinner?"

He considered, took another sip of his refilled drink before returning it to his jaw. "Dinner on Friday. Let's make it at Milano's on the Sound. Speak to Joe personally about the menu, would you?"

She made a quick notation. "I'll take care of it. Eight o'clock work for you?"

"Only if it works for you."

Angie's poise faltered for a telling instant before she gathered herself back up. "Sorry?"

"Now that Ella's out of the picture, I'll need you to attend with me. You're one of the most observant people I know. I could use your input on this." His smile drew attention to features devil-perfect and sinfully attractive, and her heart gave a sharp, painful tug. "Problem?"

She dragged her gaze away from his dark, angel beauty and focused on the tablet, pretending to make a quick notation. "I'll check my schedule and get back to you."

"Right. You do that."

She let the hint of mockery wash over her. "Next. I have several calls from a Pretorius St. John. He indicated it was a private matter. Something about a computer program he was personalizing for you. If it isn't anything you want me to deal with, I'll forward it to your PDA."

"Go ahead and do that."

She hesitated. "That name is familiar for some reason. Should I know it?"

"It's possible. His nephew is Justice St. John, the robotics wunderkind. Pretorius specializes in computer software."

Wow. "Okay, color me impressed that you have a software inventor willing to tweak one of his programs in order to fit your personal specifications."

"You know, there are some days I think you forget who you're working for."

"Oh, dear. Not again." She made an exaggerated curtsy. "I do apologize, Mr. Devlin, sir. I promise I'll be more careful in the future."

"See that you are." His eyes glittered with laughter while he studied her, curiosity spilling into the intense darkness. "I don't intimidate you in the least, do I?"

"No."

It was the truth. For some reason he didn't and never had. That hadn't been her problem, mainly because she'd been too busy fighting her attraction for him to worry about his standing in the business community. Instead, she'd done everything within her power to conceal her re-action whenever they accidentally touched. To hide how desperately she'd like to experience his hands on her. His mouth. His body covering hers with nothing between them but the damp sheen of want. She closed her eyes briefly, closed off those sort of painful, wayward thoughts— something that grew more difficult with each passing day—and fought to regain her equilibrium.

Lucius was a closed door to her. What she felt for him would never become a reality and the sooner she accepted that fact the sooner she could move on. Only one problem with that plan. She didn't want to move on. She wanted… *him*.

To her eternal gratitude, Lucius didn't appear to notice anything wrong. "Your self-possession and your natural way of behaving around me are two of the qualities I most appreciate about you."

If he only knew. "Just two?" she managed to tease.

"Fishing for compliments, Colter?"

"You bet." She pretended to cast a fishing line and reel it in, forcing out a careless grin.

"Fair enough."

He approached, circling like a shark, unnerving her

for the first time in the eighteen months they'd worked together. Until now he'd regarded her almost like a piece of office furniture. Useful. Functional. An integral, if replaceable, cog in the wheel that was Diablo. This time when he looked at her it was through a man's eyes. Her amusement faded and it took every ounce of that self-possession he'd applauded only moments before to maintain her poise and keep a calm, cool expression on her face. Her grip tightened on the electronic tablet and stylus and she could only hope he didn't notice the whitening of her knuckles or the tension pouring off her. Though, knowing Lucius, he not only noticed but would use it against her.

"Do you know why I picked you out of all the endless candidates to be my PA?" he surprised her by asking.

"Not a clue," she admitted. "I'm good at my job, but so were the other applicants, I assume."

"You're wrong," he said softly. "You're not good. You're great."

He'd stunned her. When she'd first started working for him eighteen months ago, he'd chosen her from a pool of dozens of equally efficient and qualified PAs, women—and men—who were the best in the country. Granted, Angie had worked hard for the opportunity, particularly since she'd failed in just about every other area of her life. But Lucius Devlin could afford to hire the very best, and deep down she couldn't quite convince herself that *she* was the best. And yet, here he stood, insisting she wasn't just good, but great.

"Great," she repeated faintly.

"Don't get a swelled head, Colter. Though you were great when I interviewed you, there were others who were better."

"Then why...?" Her eyes narrowed, the truth hitting

like a tidal wave. After she'd been offered the position, she'd worked longer and harder than she thought physically possible, throwing herself into the job to justify having been chosen. No doubt that's why he'd hired her. He knew she'd go the extra distance, knew on some level she'd been desperate enough to throw her heart and soul into the position. Maybe the other women hadn't been quite as committed. The knowledge that he'd used her with such deliberation gave her heart a small, painful twist. She'd been used before by Ryan and vowed at that time to never allow it to happen again. The fact that it had been Lucius who used her hurt all the more. "Damn it, Devlin. That's low, even for you."

He picked up on her intensity, caught the ripple of pain in her soft words. "If I'd known you then as well as I know you now, I'd have chosen a different method. But I needed to work you—hard—to make sure we were a good fit." An odd expression swept through his gaze, something she couldn't quite identify, but that caused her pulse rate to kick up a notch. "And we are a good fit, aren't we, Angie?"

Her mouth tugged to one side in a reluctant smile. "So far. But if you play me like that again, we won't be any sort of fit."

"Fair enough." He shot her a quick grin. "Still, you have to admit it worked. Not only did it work, but you've more than proved yourself. You've exceeded even my high standards."

"You're welcome," she murmured drily.

"That staggering paycheck you receive is my thanks. I'll even throw in a bonus if you go out and buy something decent to wear to our dinner with Moretti. I want him so focused on you that his reputation for being all business, all the time, will take a serious beating. Thanks to you, I expect him to be less business and more man. Got it?"

"I wasn't hired for that," she retorted tightly.

"You were hired to do the jobs I assign you. That's the current job."

Now what? Did she admit that she wasn't equipped to handle the current job? Or did she simply allow him to figure that out for himself? Because there wasn't a doubt in her mind that the level of excellence she exhibited at work perfectly balanced the level of mediocrity she exhibited in every other area of her life, particularly under the heading of male-female relationships. Hadn't Ryan explained that to her in no uncertain terms when he "accidentally" tripped and fell naked on top of her best friend, Britt? And in their bed, no less. What had he told her...?

Oh, right. Though she had brains and business acumen in spades, but when it came to hearth and home—particularly the bedroom portion of the home—he found her decidedly lacking. Fair enough. She found Britt and Ryan's concept of friendship equally lacking. That's when she'd decided to stick to what she was best at...work. And she had, until she'd committed a huge error. That absolute no-no of no-nos. She'd fallen in love with the boss.

She spared Lucius a single, searing look. "I don't know how, but I fully intend to make you pay for putting me through this humiliation."

That stopped him. "You consider dinner out with your boss and a client humiliating?"

"No, I consider playing the part of a seductress for my boss and his client humiliating."

Anger flared in Lucius's dark gaze. "I don't recall saying anything about seducing Moretti. Merely distracting him."

"It's not a role I'm comfortable with. And I resent being

put in that position. You know damn well that's not part of my job description." She held up a hand before he could argue the point. "And don't try and claim my job is whatever you tell me it is. That's not going to fly with me. It's whatever you tell me within the confines of the four corners of this office building. Period."

Under any other circumstance, she would have found his look of pure masculine bewilderment and frustration amusing. Instead, it tempted her to follow Ella's example and give him a good, hard smack upside his clueless head.

"You've attended business dinners before," he protested.

"Not in the sort of role you've assigned for this one."

He tossed back the last of his scotch and set the glass down with a sharp crack. "Fine. Show up looking like a piece of office furniture if that will make you feel better."

Fury sparked, spilled over. "Office furniture?"

He stalked to the front of his desk, seized one of the twin chairs positioned there and swept it in a swift one-eighty. "Office furniture," he repeated.

It took two full seconds to make the connection, to notice the simple white cream and black speckled fabric of the chair was an almost perfect match for the simple white cream and black speckled fabric of her suit. Hot color washed into her cheeks. Dear Lord. Earlier she'd thought he saw her as little more than a piece of office equipment rather than a human being. Apparently, that office equipment was furniture. Damn it! Maybe that was because she'd turned herself into office furniture.

When she'd first started work at Diablo, she'd deliberately chosen colors and designs that would help her blend with the background. Create the appearance of the perfect PA. Clearly, she'd taken the concept a step too far. Maybe a couple of steps too far.

"Well, hell," she muttered.

"Exactly."

She considered the problem for a moment. "How about this…? If I promise not to show up wearing chair uphol-stery, could I just be myself?" Something flickered to life in his eyes at the question. Sympathy? Compassion? She could only hope it wasn't pity. "To be honest, I'm not cut out to play the part of Mata Hari."

He inclined his head. "Fair enough. You can leave a few hours early tomorrow in order to purchase an appro-priate dress and accessories. Save your receipts and I'll reimburse the expense." He checked his watch. "Keesha is due with Mikey at four, so I'll need to have my desk cleared by then. Hold any calls unless they're urgent. Oh, and don't forget to forward the messages from Pretorius St. John."

"Already done."

He nodded in clear dismissal and Angie didn't waste any time retreating to the outer office. She crossed to an antique table that held a coffee and tea service and helped herself to a restorative cup of hot tea. She didn't know what had upset her more…Friday's dinner, the fact that she'd transformed herself into a chair or the discovery that Lucius was actively looking for a wife.

Idiot! Of course she knew which upset her more. She was totally, ridiculously in love with a man who com-pared her to office furniture. How would she handle it if—*when*—he found a woman willing to marry him? If she were forced, day after day to watch the two enjoying the sort of marital bliss she'd always longed to experience? She closed her eyes. She knew how she'd handle it, what she'd force herself to do if—*when*—that event occurred.

If Lucius married, Angie would quit her job.

* * *

"Pretorius? Lucius Devlin here. We have a problem."

A pained sigh slipped across the phone lines. "Don't tell me the program still isn't working."

"The program still isn't working."

"Maybe you're not waiting long enough before popping the question. How much time did you give this latest one?"

"Two weeks."

"Two…" Pretorius sputtered. "Are you nuts? No woman in her right mind is going to agree to marry you after a two-week acquaintance. Why is it that brilliant men, men who are beyond adept at conquering their small corner of the world, think every other aspect of their life should be equally as simple and straightforward. Like I told Justice, these are *women* we're talking about. Not robots. And not real estate."

"My corner of the world isn't small."

Dead silence met his claim. Then Pretorius exploded. "That's all you have to say?"

"No, I have quite a bit to say, starting with certain guarantees you made regarding the Pretorius Program. Your program was supposed to choose women receptive to the idea of marriage."

"My program did choose receptive women. You were supposed to show some patience, remember? You're just like Justice. You can't just date for a couple days, or even a couple of weeks and then pop the question."

"Why not?" Lucius spared a glance toward the door to his office, which Angie guarded with such skill and dedication. He couldn't imagine a better employee. She'd become a vital part of his organization and he didn't want to consider the possibility of ever losing her. "Your program helped me choose the perfect PA within that time frame. And Ms. Colter has proven to be an excellent employee."

"We aren't talking about an employee." Frustration bled through the line. "We're talking about a wife. The parameters for a wife are far more complicated than for an employee. In addition to personality issues and general likes and dislikes there's physical and emotional compatibility. I need to assess each woman carefully and make sure that marriage to you and caring for an infant mesh with her long-term goals and desires. Otherwise you'll find yourself dealing with an unhappy marriage, followed by a messy divorce."

"I told you I don't want any emotional involvement. I want a woman who will function in the capacity of wife and mother the exact same way Angie functions in the capacity of my PA."

"Come on, Lucius. You're being unreasonable and you know it. Why would any woman want such a cold, sterile marriage?"

Because he was cold and sterile. Because at the ripe age of twenty his father had died, and he'd allowed his desire for vengeance to rule his life. Because he didn't trust. Was constantly watching for the next betrayal. How could you build a relationship when you refused to allow anyone in? When opening yourself up to someone guaranteed a wealth of pain?

Other than his father, Lucius had fully opened himself to one other person in his life. A brother in spirit, if not by blood. Geoff. And when Lisa had come between them, she'd destroyed what they'd once shared, utterly and finally. Had shut a door he now realized had been a vital part of his life. Now he stood adrift, a lonely rock in the middle of a tempestuous sea, solid in only one regard.

He would never trust again.

"Listen to me, Pretorius…. Why my future bride would accept a cold, sterile marriage is your problem, not mine. To be frank, I don't give a damn so long as she's a loving mother to Mikey and can create an efficiently run, beautifully appointed home. Someone who is comfortable entertaining clients. Now, I've submitted my order. You assured me you could fill it. So, fill it."

Pretorius blew out a sigh. "Okay, fine. Give me a week to tweak the parameters some more. Then I'll send you a new list. But I have to tell you… We're running out of eligible women in the Seattle area."

Okay, a negotiation. He knew everything there was to know about negotiating. "Then expand the search to the Northwest section of the country. Hell, open it up to the entire United States if it means I'll have a wife within the next three months. You do that, I'll throw in a nice, juicy bonus."

"I may have to pull my assistant in on the project," Pretorius said cautiously. "Do you have a problem with that?"

"Is he discreet?"

There was a long pause, then, "She can be bribed."

"Fine. Then do it."

"I'll be in touch as soon as possible."

"With a list of women that includes my future wife."

Pretorius groaned. "Fine, fine. She'll be on there."

The instant Lucius disconnected the call, he crossed to the bank of windows overlooking a gray and rainy Seattle cityscape. It perfectly matched his mood. He planted his fists on his hips and lowered his head like a bull prepared to charge. Wanting to charge. Wanting to fight free of his current predicament.

How could Geoff do this to him? How dare he go and get himself killed, leaving Lucius with his and Lisa's son. He didn't want to be a guardian to the boy. How the hell was he supposed to raise him, turn him into the sort of man Geoff would have been proud to call his son, when it was so far beyond Lucius's abilities? What had Geoff been thinking?

He picked up his glass of scotch and drank the last of it. He didn't have the heart to be a father. Didn't have the soul for the job. Couldn't imagine years of playing the role of Dad to Mikey, despite having had the kindest, most loving father himself. The sort of father Mikey deserved. The sort of father Geoff would have been. It was so far beyond his scope and ability, he might as well have been asked to catch the moon in a butterfly net.

Damn it to hell! He swung around and heaved the glass across the room. The glass exploded, shattering against the wall, the dregs of scotch and ice raining down the wall like tears from heaven. So he would cheat. He'd hire someone—a wife—to take on his responsibilities. And he'd make her life so safe and secure and plush, she'd never leave him. Even though he couldn't offer her everything a husband should, he could offer enough. A beautiful, richly appointed home. A man who could give her pleasure in the bedroom, even if he couldn't give her love. A life filled with luxury, her every desire fulfilled, her every wish granted. It would be enough, wouldn't it?

He glanced toward the door. Well, it would be enough for most women. Maybe not for his intrepid PA since her every wish and desire revolved around her excelling at her job. Now that he could understand. Understand and admire. Just thinking about her helped him gather himself. Relax. Realize that on this front, he was in control of his own destiny.

Thank God for Angie.

Two

"Not many women can wear that dress and get away with it," Trinity commented. "It's because you're so slender."

Angie tugged at the plunging drape of the bodice. "No, it's because I'm built like a prepubescent boy."

Trinity shook her head. "Honey, that figure is all woman. True, it's not voluptuous, but no one would ever mistake you for a boy. And that shade of aquamarine is stunning on you. It really makes your eyes pop."

After Britt's betrayal, Angie had been reluctant to form a close relationship with another woman. She definitely hadn't been interested in finding another best friend. Trinity had ignored every one of Angie's defensive barricades and steamrollered right over them. It took a full six months before she'd broken through the final one, but once she had, the two became as close as sisters.

Angie gave a quick shimmy. "This dress is too tight. I think I need a size larger."

"It's perfect and you know it. It's exactly what Devlin requested."

It might be exactly what he requested, but it wasn't at all what Angie wanted to give him. Or rather, showcase in front of Gabe Moretti. Maybe if this were a romantic dinner with Lucius, and the dress were meant for his eyes alone... The instant the thought—the dream—popped into her head, she ruthlessly plucked it out again. That would never happen.

She'd heard the gossip about Lisa and her on-again, off-again relationship with first Lucius and then Geoff Ridgeway. The relationship had ended in Lisa's marriage to Geoff two short months after Angie accepted a job at Diablo, Inc.—over a year after her own split with Ryan. Rumors and gossip had flown through the office, hot and heavy, only abating when it became clear that the newly-weds were ecstatically happy. How many times had she driven that point home in an attempt to quell the rumor mill and give her boss some peace? When Lisa announced her pregnancy, and the couple had named Lucius the baby-to-be's godfather, the last, lingering whispers had finally died off.

Even so, Angie saw what no one else did, what Lucius had successfully hidden from all but the most discerning eyes. He was beyond miserable, working day by day to put a stoic face on a hideous situation, which confirmed her suspicion that he'd been madly in love with Lisa. But she knew beyond a shadow of a doubt that he'd never get over losing the love of his life to his best friend, even if Angie couldn't understand why anyone would choose the affable, slightly geeky Geoff Ridgeway over the sexy-as-hell Lucius Devlin.

No doubt losing his soul mate explained his cold-blooded attempts to find a mother for Mikey. He wasn't interested in any sort of emotional involvement; he simply wanted a permanent nanny for the baby—not that it was any of her business.

Angie forced her attention back to the task at hand and turned, frowning at the way the thigh-high skirt clung to her backside, the horizontal pleats giving the illusion of attractively rounded hips. The miniscule skirt showcased mile-long legs, while the three-inch heels made them seem even longer.

"Don't you think it's awfully short?" she asked Trinity in concern.

"Not even."

"A bit low cut?" The question carried an unmistakably desperate air.

"You have great collarbones and a pretty chest." Trinity approached, circled. "I say, show it off."

"I'm not sure this is smart."

"Hey, you said Devlin wanted you dressed to distract. Trust me. This'll distract every living, breathing man within a ten-mile radius. Maybe fifty miles. How are you planning to wear your hair?"

"Up."

Trinity planted her hands on her hips and tilted her head to one side, her spiky black hair, slanted green eyes and gorgeous golden-brown skin making her look like a cross between a cat and an elf. "I'm torn. The back is cut on the low side. If you wear your hair down, you lessen the impact of it. But you always wear your hair up." She gathered the length in her hands and lifted it into a loose and careless ponytail, the curls cascading down the center of her spine. "Okay, this might work. Hair has that flirty, windblown look and yet, you can still see plenty of skin."

"A must, I gather," Angie said drily.

"A definite must," Trinity agreed. "Go easy on the makeup. Let your body do the talking."

"My body hasn't done any talking for three full years."

Trinity shot a swift glance over her shoulder. "Girl, don't go admitting that where someone can overhear you. I mean, that's just sad."

"But true."

"Mmm. You go out dressed like this more often and your body wouldn't just be talking, it would be screaming out the 'Hallelujah Chorus' on a nightly basis."

Angie didn't dare admit that her body had never screamed the "Hallelujah Chorus." Hummed a few bars, but that was about as close as she'd come. "What about jewelry?" she asked, deliberately changing the subject.

"Earrings. Dangles. Preferably silver."

"I think I have something that might work. They're beaten silver, a cascade of twisted hearts."

"Oh, the irony."

Angie grinned. "Not that I'm obsessive, or anything."

"Hell, no. Why would you be?" She gave Angie a hip nudge. "Come on. Pay for the thing and let's go have dinner and drinks. We should celebrate your release from the land of the average and banal."

Stifling her qualms, Angie bought the dress and heels, then threw in some ridiculously expensive undergarments that were little more than scraps of lace held together by elastic threads. *In for a penny...* She found the rest of the evening far more enjoyable than the torture of clothes shopping. Trinity had a flair for distraction. Of course, it didn't hurt that they split a bottle of wine over an Italian meal.

Several hours later, she sat back, replete. "I should have bought that dress in a size larger," she confessed ruefully.

Trinity groaned. "Maybe two. It was those bread sticks. They do me in every time."

"Funny. I would have said it was the tiramisu."

"Not a chance. Desserts here don't have calories. The waiter swore it was true. I might be able to give up bread sticks—or at least cut back a little—but don't ask me to give up their tiramisu."

"Fair enough."

"So are you done brooding?"

Angie blinked in surprise. "Was I brooding?"

"He called you office furniture. That's enough to make anyone brood. But I guarantee The Devil won't call you that ever again." Trinity nudged the shopping bags with the toe of her Choos, intense satisfaction sliding through her voice. "Not once he sees you in that dress."

Angie flinched. "Don't." Though she'd never told Trinity how she felt about Lucius, there was no question her friend suspected something. "Nothing will ever happen. Not with him. He's actually thinking about getting married."

Trinity's mouth dropped open. "No way."

"It's a sensible decision. He needs a mother for Mikey."

"And has he found her or is he in the looking phase?"

"Looking."

Trinity's hazel eyes danced with mischief. "Well, then. Maybe that dress will have him looking in a whole new direction."

It was just a joke, Angie told herself for the umpteenth time, smoothly changing the subject. A tantalizing possibility, but utterly impossible. Unrealistic. And considering it as anything else could only lead to one place. Utter heartbreak. She couldn't go there. Not again. And so she chatted and laughed and tucked her heartache away until she could escape home.

The minute she entered her house, she carefully tucked her purchases into the far recesses of her closet where the outfit wouldn't be in a position to taunt her for the next few days. And even though Lucius asked for the receipts, she refused to hand them over. It didn't seem right to have him pay for the dress, not to mention the more intimate pieces she'd bought. Not when she could wear them on more occasions than their business dinner.

Friday came far too soon for Angie's peace of mind. She left work promptly for a change and refused Lucius's offer to pick her up. Easier to take a cab to the waterfront. She arrived at Milano's on the Sound exactly on time. She loved Joe's restaurant, loved the romantic ambience of it, even though tonight was strictly business. The layout of the interior appealed to her on some basic, feminine level, the overall design making clever use of spacing, angles and elegant furnishings. Joe had even created little nooks and oases that gave the diners the illusion that they were the only patrons present.

Andre, the maître d', greeted her by name as he offered to take her wrap. She could only assume he had one of those impressive memories that allowed him to pair names with faces. His gaze swept over her in a discreet manner, but one which managed to convey deep masculine approval. It gave her confidence a boost, something she badly needed considering the two men she'd soon be dealing with.

"Mr. Devlin and Mr. Moretti have already arrived," he informed her in an undertone. "They seem somewhat at odds."

"Already?"

Andre lifted a shoulder in a shrug that clearly said, "Alpha men, what else do you expect?"

She smiled. "Have they been served drinks?"

"Not yet."

"I have it on good authority that they'll be ordering beef this evening. Why don't you have a bottle of Glenrothes brought to the table. If I'm wrong and they order seafood, swap it out for Old Pulteney."

"Of course, Ms. Colter. I'll see to it immediately."

He guided her to an exclusive section reserved for VIPs. While some of the tables allowed couples to sit hip to hip in the deep, cushioned benches facing the windows overlooking Puget Sound, the table Andre showed her to was a simple round. The two men sat across from one another like a pair of combatants. A vacant chair, facing the windows was clearly meant for her. Great. She loved playing Monkey in the Middle.

She didn't know what alerted Lucius to her presence. But she could tell the instant he sensed her, his body stiffening, his gaze swiveling to narrow in on her. The patent disbelief in his gaze when he saw her almost made her laugh—or maybe cry since it told her precisely what he thought of her as a woman. He was quick to conceal his shock. Too late, she wanted to say.

He shoved back his chair and stood, approaching in order to take her hand in his and guide her to the table as though they were a couple, instead of boss/employee. "Gabe, you remember my PA, Angie Colter."

Gabe Moretti was every inch as gorgeous as Lucius, with hair as raven dark. But instead of eyes to match, his were the shade of antique gold, filled with mystery and predatory intent. He stood to greet her, his gaze sharp and appraising. Then he smiled with singular charm and offered her his hand. "It's a pleasure to see you again, Ms. Colter," he said in a voice that made her think of smoke.

"Please, call me Angie, Mr. Moretti."

He inclined his head. "Let's make it Angie and Gabe,

shall we?" Before Lucius had the chance, he pulled out the chair for her, acting the part of the host—and no doubt annoying her boss in the process. "I believe the last time I saw you, you were shopping for a house. How did that turn out?"

Impressed that he'd remembered, she rewarded him with a broad smile. "I closed on a small cottage in Ballard last month. It needs a bit of work, mostly cosmetic, but considering I picked it up for an excellent price, I don't mind in the least."

"Smart. But, then, knowing Devlin, he only hires the best." He shot Lucius a challenging glance. "Perhaps I should steal her from you."

Lucius didn't rise to the bait. "One of the qualities I look for in an employee is loyalty. You're welcome to make Angie an offer. If she accepts, it simply means my assessment of her was mistaken and I'm better off finding a new PA." He turned his black gaze on Angie and his smile smoldered like the smoke from hell. "Have I made a mistake?"

Good Lord, how in the world had she ended up in the middle of this tug-of-war? Instead of answering the question, she gave Andre a discreet nod, relieved beyond measure when he crossed to the table with the bottle of scotch. It proved the perfect distraction. With the ease of long practice, she turned the conversation to the latest financial market news. That successfully navigated them through the pouring of their drinks. Fortunately, the restaurant owner, Joe Milano, appeared just then with a platter of cold shellfish he'd prepared for them, personally.

He offered each man his hand, greeting them by name. He even took Angie's hand, kissing it with a natural ease that charmed. "You are absolutely delectable this evening. Who's going to look at my food when they can look at you?" he teased. "I should hide you away so my dishes can take center stage once again."

"I'm not sure Maddie would approve of that," Angie replied with an answering smile. At the mention of his wife's name, his brown eyes lit up and the expression that came into his face caused a pang of envy. What she wouldn't give to have a man look like that at the mere mention of her name. "Is she still trying to burn down the house?"

Joe chuckled. "Let's just say I keep her well away from the kitchen. And since our daughters all seem to follow in her footsteps—with one delightful exception—they are also banned."

"A future chef in the making?"

"Without question." Joe didn't linger after that. Wishing them *buon appetito,* he returned to the kitchen.

She didn't give either of her dinner companions the chance to cause further trouble. Once their waiter served them choice tidbits of the appetizer, she nudged the conversation ever so gently into the direction of the most recent changes to building inspections and codes, a subject dear to the hearts of both men. That got them through the appetizers, over the hurdle of a visit from the sommelier and a prolonged discussion of dinner options, before leaping directly into a terse debate over which dish was Joe's most impressive specialty.

Honestly, men never failed to exasperate her.

The instant their dinner arrived, she deliberately turned the conversation to the Richter project, hoping against hope it would get the focus off her and onto business where it belonged. "Your remodel of the Diamondt building was stunning," she informed Gabe with utter sincerity. "Are you planning something similar for this venture?"

"To be honest, I mainly handle the structural renovations." The instant he nudged his empty plate to one side, a busboy whisked it away.

"Who orchestrated the interior design? They did an impressive job of melding a forties retro feel with all the modern conveniences."

Gabe hesitated, his eyes darkening in a way that warned of some deep-seated displeasure. "I hired a San Francisco firm for the remodel. Romano Restorations."

"I'm not familiar with them."

"No, they're a fairly new firm." He glanced at Lucius. "Assuming we can come to terms, we may want to consider them for this job, too."

Lucius tilted his head to one side, his gaze shrewd. "You have reservations," he stated, picking up on the same hesitation Angie had.

"Nothing to do with their work or their owner. Constantine Romano is outstanding at his job. It's his wife who concerns me." He gave a careless shrug, drawing attention to the impressive width of his shoulders and chest. "It's a personal matter, one that has no bearing on business."

A cynical light flickered to life in Lucius's eyes and Angie could guess what he was thinking. "It's not that," she told him before she stopped to think.

Instantly, two sets of masculine eyes swiveled to dissect her. "It's not…what?" they both demanded, almost in unison, and she winced.

She sat for a split second and stewed. When would she learn to keep her big mouth shut? Granted, Lucius had included her tonight because she tended to be good at assessing people and situations. She had a knack for reading between the lines and, for the most part, coming up with accurate conclusions. Still, he probably would have preferred to have that assessment made in private. Oh, well. Too late now.

Taking a moment longer to consider how to answer their question, she went with the truth. The two businessmen were far too sharp to believe anything less. She glanced at Lucius and fought to maintain her equilibrium beneath his narrow-eyed glare. "When Gabe says it's personal, you assumed it meant he'd had an affair with Romano's wife. It's something else." She took a sip of wine in the hopes of settling her nerves. It didn't work. "Something clearly private."

"How do you know?" Again in unison.

She sighed. Could the two *be* any more like peas in a pod? She turned to Pea #1, aka…her boss. "Because he's angry, but not in a you-done-me-wrong sort of way. Plus, his anger isn't directed at both of them the way it would be if he'd had his woman stolen from him." And wouldn't that comment cut close to the bone with Lucius, considering he'd lost his woman to his best friend. She hastened to turn to Pea #2, aka…her boss's occasional competitor. "Considering the temperature just bottomed out to subarctic—shiver, shiver—it's clearly a private matter that you wouldn't talk about regardless of the incentive." She smiled brightly. "More scotch, or should we get down to serious business over dessert?"

"Dessert and serious business," Gabe decided.

"With a little more scotch," Lucius added blandly.

Unfortunately, the going continued to be as turbulent as the chop of the Sound outside the restaurant window, mainly because throughout their discussion, Gabe initiated a mild flirtation with her. His hand brushed hers when he made a point. His fingers lingering on her shoulder whenever he asked a question. He even caught a springy curl and gave it a tug during some teasing remark.

Normally, she'd have flirted right back, fully aware Gabe wasn't being the least serious. But one look at Lucius's expression warned her to play it very, very cool. It didn't make the least sense to her. Hadn't he requested she flirt with Moretti? Wasn't the goal to keep him distracted and off his game? Based on the dark looks she was receiving, the goal had changed without warning. Even worse, the only person distracted was Lucius.

By the time the last bite of a vanilla bean crème brûlée had been consumed, Angie hung from the end of her rope by a tattered thread. Gabe had somehow wrung more concessions out of her boss than she thought possible, a fact that left him smoldering dangerously. That fire threatened to burst to life when Gabe leaned in to kiss her farewell in what would have been an innocuous gesture if he hadn't taken one look at Lucius and then shifted the aim of his kiss, and slowed it, so it caressed the side of her mouth.

Angie decided it might be in her best interest to make a hasty retreat to the ladies' room while Andre ordered her a cab. With luck the two men would have already departed by the time she returned. She was half-right. Gabe was nowhere to be seen, but Lucius remained. He draped her wrap around her the instant she joined him.

She glanced toward the maître d'. "Has Andre ordered my cab?"

"*Our* cab," he corrected. "And yes, he has."

Well, damn. That's what she got for counting the minutes until she could let down her guard and relax. Cursing her luck, she piled a full thirty back onto her tally. "Isn't it out of the way for you?"

"I don't mind. Besides, I'm curious to see the house you bought."

Great. Just great. "No problem," she murmured. Big problem. *Huge* problem. And one she didn't have a hope in hell of avoiding.

"I appreciate your coming tonight," he surprised her by adding. "Ah, here's the cab now."

She followed him from the restaurant into the night air, snuggling deeper into her wrap. The scent of salt and fish flavored the breeze along the waterfront. From the direction of Puget Sound whitecaps foamed beneath a sliver of moon and ferries plied the restless chop, their lights glittering against the blackened sea. The cityscape loomed overhead, glowing with life and vitality. Lucius held the door of the cab and she slid in, praying her skirt didn't ride any higher. To her relief it stayed put, preserving her modesty. She heard Lucius give the driver the directions before joining her. Leave it to him to have every obscure detail at his fingertips, though it gave Angie an unsettled feeling, knowing that Lucius knew where she lived and could relay the address off the top of his head.

Maybe it had something to do with the thick blanket of darkness combined with the lateness of the hour, but his presence filled the back of the vehicle. Every so often a streetlight would pierce the shadows and play across hard, masculine angles. But that only served to emphasize the darkness of his eyes and make him appear tougher, more unapproachable. Like Bogey in one of his film noirs.

She searched for something to say, desperate to break the silence. Not that it was totally silent. Outside the city lived and breathed, filled with noise and lights and movement. But for some reason, it seemed distant and remote from within the confines of the cab, where his quiet breathing thundered in her ears and a visceral awareness grew with each passing moment. She peered into the night, assessing their distance from home. Still too far.

Way too far.

"I'm sorry the evening didn't work out quite as planned," she offered, desperate to break the silence.

"That wasn't your fault." His voice issued from the darkness. Quiet, yet carrying an edge that teased along her nerves, making her painfully aware of her scanty dress—and even scantier self-control. "It was mine."

"I didn't expect him to flirt with me," she confessed. "I thought that was my job."

"Yes, that took me by surprise, too." His head turned. All but his eyes remained in shadow, darkness buried within darkness. But those eyes… Heaven help her, they pierced through the night and arrowed straight into her soul. Could he see her thoughts, sense what she felt? The rational part of her knew it wasn't possible. The more visceral, feminine parts responded to the sheer maleness of him…and wanted. "If you'll recall, I did mention that you're a very attractive woman."

"With the right clothes and hairstyle, that is."

She could feel the burn of his gaze sweep over her. Strip her. "And I was right. That's one hell of a dress, Colter. What there is of it."

Her grip tightened on her wrap and she refused to look at him, afraid to look in case she lost the tenuous hold she maintained on her self-control. What would he do if she fisted her hands in that black silk jacket and yanked him to her? Kissed him in a way no employee had any business kissing her boss? Would he take her? Or reject her?

"You disapprove of my choice?" she asked.

The power of his gaze grew weightier, sharper. So tightly focused she could feel it laser into her very bones. "Hell, no. Though now that I've seen you in this, I'm not sure I can stand having you wear any more of those chair upholstery suits you favor."

"That isn't your decision." Her head swiveled in his direction and she fought to keep her voice cold and distant. "Nor do you have any say in the matter."

"And if I insist on having a say? If I claim the way you dress reflects on me? On Diablo?"

Furious words rose up, fighting for escape, trembling on the verge of utterance. To her profound relief, the cab pulled to a stop in front of her house. Not waiting for Lucius to play the part of the gentleman, she erupted from the cab. "Thank you for escorting me home. I'll see you Monday morning."

She slammed the door closed before he had a chance to reply and flew up the steps of her 1940s era Craftsman cottage. She fumbled in her envelope purse for her key, found it and was just about to jam it into the lock when she heard the slow, deliberate footsteps climbing the stairs behind her. She spun around. The cab was gone.

Lucius wasn't.

"Well?" he asked. "Aren't you going to invite me in?"

Bad idea. Very bad idea. "Sure." *Idiot.* "Would you like a cup of coffee?"

"Sounds perfect."

She fought to address him with a casual air and came within waving distance. Not that she fooled him. Lucius wasn't a man to fool, or a man to make a fool of. He continued to regard her with a watchful gaze, seeing far too much for her peace of mind. "I'll give you the grand tour while it's brewing. Not that it's all that grand," she chattered. It took four tries to get her key into the lock and the door opened. She threw a brilliant smile over her shoulder. "I guess the first improvement on my list is better lighting so I can see to open the door."

He returned her smile, though his eyes were knowing. Of course they were, damn him. Devlin never missed a thing. He stepped across the threshold and closed the door behind him, overpowering the dainty, feminine foyer with an excess of testosterone. He glanced around, nodding in approval. "This is charming, Angie."

"It needs paint. Carpets. Upgraded plumbing." *Babbling!* "But the electrical is sound, as is the basic structure."

He took his time looking around. "I like that the place has its original molding and hardwood floors. So many of the older homes have had those things stripped out and sold to restoration companies."

She led the way to the kitchen and started the coffee brewing. "Speaking of restoration, I was thinking about restoring the '40s look of the place, sort of like what Moretti did with the Diamondt building. Retro appliances. Antiques from that time period." She removed cups and saucers from the cupboard, her enthusiasm taking over. "It has two bedrooms and baths on this level, along with a powder room. One of the baths would be perfect for a claw-foot tub and one of those elegant pedestal sinks. Then there's the upstairs. It's unfinished right now and I'm not sure whether I want to put in a master suite up there or an office."

"A master suite would add more to the resell value. You can always turn one of the downstairs bedrooms into a home office."

She poured the coffee and turned to hand him a cup. He was so close she almost dumped it on him. "Sorry," she murmured, taking a swift step backward that jammed her up against the counter. For some reason she had difficulty meeting his gaze. "There are times I think this place is built more like a dollhouse than a house meant for adults."

"You're nervous. That's a first for you." He tilted his head to one side, his eyes as black as the bowels of hell. "Why is that, Angie?"

She made a helpless shrug. "You're my boss. And we're in my home."

"And we're blurring the lines?"

"Something like that," she admitted. Honesty forced her to confess, "Okay, totally that."

"Normally, we aren't the sort of people who blur lines."

"No."

But she wished she were. If she weren't afraid it would mean losing her job, she'd accept the offer she could read in his gaze. Part of her urged her to do just that. After all, what did it matter? He'd made it clear he intended to marry. If he did, she'd quit. Why not take a chance before that happened? Why not show him that she was so much more than a piece of office furniture. That she was a woman with a woman's emotions. All it would take was a kiss. A single kiss.

As soon as the thought came to her, she instantly dismissed it. Just where would that kiss lead? Straight to bed. To bed, where she'd be able to prove to him beyond a shadow of a doubt that while she excelled as his PA, she was a total disaster as the sort of woman who usually graced his bed. The stunning Lisa had managed to keep two brilliant and powerful men hooked. Angie closed her eyes. She hadn't even been able to hook one.

"Lucius—"

He lifted a hand, cut her off. "Tonight was a disaster. You realize that, don't you?"

Her brows pulled together in consternation. "You said it wasn't my fault."

"I lied. It was your fault."

"Wait a minute. Wait just one damn minute." She set her cup and saucer on the counter, the porcelain singing in protest. "You told me to flirt with him."

"I told you to distract him. You didn't distract him." It

only took a single step in her direction to have him invading her personal space. "You distracted me. And he bloody well knew it. Knew it and took advantage of that fact."

"And you blame me for that?" she demanded indignantly.

"I blame it on that damn dress." Burning flames of desire flared to life in his gaze, sweeping like wildfire across her skin, scorching in its intensity. All she could do was stare in return, bathing in the irresistible flames. "Maybe it would help if you took it off…"

Three

Lucius heard the swift, panicked catch of Angie's breath. God help him. Even that was sexy as hell. Why had he never noticed? How could he have been so blind?

"Have you lost your mind?" she demanded.

"Probably," he admitted. Definitely.

"You can't seriously expect me to strip down—"

"Expect? No. Hope?" He invaded the final few inches between them and caught the flutter of her pulse at the base of her throat, heard the swift give-and-take of her breath. "Oh, yeah."

"I work for you. And this doesn't just blur the lines. It steps way over them."

He reached for her, hooked one of the curls that had taunted him all evening and allowed it to twine around his finger. It clung to him, silken soft and utterly female. He'd watched Moretti do just that and it had taken every ounce of his self-possession not to deck the bastard. Lucius shook his head in an attempt to clear it. He didn't understand what was happening to him, couldn't make any sense out of the strength of his reaction. Angie had worked for him over the past eighteen months and not once in all that time had he ever felt the urge to connect with her on a personal level. To take her into his arms and discover whether that sexy, impudent mouth tasted as good as it looked.

Okay, once.

Nearly a year after he'd hired her, they'd been slogging through the day. It had been an unusually rough one despite the fact that Seattle sparkled beneath a crystalline sky while Mt. Rainier loomed in the distance, putting its stamp of approval on this brief slice of perfection. The September air contained the cool and crisp hint of autumn's cusp, filled with the tantalizing whispers of approaching apple and beer festivals.

But for Lucius, the day would have been better drowned beneath a torrent of wintry rain, slashing the windows at his back and driving an early darkness into his office. Lisa had just given birth to Geoff's son and the ecstatic father had raved endlessly about his newborn son and exhausted, valiant wife. Lucius sat quietly, striving to appear both excited for his best friend and interested in details he'd have just as soon known nothing about. Geoff must have talked for hours before Lucius finally sent him on his way, insisting he take the next couple of weeks off to be with his new family. And all the while guilt rode him, lashing him. He hadn't given his friend the time off out of generosity. Hell, no. He'd done it for himself, selfish bastard that he was.

He hadn't wanted to hear another word about how happy Geoff and Lisa were. Or the minute by minute, second by second details of her pregnancy and childbirth. Lisa had been wrong about one thing. It hadn't taken fifty years of wedded bliss to make him choke on their apparent happiness, but only a short nine months.

The instant Geoff left, delirious at his good fortune, Angie slipped into the room. One look at his face sent her straight to the wet bar where she poured him a stiff drink. Whether she'd heard about his involvement with Lisa through the office grapevine, or used her own deductive skills to reason it out during that first year of her employment, it was clear she knew. Knew, and set out to focus his attention on anything and everything other than Geoff and Lisa.

They worked long into the night, ordering takeout before digging into his latest rehab project. When he finally surfaced, he discovered Angie sacked out on the couch of his sitting area on the far side of his office. As always, she wore one of her godawful suits, this one in a muddy brown. At some point she'd stripped away her jacket, the simple taupe silk shell beneath escaping her waistband and draping across the sweetly subtle curves of her breasts. The skirt had rucked upward, showcasing a gorgeous set of mile-high legs. And the hair that she always pulled away from her face in a tidy knot had loosened, spilling down her shoulders in streaks of bronze and chestnut and a pale sandy brown.

For the first time, he saw Angie as a woman.

He must have made some sound. Or perhaps the undiluted concentration of his gaze alerted her on some primal level. Her lashes fluttered and she opened her eyes, the brilliant aquamarine muted with sleep, darker and more intense than normal.

Until now, Angie had always been one of the most professional women he'd ever known. He could create an endless list of her virtues—all perfect for a top-notch PA— and probably never hit all of her many attributes. But for the first time, he saw the woman behind the employee, a woman who possessed a softness and vulnerability he'd never noticed before. Her breathing sharpened, the semi-transparent flow of silk sliding and caressing her breasts with each rise and fall. For endless seconds they simply stared at each other, while a sharp, visceral awareness tugged at his gut.

Everything within him, everything that made him both a man and a predator, urged him to act. To take. To conquer. To possess. And all the while the thin veneer of civilized behavior, of propriety, kept him frozen in his chair, wanting without responding. Instinct warred with rationality. Teetered. If he went to her, pulled her into his arms, she wouldn't resist. Somehow he knew it with the sort of absolute certainty he'd perfected over his years as a businessman, his ability to assess any given situation with split-second certainty honed to a dagger's edge.

"Lucius?" His name, in a hesitant, hauntingly feminine whisper, slipped across the darkened room. Eve's call to Adam.

He clenched his teeth. "Go home. You're exhausted."

She continued to stare at him with eyes of want and he could practically see the apple cupped in her hands. "What about the prospectus?"

"It'll be here in the morning." He stood, snatched up her suit jacket and tossed it to her. "I think this is the first time I've ever seen the impeccable Ms. Colter wrinkled and out of sorts."

As he'd hoped, the comment snapped her to attention. Catching the jacket midair, she erupted from the couch with a gasp of dismay. If hunger for a fast, juicy bite of that apple weren't still dogging him, he'd have found the way she yanked her skirt into position, tucked in her blouse and jammed her arms into her jacket downright amusing. Trembling fingers attempted to shove buttons through holes. The fact that they were the wrong buttons in the wrong holes only added to her appealing vulnerability. Thrusting her hair out of her face, that long tumble of autumn browns, she made a beeline for the door, turning at the last minute.

She cloaked herself in painful dignity, but it was far too late. He'd seen what she buried beneath. Seen. Been tempted. Hungered. The serpent had invaded Eden and left its mark. "I'll see you tomorrow morning at the usual time."

"No, you won't."

He'd rattled her and he couldn't help taking pleasure in it. "I'm sorry?" she asked uncertainly.

"I'm meeting with Dolchester, remember? I won't be in until after lunch."

"Of course. I'll…I'll just leave now."

He nodded, allowing the apple to roll away, untasted. "Good night, Angie."

"Good night, Lucius," she murmured.

The initial spark of desire he felt then didn't come close to the roar of need cascading through him now. He didn't just want a taste of the apple, he wanted to consume every last, juicy bite in great ravenous gulps. His body continued to hold hers trapped against the kitchen counter and she gave a slight shimmying twist that threatened to drive him insane.

"Don't," he warned. "By all that's holy, don't."

She stilled, the cadence of her breath soft and desperate. He should let her go. He should leave. He should walk away now before they did something they'd both regret. But he couldn't walk away any more than he could stop his heart from beating.

"Lucius…"

He teetered on the brink, the foundation of his control crumbling around him while his name on her lips hovered between them like a siren's song. And then he inhaled it, inhaled her, his mouth coming down on hers while their breath became one, hers one of sweetness, his one of need. She tasted of wine and exotic flavors, her lips like velvet. Her body pressed against his in the most delicious of abrasions, lithe and slender, yet with a delicate, utterly feminine ripeness. He couldn't get enough. She invaded his senses, an intoxicating palette of scent and taste, touch and sound, and all he could think about was drinking her in, sip by sip, until he'd consumed every last drop.

"Don't hold back," he murmured against her mouth. "Let go. Show me who you've been hiding beneath those buttoned-up suits."

She laughed, the sound almost painful. "More buttons. Endless buttons."

He caught her lower lip in his teeth and tugged ever so gently, pleased with the shudder and moan it elicited. "Fortunately for you, I know all about the art of unbuttoning."

"I…" She hesitated, on the verge of telling him something, something important. But then she shook her head. "I can't do this, Lucius."

"You don't have to do anything. I'll take care of everything."

"You don't understand. I don't do this. I *can't* do this," she repeated, this time with an almost desperate edge.

He stilled. "Is there someone else?"

The question escaped with a masculine aggression he hadn't intended, though he knew the cause. Damn Lisa to hell and back for her duplicity, for destroying the one relationship he valued above all others—his friendship with Geoff. She'd left a scar when she'd cheated on him, cheated on him *and* Geoff. A festering wound, one he didn't think would ever heal.

If Angie had a man in her life—news to him—this would end here and now. Lucius refused to put another man through what he'd experienced at Lisa's hands. Nor would he put himself through that sort of pain ever again. His next serious relationship would be perfect—one programmed to order. Pretorius Programmed to order.

His question continued to hover between them, one he could tell she was reluctant to answer. "Tell me, Angie. Is there someone else?"

The question still echoed with aggressive demand. Fortunately, she'd never been intimidated by him, her unwavering directness and honesty an attribute he considered more important than any other in a PA, or a woman for that matter. She managed a laugh, though he could hear the heartbreak edging it and wondered at the cause.

"No, it's not that."

Lucius throttled back, the tension easing away. "Then there's no problem."

Before she could speak the protest forming on the tip of her delectable tongue, he kissed her again. She teetered between uncertainty and surrender, and he could practically feel her objections fading like mist beneath a midday sun. Her arms slid upward along his chest, a delicious caress, while her lean fingers sank deep into his hair, tugging him closer. With the faintest of sighs, her head tipped back in surrender, her lips opening to him. He swept inward without hesitation, diving into a sweetness beyond comparison.

He took his time, savoring everything about her. Her taste. Her scent. The stroke of her hands and the feel of her body brushing against his. His control loosened, fought free of his grasp while sheer, masculine instinct took over. He found the zipper that traced the length of her spine and slid it downward to where it stopped, just above the womanly curve of her buttocks. The dress that had tortured him throughout their evening together parted, gaped and then drifted downward to expose a creamy expanse of skin the texture of velvet.

He groaned. How was it possible that Angie could have hidden such an astonishing wealth of sensual pleasure without his ever suspecting its true extent? He'd been a fool. He eased back just enough to allow the dress to drift away. It caught at her hips, threatening his sanity before gravity stepped in and forced it to puddle at her feet.

She was beyond beautiful, a delicate confection of femininity. Her shoulders were broad and fine-boned, her breasts pert and round, tipped with nipples that made him think of raspberries on cream. Her waist curved gently inward above a boyish flare of hips. But no one could ever mistake her for anything other than a woman, not with such a beautifully rounded backside and legs that seemed to go on forever. The thought of what they'd feel like wrapped around his waist threatened to consume him. How perfectly her bottom would fit in his hands when they joined. When they moved as one. When she came apart for him.

When she was his in the most basic, primal way possible.

She stood before him, a pale blue triangular scrap of silk shyly preserving the final bastion of her modesty, while three-inch heels coyly taunted him. He wanted her. Wanted her more desperately than he'd wanted any other woman—even Lisa.

He hooked his fingers in the elastic at her hips, but before he could strip it away, she took a stumbling step backward, staring at him in open dismay. "Damn it, damn it, damn it." She snatched her dress from the floor and clutched it to her breasts. "You're my boss. We've had too much to drink. And taking this any further is a huge mistake."

He couldn't deny anything she said. It also didn't change how he felt…or what he wanted. "It would be one of the most enjoyable mistakes we've ever made."

"It would change everything and I—" Her voice broke ever so slightly, a poignant, telling little break. "I don't want our relationship to change. I think you should leave and we should forget this ever happened."

He couldn't help but laugh, though the sound contained little humor. "I think it's a little late for that." His gaze wandered over her. "I'm afraid there isn't any way I can forget what you've been hiding under those atrocious suits."

"Try," she snapped. She edged away from him, deeper into the living room. "I'd appreciate it if you'd see yourself out."

He took a step in her direction. Then another. She held her ground for a brief instant, her chin raised to a combative angle. He could see the desire in her eyes and knew she wanted him every bit as badly as he wanted her. Then he saw the heartbreak and the pride, saw the hint of fear and desperation. Oh, not of him. And not of what he might do to her. No, he could guess what caused those particular emotions. He sensed her desperation to fight the sexual urge burning through her and her fear that she'd lose her job if she didn't. Or maybe she'd feel obligated to quit, something he didn't dare risk.

All he knew for certain was it would cost her, seriously cost her, if he took this any further. To his utter shock, a protective urge swept through him, demanding he do whatever it took to shield her from hurt—even if he were the one doing the hurting. Especially if he were doing the hurting. And somehow he knew with a bone-deep certainty it would hurt her if he took this any further. Hell, he should be grateful that one of them had retained an ounce of common sense. For some reason, he didn't feel the least grateful.

"Good night, Angie. Thank you for having dinner with me."

"With you and Gabe Moretti."

That stopped him cold. "You throw gasoline on a smoldering fire, you're asking for it to burst into flames," he warned softly. "Is that what you want?"

She didn't answer. Smart woman. Instead, she turned her back on him and disappeared in the direction of one of the bedrooms. It was a more effective response than anything she could have said. Watching that glorious, nearly naked bottom twitch its way across the room on three-inch heels was a punishment worthy of the devil, himself. Lucius managed a grim smile.

And considering most people considered him Lucifer's kin, he should know.

How could she be so stupid?

Angie huddled within the comforting folds of her voluminous cotton robe and stared unblinkingly at the digital clock while it slowly ticked toward 3:00 a.m. What had she been thinking? Oh, now there was an easy question to answer. She *hadn't* been thinking. She'd been so caught up in her hormonal response to sexy as sin Lucius Devlin, to knowing in her heart of hearts that loving him was utterly hopeless, it eclipsed everything but that single, driving imperative. To have him in her bed and finally know his possession. The temptation of having just a single night with him had proved so overwhelming that she hadn't given a single thought to her precious career—the one thing in her life she valued above all else. Hadn't her mother always warned her to put her career first, that men couldn't be trusted to stick? No doubt the fact that her father had walked out on them when Angie had been a baby was responsible for that particular philosophy. But then hadn't Ryan proved her mother correct?

What would have happened with Lucius if she hadn't stepped back? If she'd allowed him to sweep her along on that mind-blowing tide of lust? He'd have discovered the truth about her, that's what. He'd have discovered she was hopeless in bed. Awkward. Self-conscious. Unable to satisfy a man.

She flinched from the thought. Damn Ryan and the cruel, careless way he'd broken her heart. The way he'd made her doubt herself as a woman. The way she'd cut off pieces of her life because he'd made her believe herself incapable. And damn her for letting him, for giving up on the possibility of having a successful sexual relationship, turning to work as both comfort and affirmation that in this area, if no other, she excelled.

It was ridiculous. She needed to get over it. She needed to find a man—a man other than her boss—who could teach her what she needed to know.

Angie frowned in concentration, the thought taking root, flourishing. It wasn't a bad idea, she slowly decided. If Lucius could entertain the idea of a cold, calculated marriage in order to provide a good home for Mikey, a contract between like-thinking adults, why couldn't she do the same? Oh, not marriage. But a cold, calculated sexual relationship, one designed to teach her the art of lovemaking, the craft of fully exploring her womanhood. It would be no different from when she'd taken classes to teach her the skills necessary to pursue a successful career, a career she now enjoyed to the fullest.

What would it feel like to be as experienced in bed and

in male/female interactions as she was at her job? To fully explore an aspect of her life she'd denied herself in the wake of Ryan's and Britt's betrayal? It would be… Tears filled her eyes. It would be heaven. All she needed was the right man. A man who would be patient and understanding. A man she could trust.

For a brief instant an image of Lucius flashed through her mind before she thrust it ruthlessly away. Don't even go there! Heading down that path offered one thing, and one thing only. Certain and total heartbreak. What she needed was a man who found her attractive and that she wouldn't mind having in her bed. But, who?

Oh, wait. Wait, wait, wait. There *had* been another man who'd shown interest in her tonight.

Gabe Moretti.

A man like Gabe, an experienced man of the world would be the perfect choice. She vaguely recalled there'd been gossip about him at the office. What had they said? Right, right. He was a man who had the reputation for caring about women and who held honor dear. And best of all, he was currently unattached. Add all that together and it made him the perfect candidate to help with her problem.

Angie snuggled into her pillow, her eyes drifting closed. Still, she could dream. She could imagine what it would be like to have Lucius free her from the pain and hurt Ryan and Britt had inflicted. A small smile drifted across her mouth. Too bad she didn't fit his criteria for the perfect wife—whatever that criteria might be. Then she'd have it all. A career she adored. A man more than capable of helping her fully explore her womanhood. And even a baby, one she found utterly adorable. Imagine having the best of all worlds.

It was perfection. Sheer perfection.

* * *

How could he be so stupid?

Lucius stripped down and stepped into the shower, inhaling sharply at the cascade of icy water sheeting over him. At least it helped cool his lust. Somewhat. Though not nearly enough, considering he could still see her, nearly nude and gloriously, perfectly female. He braced his palm against the stone wall and allowed the water to pound down on him, praying it drummed some common sense into his addled brain.

This was Angie Colter, PA extraordinaire, he was thinking about. She wasn't the sort of woman to take to bed on a whim. She was his employee, for God's sake. His responsibility.

Just as Mikey was his responsibility.

"Aw, hell," he muttered. "How could I have forgotten?"

The Pretorius Program. His plan to marry the "perfect" wife and mother. Someone who wouldn't cheat on him. Someone who wouldn't desert him or screw him over. Someone he could trust. Not that he believed he could ever have any of that. In his experience people cheated. Deliberately or otherwise, they screwed each other over. And trust was nothing more than a myth. Trust evaporated like a wispy dream at the first hard bump in the road. And usually that bump had something to do with money.

Isn't that what happened between his father, Angelo "Angel" Devlin, and Angel's best friend and business partner? The death of that trust—not to mention the theft of Angel Enterprises by that partner—had killed his father.

And hadn't it happened again with Lisa? She'd wanted money and had done anything and everything necessary to get it, even marrying someone she didn't love.

Wasn't it about to happen with Geoff's parents, a couple who'd stood like second parents to him. Hadn't they just threatened to file a lawsuit to gain custody of Mikey, claiming Lucius an "unfit" guardian?

He turned off the shower and snagged a towel, relieved that he'd regained a semblance of control and common sense. He was grateful to Angie, grateful that she'd showed such amazing restraint and put an end to a situation that would have caused endless complications on the work front. He'd been a fool to allow lust to interfere with logic. He'd finally found the perfect PA and with one foolish, impulsive act had almost ruined a perfect working environment. First thing Monday morning he'd apologize. Then he'd carefully, gently, politely return them to their former arm's length relationship. No doubt Angie would be relieved.

And then he'd devote more time and attention to finding the perfect wife to match his perfect PA.

He tossed back the covers on his bed and allowed himself to relax against a lake of silk. Punching his pillow into a comfortable mound, he folded his arms behind his head. Still, he could imagine how it would have been. He could imagine having Angie in his bed, as brilliant and amusing and meticulous in the way she made love as she was in the workplace. She'd prove just as trustworthy, too, easing the pain and hurt others had inflicted over the years. A small smile drifted across his mouth. Damn if she didn't fit his criteria for the perfect wife, as well as a PA. It was more than perfect. A multibillion dollar business. A brilliant woman more than a match for him in all the most important aspects of life. And even a mother for Mikey, a baby she found utterly adorable. Imagine having the best of all worlds.

It was perfection. Sheer perfection.

Four

"All buttoned up again, I see."

Angie offered Lucius a cool smile, one she'd practiced endless times over the weekend in order to get it just right. "Same as always."

He didn't say the words, but she could hear them loud and clear: *Not always.*

Just as she'd rehearsed for endless hours to perfect her demeanor and how she intended to act when she returned to work and came face-to-face with Lucius again, she'd also agonized over her clothing. She didn't dare select anything that remotely resembled upholstery. But she also didn't want to wear anything too suggestive. Not that she owned much that could be considered in any way, shape or form the least suggestive. Still, it made choosing the perfect outfit a challenge.

She'd finally settled on a crisp brown suit and café au lait blouse. And though she'd ultimately decided to wear her hair up, it was in a looser style than usual. She looked professional, yet approachable, she decided. The epitome of the perfect PA.

Despite that, Lucius's gaze swept her, stripped her. His eyes glittered darkly, the memory of their embrace lurking there like a menacing shadow. He held her with that single powerful look for a long, tense moment before his mouth curved upward in a knowing smile. "Buttons won't work anymore. I know what you're hiding underneath them."

With that, he disappeared into his office, leaving her with a half-dozen sharp comebacks blistering her tongue, all unspoken. Later, she promised herself. If he made one more comment, she'd cut loose with every single one of them. To Angie's relief, the morning swept toward midday without Lucius making any more suggestive observations. Instead, he filled her schedule to overflowing with a laundry list of endless tasks. Shortly before lunch, she glanced up to see an older couple approaching her desk.

"Hello, Mr. and Mrs. Ridgeway." As always, she was careful to offer them a warm, friendly smile. "Did you have a good weekend with your grandson?"

"Michael was fussy."

As usual it was Benjamin who responded, Geoff's mother cloaking herself in painful silence. Grief continued to hang on the pair, carved deep into their faces and making them appear far older than their early sixties. It had been a rough three months for them, their pain and bitterness deepened by the intense dislike they'd felt toward Geoff's wife, and the blame they heaped on her for their son's premature demise. It didn't make the least sense to Angie, but apparently they felt that the two wouldn't have died if Lisa hadn't insisted on a European vacation as a combination Christmas present and second honeymoon.

For some reason that blame also extended to Lucius

and she couldn't help but wonder if they'd somehow discovered that he'd had a sexual relationship with Lisa, as
well—knew and in some emotion-riddled, illogical fashion held him responsible for Geoff's death, too.

"Michael needs a more regular routine," Benjamin continued. "Consistent parenting. Passing him around like a
football isn't helping."

To her shock, Tabby Ridgeway spoke up, the first time
she'd ever directly addressed Angie. "It won't be for much
longer. Our grandson belongs with his own kind, assuming his responsibility for carrying on the Ridgeway line,
not raised by a man who puts his career ahead of family,
who puts riches before everything else in his life." Her
cold gaze reflected the determination sweeping through
her voice. "We'll be awarded custody soon enough and
then we'll make sure Geoff's son is raised right. Raised to
overcome the stigma of having an amoral gold digger for a
mother. Raised to resist the temptation his father couldn't."

Angie stiffened and it took every ounce of self-control
to answer civilly, though it cost her. Still, she didn't dare
say or do anything that risked putting Lucius's guardianship in jeopardy. "I know you're all trying your best under
very difficult circumstances. Do you need to see Lucius
before you leave?"

Benjamin took over again. "We do need to see him,
yes."

"I'll let Lucius know you're here," she offered. "Why
don't I take Mikey for you?"

"Keesha hasn't arrived, yet?"

Angie caught the disapproval sliding through the question and deflected it with practiced calm. "It's always a
pleasure to spend time with your grandson. I don't mind
in the least."

The couple reluctantly allowed her to take the baby,

who reached eagerly for her in clear recognition. The instant she cradled him in her arms, he grinned, grabbing at her finger and tugging it toward his mouth. Who knew she'd be such a natural with babies? Delight filled her. She'd always wanted her own children, longed to experience motherhood. But part of her—the part Ryan had taken such cruel pleasure in giving a good, swift kick— agonized over her own inadequacies. She'd ended up believing that, like in all things domestic, she wasn't capable of adequately parenting a child. Thank goodness the brief amounts of time she'd spent with Mikey had proven otherwise. A fierce determination welled up in her. She would make a great mother, and she wouldn't ever allow anyone to convince her otherwise.

Suddenly aware of the Ridgeways' intense gaze, she glanced at them. "Would you care for coffee or tea?" she asked belatedly, forcing her expression to relax into calm, dispassionate lines.

Before they could respond, the door to Lucius's office opened. He filled the threshold with forbidding power, as dark as the Ridgeways were fair. "Tabby, Benjamin. Good to see you."

It was a lie, Angie knew. In fact, they all knew it, but with the threat of a pending lawsuit, Lucius worked hard to keep their encounters low-key and polite. While he escorted the Ridgeways into his office, Angie indulged her maternal instincts. Mikey was a gorgeous baby and definitely took after his mother—no doubt an unfortunate turn of events from the Ridgeways point of view.

Mikey gazed up at her with huge inky eyes and offered a drooling grin that proudly showed off two pearly-white bottom teeth. He'd worked hard on them this past month and she suspected was working on another, which probably explained his fussiness over the weekend. She crossed to the wet bar and dampened a washcloth she kept on hand. He snatched it from her and stuffed it in his mouth, biting energetically on the cold cotton. She slid a hand down his plump, silken cheek and shook her head.

"Poor little mite. Everyone wants you, though I suspect it's for all the wrong reasons."

For the Ridgeways it was their final connection to their son—a son with whom they'd been estranged following his marriage to the "amoral gold digger" they so despised. For Lucius it was a promise made to his best friend, and a keen sense of honor and duty that demanded he fulfill that promise.

While most would have thought that was the full extent of his feelings toward Mikey, over the past several weeks, Angie had caught a glimpse of something more. Something deeper. Something more powerful. And she couldn't help but wonder if it wasn't because Lucius finally realized that the baby was the embodiment of the two people he loved most in the world, that their spirit continued to live through Mikey. She could only hope so.

The phone rang and she used her headset to answer, leaving her hands free to care for the baby. "Diablo, Inc. Mr. Devlin's office. This is Angie Colter speaking. How may I help you?"

"I thought this was the main man's private line." The voice was female, unquestionably young and brash. And oddly intriguing. "How come you're answering?" she demanded.

"Mr. Devlin is currently in a meeting," Angie explained. "The calls are routed to me whenever he's unavailable to take them."

"Huh. Most hotshot billionaires I know just use voice mail."

The comment gave Angie pause. The caller sounded

more like a teenager than a grown woman. How many hot-shot billionaires did the average teenager know? "I guess you could say I'm Mr. Devlin's voice mail. Beep." Not very professional, but something about the caller brought out the imp in Angie.

Sure enough, the girl chuckled. "Okay, fine. This is Jett. I'm working with Pretorius St. John on a top secret program for your boss man." The information had Angie nudging Jett's age a little higher, though she still sounded more like a teen than twenty-something. "You in the know about it or should I aim for enigmatic?"

Angie hesitated and Mikey chose that moment to smack her with the washcloth. And that's when two bounced against two and exploded into a huge glittering four. Her gaze fastened on Lucius's office door and she replayed that long-ago scene with Ella in her head.

"I don't know how you could possibly think I'd be interested in your insane proposal." And what had Lucius said afterward? She flipped through her memories from that day and keyed in on the one she needed. That he'd proposed to Ella after only knowing her for two weeks. *"I made a business proposition that involved marriage and for some reason that ticked her off. Go figure."* And then a little later Angie had told him, *"I have several calls from a Pretorius St. John. He indicated it was a private matter. Something about a computer program he was personalizing for you."*

She shook her head in disbelief. No. No, it wasn't possible. A *wife*? Was that what the parade of women over the past three months had been about? Why he'd proposed to Ella after just two short weeks? Not even a man as determined and ruthless as The Devil Devlin would implement such an outrageous plan…would he? Angie fought to gather her thoughts into a coherent whole, keenly aware her caller was waiting for her response.

Maybe if she asked a few careful questions, she'd be able to confirm or refute her suspicions. Preferably refute them. "Is this about the program Mr. St. John is fine-tuning for Lucius?" she asked cautiously.

"Yup."

Angie closed her eyes, struggling to control her breathing, struggling even harder to keep her voice level and matter-of-fact. Please be wrong. Please, please be wrong. Because if she wasn't, she couldn't keep her job. Wouldn't. Not if Lucius married. Not when she loved him. She refused to stay in a job where every day would be an exercise in sheer torture.

"This program…" She trailed off, steeling herself to ask the unthinkable. "It's the one to help him find a…a wife?"

"Okay, so you're in the know. Guess you'd have to be, considering that's how he picked you. See, here's the problem—"

"Wait," Angie ordered. This just got more and more bizarre. "Back up. He used this same program to hire a PA? To hire *me?*"

"Well, sure. That's what the Pretorius Program was originally designed for. To help people like Mr. Devlin hire top-notch assistants. Or apprentices. But then when Justice wanted an apprentice/wife, Pretorius tweaked it a bit."

"Apprentice…*wife?*" Was she joking?

"Yeah, it was a bit weird, but it all worked out in the end. Now Uncle P.'s got this side business going. Too busy to find a wife on your own? Let our program find her for you. So we've been on the lookout for a wife for Mr. Devlin for the past three months. Heck, we'd even be happy if we could find him an apprentice/wife." A frustrated sigh issued through the earpiece. "But unlike most of our clients, he's proving sort of tough to satisfy. We've selected tons of women for him, but for some reason none of them are right. Just between us girls, I'm beginning to think it's him. Know what I mean? Every time we turn around he's changing the parameters on us."

Angie's gaze darted to the closed office door again. The murmur of voices from inside continued, unabated. "What, exactly, are his current parameters?"

"Oh, not that much." Deep sarcasm refuted her words. "He wants a mother for Mikey, that's number one on his list. You'd think that would be good enough, right?"

"Right?"

"Wrong, girlfriend." She practically sang the words. "He also wants someone who's a top-notch cook and can entertain both clients and friends on a large scale. You know, throw a five-star party complete with gourmet food and a Vegas-worthy show with only two minutes' warning." Papers rustled and Angie could tell Jett was reading from a form. "He also wants someone classy, who can maintain an elegant home. Not sure if she's supposed to decorate it, too. That's one of my questions. She has to be intelligent. Attractive. And there's other stuff that Pretorius blanked out, which probably has to do with sex."

"Dear God," Angie said faintly. "No wonder he can't find a wife."

Jett snorted. "Ya think? Maybe Justice should just build him a frigging robot instead of driving Uncle P. crazy. I think it'd be easier. Don't suppose you know anyone who fits Mr. Devlin's criteria? Unlikely, I realize, considering I don't think she exists. Maybe in some male-oriented fantasyland, but not in any real world I'm familiar with."

The off-the-cuff question sparked an idea. A crazy, impulsive, totally outrageous idea, so unlike her, the audacity of it threatened to steal her breath away. Not only would it provide Mikey with a mother and potentially assist Lucius if the Ridgeways sued for custody, but it would give her a shot at her own female-oriented fantasyland.

Angie sat there, the possibility dangling before her like a bright, shiny diamond, just begging for her to snatch it up. Why not give it a shot? Why not take the chance? The *risk,* she was quick to correct herself. A very serious risk that could—most likely would—lose her a job she adored. Granted, if it worked out, she and Lucius would both have what they wanted. And if it didn't... Well, she planned to quit her job when he married, anyway, so what did she really have to lose?

"You still there?" Jett demanded.

"Still here. I was thinking... What if I did know someone who would be the perfect wife for Lucius?" she asked.

"Get out. You know someone who can cook, clean, do the party thing and take care of a baby? Seriously? Like a real human woman?"

"Not exactly." She stared down at Mikey and cuddled him closer. "We might have to alter the woman's abilities just a tad."

"Uh-huh." Cynicism replaced excitement. "How much is a tad?"

"Well, totally, since this person can't cook or clean. At least, not on the scale you're suggesting." Yet. "The parties might be on the table. And she flat-out adores Mikey, even if she's a bit inexperienced when it comes to babies."

"Well, thanks for getting my hopes up for nothing," Jett complained. "Who is this person and why would I pick someone so completely wrong?"

Angie took a deep breath. "The person is...well...me. And I don't think I'm wrong at all. In fact, I think I'm the perfect choice."

* * *

Rain beat down on them for the rest of the week in a seemingly unending gray curtain. Friday, the sun made a brave reappearance, battling back the storm clouds, and by late that afternoon gained strength, flowing triumphantly through the window behind Lucius's desk. Streams of soft gold flooded the room and he tilted the printout he held to catch the tidal wave of light. He read the name the computer had kicked out for the umpteenth time.

"How is this possible, Pretorius?" he demanded in disbelief, his hand tightening around his cell phone. "Answer me that. How?"

"I don't know. I'm as stunned as you are."

"You programmed the damn thing. Are you telling me you don't know how your own program works?"

"It must have been the result of this latest tweak in parameters," Pretorius insisted doggedly. "But she's your perfect apprentice/wife."

The name of the "perfect" woman danced across the page in a taunting tango. Angelique Colter, Angelique Colter, his *dammittohell* PA, Angelique "Angie" Colter. "How was her name even picked up by your program?"

"Not sure, but I can guess," Pretorius said cautiously.

"Fine," Lucius snarled. "Guess. But make it an accurate one or I swear I'll reach through my computer and peel your circuits right off your mainframe. Then I'll get really mean. Now explain."

Pretorius erupted into speech. "It's possible that the new program, the program designed to find you the perfect wife, was accidentally connected to the old program, the one designed to find you the perfect PA. Apparently, Ms. Colter is an acceptable candidate for both positions."

"Both."

"Exactly. I guess that makes her more than perfect,

doesn't it?" Pretorius gave a quick laugh, then cleared his throat when Lucius didn't join in. "So the real question is… Would you prefer her for your PA, or for your wife?"

For some reason that one simple question hit Lucius like a towering wave, sweeping his feet out from under him and tumbling him over and over. "I'll get back to you," he said and disconnected the call.

An image of Angie in a tiny triangle of blue blossomed fully formed in his mind. So did the rest of her, a very naked rest of her. He saw her again as he had a week before. Her small, pert breasts—Eve's apples, perfect and perfectly tempting. Those killer legs that went on forever. That long, supple flow of her naked back. That glorious backside, round and biteable. The way that glorious backside twitched when she stalked away from him.

His hand clenched around the printout. Dear God, he could have it all. He could have Angie, probably the most trustworthy woman he knew—not to mention drop-dead gorgeous. He could have a mother for Mikey and, hopefully, an end to the Ridgeway's impending lawsuit. He could have Angie in his bed. A suitable hostess. Angie in his bed. Someone to welcome him after a hard day's work with home-cooked meals. And best of all, Angie in his bed. How perfect would that be? It was every man's secret fantasy. And it could all be his.

He shook his head. Forget the fantasy. He needed to consider more urgent issues than personal gratification, the most important of which was Mikey's welfare. If he believed for one minute the boy would be better off with the Ridgeways, he'd have discussed terminating his guardianship in their favor. Had seriously considered it. But in the three months since the death of Geoff and Lisa he'd had ample opportunity to speak to Mikey's grandparents and watch how they cared for him. And one overriding fact had become painfully clear. They were more concerned about the boy's "tainted" blood and the need to suppress that taint than they were about any other aspect of child-rearing.

Not only that, but they were a cold, hard couple, totally unlike Geoff. Maybe that was why his friend had spent so much time hanging out at the Devlins. Memories of those days gathered around Lucius, as faded gold as the sunlight at his back. A bittersweet smile carved his mouth. His father and Geoff had been as alike as two peas in a pod. Open. Trusting. A friend to all. The irony didn't escape him. Maybe they'd been accidentally switched at birth, he the offspring of the emotionally compromised Ridgeways, Geoff the son of Angel Devlin.

He shook his head. It didn't matter. Not any longer. All that mattered now was Mikey and Lucius's determination to save him from the Ridgeway's tender, loving care— or lack thereof. That left only two questions to consider. First, was Angie an appropriate mother figure for the boy? It didn't take any thought at all. He'd seen how she inter-acted with Mikey. Seen her light up whenever she held him. Witnessed the ease with which she held him. Fussed over him. How her eyes would track him whenever Keesha was around. She was as maternal as they came. And ac-cording to the computer printout, experienced with chil-dren.

Which brought him to his second question… How did he convince Angie that she'd rather be his wife than his PA?

He shoved back his chair and paced the length of the office. *Face facts, Devlin.* No one would want to take him on full-time. He was a workaholic. Emotionally compro-mised. Hard. Ruthless. Not the best attributes in a hus-band, even a temporary one. So, what did he have to offer a woman like Angie that would induce her to accept the position? Money. That was a given. But from what he could tell, financial gain had never been a driving force in Angie's life. Her career had always been her main focus. So, how did he convince a woman dedicated to her career that marrying him was a better option? There was one lever available to him, though he'd rather not use it.

Angie was crazy about Mikey. If she believed the Ridgeways would win custody of the baby if she didn't agree to his proposition, it might put just enough weight on his side of the scales to convince her to go along with his plan. Well, there was only one way to find out whether he could make an offer Angie wouldn't refuse. Ask her.

He touched a button on his phone and an instant later she appeared in the doorway of his office, electronic tablet in hand. Ever since the night they'd had dinner with Gabe Moretti, she'd subtly changed her appearance. She wore her hair looser, the style more flattering to her delicate features. She'd also changed the type of suits she wore from boxy to tailored. And though she hadn't quite broken loose when it came to the color of the suits, they were far more attractive than they had been.

Of course, ever since that night all he could think about was the earth-shattering kiss they'd shared. The softness of her skin. The perfection of her breasts. The taste of her mouth. And all that could be his. He only needed to convince her that she wanted a different sort of career.

"Come in and close the door," he requested. The minute she'd done so, he crossed to the wet bar and poured her a glass of wine. Her brows shot upward when he exchanged the drink for her electronic tablet.

"Am I going to need this?" she asked uneasily.

"Possibly." He shrugged, setting the tablet aside. "Probably."

Her face paled. "Have I done something wrong?"

He allowed a brief smile to touch his face, despite the seriousness of the situation. "I don't usually offer wine to someone I'm about to fire."

"I'll make a note of it," she murmured. "Or I would if you hadn't taken my tablet."

"You won't need it for this."

She took a tiny sip of wine, probably to fortify herself. "And *this* is…?"

"I have a proposition to offer."

She stilled, an odd expression crossing her face, almost as though she were bracing herself. "A business proposition?"

"In a sense." He poured himself a drink, as well, then gestured her toward the sitting area of his office. He could only hope that this discussion wouldn't end the same way it had with Ella. "Let's discuss it."

Angie gripped the wineglass so tightly it was a wonder it didn't shatter. She knew what was coming and could only pray her expression didn't give her away. Guilt threatened to overwhelm her. Ever since she and Jett had concocted their plan and "accidentally" slipped her profile into Pretorius's ongoing search parameters—with a few vital adjustments—she'd second- and third- and fourth-guessed herself.

Lucius needed a wife. A real wife. One who knew all about babies and running a home and entertaining clients. She didn't qualify at all for the first two of those, and barely scraped by on the third. Angie closed her eyes. But there was one thing the computer couldn't program, that Lucius hadn't thought to add to his precious parameters.

It couldn't program love. Whomever the Pretorius Program chose as Lucius's perfect mate, she wouldn't love him. Nor would she love Mikey, even if she excelled in all those other areas. How could she love a man and a baby she'd never met before? Oh, knowing Lucius, he'd find a capable woman. Tears pricked her eyes. As capable as his PA. But he wouldn't find what he didn't even realize he needed.

Love.

Aware that a tense silence had fallen, Angie opened her eyes to find Lucius staring at her through narrowed black eyes. "I told you I wasn't planning on firing you."

"But…" she prompted softly.

"But I'd like to offer you a different position."

"Within Diablo, Inc.?"

"Not exactly."

She refused to act coy. Not about this. "Is this a position along the lines of what you were offering to Ella?"

She'd caught him by surprise and he took a moment before inclining his head. "You're a smart woman, Angie. One of the many qualities I've always admired about you."

Maybe too smart for her own good. "Tell me what you're offering. And tell me why I'd want to give up the job I currently have—and love—for one that won't advance my career."

"First, the position I'm offering is…" To her surprise a hint of color carved a path across his impressive cheekbones. If circumstances had been different she'd have been amused by it. "Well, I suppose you could call it 'temporary fiancée.'"

"A fiancée," she repeated, tensing. Not what she'd expected. Not at all what she'd expected. "A *temporary* fiancée." What happened to his wanting a wife?

He hesitated. "With so much at stake, I thought it reasonable to employ caution. A trial run makes certain both parties are satisfied with the arrangement. If you'll recall, there was a trial period when I hired you as my PA. It's even more crucial to have one for this position." He blew out a sigh. "God, that sounds so cold and calculated. Sterile."

"Is that what you want?" she dared asked. "Cold, calculated and sterile?"

His eyes fired. "No, of course not. But what *I* want to get out of this arrangement isn't what's important. This is about Mikey."

"Believe it or not, I understand that. I'm not a fool, Lucius. I didn't think you were proposing a real engagement." She fought to remain calm, to ignore that flame building in his gaze. To ignore the nerves clawing at her composure. "What happens if we're both satisfied with the probationary period of our engagement? What then?"

"Then we marry."

It was her turn to hesitate. "Again, other than the honor of becoming your wife and a mother to Mikey—"

"Ouch."

She didn't back down or curb the hint of sarcasm she'd allowed to drift into her comment. Didn't dare. If he ever suspected what she and Jett had done, The Devil Devlin would make her life a living hell. And then he'd get really mean. "Seriously, Lucius. Why would I agree to such an insane arrangement? Why would any intelligent woman?"

"First, I'll pay you far more than what you're currently receiving as my PA."

"Okay, ouch right back at you."

He waved that aside with an impatient air. "Look, I know that money doesn't drive you. But it's a start. Let's discuss what the job entails and then you tell me what you want in the way of compensation."

"Fair enough. What would my duties include?"

"First and foremost, as you've already guessed, I require a mother for Mikey. I'm sure you're aware the Ridgeways are talking about suing for custody. So far, I've convinced them to hold off, but one of their arguments is that I don't have a stable home life. I'm dependent on outsiders for Mikey's care. Having a wife whose primary duty is to raise the baby would go a long way toward appeasing them. You have an excellent rapport with Mikey already and you've been very good with the Ridgeways, something they've both noticed and commented on. And it's obvious that your maternal instincts and your kindness are a genuine part of who you are as a person."

"I'm not sure how kind I've been toward the Ridgeways, but they're Mikey's grandparents and Geoff's parents. They deserve my respect, even if I don't agree with their parenting style," Angie stated simply. "Plus, I flat-out adore Mikey."

Lucius grinned. "Even teething?"

She relaxed enough to return his smile. "Even teething." She gestured for him to continue. "What's next?"

"I currently have a housekeeper who takes care of maintaining the house and providing meals. But she's informed me she plans to retire."

Angie lifted an eyebrow. "You want me to cook and clean as well as care for Mikey? Seriously?"

He frowned. "I understand you're a gourmet chef."

Time for a little honesty. "That's a gross exaggeration. I putter in the kitchen." Boiling water. Throwing together a prepackaged salad. Fixing a decent cup of coffee. "But if you're expecting gourmet meals, you have the wrong woman. You're a billionaire, Lucius. Is there some reason you can't hire a housekeeper to handle the general cooking and cleaning?"

"No, no of course not." She could see him making a swift alteration to his game plan. "What about staging events for entertaining large groups of people?"

She could learn. How different could it be from some of the business events she'd helped plan for Diablo? "Sure."

He relaxed ever so slightly. "And you can oversee the domestic end of things."

"I haven't agreed to anything, yet."

Lucius inclined his head. "True enough."

"So far we have the care for Mikey, the organization of the house and entertaining friends, clients and business associates. What else?"

"One final requirement." He set his drink aside, untouched. "As you're probably aware, I live in the penthouse apartment of this building. My plan has always been to find a house better suited to entertaining. With Mikey's advent, I've moved those plans forward. I recently purchased a home on Lake Washington, but it needs a facelift. It needs a creative woman with an eye for color and design, who also possesses impeccable taste, to oversee those improvements."

Uh-oh. Angie could see where this was heading. Straight off a cliff and into a vat of hot water. Scalding hot water. What the hell had Jett been thinking to add that particular talent to her curriculum vitae? And why in the world would Lucius buy into it? Or had it not occurred to him that a woman who dressed like chair upholstery might not have the best eye for design and color, let alone impeccable taste?

"Are you insane, Lucius?" she inquired politely. "I mean, seriously. Your little laundry list of requirements is a lovely dream. The perfect male fantasy, no doubt. But that's all it'll ever be. It's the height of arrogance to expect one woman to do all that, especially a woman with an ounce of brains, common sense or self-respect. There isn't one item you've detailed that isn't, on its own, a full-time position. Expecting a single person to handle all of them…?" She shook her head. "That's not going to happen. It's certainly not going to happen with me."

He nodded, almost as though he'd anticipated her objection. "Fine. Let's open negotiations. If we hire a housekeeper to handle the domestic chores—cooking and cleaning—all you'd need to do is delegate and supervise."

"That would be a definite improvement. As for Mikey, you still need a part-time nanny to cover for—" She started to say "me" and smoothly changed gears. "To cover for your fiancée/wife when she's entertaining or meeting with the decorator. Or knowing you, dealing with the slew of additional tasks you'll undoubtedly dump on her."

"Keesha is a temporary full-time hire. She made that clear from the beginning. Apparently, she has a mother who isn't well and needs her assistance. But I've already asked if she'd be available for part-time work and she's agreed. Does that satisfy you?"

Angie inclined her head. Now for the more distasteful part of the arrangement. Though she didn't want to ask about the financial end of their bargain, if she didn't address the issue, he'd suspect something was off. "You mentioned payment. Just out of curiosity, how much are we talking?" He named a figure that made her grateful she was sitting. It took her an instant to gather her wits sufficiently to ask, "And if the job doesn't work out?"

He shrugged. "Then you could return to your position as my PA, with a comfortable bonus for your efforts. No hard feelings on either side."

She simply looked at him. "You know better than that, Lucius. If our relationship falls apart on the personal side of things it would have a serious effect on any future working relationship. What happens if one or the other of us wants to sever all ties? I'd be giving up a job I love, a career that's important to me, and for what? To be your domestic goddess?"

He chuckled, the sound sliding through her like a velvet touch. "Is that what I'm hiring? A domestic goddess?"

"Actually, the job title should be domestic slave." Angie leaned back, relaxing for the first time since the start of their discussion. She took a bracing sip of wine, a cool, refreshing Fumé Blanc. It helped steady her for the next topic of conversation. "There's one part of this job we haven't discussed."

"Which is?"

"Sex."

"Ah." An expression came into his eyes, one that had her throat going dry and a hot pool of want forming in her belly. Waves of it lapped outward, roiling and seething in endless demand. "How could I have neglected something so vital?"

"I gather that's a 'yes.'"

"No."

She stiffened, shocked by his answer. Had she miscalculated? Had she read more into the night they'd had dinner with Gabe Moretti? Had he considered their kiss a mild and forgettable flirtation, easily dismissed, while she'd built it up into something far more serious and memorable?

"Not a yes?" she asked faintly.

"No, not a yes," he responded gravely, "but rather a *hell*, yes."

Her mouth twitched and a laugh escaped before she could control it. Then she realized that it wasn't funny. Not considering her issues. Not considering that she'd planned to approach Gabe Moretti over this very problem. Her laughter died and she regarded him with nervous apprehension.

"What's wrong?" His eyes narrowed. "You must realize that if we're going to become engaged, probably married, that a sexual relationship would be an important part of the equation."

She lifted a shoulder in what she hoped was a casual shrug. "You didn't mention it as one of your conditions, so I can only assume it's not a very important part."

"Allow me to prove otherwise."

Before she could react, he took her hand and gave a quick tug. Unable to resist, she tumbled straight into his arms, straight into his mouth…and straight into heaven.

Five

It took only that one kiss for Angie to confirm that her first embrace with Lucius hadn't been a fluke. That if anything, the explosive desire was more intense, searing them in endless heat. She couldn't get enough, didn't think she'd ever get enough. Not of Lucius. Not of his touch, his unique taste.

His mouth moved on hers, a blatant taking, and she moaned in pleasure. He offered endless possibilities on every front. The chance to be a mother. To be a wife. To form a relationship with the man she loved. And maybe, just maybe, she'd be able to explore the sexual side of her nature without fear of rejection.

Her blouse fell open beneath his busy hands and he cupped her breast, stroking the pad of his thumb across the sensitive tip. She shuddered, helpless beneath the onslaught of sensations. How could she have thought, even for one tiny minute, that she could give herself like this to Gabe Moretti. The mere idea now seemed obscene. It was Lucius she wanted. Lucius she loved.

Lucius who might reject her the way Ryan had.

She stiffened in his arms, fighting her way free of the embrace. Lucius released her without protest, but something in his expression warned that next time he wouldn't show such consideration, let alone restraint. "We need to finish our discussion," she informed him. "Nothing is settled and until it is…" She trailed off, heat washing into her face.

"No sex?"

She turned on him. "You're still my boss, Lucius. If we can't come to terms, that isn't going to change. I can't… We can't…" She spun away, struggling to refasten her bra, fumbling with buttons and buttonholes. Why was it that every time she was with him, she came undone? Literally. "If we make love and you end up with someone else as your fiancée/wife it would be more than awkward and you know it. It would mean I'd have to find another job." Of course, she'd have to do that, anyway, one of the primary nails in the coffin she was busily building.

"Why?"

Was he kidding? She turned, glared. "Don't be an ass, Lucius. You know damn well why. Do you really expect to take me to bed one night and then marry another woman the next?" Apparently Ryan had thought so. "And I'm supposed to be okay with that? Well, news flash, ace. It's not okay with me. And it shouldn't be okay with you."

Something in his reaction acknowledged that her words had impacted harder than she'd anticipated. Temper flared, though she didn't think it was aimed at her. "Angie—"

But she wasn't finished. "You know, I was considering having an affair with Gabe Moretti." She had no idea where the words came from, just that anger drove her toward recklessness. "Maybe I should have a quick fling with him before starting this new job you're offering. I'm sure you wouldn't mind. After all, that wouldn't be the least awkward, would it? You wouldn't want to end all association with him. With me. Would you, Lucius?"

Dead silence followed and she shivered, belatedly closing her mouth. Oh, damn. Slowly, Lucius rose, more intimidating than she'd ever seen him. His eyes burned with hellfire, his expression carved into taut, furious lines. Tension and blatant male aggression poured off him. Unable to help herself, she stumbled backward a step. Her gaze shot toward the door, desperate for escape. But it was far too late for that. Far too late to do anything other than watch him come for her, striding across the room like vengeance incarnate.

"I swear to God, if you go anywhere near Gabe Moretti—"

Cornered, she fought back. "You'll what? Fire me? Why, Lucius? Oh, wait. It couldn't possibly have anything to do with what's happening between us. With how you'd feel if I took another man into my bed when we were in the middle of 'negotiating'—" she encased the word in air quotes "—a sexual relationship. If our negotiation falls apart, what is it to you if I sleep with someone else?"

He swept her comments aside as though they were of little to no consequence. "Why were you considering an affair with him?" he demanded.

"Oh, that is so typical of a man," she stormed at him in response. "Ignore my points because the only thing that matters is marking your territory. Well, I'm not a fire hydrant, Lucius. So, back off."

To her amazement, he did. Just a single step. But at least it gave her a tiny amount of breathing space. "When did you come to this decision?" he asked. "And why?"

"My reasons are private. As to when…" She gave it to him straight, even though the truth would only escalate the situation. "I decided the night you kissed me."

His back teeth snapped together and the muscle along his jaw twitched. "Why?"

"You're my boss. I can't have an affair with my boss."

"He's my competitor."

"On occasion. On rare occasions. Shortly, he'll be a business associate." She struggled to remain calm and poised. "And news flash… He's not *my* competitor. He's not *my* business associate. And most important of all, he's not *my* boss."

"It's a conflict of interest."

"You're grasping at straws. I know how to keep my mouth shut when it comes to business matters. You know it, too, or you'd never have hired me or kept me as your PA these past eighteen months. I would never give Gabe Moretti inside information and you damn well know it."

He spun around and paced the full length of his office before turning to face her again. He'd regained a modicum of his legendary control, though she could still see the fury smoldering just beneath the surface. "Why, Angie? Of all the men in the whole of Seattle, why him?"

A choice loomed before her. She could tell him the truth, humiliate herself in front of a man who was her employer—potentially her fiancé. Or she could refuse to answer and risk losing her current job, as well as the one he was offering—a position she wanted more than she could express. Tears filled her eyes and she blinked them back, refusing to allow them to fall.

But he caught her distress. His anger faded, replaced by bewildered concern. "Hell, Angie, don't cry. I couldn't handle it. Not from you." When she simply shook her head, he approached. "What is it? I'm missing something here, something important. What?"

"It's personal. Private."

That gave him pause. She could see his brilliant mind sifting through possibilities. "Something you thought Moretti could help you with?"

She didn't bother denying it. "Yes."

"By having an affair?"

Her mouth compressed. "Yes."

"Why him?" he asked again. Pure masculine frustration ripped through his words and she could hear the real question behind the one he asked. *Why him and not me?*

She chose her words with care. "Because we would both know the score going in. We would both understand that it's a temporary, mutually satisfactory arrangement. Because there wouldn't be any hard feelings or emotional fallout afterward."

Lucius froze and his expression closed over, preventing her from reading his thoughts. He'd always been good at that. No doubt it was part of his success, part of what helped him build a billion-dollar business. "And that's enough for you? Is that part of your reluctance to accept the position I'm offering? You don't want anything more than a sexual relationship?"

She couldn't answer him for fear she'd cry. *No!* It wasn't what she wanted. Not at all. That's what she wanted with Gabe, not with Lucius. But how did she explain that? How could she explain to him that she'd fallen in love with him, wanted more than anything to have a long-term personal relationship? She couldn't. Not without revealing how she truly felt. No way would she give him that sort of power. She didn't dare.

"I don't see any purpose in discussing what I want or don't want from a relationship—specifically, *our* relationship—until we've worked out an agreement," she informed him as calmly as she could manage. "And in case you hadn't noticed, we seem to have gotten off point on some of the terms currently under debate."

He cocked an eyebrow, his mouth taking on a sardonic slant. "I'm impressed, Colter. You've managed to reduce sex to a business addendum." He noted her blush, clearly took grim satisfaction in it. "It's called a kiss. Something I found very much on point considering the nature of the position I'm offering."

Is that all it had been to him? A kiss? How was it possible that one kiss from Lucius Devlin managed to leave her totally undone, while his control remained absolute? It wasn't fair. Even worse, Lucius was a brilliant man. Eventually, he'd cop to how she felt, which made her more determined than ever to hold him at arm's length until they'd hammered out the details.

She lifted her chin and shot him a cool look. "Kissing me isn't on point until we reach an agreement." When he would have argued, she held up her hand. "How many times have you told me that a deal isn't consummated until the contracts are signed, sealed and delivered?"

"And the money transfers hands."

She tried to conceal how much his comment hurt. "You know what I mean."

"No consummating until it's a done deal?" he asked drily.

Relief flooded through her at the reluctant acceptance his question signaled. "Exactly."

He crossed the room and retrieved the drink he'd set aside when they'd started the conversation. It seemed hours ago, yet couldn't have been more than twenty minutes. His gaze remained fixed on her in a manner she'd seen all too often. He was considering the problem from all its various angles. Right now she was an opponent in a business negotiation, which put her at a severe disadvantage. He proved it by approaching like a predator stalking its prey.

"Point One," he began. "Even if you refuse the job offer, I still don't want you seeing Moretti."

"That isn't your decision and you know it." She held up her hand before he could argue. "Stop it, Lucius. You cannot dictate my personal relationships and that's final."

"Yet," he corrected, "that changes the minute I put my ring on your finger."

"Just remember that goes both ways," she shot right back.

The minute he absorbed the comment, he stiffened. "I wouldn't cheat on you."

She didn't respond, simply fixed him with an unflinching gaze.

"Son of a bitch," he said softly. "Are you talking about my affair with Lisa?"

No way was she touching that one. "Not at all. I'm talking about a crucial deal breaker to the job currently under discussion."

He simply shook his head. "Somehow I think we're talking about Lisa. Just in case, let's address it so there aren't any lingering questions." His expression remained empty, still giving nothing away, making it impossible to get a read on him. "Lisa and I had an affair. After it ran its course she turned to my best friend, Geoff. When that relationship didn't work out, when it ended badly, as well, she dropped by my apartment. She claimed her affair with Geoff had been a terrible mistake. I compounded that mistake by giving her a shoulder to cry on. As I'm sure you can guess, one thing led to another. It wasn't planned. It was one night and only one night. In retrospect, it wasn't one of my smarter decisions. In fact, it was damn stupid."

"I wasn't asking." Didn't even want to hear. She got that Lisa was irresistible to men. That she had something that Angie couldn't possess if she lived to be a hundred. That she was the type of woman Lucius wanted, a type Angie would never be. Could never be. And it brought home the brutal fact that he would never love her. She fought to keep her voice level, when all she wanted was to weep. "To be honest, I'd rather not know."

"If we're putting our cards on the table, you deserve to know. Now you do." He lifted an eyebrow. "Any cards you'd care to throw on the pile?"

Oh, God. She struggled to conceal her alarm behind a calm facade. "Not right now, thanks."

"That suggests there are cards."

"We all have cards. Right now, mine remain facedown."

"Fair enough." He gestured to the sitting area. "Are you interested in continuing our negotiation, or should we walk away from the table and resume our former business relationship?"

That wasn't possible, not after their latest kiss. He had to suspect as much. But if she continued with their negotiation it would be with eyes wide open, aware he'd never feel for her what she felt for him. If she couldn't accept that, better she walk away. Now. There existed an outside possibility they could return their working relationship to status quo. Well, almost status quo. This second kiss would make it far more difficult to find their way back to familiar ground. That didn't change her options. Retreat… or gamble everything. Not that there was any real question.

She summoned a cool smile. "I'd like to hear the rest of your offer and see if we can't come to terms. I think we've resolved your first point. Shall we simply agree to a fidelity clause?"

He approached again, invading her personal space, watching her helpless reaction to his proximity. "That would be acceptable."

"What's your next point?" she asked, fighting for equanimity.

He took a long swallow of his drink before setting it aside. Hunger glimmered in the depths of his inky gaze, a clear warning of what his next point would be before he even opened his mouth. "Point Two. Sex."

"Why doesn't that surprise me?" she asked wryly.

"I don't know, since it's surprising the hell out of me." He tugged at one of the loose curls dangling along her neck. "I assume we're also in agreement there? If it makes you feel any better, I'll even agree not to expect anything more from you than a purely physical relationship. Will that satisfy you?"

No! "Yes. That would satisfy me." She wanted to weep at how neatly she'd been boxed in, or rather, out of a personal relationship with Lucius, though she didn't have a single doubt he was delighted by the arrangement. Sex without strings. The perfect fantasy. She stepped away from him, forcing him to release the lock of hair he'd twined around his finger. She resumed her seat in the sitting area, anything to give herself some space from the strength of his personality. She needed to think straight if she were to win any concessions in this devil's bargain. "Assuming the trial period goes well, we'll marry?" she asked.

"Absolutely. Point Three. I don't want too long a trial period." He followed her, also sat. "The Ridgeways are on the verge of suing for custody of Mikey."

She frowned in concern. "It's gotten that contentious?"

His mouth tightened. "I suspect they hired a private investigator who uncovered the fact that I had an affair with Lisa. They informed me they're concerned that between Lisa's bloodline, as they refer to it, and my own questionable judgment, Mikey's welfare is at risk."

"Yes, they said something similar to me," she murmured. "I don't like the sound of that."

Their gazes met in perfect accord. "Nor do I."

"What happens to our arrangement if guardianship is awarded to the Ridgeways?"

"I believe that's Point Four. If I can't get it reversed, our marriage will be dissolved. In addition to your salary, you'll also be suitably compensated for your time and for the interruption to your career." He mentioned an amount that stunned her.

"Don't be ridiculous, Lucius," she protested. "That's… that's obscene."

He chuckled, the sound low and warm and strangely intimate. "It's not obscene. A trifle extravagant, but I suspect you're worth it."

"I'm not sure I like the sound of that."

His brows snapped together. "I'm not paying you for sex, if that's what you're thinking. I'm paying you for precisely what I said. Your time and the hit this job will mean to a career that's a vital part of who you are as a person. The money will allow you to pursue a course of study after the dissolution of our marriage so you can once again enter the workforce with marketable skills. Or you can sit at home and twiddle your thumbs, for all I care. If you invest the funds intelligently, you'll be in a position to choose what you want to do with your life from that point onward, while living quite comfortably for the rest of your life."

She edged away from the topic. "And if you're awarded

permanent custody of Mikey? What happens to our marriage?"

"Fair warning, I fully expect to be awarded custody, which brings us to Point Five. I'll require a guarantee that you'll remain with me for at least six years. Mikey will be of school age by then, which puts him at a less vulnerable age. After that, we can renegotiate terms."

"Very businesslike," she observed. Painfully businesslike. "Very cut and dried."

"Would you prefer me to lie?" A hint of irritation swept through the question. "To wrap everything up in a pretty tissue of fantasy tied together with fancy ribbons of pretense? Will that make our agreement more palatable?"

"No. Of course I don't want that."

She wanted a pretty truth tied together with ribbons of love. But he wasn't offering that and she was an utter fool if she thought that by agreeing to this devil's bargain he might one day come to love her. Determination filled her. But she could try. She would definitely try.

"So, what's left to discuss?" he asked.

She did a swift, mental run-through of their points so far. "Point Six? Is that where we left off?"

"Sounds about right."

"Let's label this one 'My Responsibilities.' I want to clarify what you expect of me," she said and proceeded to tick the points off on her fingers. "I will have the full-time responsibility of Mikey except when family obligations require a part-time nanny." She used the word *family* with deliberation, relieved when he nodded his acceptance. Might as well start the way she intended to proceed. "You'd like me to handle all aspects of entertaining friends or clients, but you agree to my hiring a housekeeper to handle the cooking and cleaning. And you want me to decorate your Lake Washington house. You do realize that I'll also require the assistance of a design firm in order to make the necessary improvements to your home?"

"*Our* home. I have no problem with that."

She warmed at his correction. "And anything we've forgotten to cover we can negotiate during our trial period?"

"Absolutely." He tilted his head to one side. "Do we have an agreement, Ms. Colter?"

She took a quick, steadying breath and took a reckless leap off the proverbial cliff. "We do, Mr. Devlin."

"In that case, there's nothing stopping us from doing this…" She realized his intentions a split second before he repeated the same maneuver he'd used earlier, and yanked her out of her chair and into his arms. "You have no idea how badly I want to see you naked again."

Finally.

Lucius would finally have Angie back in his arms. And in very short order he'd have her naked and in his bed. He could see the shock and protest building in her stunning—and stunned—aquamarine eyes. But he could also see the desire. The delicious memory of their almost tumble shyly peeking around the sensible restraint she normally possessed. About damn time.

"The Ridgeways asked to have Mikey again this weekend because it would have been Geoff's birthday. I felt the most diplomatic option was to agree. Since I'm through with my appointments for the day, we can slip upstairs to my apartment and consummate the deal with no one being the wiser."

"Lucius, I'm not sure—"

He couldn't contain himself another minute. He captured her bottom lip between his teeth and tugged. She rewarded him with a soft, hungry groan, one that instantly had him turning hard as a rock. His tongue flirted with hers, then sank into unbearable sweetness while his fingers plunged into the weighty thickness of her hair. He combed it loose, the silken curls tumbling free around her shoulders. The color never ceased to amaze him, an endless spectrum of browns from tawny to bronze.

Lucius managed to gather Angie up and urge her toward the private elevator that accessed the penthouse suite. The doors opened and they practically fell into the car. He fumbled for his access card, all the while deepening the kiss. He had no idea how he managed. Sheer desperation, no doubt. The instant the doors parted, accessing the penthouse foyer, Lucius swept Angie into his arms and carried her directly toward his bedroom. And then he did what he'd been wanting to do ever since he'd last kissed her.

Piece by piece, he stripped her. First, her suit jacket. Then her skirt. Her blouse was next, allowing him to see her as he'd dreamed endlessly of seeing her. She stood before him in nothing but garter and stockings—color him surprised—and panties and bra, the set a lovely shade of bronze that somehow mated with the streaks running through her hair and made her appear like some sort of bewitching autumnal goddess. Slender as a willow, he could only look…and want. Only, this time he would also possess.

He shrugged off his own jacket, ripped at the tie constricting his neck. She tackled the buttons of his shirt while he unbuckled, unzipped and ripped away clothing with impressive speed. And then time stilled. Late-afternoon sun slipped through the window of his bedroom and splashed across the room to where Angie stood, painting her in muted gold.

Once again he saw it, a painful and utterly feminine vulnerability that went to the very core of her. It brought out his protective instincts, the strength of them catching him by surprise. When had that happened? Why had it happened? What was it about her, a woman far stronger in some regards than Lisa, and yet far more fragile in other ways, that caused the most primal of masculine instincts to well up inside of him? She didn't want that from him. She'd made that perfectly clear. She wanted a sexual relationship and no more.

Well, he could give that to her. He was only too happy to give it to her.

But that didn't change how she affected him, the quiet urge to treat her tenderly, with a passion that transcended a mere sexual encounter. How was that possible? Unable to resist, he reached for a lock of her hair and wound it around his fist, drawing her to him. He inhaled her, drew in her essence and allowed it to brand him inside and out, to mark him in some way that would make her forever-more a part of him.

"How could I have worked with you for a full year and a half and never seen?" he murmured.

How could he not have seen who she was at her very essence? How beautiful she was, when stripped of her camouflage? The sheer force of woman that made her eclipse every other woman he'd ever been with. Made them seem…less. Made them seem shallow and incomplete, a meal that no longer satisfied. How could he not have seen the veils upon veils of her that tempted and taunted and urged him to strip them away, one by one, until he knew her as intimately as she knew herself?

"You're seeing me now," she whispered. "I just don't know if you're seeing the real me."

He nudged her chin upward and kissed her, slowly this time. Gently. She was like the first sip of a rare and delicate wine, an explosion of subtle flavor that blended into an intoxicating whole. "You taste real." He released the clasp of her bra and watched it slide away. "You look real."

She swallowed and he saw a hint of nerves. "Touch me and see if I feel real."

Hardly daring to breathe, he cupped her breast, kissed each tip, watched as the nipples tightened and pearled for him. "Oh, you feel real. Very real."

He crouched in front of her, taking his time to release her stockings and slide them down endlessly long, lean legs. They were gorgeous legs, fine-boned and supple, with strong, sweeping lines. He traced the silken length with his fingertips, from narrow ankle to inner thigh. She shuddered beneath the stroke and he heard the breathless moan explode from her. It only took a moment to unfasten the garter and discard it, leaving one final barrier between them.

Instead of a blue triangle like before, this one was bronze, just a tissue-thin silk and lace bastion of modesty, begging to be breached. He pressed his mouth to the center, inhaling her, warmed by her, drinking in the perfume of her desire. Gentle, gentle, gentle, he eased the elastic from her hips and bared her. Wanted her. Needed her. Would do anything to have her.

And then he ravished her, sending her over before she could draw breath to cry out. Her back bowed in reaction at the same instant her knees buckled and he tipped her backward as she flew apart, so the silk duvet cushioned her fall. He stood for a moment, looking his fill at the woman he intended to make his.

Her lashes fluttered against her cheeks and then she lifted her gaze so it clashed with his. He didn't think he'd ever seen anything more glorious than those eyes, drenched in wary shadow and a painful want. They overwhelmed a face edged with elegance and a classic, ageless beauty. Understated, like her delicate bone structure and graceful feminine curves, a shimmer of pale light against the darkness of the duvet. She was a flawless diamond of incalculable value, eclipsed by gemstones who appeared larger and flashier, but were infinitely less precious.

And she was his.

He took her mouth in a nibbling bite. Sank inward. He couldn't get enough of her, didn't think he'd ever get enough. Angie shifted beneath him, her arms stroking upward along his arms, then cupping his face.

"Lucius…"

Just his name, that one word a whisper that slipped from deep inside her to deep inside him. Her fingers slid into his hair, anchoring him, and she lifted her leg, gliding it along the length of his own leg. He shuddered beneath the slow, relentless stroke. She bewitched him. Stole sense and sensibility. All he wanted was to lose himself in her, to make her his in every sense of the word. But a small alarm sounded in the back of his head, growing progressively louder with each moment that passed, until the reason finally penetrated.

"Protection." The word escaped between kisses. "Give me a minute…"

"Hurry." The word was both demand and plea. "Please, hurry."

Lucius reached to one side, fumbled in the drawer of the bedside nightstand. Groped for the packet. Swore when it took three tries. Swore again when it defied his attempts to open. She dared to laugh, scooping the wrapper from his hands and somehow getting it open. And then her cool, skillful hands were on him, rolling along the length of him as she sheathed him, threatening both sanity and control.

"Better?" Angie asked.

"Hell, no." He palmed her lovely bottom and settled between her parted legs. In one swift stroke he mated them, a joining of such utter perfection it took him a moment to speak. "There, that's better. Infinitely better. Unimaginably better."

With a sigh of pure pleasure, she gathered him up, wrapping those endless legs around him and twining her arms tight, tight, tight. And then she moved with him, revealing a charm and style he'd never experienced with another, blending male and female in a dance of perfect synchronicity. *Mated. Branded. Joined.* The words became new to him, the definition honed to a meaning that would forevermore include her at its heart. And through that mating, that branding, that joining, he absorbed her. She became part of him, melded into the very fiber of his being.

Lucius didn't know if she understood what had happened, this claiming. Couldn't do more than state it in a single word of utter possession. "Mine."

"Always."

It was enough. For now it would do. His hands swept over her, a burning desire to explore every part of her, to know it quickly and thoroughly. But he couldn't. It wasn't possible. He couldn't hold back long enough and even as he took her, satisfied his initial hunger, he knew it would return. That it couldn't be sated, not tonight. Not anytime soon. One helping would never satisfy him…or her. She called to him, her voice an irresistible siren's song that made him deaf to any and all women—those who came before and those shadows of tomorrow who would never be. On some level he sensed himself incapable of hearing them the way he heard her. Could never respond to them the way he responded to her.

And with that knowledge, he let go. Let go of a lifetime of restraints and caution. Sliced through the Gordian knot of his control. For the first time, he gave himself fully to a woman, holding nothing back. Gave himself up to the fury and passion. He could tell the instant she let go, as well. Heard her cry of surrender, felt the shift as they climbed. Felt that breathless moment of ecstasy as they hovered at the peak. Felt the explosive climax. And then they tumbled into the wild and uncharted.

But he wasn't alone there. He had Angie.

Six

"I gather we're now committed to this course of insanity?" Angie asked, her voice satisfyingly breathless.

Lucius rolled onto his side, facing her. "So it would seem."

Unable to help himself, he traced the length of her neck. Unbelievable how much her skin felt like silk. He glided his fingertips across the hollow at the joining of neck and throat and farther, to the gentle curve of her breast. She shivered at the touch, and with their bodies still intimately linked he could feel the abrupt kick to her heart rate. Instead of being amused by her reaction, it humbled him. His touch alone could do that. And he had a sneaking suspicion her touch alone affected him the exact same way.

Aw, hell. It wasn't supposed to be this way. Sure, he'd hoped for a mutually satisfying sexual relationship. But this felt like more than that. This felt dangerous. Serious. It was time to adjust course, because going down this road led straight to disaster, particularly when Angie had been crystal clear about her disinterest—hell, her distaste—for anything too personal. And after Lisa... Well, he knew better than to look for something that didn't exist.

And yet, still he wanted Angie. Still, he touched. And touching, possessed. She didn't hesitate when he turned to her, gathered her in. Her initial acquiescence became demand, her demand an intriguing combination of uncertainty and aggression. And something else. Something he couldn't quite put his finger on. Then it hit him. Infuriated, challenged, defied him. *Reticence.* She was holding back, refusing to give herself fully to him, and the knowledge drove him wild.

"Look at me," he demanded. He speared his fingers into the thick tumble of her hair, anchoring her so she had no choice but to meet his gaze. "I want you to see who you're in bed with."

A laugh broke from her, a heartbreaking sound. "I see you. I've always seen you."

"You're holding back and I won't have it. I'm not Moretti. I'm not a one-night stand. I'm not some convenient body in the dark you can use for a night's worth of temporary pleasure and then toss aside come morning."

"I know you're not. I've never—" She shook her head, fighting him. "I don't *do* one-night stands."

He throttled back, allowed his voice to go low and soothing. "Then trust me. Let go. I won't hurt you. I swear I won't."

Her eyes sheened with tears and one escaped, sliding down her temple to lose its way in her hair. "You don't understand. I don't think I can. I don't know how."

"Don't think. Just feel."

He slowed the pace, drew out each caress, each kiss. Lingered and wallowed until he felt the slow give of her body. He explored her, the uncharted territory as well as the familiar, delighting in the sleek and toned, tracing from subtle curve to quiet valley. He still sensed a certain resistance, but inch by inch he soothed and encroached his way through her barriers, not giving her time for defense or withdrawal. And all the while he talked to her, a gentle, soothing whisper of words that eased him closer and closer to the true heart of the woman he held.

The instant the last bastion fell, he joined their bodies, one to the other, taking her in every sense of the word, penetrating with one devastating stroke. Her cry of surrender shattered the air and the moment she let go was also the moment she fully awoke. He didn't understand how or why. He didn't understand what past issues had caused such caution, although he swore to himself that he would. He simply matched her. If he'd thought what had come before had been life altering, it bore no comparison to what they now shared. He could only ride the wave with her, fighting to stay ahead of the tumble, to draw out the experience to its ultimate degree. To show her the possible. The impossible. The transcendent.

He had no idea whether they slept afterward. More likely, passed out. When consciousness returned, he found them so tangled together he suspected it would take a herculean effort to separate male from female. She stirred, though she made no attempt to shift away from him or begin the untangling process. He hoped she'd lost the ability to raise any further barricades against him.

"Why?" she asked simply.

"I wanted all of you," he replied just as simply. "I wanted more than you would have given Moretti or any other man."

She shifted, just enough to put a whisper of cool air

between them. "And did you give me more than you gave Lisa or any other woman?"

He didn't even attempt to lie. "Yes." He cupped her cheek—heaven help him, but she had skin like velvet—and leaned in for a slow, thorough kiss. "I didn't plan to. But it only seemed fair, all things considered."

He caught it then, that flash of vulnerability, secrets dimming her eyes to a sunset aquamarine. "I've never found sex fair or safe. I'm not sure it can be."

Ah, finally. He'd gotten to the root of the matter. "I don't disagree, though I'd love to be proved wrong." He paused a beat. "Who was he, Angie?"

Her eyes swept closed in momentary resistance before she looked at him again. One more small surrender. "His name was…is…Ryan. We lived together for a while. We planned to marry."

"And who was she?" Because he didn't doubt for one tiny minute that another woman came between them.

"My best friend, Britt," she confessed. He could hear the effort it took to keep her voice level and dispassionate. "I found them in bed together."

Ah. Which must have struck at the very core of her womanhood. Made her question everything about herself, particularly her own sexuality. Not that she should have any concerns on that front. He released his breath in a long sigh, the similarities between her situation and his resonating more keenly than he'd have liked. "We are a pair, aren't we? Both betrayed. Neither willing to trust. Maybe we can work together to get past all that, assuming we can continue to trust each other."

For some reason his comment caused her to stiffen, a hint of alarm to flicker across her expression. "Lucius—"

"Don't take it personally, Angie. In fact, you're one of the few people I do trust. At least, as much as I trust anyone. You. Geoff. My dad." His mouth twisted when he realized she was the only one left of those he'd named. "Did you ever meet Geoff?"

"Yes," she whispered.

"He was a lot like my dad. Just…" He moved his shoulders in a shrug. "Decent, you know? Down to his bones decent, like Dad. I guess that quality allowed people to take advantage of them both. Unlike me, they weren't suspicious enough. They regarded everyone as a potential friend instead of trying to figure out the angles, figure out what the other person wanted."

"But you always try and figure out the angles. You look for the underlying motivation."

"Every damn time," he confirmed. "My father lost his business because he trusted his business partner. Was blind to Lynley's agenda."

Her gaze traced his face, no doubt looking for a soft place to land. She wouldn't find it. "I heard Lynley took the company from your father."

"The betrayal gutted my father. He wasn't the same man afterward." Lucius swallowed past the acid eroding his throat. "He wasn't bitter like me, nor vengeful. He was…confused and bewildered. And later, hurt beyond measure. After that, he just gave up, let the betrayal kill him."

"They say…" She pulled away from him another inch or two, more than just a whisper this time. "They say you went after Lynley. Took him and his company down. That's how you acquired the nickname Devil Devlin."

He didn't pull his punches. "Guilty as charged. And I'd do it again without hesitation."

"And Lisa?" She withdrew a little farther, widening the breach between them until he could see the beginnings of a chasm. "Did she betray you?"

Had she? He considered, surprised to discover that she hadn't. He'd always known what she wanted. Hell, it hadn't been a secret. "Lisa wanted marriage," he replied slowly. "She didn't particularly care who she married, so long as he possessed a healthy bank account. I was her first choice, but only because I had more money than Geoff. Once she realized I wouldn't marry her, she moved on."

"To Geoff." A frown darkened Angie's expression. "I imagine you felt quite protective toward him. After all, he was your best friend and a lot like your father. Do you think on some level you were determined to save him, especially since you couldn't save your father?"

Lucius had considered the possibility when Lisa first went after Geoff. He suspected it also played a big part in that final night he'd spent with her, and his willingness to bed her one last time. Even though he knew it risked his friendship with Geoff, he'd taken that risk in order to reveal her true nature once and for all. "I tried to get Geoff to see Lisa for what she was. Not that it did any good. In the end it was his choice, his life, and I had to respect that."

"At some point would you have taken her down, too?"

And there it was, the true motivation behind Angie's questions. She feared his ruthlessness, and not without good cause. "No, sweetheart. I never would have touched Lisa, not once she married Geoff." He could tell his blunt, starkly honest response eased her concerns.

"Because you still loved her?"

Unable to help himself, he escaped the bed and put some distance between them. For some reason the question disturbed him, ripped a scab off a wound only half-healed. And then it hit him and he closed his eyes.

"Lucius?" His name contained a hint of uncertainty. "What is it?"

He turned around. Faced her. Found it the height of irony that he stood before her, stripped naked in every sense of the word. "I didn't love Lisa. I loved Geoff. He was my brother in all but blood. He's the reason I'd never have taken her down. Out of respect for him, for what he hoped to build with her." He shook his head, gutted. "It doesn't make any difference, anyway. They're all gone now. My dad. Geoff. Lisa."

"Everyone you loved." He closed his eyes to hold at bay the compassion he read in her voice and expression, rejecting it. "There's still one more person, Lucius. There's Mikey." Urgency raced through her words, hammered at him. "He needs you. He needs your love."

And perhaps that bothered him most of all. "I'm not sure I'm capable of love anymore." He didn't give her time to debate the issue. He checked the clock by his bedside table. "It's getting late. I don't know about you, but I'm starved. I'm going to call for a meal to be brought up. Your choice whether they serve it while you're still naked."

The comment accomplished just what he hoped. It served to catapult Angie out of bed. She hastened around the room, gathering up her clothing. Watching, he had the almost-overpowering urge to snatch all that gorgeous nudity back into his arms and return her to his bed. To make love to her all over again, long into the night, until he'd found a way to sate the desire that continued to infect him, that simmered through his veins and pooled in his loins and demanded he take. Possess. Stamp repeatedly with his possession.

"Do you mind if I grab a quick shower?" she asked, clutching her bundle of clothing to her chest.

He fought to make sense of her words. But all he could

see were those legs. That pearly skin. The tumble of soft curls that haloed her lovely face. Those huge, haunting aquamarine eyes. Silently swearing, Lucius forced his brain into gear, dissected her words one by one and shoved out a response.

"Go ahead."

She turned, presenting him with that perfect, round backside. If she hadn't been moving at such a swift clip, he would have lunged for her. Yanked her back into his arms and his bed and taken her in a helpless frenzy of need.

Mikey. Remember Mikey. The boy had to come first and foremost. He was the only reason Lucius had taken Angie to his bed. Was considering marrying her and making her an intimate part of his life. He must never forget that. Geoff's son came first. The side benefits of marrying Angie were just that. Side benefits. A tasty appetizer to enjoy, but not the main meal. He couldn't allow himself to become distracted by a pert bottom, stunning legs, an elegant face or wary, vulnerable eyes. Eyes that made him want to wrap her up in an endless embrace and protect her against…

Against what?

Himself, he realized. Against using her. Hurting her. Causing her the sort of pain Britt and Ryan had. The sort of pain Lynley had caused his father. The sort of pain, ultimately, Lisa would have caused Geoff simply because it wasn't in her nature to remain faithful to any one person. He needed to remain dispassionate and focused on Mikey, to the exclusion of everything—and everyone—else.

And yet, still he wanted. Yearned. Fought to control what shouldn't matter…but did.

Blistering the air with his frustration, Lucius swiftly dressed, then placed their dinner order. He made a beeline for the living room, aware if he didn't get the hell out of the bedroom—and now—neither of them would leave anytime soon. How was it possible that something so simple had taken such an unfortunate turn?

When he'd first considered using the Pretorius Program to help him find a wife, he'd been determined that his marriage would be one of pure convenience for both parties. That any sexual involvement would remain physical, uncomplicated by any sort of emotional connection—exactly what Angie wanted, which should have made it perfect for them both. In fact, that particular requirement had been one of the most difficult to fulfill, according to the program's designer. For some reason, women entering the marital estate wanted love, something he couldn't and wouldn't offer.

Even when Angie's name had been raised, he'd experienced a swift wash of relief. He'd marry someone he respected, with whom he had a comfortable relationship. A woman he trusted. Someone he wanted sexually and who, based on her response to their kiss after the business dinner with Moretti, wanted Lucius, but without the added obstacle of messy emotional demands, a prerequisite that worked well for them both.

But something had happened when he took Angie to bed. Something he didn't want to examine too closely. Something he didn't dare analyze. Ever. All he knew was that he'd never experienced such perfection with any other woman. Lisa, with whom he'd enjoyed a very passionate, energetic sex life, paled in comparison. And he knew why.

Once he broke through her restraint and Angie gave herself to him, she gave everything, unstintingly, just as he'd demanded. She held nothing back. Every part of her was open to him, gifted to him with a generosity that unmanned him.

Damn it! Hadn't he just promised himself he wouldn't

analyze what made Angie different from the other women he'd known?

She appeared in the doorway between his bedroom and the living room just then and he fought not to laugh at the irony. Angelique, the tempting sex goddess he'd been so busily fantasizing about had been replaced by Ms. Angie Colter, PA Extraordinaire, fully zipped, buttoned and un-creased, from the painfully tight knot of hair at her nape to the sensible heels concealing her pretty painted toes. Despite that, he caught the merest hint of nervousness eroding the edges of her composure.

"Dinner's not here yet?" she asked.

"Not yet." He lifted an eyebrow. "You okay?"

"Fine."

But she wasn't. Not totally. "Except for…?"

Before she could respond, a panel by the elevator buzzed. "I assume that's our dinner," she prompted, her relief almost palpable.

Lucius nodded in confirmation. Fine. He'd save the postcoital interrogation until after dinner. He crossed to the panel in the foyer and punched in a code. A few min-utes later the doors opened and a young man in his late teens stepped from the car bearing a cardboard box, a cocky grin and a long golden braid that flowed all the way to his waist. It twitched rhythmically to the music pouring from the earbuds dangling from his ears.

"Thanks for being so prompt, Tuck," Lucius said.

"Anything for you, Mr. D. You want it in the dining room, as usual?"

"If you wouldn't mind."

He started in that direction, his stride catching in a brief hitch when he caught sight of Angie. To Lucius's amusement, he gave her a quick, flirtatious wink before continuing on his way. He made short work of setting up their meal, then returned with the empty box. "Nice one, Mr. D.," he murmured under his breath. "I live to be you."

He handed the kid a generous tip and jerked his head in the direction of the elevator. "Just live to be yourself, Tucker," he advised.

"That was my second choice," the teen replied. Hopping onto the elevator he punched the button for the lobby. Just as the doors slid shut he waggled his brows in Angie's direction and gave her a low wolf whistle.

"Interesting character," she said with a laugh.

"He takes a little getting used to, but he's harmless." Lucius led the way into the dining room and held the chair for Angie. "Smart, too. He received a full scholarship to U-Dub. Wants to be an engineer."

"Did you attend the University of Washington?"

"Yes. Or I did until my father died," he qualified. He selected a bottle of chilled white wine that would mate well with their meal, made short work of opening it. "I dropped out at that point to salvage what I could of his business. Not that there was anything left to salvage. Lynley had gotten it all by then."

"And then you started Diablo, Inc.," she prompted.

"That took a few years to get off the ground." He transferred some chicken stir-fry to her plate. "I think you'll like this. They use an excellent blend of spices."

She took a bite, her startled gaze flashing to his. "Oh, wow."

He smiled. "Told you."

They ate in silence for a few minutes. Drank wine. He watched while she pushed a bite of dinner around her plate, working up the nerve to speak. Finally, she glanced at him and caught him looking. She released a low laugh. "Aren't you going to say, 'Out with it, Colter'? You don't normally show such patience."

He shrugged. "I knew you'd work up to it in a bit. It gave me a chance to eat before you grilled me again."

"I'm not going to grill you. To be honest, I just wondered… Where do we go from here?"

Back to bed, he almost replied, but refrained. She must have guessed the direction of his thoughts, though, because warm color swept across her cheekbones.

"Other than there," she added drily.

He sipped his wine. "Tomorrow's Saturday. We'll spend the day picking out an engagement ring. Make it official. We'll break it to the Ridgeways when we pick up Mikey on Sunday."

"We?" A part of her loved the way he connected them with such ease. Another part struggled to deal with the speed with which they were moving forward. "You want me to come with you?"

"From this point forward, we're joined at the hip," he confirmed. "We present a unified front in every regard. Got it?"

It made perfect sense. The Ridgeways needed time to assimilate the changes. Even more important, they needed time to buy into those changes. To believe without question that she and Lucius were a couple, and would make excellent parents for Mikey. Although, no question, that would take quite a bit of convincing. She nodded in agreement. "Got it."

"Excellent." His cell phone rang just then. He checked the number and frowned. "I better take this. It's the Ridgeways." He connected the call. "Benjamin? Oh, Tabby. Is there a problem? Mikey?"

To Angie's concern, his expression closed over and she stood, crossed to where he sat. Unable to help herself she slid a supportive hand onto his shoulder, praying nothing had happened to the baby.

"We'll be right there." He snapped the cell phone closed. "She thinks Benjamin has had a heart attack. They're at the hospital and she's requested that I pick up Mikey."

"Let's go," she said simply.

"One quick adjustment first." He stood, ran his gaze over her in a manner that had her stiffening. "I'd hoped to have this weekend to set the stage a little better."

For some reason she found herself falling back a step. "What does that mean?"

"It means, when we get to the hospital, try gazing at me adoringly rather than like you are now." At her look of utter confusion, he clarified, "As though I'm about to steal your chastity, run off with the family jewels and give a boot to your little pet dog on my way out the door." He approached, looking entirely too dark and dangerous. "From now on you need to look a bit less professional and a hell of a lot more like my future wife."

Her breath quickened. "Perhaps the engagement ring we purchase tomorrow will be sufficient. Besides, Mrs. Ridgeway will be too distracted by concern for her husband to pay attention to me."

"Don't be so sure, not when it comes to Tabby. She might not consciously notice, but in retrospect she'll pick up on the clues. Assuming we give her a few to pick up on." He paused in front of Angie, so close she could feel his warmth and catch a hint of his scent, a scent he'd somehow imprinted on her in those hours they'd shared in his bed. Before she could stop him, he reached for her hair, tumbled it free of the tidy knot she'd settled for after her shower. "Better."

"Lucius—"

"Much better. Keep saying my name like that and there won't be any question about our relationship."

He reached for her, drew her up for a slow kiss, one that had her melting against him. And then another, deeper, more thorough. She didn't have a clue how long the embrace lasted. Minutes. Forever. When he finally released her she discovered he'd somehow freed the first few buttons of her blouse, exposing the lacy edge of her bra. She fell back a pace, fumbling with the buttons, only to have him stop her.

"Leave it," he ordered.

"You can't expect me to go around like this. What will people think?"

"Exactly what we want them to think. That we're a couple who can't keep our hands off each other. A couple who were caught in bed when Tabby called and threw on the first things that came to hand before rushing off to the hospital."

She could feel warmth burning a path across her cheekbones. "I don't think I can do this."

"You don't have a choice. I don't want there to be any question that our marriage is a love match. I don't want the Ridgeways to have any grounds for suggesting otherwise." He tipped her chin upward, his black eyes burning into hers. "When we rush into the hospital together I want on some level for Tabby to believe we just rolled out of bed."

"Not much of a stretch considering we did," Angie muttered.

His mouth twisted to one side. "Unfortunately, my dear Ms. Colter, you have an innate knack for presenting a calm and unruffled front. Excellent when it comes to a work setting, but not at all what I need right now."

She glared at him in exasperation. "And you think undoing a few buttons and wearing my hair down will change that?"

"It'll help. So will a carefully staged embrace."

She stared at him in open dismay. "Oh, Lucius, no. Not tonight."

"Of course not tonight," he retorted impatiently. "But soon."

"Is that really necessary?"

Irritation flashed across his face. "What the hell difference does it make if the Ridgeways catch us kissing? We will be kissing. In case there's the least doubt in your mind, we'll be kissing on a regular basis. We'll also be sharing a bed from this point forward."

"You're moving too fast."

"Then catch up," he snapped. "I don't have time to go slow with you, not considering this latest development. Nor is there time for you to turn coy at this late date. I explained what I needed going in. And you know damn well what's at stake here."

Angie's chin shot up. "Back off, Lucius. You're pushing too fast, too hard. We're not married, yet."

"Another fact that I plan to change at our earliest possible convenience." He checked his watch and swore. "We need to go. We can argue about this later."

He was right. They did need to go. She held her tongue while he whisked her into the elevator. The ride to the garage level took next to no time. He led her to a new BMW sedan that took her by surprise. She wouldn't have associated the car with him, vaguely recalled he drove something far sportier, until she caught sight of the car seat in the back. It hit her then. He'd purchased the car with Mikey in mind. And she'd bet the title on her pretty little house in Ballard that this particular model possessed one of the highest safety ratings around.

They pulled out into the misty Seattle night, the dampness causing the tires to softly hiss against the pavement.

Darkness clamped down on them, intensifying the intimacy within the confines of the car. To Angie's relief, Friday night traffic proved light, perhaps because it was well past rush hour, also well past the time when people would be heading out for dinner dates or theater engagements. The darkness and intimacy also gave her the courage to address an issue she'd neglected to ask Lucius about, an issue that continued to nag at her. She decided to get it out into the open before committing herself to her role as his fiancée.

"Would you mind if I asked you a question about Mikey and your guardianship of him?"

He spared her a swift glance before returning his attention to the road. "Since you'll soon be his mother, I don't mind at all."

"His mother," she repeated faintly. "I…I hadn't thought of it quite that way."

"Start."

She gave a quick nod. "Okay. I can do that. I think."

"What's your question?"

"Why?" she asked simply. "Why did you agree to take Mikey and why are you so determined to keep him—to the extent of marrying a virtual stranger? Why not just let the Ridgeways have him? It would certainly be simpler."

"Excellent question and one I've asked myself countless times over the past three months." His mouth compressed and a frown of concentration etched a path across his brow. "There are several reasons, to be honest. First, I made a promise to Geoff, and I don't ever—*ever*—renege on my promises."

"There's a reason for that, isn't there? Your father?" she hazarded a guess. "And what happened between him and Lynley?"

"I will never be Lynley," he confirmed. "I will never break a promise, once made."

She didn't doubt him for a single moment. Lucius Devlin might be one of the most ruthless men she'd ever met, but he had a code of honor as inherent and unalterable as the color of his eyes or the hard, uncompromising angles of his face. Even with Lisa, if she and Geoff had still been a couple when she'd come crying on his shoulder, he'd never have laid a finger on her. Angie knew that with utter certainty.

"And your other reasons?" she prompted.

"The Ridgeways aren't fit guardians." He made the statement in a flat, absolute voice. "They despised Lisa, and there's not a question in my mind that Mikey will ultimately pay the price for their attitude toward his mother."

"I agree," Angie murmured unhappily. "Mrs. Ridgeway, in particular, seems almost zealous in her determination to make sure Mikey doesn't take after Lisa in any fashion."

"Lisa had her flaws, but one thing I know for certain. She adored Mikey. She was like a lioness with her cub when it came to her son."

Angie regarded him with grave eyes. "But there's another reason you've decided on this course of action. I can tell."

"That's none of your business," he stated gently.

"I disagree. If I'm to be your wife, if I'm to be Mikey's mother, I think it is my business."

He had zero intention of answering her, she could tell. But then to her utter astonishment, the words escaped in a whispered confession, full of pain and regret, spilling into the heavy darkness of the car.

"Mikey could have been mine."

Seven

Angie stared at Lucius in disbelief. *"What?"*

He flicked her with a brief glance with pit-black eyes, enfolding himself in remoteness.

"Lucius… The timing was that close?" she pressed.

"Yes."

"Did you… Has it occurred to you—"

"That Mikey might be mine? Of course. After Lisa announced her pregnancy I approached her privately and asked. She promised to have a DNA test done after Mikey was born."

"Talk about awkward." Angie caught her lip between her teeth. "I assume Geoff knew about—"

"Our encounter, for lack of a better word? Yes. Our friendship survived it. Barely. After Mikey was born, Lisa was quite up-front about the test. She arranged for it to be conducted, all very discreet and private, all of us very polite and sophisticated about the situation. Geoff was certain Mikey was his. As it turned out, he was right. But that doesn't change anything. I could have been the father just as easily as Geoff. And if our situation were reversed, I would have wanted him to stand for me if I'd orphaned my son. And Geoff would have done it, too. He was that sort of man."

Angie caught the black pain underscoring his words and her heart went out to him. More than anything she wished she could take him in her arms and soothe the hurt. But she couldn't. Not only were they in a moving car, but they didn't have that sort of relationship. She fought back a pained laugh, one she didn't doubt would be edged with hysteria. They'd made love. They planned to marry. But she didn't dare comfort her future husband. Could it get any more bizarre?

They arrived at the hospital just then, putting an end to the conversation. Parking proved more problematic since visiting hours hadn't yet ended. Lucius finally slipped into a space a good hike from the emergency room entrance. Right before they walked through the sliding doors, he annoyed her by giving her hair a quick ruffle, tumbling the curls into just-out-of-bed disorder.

They found Tabby Ridgeway in a jam-packed waiting area. Somehow she held herself aloof from the noise and bustle and misery. She cradled a sleeping Mikey in her arms and sat with her eyes closed, the deep lines carved into her face revealing age and exhaustion and fear in equal measure.

Sensing their presence, she glanced in their direction and drew herself up as though steeling herself, a regal hauteur snapping into place along with her spine. Her gaze shifted from one to the other of them and in that instant Angie realized Lucius had been right. As usual. A woman's awareness filtered through Tabby's obvious distress, one that took in Angie's hair, the not fully fastened buttons of her blouse, the lack of makeup. A hint of outrage flashed through her cold eyes, then was gone.

"How's Benjamin?" Lucius asked. He gently unburdened Tabby, ignoring her instinctive flinch to prevent him from taking the baby. Mikey stretched and opened his eyes, grinning and babbling excitedly when he saw who held him. "Is there anything we can do to help other than take Mikey?"

She registered the word *we* by switching her attention to Angie and narrowing her eyes. "I shouldn't have called. Clearly, I've interrupted something."

"You did. Angie and I were celebrating our engagement," Lucius replied easily. "But don't worry about it. All that can wait. It's not like it's come as any surprise to either of us. We'll celebrate tomorrow when we pick out the ring." He switched his attention to the baby. "You can come along and help us decide which one is best, can't you, little guy?"

"Engaged?" Angie caught the confusion, followed by a reassessment. "You two are engaged to be married?"

Lucius nodded. "It's been in the works for a while." Angie couldn't get over the gentleness of his tone or the effortless way he held the baby, bouncing him in a light, rhythmic motion that spoke of experience in quieting a fussy infant, or entertaining a happy one. "Since she works for me—for the moment—we haven't wanted to say anything. It didn't seem…appropriate."

Angie deliberately changed the subject. "Is there any news about Mr. Ridgeway's condition?"

Fear invaded Tabby's features once again. "Not yet. They're taking so long. Too long."

"Let me see what I can find out." Lucius transferred the baby to Angie. "I'll be right back."

Angie cradled Mikey against her shoulder and took the seat next to Tabby. "If you want to get yourself a drink or some food, I can wait here and watch your things."

"No. No, I don't want anything." She twisted her hands together, waves of disapproval emanating from her. "How long have you and Lucius…?"

Oh, dear. They hadn't discussed the details of their cover story, yet. "About nine months," she improvised, deciding Lucius would want the relationship to predate his guardianship. "We were going to announce our engagement sooner, but…" She trailed off in the hopes that Tabby would assume the announcement had been postponed after Geoff's and Lisa's deaths.

She nodded. "Very considerate of you," she said in a stiff voice. "I'm surprised you'd be willing to take on a man like Lucius, especially now that he has the responsibility of my grandson."

"I adore Mikey. I have from the moment I first saw him."

"We—Benjamin and I—don't feel Lucius is a fit parent."

Angie tiptoed through the minefield which had opened up so unexpectedly in front of her. "Perhaps with time, you'll discover otherwise. I know he has a reputation, but I've found that reputation to be a bit of an exaggeration." She offered a conspiratorial smile. "You know how businessmen are. If people think you're ruthless, they're more respectful and cautious in their dealings with you. I'm sure Geoff would never have appointed Lucius his son's guardian if he didn't have complete faith in his best friend's character."

"Geoff was under the influence of *that woman,*" Tabby retorted. "I'm not sure he was in an adequate frame of mind to judge."

Okay, Angie decided. Clearly, she wasn't going to win this particular argument, not that she'd expected to. Heavy silence settled between them, as chilly and bitter as the breeze that gusted through the sliding doors whenever they parted to cough out a new arrival. She glanced in the direction Lucius had disappeared, relieved to see him striding in their direction, a doctor at his side.

"This is Dr. Sanji," he explained, making the introductions. "He's the cardiologist who's been taking care of Benjamin."

The doctor sat beside Tabby and gathered her hand in his. Brave man, was all Angie could think. "All is well, Mrs. Ridgeway. Your husband did not suffer a heart attack, but a panic attack."

Tabby's chin trembled. "Not his heart? You're certain?"

"Quite certain." His light brown eyes stayed fixed on her, their expression calm and reassuring. "I understand you are both under considerable emotional distress. This weekend would have been your late son's birthday, is that correct?"

Tabby nodded, pressing her lips tightly together. "He would have been thirty-two."

"No doubt this is the root cause of your husband's problem. Panic attacks often mimic the symptoms of a heart attack. The nausea, dizziness, shortness of breath."

"I didn't know what to do," she confessed, "so I called 9-1-1."

"As you should have. We have put him on a mild antianxiety medication, which will ease his distress. You should be able to take him home in a few hours. Until then, why don't you come sit with him?" He offered a charming smile. "I'm sure having you at his side will do far more for him than any medication."

Tabby spared Mikey a worried glance. "My grandson?"

"Don't worry about that." Angie leaped into the breach. "Lucius and I will take good care of him."

Tabby retreated behind her wall of reserve. "See that you do." Sweeping to her feet, she collected her handbag. "Please return the diaper bag the next time we have visitation." She didn't bother waiting for an answer, but stalked away without a backward glance.

"Let's get out of here," Lucius said. "Are you okay with Mikey?"

"If you'll grab the diaper bag, I'm fine." She traced her hand across the baby's soft dark curls. "It's so noisy here, I can't believe he's fallen asleep again."

"He's a good kid, just like his dad." After making sure Mikey was protected against the elements, they exited the emergency room and headed for the car. Lucius hit the remote to disengage the locks. "Did she buy the engagement?" he asked, shooting Angie a searching glance.

"Seemed to."

"Let's see if we can't find a way to shift that to 'completely sold' on the concept." He took Mikey and slipped him into the car seat with the ease of three months' worth of practice. Angie watched carefully while he took care of the various buckles, committing the process to memory in case she was called on to do it in the future. "Let's get home. I don't know about you, but I'm exhausted."

The return trip didn't take long. Mikey woke up just as they were parking the car, his whimpers increasing to wails with each passing minute. The instant they reached the foyer, Lucius inclined his head in the direction of the kitchen. "He sounds hungry. I'll warm up a bottle."

"I'll check his diaper and get him ready for bed."

"His bedroom is opposite mine. Ours," he corrected himself. "You'll find everything you need in there."

She located the room without any trouble. Before

Mikey's advent it had been used as an office. A crib occupied one corner of the room, while a huge mahogany
desk had been transformed into a changing table, the surface boxed in with a wooden topper to prevent the baby
from rolling off. His pitiful wails eased off the instant
she stripped him of his sopping disposable diaper. She'd
have been a bit more uncertain about the process if she
hadn't had the opportunity to help out with Mikey's care
over the past dozen weeks. She hadn't been called on to
assist often, just enough to refresh her memory from her
babysitting days. With luck, Lucius wouldn't pick up on
the fact that she wasn't quite as experienced as her résumé
claimed.

To her amusement, she found sleepwear in a gorgeous
mahogany file cabinet that matched the desk, clearly
repurposed to serve as Mikey's dresser. Fighting flailing
limbs, she managed to get him snapped together. Then she
scooped him up and carried him into the living room.

A couple minutes later, Lucius entered with a baby
bottle. "Want me to take him?"

"I don't mind feeding him." She took a seat on the
couch and smiled down at Mikey. "I don't often get the
chance."

"That's about to change." He tested the temperature of
the milk a final time and handed her the bottle. "A lot of
things are about to change."

Mikey latched onto the nipple and she chuckled at his
greedy enthusiasm. "At least we got the hard part over
with. Now that the Ridgeways know about our engagement, maybe they'll hold off suing for custody."

He turned off the overhead lights, allowing the illu-
mination from the city to bathe the room in a soft glow.
"They might hold off. Especially if we follow it with a
wedding as soon as possible."

It took a moment for his words to penetrate. The instant they did, her head jerked up and she looked across the room at him. He stood in front of the bank of windows that marched along one full wall of the room, his forearm braced against the glass. He kept his back to her while he stared out at the city. Even though his stance gave the impression of casual indifference, she caught a line of tension sweeping across his shoulders and a dangerous stillness that usually came before the predatory pounce.

"As soon as possible?" she repeated uneasily. "What sort of time frame are we looking at?"

He shrugged, a swift, restless movement. "Days. No more than a week or so."

Angie lifted the baby to her shoulder and rubbed his back, struggling to pinpoint the quality in his voice that sounded off. "Why the rush?" she asked.

He turned to face her. Even then she couldn't read him, his expression buried within the thick shadows consuming the room. "I want this tied up. A done deal."

This time she didn't need to read his expression. She could hear the fierce determination in his voice, the intent lurking beneath the words. "You mean, you want *me* tied up."

"If that's how you prefer we do it next time." A blatantly sexual undertone rippled through his dark voice. "I'm sure I can accommodate you."

"Cut it out, Lucius."

"I don't think I can." He approached, his movements as sleek and graceful as a lion on the prowl. "I want you tied up, tied down, tied to me. I don't want to give you room to escape."

She stared at him in bewilderment. "Who said I planned to escape?"

"I'm committed, Angie. *We're* committed. We just

made the big announcement to the Ridgeways. There's no going back now and I can't take the risk that you might change your mind."

What in the world was going on? "I understand that, and I have no intention of going back or changing my mind."

"I intend to make certain of it. Tomorrow the ring. Monday, we'll apply for a marriage license. I have no idea if there's a waiting period. If so, we wait. If not…" He shrugged. "No point in wasting the opportunity. We can have it over and done with right then and there."

"Over and done with?" She felt her temper slip and slowly stood. Mikey had fallen asleep once again, and without a word, she set the bottle aside and carried him to his crib. She sensed Lucius following, and turning, found him leaning against the doorjamb. "Lights on or off?" she asked crisply.

"Off. There's a night-light that comes on automatically when the sensor registers the darkness."

Sure enough, it flickered to life, a cute little teddy bear, holding its paw to its muzzle in a *shh* gesture. Without a word Angie brushed past Lucius and returned to the living room. There, she spun around to face him.

"I realize I entered this devil's bargain with my eyes wide open when I agreed to take on this new job." She used the final word deliberately, because despite everything he'd said, that's really how he saw it. "And that our marriage isn't what anyone would remotely consider normal. But it isn't something I plan to get over and done with. I won't be rushed. Nor will I be treated with such casual indifference."

"So you do want a few ribbons and bows, despite what you claimed."

It hurt. His callous disregard hurt more than she could

possibly express. And it was her own fault. He'd been totally up-front about what he wanted from their marriage.
He hadn't pretended to love her or have any feelings for
her other than pure sexual desire.

Anger warred with hurt. "I need you to back off and
stop rushing me. I need time to get used to this crazy idea
I've agreed to. It hasn't even been twenty-four hours since
you asked me to marry you. I'm not sure it's even been six!
It's all happening too quickly. I need you to slow down,
give me time to adjust."

Frustration flashed across his expression and he paced
the length of the room. "Benjamin isn't well. Fortunately,
it's not his heart, but it's clear the stress of losing Geoff is
affecting him. Affecting them both. If we marry—soon—
they may realize they can't argue I'm unfit or that Mikey
won't have a stable home life. In addition, they like you.
They may conclude that, although it's not what they originally wanted, they can live with our retaining custody if I
grant them liberal visitation rights. Maybe they'll finally
realize trying to take on a baby at this stage in their life
would be too much for them, particularly after Benjamin's
anxiety attack."

"All excellent points. That doesn't mean we need to
marry first thing Monday. We have time."

"No." He cut her off with a slashing jerk of his arm. "I
don't want to give them that time. I want to push forward
while—"

"While what, Lucius? While they're weak? Hurting?"

He swore. "Damn it, Angie. I have my reasons for
moving up the timeline and they're sound. I expect you
to respect my decision without arguing." He thrust a hand
through his hair, regarding her with open frustration. "You
never gave me this much trouble when you were my PA.
Stop fighting me on this."

"Stop pushing." She planted her hands on her hips. "I'm warning you, Lucius Devlin. If you don't want your apprentice/wife to become your ex-fiancée before you even have a chance to buy an engagement ring, I suggest you give me a little breathing room."

For some reason his eyes narrowed and it took a moment for her to realize what had caused his reaction. The instant she did, the breath stuttered in her lungs. Oh, no. No, no, *no*. She'd said *apprentice/wife*. There was only one way she could have known that term. From Jett or Pretorius. How could she have been so stupid? He continued to stare at her and she couldn't look away, trapped within the ice and fire.

"How long have you known?" Soft. Deadly. The slicing flick of a lash.

She didn't prevaricate, didn't dare. "Since last Monday."

"Who told you? How did you find out?" he demanded. The questions came fast and furious, his expression as hard and relentless as his voice. "Why didn't you tell me you knew?"

She eyed him warily. "Jett let it slip. She assumed I knew and I didn't correct her assumption."

"Son of a bitch."

Maybe a bit of damage control was in order. "I didn't mention it to you because I assumed it was personal and therefore none of my business. When you called me into your office today and said you had a business proposition to discuss with me, I began to suspect it had something to do with the Pretorius Program." She wrapped her arms around her waist. "I understand you used a similar program when you hired me."

It was his turn to hesitate and he made a concerted effort to curb his temper. "Yes. It's how you ended up on the short list for a potential wife. Apparently there was a computer glitch and the two programs were linked. It would seem you were the perfect candidate for both positions."

She couldn't help herself. The lies she'd set up with Jett's help caused her to flinch.

He instantly apologized, mistaking the reason for her reaction. "I shouldn't keep referring to our marriage as though it were a job. I'm hoping it'll become far more than that for both of us."

"But not real," she couldn't prevent herself from saying.

"I promised you I wouldn't make any emotional demands on you and I won't." His words took on a tight, impatient edge. "Does that reassure you?"

No, the comment made her want to cry. She was a fool. A total idiot. She'd locked herself into this travesty of a job—because despite what he said, it *was* a job—in the hopes that he would fall in love with her the way she'd fallen in love with him. Not that he ever would. Lucius Devlin possessed far too much self-control to ever allow such a thing.

"So, where do we go from here?" Angie asked.

He didn't hesitate. "Forward."

She nodded. "Okay." She dared to approach, to run her hand along the impressive ridge of muscles lining his arm. "I promise I'll go through with our marriage, Lucius. I promise I won't back out. All I'm asking is that we take this a little slower. Just a little."

"Tomorrow the ring?"

She nodded. "And Monday we'll take care of the marriage license. That way we're ready should the need arise sooner than anticipated. Fair enough?"

She felt his tension drain away, the muscles beneath her hand gradually relaxing. "I can live with that." He hesitated, then added, "You should have told me you knew about the Pretorius Program."

"You're right. I should have." Time to put a quick end to the conversation before he had time to think of any more questions. She made a point of checking her watch. "It's late. I should head home."

"Excellent idea." Then he surprised her by swinging her into his arms. "Welcome home."

She couldn't help laughing. "Lucius, seriously. I need to go."

He shouldered his way into his bedroom. Depositing her onto the bed, he followed her down. "Trust me, my lovely Angelique, when it comes to having you in my home—and in my bed—I'm dead serious."

And then he consumed her.

"Your assistant has a big mouth, Pretorius."

"She's…young. I'll speak to her."

"Fortunately, the person she slipped up with is Angie, who's discretion personified. If it had been anyone else…"

"Yeah, yeah. Got that." Pretorius hesitated. "The important question is, has the Colter woman agreed to marry you? On paper she's perfect. More than perfect, in fact."

"Amazingly, she has agreed," Lucius confirmed.

"An unusual woman."

No question about that. "One of a kind."

"Sort of surprising she'd go along with the plan this fast. Not something most women would do, as you've discovered for yourself, especially when you're not interested in a…" Pretorius groped for a word both appropriate, as well as tactful. "A traditional marriage. Yeah, that's it. Traditional. You must have offered quite an incentive package."

Lucius hesitated, his eyes narrowing. "Not really."

In fact, now that he thought about it, the terms were heavily weighted in his favor. He attempted to run through their conversation in his office, when he'd first outlined their devil's bargain, as she'd referred to it. Why *had* she agreed? Money? Maybe that played a part in it, though she'd never betrayed any avaricious traits before. And he'd have noticed. A man in his position possessed impeccable radar when it came to greedy women.

Career advancement? Also unlikely. She'd be tied to him for the next five to six years, caring for house and home. Not the smartest way to advance your career, regardless of the payout at the end of their contract. She'd need to retrain. Work her way back up the corporate ladder. Even with his assistance, that would take time. He'd always sensed she took pride in her abilities on the work front. That it was somehow tied to her self-esteem and sense of overall accomplishment. Why give that up to become a wife and mother?

So, why had she agreed to his proposal? He couldn't actually remember her ever saying.

"I've got to go," he informed Pretorius, a trifle abruptly. "Speak to your assistant about her discretion issues. Or should I say, indiscretion?"

"Will do. And congratulations. I hope you and Ms. Colter will be very happy together."

Lucius hung up the phone and glanced toward the elevator. When he'd left his bed, Angie had still been out cold. And with good cause. They'd made love into the deepest, richest part of the night, entwined in passion, then in sleep, lost in an endless embrace as the star-studded inkiness of the dark released its hold to the burning reds and purples of a new dawn. It was as though neither of them could get enough of the other. Even when sleep claimed them they'd remained locked together, craving the intimacy that came through touch and scent.

He crossed to the elevator and returned to his apartment. Angie's voice came from the direction of the kitchen and he found her there with Mikey. The baby sat cushioned in a high chair, and it seemed to Lucius that his balance improved by the day. She offered him a bite of cereal mixed with mashed banana, laughing when he grabbed the spoon and attempted to feed his cheek.

"Close, but no cigar, champ," Angie informed him, gently wiping him clean with a damp washcloth.

She took renewed aim at his gaping mouth, allowing him to assist, and this time the food found its way home and he ate as if they'd been starving him. She must have heard or sensed Lucius's presence because she glanced over her shoulder and smiled. "Morning."

"I'm sorry he woke you," Lucius said. "I planned to feed and change him, but thought I had time to make a quick phone call first."

"No problem. I found the list of safe foods for him on the refrigerator and took it from there."

"It's a system Keesha and I worked out."

"Smart."

Angie wore one of his T-shirts and a pair of sweat shorts he used for workouts. The black cotton tee was too big for her, the neckline slipping off one narrow shoulder. It made her appear even more delicate and feminine. Fine-boned and fragile. Someone to protect the way he needed to protect Mikey. She hadn't taken time to brush her hair and the tousled curls tumbled down her back. She shoved absently at them, hooking the strands behind her ears, not realizing she'd smeared a bit of cereal and banana on her cheek.

Lucius steeled himself against a sight that impacted in

the region of a heart he'd thought long dead. Steeled himself against the craving to take. To hold. To safeguard.

"Why did you agree to marry me?" he asked abruptly.

Eight

For a split second Lucius caught a glimmer of panic in Angie's expressive eyes.

Then she laughed. "Pity."

He struggled to process the word. *"What?"*

"Yup, it's true." She turned back to Mikey. "I was overwhelmed with pity. Poor you. Couldn't even buy yourself a wife. Thank goodness I felt sorry for you or you'd still be trolling for a bride."

"You're marrying me because you *pity* me?"

She released a sigh. Standing, she cleared away Mikey's breakfast. After rinsing the washcloth she'd used to wipe his face, she returned and gave him a gentle scrubbing, one that had him crowing in vehement protest. She released him from his high chair, swept him up and dumped him into Lucius's arms.

"Why don't you get him ready to go outside while I shower? I'd like to swing by my house and change, pick up some clothes to stash over here before we shop for an engagement ring." She waggled her left hand at him. "You do remember you were going to stick a rock on my finger, don't you? And it better be an impressive one. I have a reputation to uphold as Mrs. Lucius Devlin. Because, apparently, not only do I pity you, I'm greedy as hell."

With that, she turned on her heel and presented him with her pert backside showcased by his sagging, oversize sweat shorts. He couldn't help grinning. "She gets high marks for the exit line," he informed Mikey. "Afraid we'll have to deduct points for the shorts, though if she twitched those hips any more she wouldn't have a pair of shorts to worry about."

Then it occurred to him that she hadn't answered his question, which caused him to wonder. Damn it all, why *had* Angie Colter agreed to marry him?

The day sped by. After filling the trunk of his BMW with Angie's possessions, they returned to Seattle's jewelry district to shop for a ring. After the fifth store and an odd reluctance on Angie's part to settle on one, he tugged her into his arms with a growl of exasperation.

"Try showing more greed and less pity," he ordered, drawing her up for a swift, thorough kiss.

She gave herself up to the unexpected embrace without the least hesitation or reticence. He couldn't explain it. How had they gone from a polite working relationship to one so sexually charged that even in the middle of a busy Seattle sidewalk he couldn't keep his hands off her? It didn't make the least sense. He was marrying her for Mikey's sake. Because she was the perfect, most logical choice for a temporary mate. She was intelligent. Gorgeous. Sensible. Sexy as hell. And he wanted her more than he'd ever wanted any other woman.

The intensity of his feelings were dangerous, he acknowledged, and he'd better find a way of throttling back—and fast—or he'd find himself in deep, deep water with no land in sight. He deliberately released her and stepped back. She continued to stand with her eyes closed, swaying for a moment before her lashes fluttered and she looked at him, dazed. It was almost too much to resist. Almost.

"What was that for?" she asked, pressing her fingertips to her swollen mouth.

He had no idea. None. "A reminder," he improvised.

"Okay. Um… What was I supposed to remember again?"

"To pick a damn ring. Make it snappy, Colter. You've always been a reasonable, decisive woman. What is it about an engagement ring that's had you go all…all female on me?"

She lifted an eyebrow, the passion draining from her eyes, replaced with a crisp, cool look of displeasure. "I *am* female, in case you haven't noticed."

"Oh, I noticed," he murmured. That was the problem. He spent entirely too much time noticing.

Her eyes only narrowed, the comment not helping his cause any. "When I see the ring I like, trust me, Lucius Devlin. Your credit card will go from subzero to blazing hot in one fast swipe."

If she hadn't opened the door to the next jewelry store, and stalked inside, he'd probably have kissed her again. He didn't know another human being alive who faced him down with such ease and with such a wicked edge to her tongue. Who would have guessed he'd appreciate that particular quality in a woman? Lisa had always attempted to get her way through wiles. Other women through sex. Still others, with tears. But not Angie. He always knew right where he stood with her. Unfortunately, right now he stood square in the middle of the proverbial doghouse.

He jostled Mikey's stroller through the door and lifted an eyebrow. Did she realize she'd just walked into the Seattle branch of Dantes? He doubted she had any idea what a Dantes original wedding ring cost or she'd have walked by. Hell, she'd have sprinted past. He found her examining a display case, a salesman standing at a discreet distance, ready to assist if needed.

"See anything you like?"

"I'm looking," she said, the words having enough bite that the salesman's eyes widened.

Lucius attempted to look suitably henpecked. "Yes, dear," he murmured. "I'll just take care of the baby while you make up your mind."

Her head jerked up at that and she swiveled, spearing him with a look. Then her anger dissolved and she burst out laughing, utterly confusing the clerk. "See that you do," she ordered with impressive arrogance, falling into the character she'd been assigned. She switched her attention to the display case and pointed. "I'd like to see this one, please."

Lucius came up beside her. "Don't be so polite," he whispered in her ear. "You'll spoil his image of you."

She turned her head, her lips zeroing in on the side of his face in response. Time slowed and he heard the soft give and take of her breath. Inhaled the light fragrance that was so uniquely hers. Felt the faintest brush of her smooth, silken cheek against his more abrasive one. She said something in return. Something that took forever to slip from ear to brain for analysis and interpretation.

"Right back at you, ace. Henpecked husbands-to-be are required to stand a full pace behind their Bridezillas."

She looked at the ring the salesman removed from the

locked display and shook her head. "Close, but not quite what I'm looking for," she confessed. "I don't suppose you have any more by this designer?"

Lucius took a quick look at the ring. Beautiful, of course, considering it was one of Dantes, but definitely not right for Angie. Time to drop the subservient act. He removed a business card and handed it to the salesman. "We'd like to see what you have in the Dantes Exclusive line," Lucius instructed crisply.

The salesman took his card, glanced at the name and stiffened. "Yes, sir, Mr. Devlin. Right away, sir. Mr. Arroya will see to you personally. He's the manager. If you'll just give me a minute to arrange for a showing?"

"We'll wait."

Angie watched the byplay with a small smile of bemusement. "No more role-playing?" she asked.

"No more role-playing," he confirmed. "Tell me what you didn't like about the ring."

"It was elegant, but a little too flowery." She gave an uneasy shrug. "It's probably close, though. Maybe we should go ahead and take this one."

"It's one of the wedding lines created by Francesca Dante, aimed for the average consumer. I think you'll find some of her exclusive collections more to your liking. I should have thought about coming here first."

Angie stirred uneasily. "Exclusive collections?" she repeated. "That sounds pricey. The ring I chose is close enough. I don't mind—"

He cut her off without hesitation. "I do mind." He softened his words by linking their hands. "Your instincts are right on, Angie. You need something elegant, but stunning. Something that makes a statement, and yet suits your personality. People will judge your worth, as well as your value to me, by the ring you choose."

He'd shocked her. "That's horrible."

"I agree, but it's life. Trust me on this."

The salesman returned and escorted them to a sweeping staircase. Lucius removed Mikey from his stroller, while Angie slung the diaper bag over her shoulder with the sort of loving panache that would have befitted a Fendi handbag. Once upstairs, they were shown into a private room with a view of the city.

The room, accented with a wealth of plants and gorgeous fresh flower arrangements, featured a plush, ankle-deep carpet in a pearl gray, giving the impression of luxury combined with warmth. They were shown to a sitting area that consisted of a love seat covered in a discreet pinstripe of gray and white, accented with narrow bands of black, and silk chairs in a rich ruby red. A glass table fronted the love seat and chairs, positioned slightly higher than a conventional coffee table. Overhead spots creating brilliant puddles of light, focused on the table in order to showcase the merchandise.

"I informed Mr. Arroya that the lady finds our Francesca designs most appealing," the salesman explained to Lucius. "He's selecting a few of her pieces with that in mind. In the meantime, may I offer you refreshments? Wine? Champagne?"

"Champagne sounds perfect," Lucius replied, positioning Mikey so he couldn't grab at anything harmful. Not that he need worry. Mikey simply stared at his surroundings, occasionally offering a babbling commentary in a serious tone, one Lucius answered in an equally serious tone.

The salesman returned almost immediately with a silver tray service that included a selection of hard cheeses, a dish of berries and even a small plate of sushi. He opened the champagne, poured. Then indicated the accompanying food. "Shall I serve you or would you prefer some privacy?"

Lucius inclined his head. "We're good, thanks."

The instant he left, Angie turned dazed eyes in Lucius's direction. "Okay, wow."

He handed her a flute. "Get used to it, at least when we're out in public. In private, I prefer leading a far simpler lifestyle."

She helped herself to some cheese, nibbling in what he took to be a nervous manner. "I hadn't thought... Didn't anticipate—"

"You've been part of my life for eighteen months, Angie. You've seen this side of things."

"To a minor extent, yes." She closed her eyes and confessed, "I'm feeling a bit out of my depth."

"You'll get used to it."

She impressed him by nodding, straightening in her seat and taking a deep, calming breath. "Okay, I can handle this." She studied the tray. "Would you like something to eat? The fruit mixture looks incredible."

"Are there currants in there?"

"Yes, and color me impressed that you even know what a currant looks like."

"No choice but to learn. Either that or make sure I carry around a supply of antihistamines."

She regarded him in surprise. "You're allergic to gooseberries? How could I have worked for you for so long and not known that?"

"It's a mystery. I thought you knew everything."

She offered a casual shrug. "I do now. I assume you're not allergic to sushi and cheese?"

He took the plate she offered. "That I can handle."

Tomas Arroya joined them just then, accompanied by an assistant. They exchanged the requisite amount of small

talk before getting down to business. He had to give Angie
credit. Even though this world was miles out of her realm,
she handled it with a quiet poise that impressed the hell
out of him.

She took her time examining the rings on display. He
was probably the only one to catch the slight hitch in her
voice and uncontrollable tremor of her hand when he
slipped each ring on her finger. He could also tell that
none of the choices was quite right, and sensed she teetered on the verge of choosing one, any one, just to be done
with it. Mr. Arroya proved equally astute.

"These all look lovely on you, Ms. Colter," he said
gently. "But none suit the way Francesca would insist they
must."

"Oh, but—" Angie started to say.

Arroya simply shook his head. "No, no. They won't
do. Tonya, bring me Utter Perfection." He patted Angie's
hand. "I think this next one may work. It wasn't designed
as an engagement ring, but as part of a set. Even so, I suspect it might be right for you."

Tonya returned with a large velvet box. Tomas gestured toward Lucius and the assistant offered him the box.
Fire diamonds shimmered beneath the light, exploding
in shards of flame in a manner unique to the stones. The
pieces were utterly exquisite—a necklace, bracelet, earrings and ring. The sheer simplicity of them would have
caused most women to pass over the set in favor of something more ostentatious. But the instant he saw it, he knew
it was not only Utter Perfection, but utterly perfect for
Angie.

Lucius removed the ring from the case and took Angie's
hand in his. Sliding the narrow band of white gold onto
her finger, he nodded. "This is the one. We'll take them."

He shot Arroya a look, one that had the manager's eyebrows shooting skyward and had him nodding in instant understanding. Angie remained oblivious to the byplay, one hundred percent of her focus on the ring he'd selected.

"It's…it's the most beautiful ring I've ever seen," she murmured.

And it was. The ring had a curving flow of small, perfect fire diamonds that seemed to float across her finger, like a trail of stars across the night sky. On one side of the pathway of diamonds was a huge, stunning solitaire, set slightly off center. Balancing it on the opposite side was a brilliant sapphire, the two stones like a pair of dancers, twisting around each other across the cosmos, their passage marked by the trail of diamond stars.

It was as unique and individual as the woman on whose finger he'd placed the ring. Even Mikey appeared riveted by the brilliant sparkle, babbling his excited approval. "I couldn't agree more," Lucius said and lifted Angie's hand. He kissed her fingertips, then her mouth. A hint of tears flavored the kiss, revealing one more intriguing facet of her personality. He had a feeling the next few years would prove fascinating as he worked his way through all the interesting layers that comprised the woman soon to become his wife.

"Thank you, Lucius," she said. "It's the most gorgeous ring I've ever seen. Perfect, of course. Utter perfection." She laughed through her tears and held out her hand to admire the flash and burn. Where before there'd been the slightest of tremors, now they visibly trembled.

Lucius's gaze shifted from the ring to the confused delight reflected in Angie's expression. He didn't think he'd ever been with a woman quite so open in her attitude and responses. It pleased him. It more than pleased him. And he was glad they'd taken the time to find the perfect ring.

The perfect ring for the perfect woman, came the way-ward thought.

"You're quite welcome, sweetheart. Here…"

He handed Mikey to her while he arranged for payment. She took the baby into her arms and hugged him close while he followed the manager to another room where the business end of the transaction could be completed. The sale was accomplished as discreetly as everything else. Fortunately, the ring didn't require sizing, so Angie could wear it home. He arranged to have the rest of the set mes-sengered to him the next week since he preferred not to walk out the door carrying jewelry that cost the equiva-lent of a medium-size South Pacific island. Maybe even a small European country.

He rejoined Angie a short time later, and found her leaning against the back of the love seat with her eyes closed. Her left hand cradled Mikey's head, her fingers sinking into the short, dark curls and gently stroking. For some reason, seeing his ring on her finger, the baby he'd taken as his own held tight within the warmth of her em-brace, stirred a deep, relentless craving to make the pic-ture she created more than just a business contract.

He felt the image of her and Mikey imprint itself on his mind and on what remained of his heart. And he wanted. Wanted to have the life that image promised. Wanted it to be real. Wanted it to last forever. He backed away, forcing himself to reject a temptation he didn't dare surrender to.

He'd made a promise to her—that he wouldn't force her into an emotional relationship, and he was honor bound to keep that promise. Besides, he wasn't after an emotional involvement any more than she was. Opening himself up, meant trusting. And trusting meant eventual pain and dis-illusionment. Better to remain above all that, to avoid the bitter fall that would inevitably come if he were foolish enough to succumb to the fantasy.

Deliberately, he turned his back on possibility. "We're done here," he announced.

And that said it all.

He'd been quiet. Far too quiet for Angie's peace of mind.

She glanced up from her book and studied Lucius. He sat on the opposite end of the couch, papers piled around him, Mikey on his lap. It never ceased to amaze her how at ease he was with his parental duties. And yet...

She sensed something, something that worried at the edges of her mind. She'd noticed it on several occasions and tried to call them to mind in the hopes of finding the connecting thread that ran through whatever it was that bothered her. The first time had been before he'd offered her the job of "wife," though not long before, three months after accepting guardianship of Mikey. They'd just finished up work for the day and Keesha had dropped off the baby. As always, the baby greeted Lucius with a huge grin, reaching eagerly for the man he'd someday call "Dad."

And Lucius had grinned back, actually crossing to the sitting area to give Mikey some one-on-one attention. She stood in the doorway to his office, resting her shoulder against the doorjamb while she watched, unnoticed. Since he'd inherited Mikey, she'd discovered that they had a little routine. First, Lucius would tickle Mikey's belly which elicited gales of gurgling laughter. Then he'd play a quick game of peekaboo. And finally, he'd do something that caused an aching tightness to grip her throat. He'd count fingers and toes, as though reassuring himself everything was still safe and sound and accounted for.

This time was no different, except when he started to

pull off Mikey's tiny Seahawk football socks, he stopped and shook his head. And she could see, bit by bit, the way he closed down. Briskly, he checked Mikey's diaper, handed him his favorite rattle and slipped him into his bouncy chair, one guaranteed to keep a baby entertained by playing a dozen different songs and featuring an overhead mobile of various farm animals. It even—heaven help her—vibrated.

The second time had been tonight at dinnertime. He'd taken Mikey into the kitchen to feed him and she'd been highly amused by the noises emanating from that direction. Sounds of planes, trains and cars. Baby giggles. Mealtime was clearly bonding time for the two boys.

And yet, after several moments the tenor had changed and when she entered the kitchen under the pretext of fixing coffee, she discovered it had become all business. Lucius sat with a cool, remote expression on his face, making steady inroads into shoveling food from plate to mouth, while Mikey watched with huge, painfully serious dark eyes.

Angie turned a page in the book she was pretending to read and continued to surreptitiously study the two men her life now revolved around. Where before Lucius had been playing with Mikey, now he studied a contract. She wouldn't have thought anything of it if she hadn't happened to glance up at the exact moment Lucius had transitioned from play to business. And then it hit her.

It was as though he'd caught himself doing something he shouldn't. He'd gone from unselfconscious pleasure to abrupt awareness in the blink of an eye. And in that split second of time he'd barricaded himself off, distancing himself not only from his actions, but from whatever emotions he experienced while interacting with Mikey.

Why? Why would he do that?

He'd also barricaded himself off from her, she suddenly realized. It was after he'd paid for the ring. Up until then, he'd been involved. Engaged. Connected and connecting. She'd assumed the abrupt withdrawal had been the result of the ring costing more than he'd wanted to spend. But now she couldn't help wondering if there weren't another reason altogether.

Maybe he'd allowed himself to become emotionally compromised. Maybe he'd allowed himself, for one short moment, to believe their engagement was real. She couldn't help but wonder if on some level he possessed a sort of internal warning sensor, one that went off whenever he became too personally involved—even if that involvement was with a small, helpless baby.

Even if that involvement was with the woman he intended to marry.

Not that it changed anything. She'd seen the true heart of the man and sensed the depths of emotion he worked so hard to deny. It was because he possessed those depths that he built walls to protect himself, locked himself safely away so he didn't have to feel. Didn't have to suffer the pain of loss or disillusionment.

She had a choice. She could allow him to continue to cement barriers in place until he became so swift and experienced at the process that she'd never find a way to break through. Or she could start undermining those barriers right here and now.

She made her choice even before the options were fully considered. Tossing aside her book, she crossed to where he sat and picked up the sleeping baby. In no time she had Mikey changed and tucked into bed. Then she returned to the living room and turned out the lights, just as Lucius had done the night before. And there, caught within the soft city glow and glitter, she slowly, tantalizingly removed her clothing, piece by piece.

Once again, she couldn't see his expression. But she heard the tenor of his breathing change. Heard it deepen, thicken, grow heavy with desire. And she smiled. When had it happened? When had she lost her nervous dread, her insecurity about satisfying a man? She stood before him wearing only a tiny scrap of silk and lace clinging to her hips and reveled in her femininity, knowing that Lucius wanted her above all women. Not just for her body, though he'd left her in no doubt how he felt about that. But for her intellect, for her personality. And soon, if she had any say in the matter, for her heart.

"Finish it," he practically growled.

She laughed, the sound soft and low. Ripe. Womanly. She skated her hands down her hips and shimmied free of the last of her clothing. And then she stood before him wearing nothing but the ring he'd placed on her finger, the flash a beacon calling him home. She traced her hand across the slight curves of her breasts, allowing the diamond's fire to beckon. Traced her hand downward over her belly to the shadowed valley between her thighs where the fire became a flame.

With a muttered oath, he shot from the couch and caught her in his arms, tumbling her to the thick carpet at their feet. They fought through his clothing, his hands and hers colliding. Tearing. Ripping. Desperate to feel flesh against flesh. And when they were both stripped bare, open and vulnerable, one to the other, they came together.

"No more walls between us," she demanded. "No hiding. No barriers. Just the two of us, allowing the other in."

He shook his head. "It's not what you want." He nuzzled her breast, captured her nipple between his teeth and gently tugged. "Not what either of us wants. We're too damaged to open ourselves like that again."

She shuddered beneath the delicate touch. "How can you say that when this is what happens whenever we make love?" The words hung within the softness of the night, powerful and bright against the darkness. "It *is* what I want. What you want. What we both want from each other. To try again. To feel again. Admit it."

His fingers danced low, sliding into the source of her heat and making her moan in longing. "You're not Lisa...I get that. You're not like any other woman I've known. But I lost the capacity to feel long ago."

How could he say that? He tried to be that dispassionate man, no question. But he was so much more. She'd seen it. Sensed it. "Are we going to live like strangers for the next half-dozen years? Opening ourselves physically, but nothing more? Is that what you want for yourself? For Mikey?" She trailed her hands across the dips and ridges of his abs, following the crisp curls that guided her downward. He was hard and slick, the epitome of masculine strength and virility. She circled his length, guiding him to her heat. "Or do you want everything, everything I have to give?"

Lucius shook his head. "I can't give what I don't have," he claimed.

And yet... And yet she felt the slip. The reluctant easing. The subtle collapse of barriers shifting and trembling. It wasn't a surrender. But it was a start. They had time. Endless time to transition from a place of hurt and suspicion to trust and certainty.

She lifted her hips, took him in, crying out at the sheer perfection of fit and rhythm. "Lucius!" His name became both prayer and demand.

He took her mouth in an endless kiss, then pulled back

ever so slightly. "Look at me. I want you with me on this ride."

Their gazes met, clung. And what she saw there gave her hope. A spark. Just a spark of it, but it was enough. She let go, gave herself up to the heat and fire that burst into life whenever they came together. The flame became an inferno, unstoppable in its power. Branding them. Joining them. Binding them, one to the other—the fit, utter perfection.

Possibilities. He'd stopped believing in possibilities so very long ago.

Lucius gathered Angie up in his arms and carried her to their bedroom. *Theirs.* He shook his head, amused by the speed with which he'd transitioned from "his" to "theirs." And he could pinpoint precisely when it had all changed. It had stopped being his bedroom the first night she'd shared his bed, just as he'd stopped being alone that very same night.

He'd resisted involvement. Would probably continue to resist…for now. But he could see that this time, because of this woman, his life would never be the same again.

She'd shown him a road he'd never noticed before, was utterly surprised to find it beneath his feet and himself some distance along its path. He hadn't anticipated that occurring. Would have vehemently denied the possibility of it ever happening. And yet, here he stood with a woman in his arms and a longing in his heart he hadn't felt in…

Forever.

Possibilities. For some reason his life had become filled with endless possibilities and they were all because of one woman. The woman who wore his ring on her finger. And if he had anything to say about it, it was a ring she'd continue to wear for the rest of her life.

Nine

"I realize this is bad timing, but I have a business trip to New York that I can't postpone," Lucius announced one morning over Sunday breakfast.

To his relief, Angie nodded, not revealing any hint of concern that she'd be left in charge of Mikey and the home front. She poured herself a cup of tea and took a seat beside him. "The Tobias project, I assume?"

"It's reached a crucial point and I need to meet with the investors before moving forward with it."

She took a sip of tea and sighed in unconscious pleasure. He noticed she always did that with her first sip, made that soft, semimoan that caused him to clench his muscles in helpless want. No doubt it had something to do with the ecstatic expression that slid across her face when she drank. He recognized it as a pale reflection of how she looked when he made love to her, the resemblance just close enough to tempt him to sweep her into his arms and closet them in his bedroom for the next several hours. Maybe he'd get used to his reaction to her, to the relentless desire that filled him whenever he looked at her. Maybe he wouldn't respond to that sigh each and every morning for the rest of his life. Maybe. Though somehow he doubted it.

It had been two weeks since they'd become engaged. Two incredible weeks during which, with a fast assist from the Pretorius Program, he'd put a new PA in place, freeing Angie to slip seamlessly into her new responsibilities. Granted, the new PA wasn't Angie, but the motherly woman would do.

When it came to his home life, he couldn't quite get over how well he and Angie fit together, blended, and he'd realized a few days earlier that he no longer thought of their engagement as a position he'd hired her to fill. He couldn't say when the transition had occurred. Like everything else about Angie's advent into his life, it had been equally seamless. He simply recognized that life was different. Better.

He could even fool himself into believing their engagement had come about the way normal engagements did—with two people falling in love and deciding to link their lives through marriage. And though he wouldn't go so far as to claim they'd fallen in love, they'd certainly fallen in lust. Even more important, they enjoyed each other's company. Respected one another. There was such an amazing naturalness to their interactions, a comfortable fit to how their lives had blended. And yet they could exchange a single glance and have passion explode instantaneously between them.

He removed Mikey's breakfast dishes and dumped them in the sink before grabbing one of the neatly folded washcloths on the counter. "I also wanted to warn you that, according to my sources, the Ridgeways still plan to file for custody." He dampened the washcloth and returned to the table to apply it to Mikey's hands and face, ignoring the baby's squirming protests at his mistreatment. "I want our wedding to take place before that happens so no one can accuse us of marrying as a countermeasure."

"You have sources who have inside information regarding the Ridgeways and their lawyer?" At his bland stare, she nodded. "Okay, I guess you do. Why are they delaying?"

"They've arranged for a cardiac specialist to give Benjamin a full workup."

"So you won't have grounds to argue any possible health issues impeding their ability to raise Mikey," she surmised.

"Shrewd as always," he said with an approving nod. "That's precisely their plan."

"Okay." She lifted her shoulder in a casual shrug. "How do you want to handle the wedding?"

The level of relief Lucius experienced at her immediate understanding and willingness to fall in with his plan, caught him off guard. He'd anticipated her arguing the need to marry quite so soon, had his arguments lined up like little ducklings following the mama duck. Or in this case, the papa. He'd been determined to bend her to his will with logic and reason, and if that didn't work, with emotion. He'd even been prepared to commit the ultimate sacrifice and take her to bed and wring an agreement from her once he had her naked and helpless and vulnerable to his influence. Of course, considering those moments of ecstasy left him equally naked and helpless and vulnerable to *her* influence, put him at a small disadvantage. Not that it mattered.

Bottom line, he wanted Angie tied to him in every possible way, wrapped up in inescapable bonds, though he didn't want to look too closely at whether it was strictly for Mikey's sake or if there were another, more personal reason for the sudden rush.

"I'd prefer a small, private ceremony," he said. "Tasteful, with a few close friends and family invited." A sudden thought struck him. "You've never mentioned your parents. Will they attend?"

She shook her head. "My father walked out on my mother when I was Mikey's age. Mom died in a car accident shortly before I started working for you." Her smile held a heartbreaking stoicism. "There's just me."

"I'm so sorry, Angie."

"That's okay."

But it wasn't. He could see it wasn't. One more abandonment. One more relationship that had slipped away, never to be recovered. Could they be any more alike?

"I do have a couple of friends I'd like to include if that's acceptable," she continued. "Trinity, in particular. She's my best friend."

"Of course. Anyone you want. How about a sunset ceremony followed by a small dinner reception? Would that appeal?"

"Very much." Her smile was radiant. "Will you be inviting the Ridgeways?"

"Definitely, though I doubt they'll attend. I'm thinking engraved invitations, the Dorchester Chapel for the service, followed by a private dinner for our guests at Milano's on the Sound. Joe has a room for events like these above the main dining room."

"I'll get on that right away."

She immediately fell into PA mode, opening a kitchen drawer and rummaging around for a pen and notepad.

Lucius took them from her and tossed them aside. Then he drew her into his arms. "You're not my PA anymore."

She settled into the embrace, releasing her breath in a laughing sigh. "That's a good thing since I don't believe our antics last night fall under the heading of proper office decorum."

"Not in any office I've been in charge of." He kissed her, tasting the tea that flavored her lips. "Nor any office I haven't been in charge of."

She settled into his embrace, her trim curves growing more familiar by the day, even as they grew more tempting. "I can't begin to tell you how relieved I am to hear you say that. So, when are you thinking we should marry? I can't send out engraved invitations without a date."

"Good point." He frowned in concentration. "Let me call Joe regarding the dinner and make the arrangements with Dorchester Chapel. I think they'll both be willing to accommodate me."

She stroked her fingers along the jutting curve of his jaw, causing his blood to heat. How did she manage that with just a single touch? "They'll be accommodating because it's you?"

He laughed, the sound ironic. "No, more because of my bank account. It does come in handy at times like this. Once I have that set up, do whatever it takes short of offering sexual favors to get those invitations printed and out as quickly as possible."

She tempted him with a laughing pout. "And here I was looking forward to offering sexual favors."

He chuckled. "You can offer them to me, instead. Or maybe I should offer them to you out of sheer gratitude."

"I have to admit, I like a grateful man," she teased. "Once the venue's set, I'll take care of the rest of the details."

"Thank you, Angie." He couldn't help himself. He took her mouth in a slow, thorough kiss. He vaguely heard Mikey squeal in approval, banging his hands against his high chair tray as though in applause. "I agree, munchkin. That definitely deserved a round of applause."

As always, it took Angie a few seconds to surface and her open passion and lack of artifice never failed to humble him. She moistened her lips as though still tasting him. "You leave tomorrow, right? Monday? How long did you say you were going to be gone?"

"Five days. I'll see if I can't cut it to four. Three. Maybe I can rearrange my schedule and get back here in three."

"I'll see what I can get accomplished in the meantime." She lowered her head to his chest and held on as though it hurt to let go. "Why don't you leave me the key and directions to your Lake Washington house. I'll swing by and start working on some preliminary ideas on that front."

"Do you think you'll have enough time?"

Angie looked up at him and what he read in those soft, aquamarine eyes sent a shaft of desire spearing through him. "I need to stay busy while you're gone, Lucius. Maybe if I fill every minute I won't miss you quite as much."

He cupped her face and feathered another kiss across her mouth. "Liar."

And she was a liar, Angie readily conceded the instant he left. Guilt threatened to overwhelm her at the way she'd set herself up as the "perfect" woman for Lucius. She would have been tempted to tell him the truth except for two vital facts. First, though she might not be "perfect"— who was?—she didn't have a single doubt that she suited him right down to the bones, just as he suited her. They fit together in every possible regard, from the way they related to one another, to emotional needs, to sexual compatibility. She'd never anticipated they'd bond so well, so fast.

But they had and she refused to feel guilt over one small lie if it forced Lucius to see what had been right under his nose all along.

Second, Mikey needed a mother, someone who would love him as much as she would her own child, love him in a way the Ridgeways would never offer due to what they perceived as the "stain" on his bloodline. Though she hadn't anticipated falling head over heels for a six-month-old, she had. And if it had taken one small lie to bring the three of them together as a family unit, well… She could live with the guilt. Besides, what did it matter how she and Lucius married, if the end result not only met their expectations, but exceeded them? Wasn't that the actual intent and purpose of the Pretorius Program?

She presented those same arguments over dinner at Trinity's apartment later that night. "Yeah, it sounds all nice and logical," her friend allowed. "But I have a feeling Devlin won't take your view of things. All he's going to see is a big, fat lie and hang you with it. You know he has trust issues. This isn't going to help him get over them."

Trinity pinpointed the one detail that continued to gnaw at Angie. "I keep hoping the ends justify the means," she muttered.

"A popular defense, but historically, it's one that tends to get people hanged." Trinity swept up their dinner plates and carted them into the kitchen. "I made cobbler. You want?"

"Did you make hard sauce to go with it?"

"Of course."

"Then I want."

Trinity laughed. "Just like my granny used to make with one small exception." She set a small dish of cobbler in front of Angie. "In addition to the butter and sugar, there's also a tablespoon of whiskey."

Angie stabbed a finger at her friend. "You're evil. I never noticed that about you before, but it's true."

"More like an evil genius. Since I don't hear you rejecting the offer, even with my small addition, I'll get the hard sauce."

Angie tucked Mikey more firmly in the crook of her arm and offered him another bite of the cooked carrots she'd brought for his dinner. He scrunched up his face and shoved the spoon away. "Got it. No more carrots. Dessert time, right? Give me a minute and I'll get your applesauce."

He didn't wait. Instead, he made a grab at her cobbler. Before she could whip it aside, he snatched up a small helping and shoved it into his mouth, crowing in approval at the flavor.

"The kid's got good taste," Trinity observed, setting a small bowl of hard sauce on the table.

Angie nipped her dessert plate clear of Mikey's reach. "The kid isn't allowed cobbler. He's too little. And make sure you keep that hard sauce on your side of the table. If the Ridgeways ever found out he ate something containing alcohol they'd slap Lucius with a lawsuit so fast they'd hear the sonic boom in the Antarctic."

Trinity obediently shifted the bowl. "So, when's the wedding and do I get to help pick out the dress?"

"This is Monday... The date's been set for a week from Friday."

"Nine days!" Trinity stared, nonplussed. "How are you supposed to pull everything together in nine days?"

"Apparently, Lucius has solved that problem by throwing money at it." Angie helped herself to a bite of cobbler. "One call and the invitations that couldn't possibly be ready for two weeks were available the same day. They go into the mail first thing tomorrow morning. The flowers have been ordered. Joe Milano is taking care of the cake. It's amazing how much you can accomplish in a single day when money is no object."

"What about a tux?"

Angie made a face. "Lucius must own a half-dozen tuxes, so that won't be a problem."

"Which leaves your wedding dress."

"Which is a problem," Angie acknowledged with a sigh.

"Not for long." Trinity dropped a generous dollop of hard sauce on her cobbler and dug in. "The day after tomorrow you, me and Mikey will hit the stores and we won't give up until we find the perfect gown. I'd drag you out shopping the first thing tomorrow—"

"But Mikey has his six-month checkup on Tuesday." Angie sighed. "Why don't you torture me instead of taking me shopping? It would be less painful."

Trinity shook her head, her expression turning serious. "You only have one first marriage, Ange. If you're lucky, only one marriage, period. You want it to be a day you'll remember for the rest of your life." She polished off the last of her cobbler and waved the purple-stained fork in Angie's direction. "And that means the perfect wedding dress."

Trinity was right, of course, and Angie couldn't explain her reluctance when it came to buying a gown. Maybe it went back to the feeling she'd cheated when it came to her marriage to Lucius. That because she'd asked Jett to alter the Pretorius Program, she'd manipulated him into marrying her. After putting an unusually cranky Mikey to bed for the night, she faced the unpalatable truth.

She wanted Lucius to marry her because he loved her, not for expedience.

Angie stood at the foot of the mile-wide bed—a cold and empty bed without Lucius—and struggled not to cry.

She'd made this bed. Time to lie in it. Based on their interactions to date, chances were excellent that it would be a good bed and a good marriage. She just needed to give them both time to develop their relationship a little more. To finish the process she didn't doubt they'd already started…and fall in love. Stripping off her clothes, she crawled beneath the covers. She missed Lucius. Missed him unbearably. Tugging his pillow into her arms, she buried her face in it. A faint trace of his scent clung to the fabric. Crisp and distinctly male with the merest hint of forest cedar.

She'd just started to drift off into a lovely dream that involved Lucius and a wedding in the clouds, when the phone on the bedside table rang. She rolled over to snatch it up before the sound woke Mikey. "Hello?"

"Did I wake you?" Lucius asked, his voice dark and rich, though she could hear the exhaustion running through his words.

"It's okay. I was just drifting off." She checked the clock, made the swift calculation between West Coast time and East and frowned. "What are you doing still up? It's nearly three in the morning."

"Just going over some last minute reports before turning in. I've been trying to sew everything up early, though it's not looking too encouraging."

Disappointment flooded through her and she struggled to keep the sound of it from filtering through her voice. "When will you be back?"

"Closer to the end of the week. Thursday, if I'm lucky, but I'm not sure if I can make it."

She plumped the pillows behind her and relaxed against them. "Where are you?" she asked.

His soft, knowing chuckle had her toes curling and sent shivers racing down her spine. "In bed. You?"

"The same."

"Ah… Give me a second to get an image." He released a sigh she'd only heard when they were both naked and he first slipped inside her. "Yes, there it is. What are you wearing?"

"Your pillow."

He groaned. "You're killing me."

"It smells like you, not that that's much help," she confessed. "I miss you."

"I miss you, too, sweetheart. It won't be much longer, I promise."

Silence settled between them, while the want grew thick. "Lucius…" she whispered.

"Me, too." He cleared his throat. "Okay, if we don't change the subject, I'm not going to get any sleep tonight. You…you remember Mikey has a checkup tomorrow?"

She strove to divorce herself emotionally, but it was far too late for that. Longing clung to her like Lucius's scent to his pillow. "Nine o'clock," she confirmed. "It's on the calendar."

"I wanted to be there for it. I almost postponed it a week, but it would have given the Ridgeways more ammunition to use against me."

"I'll take notes during the appointment. Fortunately, I'm really good at it."

"I appreciate it. You know that, don't you?"

"I do know." A plaintive cry came through the baby monitor beside the phone. "I think Mikey misses you, too."

"I hear him. Anything wrong?"

"He's just a little fussy tonight. Maybe he's cutting another tooth. Or maybe he knows I'm talking to you and wants his fair share of your attention."

"I know you have to go. Give me a quick update before you do. How are the wedding plans proceeding?"

"Good. Great, in fact. I think we have everything covered except for my dress. Trinity and I will be shopping for that on Wednesday." She released a sleepy laugh. "Technically, I guess that's tomorrow since it's now Tuesday morning."

"Get something beautiful. Money's no object."

"Lucius—"

He sighed. "Just do it, Angie. It's only money."

"Okay." There was so much more she wanted to say to him. So much she didn't dare. At least, not yet. "Mikey says I have to go now. Call me tomorrow?"

"I'll try." He hesitated, the words they both longed to speak hovering between them, hanging in the airwaves across the three thousand miles separating them. "Give our boy a hug from his… Aw, hell, from me. Good night, sweetheart."

"Good night, Lucius."

He couldn't say it, Angie realized. He still couldn't say the words he longed to. *Give our boy a hug from his daddy.* That's what he'd meant, what was in his heart. She could only hope that he'd soon be able to say them aloud putting words to the emotions he still denied.

She crossed to Mikey's bedroom and lifted him out of the crib. "Daddy says good-night, little guy. Is that why you're fussing? Because he wasn't here to tell you in person?"

Flipping on the overhead light, she carried him to the changing table. He blinked through his tears, his crying jag leaving his face red and blotchy. Or she assumed it was from the crying jag until she unsnapped his sleeper and saw that his face wasn't the only part of him all red and blotchy. Panicky fear swept through her. Something was wrong. Seriously wrong.

Scooping him up, she made a beeline for the kitchen

and the doctor's emergency number listed on the sheet taped to the refrigerator. She punched in the number, filled with relief when her call received an immediate answer, even though it was an answering service. The operator reassured her in a calm, soothing manner, promising the doctor would phone back within a minute or two. Sure enough, she'd no sooner hung up than the phone rang again.

"This is Dr. Graceland. Describe the symptoms," the pediatrician requested briskly. He listened, then asked, "Is Mikey having difficulty breathing?"

"No, not that I've noticed."

"Do you have a liquid antihistamine on hand, preferably dye-free?"

Holding the phone to her ear with her shoulder, she hurried to the medicine cabinet in the bathroom, found an unopened box and scanned the information. "Yes. Yes, I have it and it says it's dye-free."

After verifying age and weight, the doctor said, "Give the baby one quarter teaspoon. Wait half an hour and call me if there's no improvement. In the meantime, try a cool bath in case it's a reaction to something he's come into contact with physically, like pet hair or a new detergent. And make a list of everything he's eaten the past twenty-four hours."

"There's nothing he hasn't tried before," she started to say. Then remembered Mikey's grab for her cobbler. "Wait. He managed to get a handful of my cobbler at dinner."

"That's a possibility, particularly if it contained egg, dairy, nuts or wheat. Even more likely if one of his parents exhibited a similar allergy. Do you know of any allergies that run in the family?"

"I have no idea," she admitted. "Both his parents are deceased."

"Yes, of course. I remember now. Give him the antihistamine and if his symptoms don't improve, call me back and I'll meet you at the hospital. If they do improve, come into the office at eight and I'll bump you to the front of the line."

"Thank you, Dr. Graceland."

The next half hour felt like forever. A dozen different times she reached for the phone to call Lucius, each time resisting the urge. There wasn't anything he could do to help except worry. And he had enough to worry about without this. Besides, she could see an almost immediate improvement as soon as she administered the medication. It would have been a different story if she'd needed to rush the baby to the hospital.

It wasn't until she'd finished bathing and redressing Mikey that another thought occurred, one that shocked her to the core. This time she did snatch up the phone.

"Wha—?"

"Trinity, it's Angie."

"Wha—?"

"Look, I'm sorry it's so late, but it's important. Tell me what was in the cobbler we ate tonight."

Trinity groaned. "Are you kidding me? Do you have any idea what time I have to get up in the morning to go to work? You woke me because you couldn't wait a few more hours to get my recipe for cobbler?"

"No, I woke you because Mikey may have had an allergic reaction to your cobbler. What was in it?"

"Oh, hell." Her friend suddenly sounded more alert. "Okay, okay. Ingredients for cobbler. Um, sugar, blueberries, raspberries—"

"Currants? Did you use currants?"

Trinity gave a quick laugh of surprise. "As a matter of fact…"

"Thanks, that's all I needed to know."

"Wait, what—"

"I'll explain later. Go back to sleep."

Angie hung up without waiting for a response. Currants. If that turned out to be the cause of the allergic reaction, and the allergy ran in the family… Was it possible? Could Lucius actually be Mikey's father? She fought to think it through logically, to try and figure out her next step. If the two were father and son, how did she prove it? Another DNA test, obviously. But that would involve informing Lucius of her suspicions. She hated getting his hopes up only to have them dashed if she was wrong.

So, how did she work around that minor detail? Whenever faced with a new situation she didn't understand, she gathered facts. Researched. That was easy enough. She carried the baby to the computer and booted it up, then ran a fast search on DNA testing. To her relief, Mikey nodded off in her arms, the hives fading with each minute that ticked by.

"Well, look at that," she murmured. "I had no idea it was so easy. Or that you could do a home paternity test. Best of all, I can get the results by the time Lucius returns on Friday."

The website provided a long list of items from which they could extract DNA, examples of which she could find around the apartment without involving Lucius directly. She just had to pick one, send it in and wait for the results. And if the test results confirmed he fathered Mikey? She leaned back in the chair and cuddled the baby close. It would mean that Lisa had somehow falsified the results of Mikey's paternity test. Another thought struck. If she was right, Lucius wouldn't need her any longer because the Ridgeways would no longer have a viable claim on Mikey.

"Damn," she whispered. "What do I do now?"

There wasn't really any question about what she'd do. She'd let Lucius off the marital hook by ending their engagement gracefully and without complaint. Tears filled her eyes. Maybe, just maybe he wouldn't want to be let off the hook. Maybe he'd demand she stick to the agreement they'd made because he… She buried her head against Mikey's curls. Because he *what*? Because he wanted to be married to her? Because he *loved* her?

Foolish, foolish girl. Lucius had been up-front about what he wanted from the beginning. He'd offered marriage in order to ensure he retained guardianship of Mikey. Sure, he enjoyed the fringe benefits of their relationship. The companionship. The sex. A wife to take care of all the little wifely duties. But not once had he said anything about love. In fact, he'd gone out of his way to tell her he didn't think himself capable of that particular emotion. Was it his fault that she'd fallen head over heels for him?

She swept the back of her hand across her damp cheeks. Enough. She didn't even know if Lucius was Mikey's father. Once she'd settled that issue, she'd worry about the next step. In the meantime, she'd keep a close watch on Mikey in case he suffered a relapse from the allergen he'd come into contact with. And on Wednesday she'd choose a wedding gown, even knowing she may never wear it. She sighed.

Better make it returnable.

He didn't think Friday would ever arrive or that his meetings would ever come to an end. He boarded his private jet by noon, delighted he'd soon surprise Angie with an early arrival. He'd made a startling discovery during his five days in New York, one he'd tried for weeks to deny, but no longer could.

He'd fallen utterly, hopelessly, completely in love. And it wasn't with just one person, but two. His feelings for Mikey had been steadily growing, bit by bit, over the past three months until he had no choice but to concede that he flat-out loved the baby, had even come to regard Mikey as his own son. But his feelings for Angie hadn't crept up on him. They'd hit him with all the power and fury of a Cat 5 hurricane, flinging him into the midst of an inescapable storm of emotion.

He'd discovered something else during his trip to New York. He didn't just want Angie for the sake of his son—and Mikey was as much his son as Geoff had been his brother, Lucius now admitted. No, he wanted her in his life…for himself. A permanent part of that life. And the minute he saw her again, he intended to tell her so.

The only remaining question was… Could he convince Angie to change her mind, too? Could he convince her to give their marriage a chance, a real chance? To accept the ring on her finger as a sincere promise of intent, and the wedding they'd organized as the start of a true marriage.

His cell phone rang while they were waiting for permission for takeoff and he checked the caller ID. Pretorius St. John. Flipping open the phone, Lucius greeted the programmer. "How's it going, Pretorius?"

"To be honest? Not good."

"I'm sorry to hear that. How can I help?"

"It's not how you can help me. It's how I can help you." Pretorius sighed. "Listen, there's something you need to know about your 'perfect' wife-to-be. Unfortunately, it involves my former assistant, Jett."

Ten

Angie stood in front of the mirror and ran a trembling hand across the skirt of her wedding gown. She didn't think she'd ever seen anything more stunning in her life. It made her look…amazing. Beautiful. Elegant. Like some sort of storybook princess.

The pale ivory gown possessed an Empire waist and squared-off bodice, studded with Swarovski crystals and a skirt that fell in a straight column, the material so light and airy that it made her appear as though she were floating. Even with a flowing train, she found she could move without any problem.

She'd been experimenting with her hair to see what style best suited the classic lines of the gown, the decision easily made the second she'd pinned her curls into a loose knot on top of her head, allowing little tendrils to drift about her neck and temples.

"All you need is a tiara," came a voice from behind her.

Angie spun around with a gasp. "Lucius!"

"Surprise, surprise."

Why, oh why, had he chosen this particular moment to return? Fifteen minutes earlier and she wouldn't have yet donned the gown. Fifteen minutes later and she'd have finished trying it on and it would be safely tucked away in the closet. "You aren't supposed to see me in my wedding gown before the ceremony."

A small smile played at the corners of his mouth, one that caused a tremor of unease to shoot through her. "In our case, I don't think that's an issue," he said, the extreme gentleness of his tone causing her nervousness to increase. She knew that tone. It was a bad tone. A dangerous tone. One he used when he was about to take down one of his competitors.

Then his comment sank in. Seeing her in her wedding gown wasn't an issue for them because they weren't marrying for normal reasons, such as love. Perhaps that explained the tone. Why did she keep forgetting their marriage wasn't a real one, especially when she doubted the marriage would even take place? Ever since receiving the results from the DNA test this morning, results which proved with 99.99% certainty that Lucius was Mikey's father, she'd accepted the strong likelihood that next week's wedding ceremony would be the first casualty.

Angie had no idea how Lisa had manipulated the results in the first place. Perhaps she'd faked the test from the get-go, hiring actors to play the part of technicians. Or perhaps she'd paid one of the technicians to falsify the results at whatever lab they'd used. Or maybe it was a simple clerical error, the lab accidentally switching samples by mistake. All that mattered was that Lucius now had enough probable cause to have another test done, one that would hold up in a court of law.

Which meant…he wouldn't need to marry.

Which meant…she stood before him in a wedding gown she'd never use, at least not for its intended purpose.

Oh, what did it matter? "You're right, of course. It's not an issue for us." Angie started toward Lucius, her hands held out, a smile of sheer delight spilling free. "I'm so glad you're home early."

"Are you? Are you really?"

The barely audible questions contained an unmistakable bite and dismay swamped her, checking her forward momentum. She hesitated in the middle of the room, filled with uncertainty. Her arms slowly fell to her sides. What in the world was going on? "I…I should change," she murmured. Because whatever was wrong, she'd rather not deal with it while wearing a wedding gown.

"Don't. I think I'd prefer having this conversation with you dressed just as you are."

She stilled. Something was off, seriously off. She'd suspected it when he first spoke. Now she didn't have a single doubt. "Lucius? What's going on?"

"An excellent question. Perhaps you could answer it for me."

She shook her head, feeling the curls around her neck dance in agitation. "I don't understand. Is something wrong?"

"Yes, Angie. Something is wrong. Something is very wrong." He approached. Circled. "I don't think I've ever seen you look more beautiful. Not at all like office furniture. You've certainly come up in the world this past month."

Her chest felt as though it were squeezed in a vise, and her breath came swift and shallow in response. Every instinct she possessed compelled her to run. Instead, she could only stand, frozen in place, while he circled, circled,

circled. She caught a brief glimpse of herself in the mirror, saw the crystal beads fracture beneath the overhead light, shooting shards of desperate color into the room and realized it was because she was trembling.

"That should sound like a compliment." She moistened her lips. "Why doesn't it sound like a compliment, Lucius?"

"Do you know, I never saw it coming. I really have to applaud you. I'm not easily fooled, but I must say you played your part exceptionally well. Better even than Lisa."

Oh, God, he knew. Somehow he'd found out that she and Jett manipulated the Pretorius Program. "Lucius, I can explain—"

He stopped his endless circling, pausing in front of her, and what she read in his face eviscerated her. She'd never seen such ruthless intent. Instead of fury, as she would have expected, she saw that he'd encased himself in ice, staring at her from eyes so cold and remote and deadly she didn't have a chance in hell of ever getting through to him. That didn't change the fact that she needed to try.

Before she could begin an explanation, he spoke again. "Seriously, Angie. I'm impressed. I really am. I've worked with you on a daily basis for eighteen months. And not once, not one single time, did you deviate from your role. That's truly an amazing feat. Very difficult to sustain, long-term. And I must say that choosing suits to match my office furniture was probably the coup de grâce. A stroke of brilliance. It was the final detail that sold the entire scam." He slowly clapped his hands. If the sound of clapping could be described as sarcastic, he'd perfected a sarcastic clap. "Brava, Angie."

"You know about the Pretorius Program."

He smiled in genuine amusement. "Why, yes. I do know."

She swallowed past the thickness clogging her throat. "How…?"

"Pretorius discovered Jett tampered with the results. As soon as he put it together, he called me." He folded his arms across his chest, stretching the fabric of his black suit across the impressive width of his shoulders, underscoring the sheer physical strength and power of the man. "I'm curious… I assume when you accepted the position of PA you hoped the job would eventually transition into that of my wife. How would you have attempted to trick me into marriage if I hadn't been foolish enough to offer you the perfect opportunity with the Pretorius Program?"

She couldn't control the soft laugh that bubbled free at the bizarre turn the conversation had taken. "Oh, gosh, let me count the ways. Maybe I'd have done a striptease on your desk. Gotten accidentally pregnant. Found some deep, dark secret hidden away in your files and blackmailed you into marriage. I'm sure I would have come up with something."

"None of those things would have worked. Not on me."

She blinked. Good grief, he actually believed her. "Well, damn, Lucius. Now I'm really disappointed, because God knows marrying you just has to be the ultimate goal of every woman in Seattle. Maybe in the entire Northwest." She snapped her fingers. "Maybe even in the whole of the good ol' U.S. of A."

"You think this is funny?"

His voice flicked like a lash, cutting painfully, and she flinched. "Not even a little. Explain something, Lucius. Why are you so angry? I thought you wanted a wife. What difference does it make how you got one if she fulfills your requirements?"

"But you don't fulfill my requirements. You lied about your abilities. Pretorius discovered that, as well."

She released a sigh. "True enough. I did lie. Though if you don't mind my saying, they were ridiculous requirements."

"That's not for you to decide!"

"Oh, right." She planted her hands on her hips, her anger rising to meet his, exceeding it. "And we both know how well those requirements were working before I agreed to marry you, don't we? How many women did you go through, Lucius? How many of them told you to go to hell like Ella? Do you think you'd have found someone else by now, your *perfect* wife, if I hadn't stepped in?"

"How the hell do I know? Maybe she would have been the next name on the list."

"And maybe she doesn't exist." Angie ticked off on her fingers. "A gourmet cook. A superb housekeeper. An excellent interior designer. A mother. A wife with fringe benefits. Come on. Are you kidding me?"

A hint of color swept across the arch of his cheekbones. "Those aren't unreasonable requirements."

She swept them aside with a wave of her hand. "They're ridiculous requirements. The only important ones, the only ones you should have been focused on were acquiring a wife who would love and care for Mikey and who would—" She broke off, her throat closing over, preventing her from finishing her statement. She stood in front of him, utterly exposed, aware he'd have no problem deducing the rest of her comment. ...*and who would love and care for you.*

He shook his head, fury melting through the ice and burning across his expression. "Don't. Don't try and turn this into some sort of grand romance. What we shared was purely physical. Sex and nothing more. Our marriage is for Mikey's sake, not for any other reason. Are we clear on that point?"

"Crystal." She tugged off the engagement ring and held it out to him.

He took her wrist in an unbreakable hold and thrust the ring back on her finger. "Our engagement doesn't end until I say it does. You will marry me, Angie. Only now you'll do it on my terms, as per our contract."

"That's where you're wrong, Lucius." She didn't attempt to pull free. She simply met his gaze head-on, refusing to back down. "The gown is returnable. I haven't mailed out the invitations. Both the floral shop and Joe Milano have been called and instructed to put the flowers and reception dinner on hold. The Dorchester Chapel is also on hold pending your phone call to either move forward with the ceremony or cancel."

He stared at her a full thirty seconds, his black eyes narrowed in assessment. She could practically see him picking his way through the information, searching for the catch, struggling to evaluate what advantage canceling the wedding gave her. "You work for the Ridgeways," he finally said. "It's the only explanation. String me along, get inside information on me and then back out of our wedding right before they hit me with a lawsuit. Stand up in court and tell the judge about the Pretorius Program and my attempts to buy myself a wife. Custody of Mikey goes to the Ridgeways. End of game."

She couldn't help herself. She laughed. It was either that or burst into tears. "There are times you break my heart, Lucius."

"What other explanation could there be?"

"An excellent question. Let go of my wrist, please."

She continued to hold his gaze until he complied. And then she removed the ring for a second time. Instead of handing it to him, she crossed to his dresser and placed it dead center on the gleaming wood. The fire diamond flashed in reaction, sending out rays of hope that faded with each passing moment, along with a promise that would never be kept.

Angie glanced over her shoulder at Lucius. "Would you mind unbuttoning me? I had so much trouble getting it buttoned, it'll take me all night before I can change back into my office furniture."

Without a word, he approached. He released the column of tiny crystal buttons one by one, his fingers skimming the length of her spine. She fought to conceal her shiver of reaction, fought harder to divorce herself from the emotions clamoring for release. His warmth caressed her back and she gripped the edge of the dresser in an effort to steady herself. He swept the dress from her shoulders, baring her to the waist.

She wore a bra with barely-there cups specifically designed to work with the bodice of the dress, one that took what little she had and made it appear… Well, if not impressive, at least adequate. Based on Lucius's reaction, possibly more than adequate. Angie caught the change in his breathing, the subtle catching hitch followed by a deep, dragging inhale. Bending forward slightly, she allowed the dress to drift toward the floor to pool at her feet in a puddle of ivory silk tears.

She'd hoped—how she'd hoped—they would be married by the time Lucius saw her in the delicate undergarments. The soft bridal ivory of the scraps of silk and lace matched her gown and were held together with tiny bows that coyly promised, with one gentle tug, to bare her to his gaze. She stepped free of the gown, fully aware of how she appeared in heels, garter and stockings. Let him look, she decided. Let him get a good, long look…and regret.

Ever so gently, Angie gathered up the gown and carried it to the closet, replacing it in the protective bag the shop had provided. She continued to ignore him, removing one of her older suits from its hanger, the outfit he'd once upon a time compared to chair upholstery. She started to dress, but before she could do more than reach for the skirt, Lucius stopped her.

"Don't."

He turned her around to face him. For a split second the barriers between them fell and he swept her into his arms, his fingers forking deep into her hair, loosening the topknot. And then he consumed her. The kiss held endless passion, combined with an underlying anger and hurt. She could taste his pain, his disillusionment, and tears filled her eyes.

One last time. For this brief moment, she'd take whatever he offered. Take it and imprint it on her memory so in the painful days to come, she could slip it out and remember. Just one last time.

Her lips parted beneath his and he swept inward, taking her. Marking her. Telling her with his kiss what he didn't dare say aloud. He loved her. She didn't have a single doubt in her mind, just as she didn't have a single doubt that their love was doomed. He didn't trust. Couldn't. Not that she blamed him. She'd lied. Broken faith with him, which was the one thing he couldn't forgive.

"Why?" he demanded against her mouth, the question escaping between deep, passionate kisses. "Why would you betray me like this?"

The tears escaped despite her best efforts to control them. "It's not a betrayal. I swear it isn't."

"It can't be anything else. Not when you lied to me. Not when you pretended to be something you aren't."

Her laugh splintered on heartbreak. "I never pretended

to be anything other than I am. You were the one looking for the perfect wife. What you don't realize is you ended up with someone who's more than perfect...at least for you. Don't throw it away now."

But he was already pulling back, shaking his head. He stepped clear of her and tossed her suit into her arms. "Get dressed. Then we'll discuss where we go from here." With that, Lucius turned on his heel and left the bedroom.

Angie pulled on her clothing without a word, not bothering to change out of her wedding undergarments. Pointless now since they'd never be used for a wedding. She took a final look around, attempting to determine if there was anything too urgent to leave behind. There wasn't. Just one final stop before she left the apartment, left behind the life she'd hoped to build here.

She walked into Mikey's room and found him batting at dust motes, having just woken from his nap. "Hey, there, little guy," she greeted in a soft voice. She lifted him from his crib and cradled him close, tears clogging her throat. "You have no idea how much I'm going to miss you."

He smelled of sweet, clean baby with a hint of powder. He grabbed the loosened tendrils of her hair and tugged them toward his mouth. She untangled her hair from his chubby fist with a tearful laugh. He was so beautiful. Had managed to become such a vital part of her life. She didn't think she'd ever recover from the loss of both Mikey and Lucius, the two men she'd come to love with all her heart.

"I tried. At least I tried," she whispered against the top of Mikey's head. "I thought I'd be... I wanted to be... Oh, Mikey, I'd hoped I'd be your mother. To care for you. Nurture you. Watch you grow to manhood." She held him for endless minutes, absorbing his baby warmth, his baby scent, the quick, eager heartbeat thumping against her breast. "I love you. I'll always love you."

She needed to go. A quick, decisive end to it before she lost control, altogether. She carried Mikey into the living room. Lucius stood in front of the bank of windows overlooking the city, the light streaming behind him settling on her and the baby, while framing him in darkness. It was a calculated maneuver, one she'd seen him use before. She negated his advantage by crossing to his side and settling the son in the father's arms. Now that she knew the truth, it seemed so obvious. The set of the eyes, the curve of the mouth, that stubborn, authoritative chin, one a miniaturized mirror of the other.

"Before we take this any further I want to know, once and for all, whether you're working with the Ridgeways," Lucius announced, taking immediate charge. Devil Devlin at his most intimidating.

She released a distracted sigh, glancing around for her purse. She spotted it on the couch and retrieved it. Then she walked to the foyer and stabbed the call button for the elevator.

"Where the hell do you think you're going? Don't you even think of walking out on me, Angie." He took a step in her direction, seemed to suddenly realize that holding Mikey in his arms prevented him from physically stopping her. Frustration bloomed across his face. "You aren't leaving until you explain why you did this."

"Actually, Lucius, you should already know why I did this. You asked often enough." The door slid silently open and she stepped into the car. Turning, she pushed one of the buttons on the panel. "You just never listened to my answer."

And with that, the door closed between them.

Lucius glared at the elevator doors. "How am I supposed to hear something she never said?" he demanded of Mikey. "If she thinks this is the end of it, she's about to learn otherwise."

Mikey leaned in the direction of the elevator and held out his arms, making clear his displeasure at Angie's disappearance.

"You and me both," Lucius muttered.

He continued to bore holes through the elevator doors as though they held all the answers to the universe and were deliberately keeping them from him. Ever since the call from Pretorius, Lucius had stewed over what Angie had done, the coast-to-coast flight providing him with all the time in the world to first whip himself into a full-blown, brain-melting, self-righteous rage, before chilling into the sort of bitter cold reserve he'd perfected ever since Lisa's marriage to Geoff. It had been his only defense during that bleak time.

When he and Angie had first made their devil's bargain, somehow, someway, she'd managed to release him from that. How had it happened? *When* had it happened? Without him even being fully aware of it, she'd infiltrated his life, knocking down barriers, easing that long, lean glorious body of hers into every aspect of his world, even the private corners where she didn't belong. He closed his eyes. Where she'd become so damn necessary. Vital. Needed. Oh, *hell.* Where he'd fallen in love with her and slowly—like a tender shoot shoving its way through an earth still half-frozen from winter's barren chill—ever so slowly, come alive again.

Which only made her betrayal all the more cutting. Then he'd arrived home and found her in a wedding dress. God in heaven. She'd been breathtaking. Radiant. And the expression on her face... It had been that of a woman caught in a moment of perfect happiness. Until he'd stolen that moment from her. Until he'd stripped her of the dream the way she'd stripped herself of her wedding gown. And if the sight of her in that gown had threatened to bring him to his knees, it didn't begin to compare to what he'd experienced seeing her in those filmy bits of ivory, barely held together with satin bows of promise. Bows he'd have given anything to untie, one by one by everlasting one.

Frustration welled up inside. "Damn it, if she didn't betray me, why didn't she stay? Why didn't she fight?"

There had to be a reason and the only one he came up with was that he'd been right about her working for the Ridgeways. And yet… Now that he'd had more time to reflect, seen the quiet pain and hurt anger of her response— or lack of response—it simply didn't add up. He blew out a sigh. Mikey glanced up at him and babbled out a question.

"Yeah, we're going after her. And this time we're not leaving until she tells us why she had Jett set her up as my perfect wife. And then there will be bows to untie." He gave Mikey a man-to-man look. "That's a bit like hell to pay, only a lot more fun."

He snatched up Mikey's diaper bag, intent on giving chase and that's when he saw the envelope poking out of one of the zippered pockets, his name neatly scripted across the outside. He instantly recognized Angie's handwriting. Finally. An explanation.

"Let's hear what she has to say for herself." He slid a hip on the arm of the couch, tucked Mikey more securely into the crook of one arm and opened the envelope. It took him almost a full minute to process the information. "Oh, God."

The test results drifted from his grasp and his second arm wrapped solidly around Mikey. Around *his son*. He reached out a trembling hand, stroking it along Mikey's downy cheek, his black gaze locking with an equally black gaze. He had a son. All this time, Mikey was his and he never knew. Never even suspected, not after that initial paternity test. Worst of all, he'd had his son in his life for a full three months and refused to allow himself to get too close, to open himself up to the bond steadily growing between them. And why?

Fear.

Fear of abandonment. Fear of giving himself over to love. Fear of losing control.

Fear of allowing another person in, a person who could hurt him, compromise him emotionally.

He closed his eyes. How close had he come to losing his son? If the Ridgeways had won custody of Mikey would it even have occurred to him to demand a second paternity test? Highly doubtful. If it hadn't been for Angie...

He slowly straightened. Angie. How the bloody hell had she known? And how had she gotten a sample of his DNA to have tested in the first place? If Mikey truly was his son and she'd figured out what no one else had, then it didn't make sense that she was in the employ of the Ridgeways. Nothing made any sense anymore. Only one person possessed the answers he required.

Angie. He needed to find Angie.

It had been an endless night, one in which Angie had gotten next to no sleep. She'd returned home after her fight with Lucius, not quite certain what to do with herself in the little cottage that was her home, and yet, wasn't anymore.

She'd wandered from room to room while minutes ticked into hours and evening transitioned to night. Little by little, she realized Lucius wouldn't come. Night deepened into that still, dense time where hope slipped away while fears gathered and wandered freely. And still he didn't come. Not until dawn chased away the darkness that seemed to have seeped into the walls and furnishings, into the very pores of the house, did Angie finally fall asleep on the couch, curled into a tight ball, an afghan wrapped around her for warmth and comfort.

And that's where he found her.

She woke to Mikey's demanding cry, groggy and confused. "I'll get him," she muttered, her eyes refusing to unglue themselves. What in the world had happened to their bed? It felt like someone had filled it with rocks during the night. She yawned. "Probably needs his diaper changed."

"Not really. I think he just needs his mother."

Dishes rattled nearby and she caught the subtle fragrance of her favorite tea. Memory slammed through her. Lucius. Mikey. The Pretorius Program. Oh, God, their fight. Her eyes popped open, fighting to focus through the blur of a sleepless night and too many tears.

And there was Lucius, crouched beside her, steam wafting from the translucent porcelain cup and saucer he held. Mikey sat at his feet in a carrier, pumping his little arms and legs as though trying to swim through the air in order to reach her.

"What…?" She struggled to get her brain cells to fire. "How…? How did you get in?"

"You left the front door unlocked—an oversight we'll discuss later. So, I made myself at home." He handed her the tea. "Drink."

She'd have refused, just on sheer principle, but the tea smelled too delicious. Plus, if she had a hope in hell of dealing with Lucius, she'd better get some caffeine in her. She took a restorative sip and nearly moaned. Or maybe she did. For some reason, the sound caused Lucius's eyes to flare. Once upon a time she'd have said it was passion. Not anymore. Not considering how they'd parted.

She sat up, painfully aware she only wore a thin night-gown. Great. Just great. Could she be at any more of a dis-advantage? She took another sip of tea before shoving her hair out of her face. And then she forced herself to meet his gaze. He continued to crouch in front of her, which put him far too close for comfort.

"Why are you here, Lucius?" she asked, seizing the of-fense. "If it's to make more accusations—"

"I'm here to apologize."

"And I've already told you…" Wait. What? "Did you say *apologize?*"

"Yes." A smile twitched at the corners of his mouth though he answered gravely enough. "I'm sorry, Angie. I should have trusted you. I should have known that even if you and Jett did put your heads together in order to ma-nipulate the Pretorius Program, it was with the best of in-tentions."

Angie scrubbed trembling hands across her face. "Either I'm dreaming or…" She shook her head, strug-gling to focus through the pain and fatigue. "I can't think of an or," she admitted in a heartbreaking voice.

"You're not dreaming. I'm really here. And I'm really apologizing, most sincerely apologizing."

Tears burned her eyes and throat. "Don't," she begged. "Don't do this to me. Not unless you really mean it. I can't bear—"

The sound of her broken plea proved too much for him and he swept her off the couch and into his arms. He cupped her face, took her mouth in a soft, tender kiss. "I love you. And I'm sorry."

"Sorry you love me?"

He laughed softly. "I can never be sorry for that, regardless of your feelings for me. You gave me my son. A son I'd never have known I possessed if not for you."

"Oh, Lucius." She burrowed against him. "Why didn't you come last night? I hoped you would. I waited and waited and you never showed up."

"I had a stop I needed to make first. It took me longer than expected."

Her head jerked upward. "The Ridgeways?" At his nod, she asked, "How did they take the news?"

"They demanded another DNA test. I agreed, of course. But I could tell they believed me, and it devastated them." His mouth tightened. "It devastated them at first. Then they demanded I reimburse them for all the expenses they'd incurred while taking care of Mikey over the course of the past three months."

"Oh, Lucius."

His eyes went stark. "I wrote them out a check then and there."

She hesitated. "So... What now?"

"Now we talk. Now we're totally honest with one another, starting with... Why did you change the Pretorius Program? Why did you agree to marry me?"

She remained silent. And waited. Hope crept into her heart and took root there, which terrified her. What if she were mistaken? She didn't think she could handle it if he got this part wrong. She didn't have to wait for long.

"You agreed to marry me because you love me."

He made the statement with an absolute certainty that devastated her. She closed her eyes and allowed the words to wash over and through her. To fill her to overflowing. It took three tries to respond. "Yes, Lucius. I agreed to marry you because I love you, and for no other reason. I've loved you almost since I first came to work for you."

"And I've been an ignorant ass almost since you first came to work for me."

She smiled, her smile growing to a grin. "I won't argue with that."

"I'm sorry, Angie. I should have trusted you."

"I did lie to you. And collude with Jett. But I hoped that someday you'd feel what I've felt all this time and realize what I've realized."

"Which is?"

She cupped his face and feathered a kiss across his mouth. "Why, that I'm the perfect woman for you, Lucius Devlin."

He reached into his pocket and removed the engagement ring she'd left behind. Taking her hand in his, he returned it to her finger where it belonged. Where it would remain forevermore. Where soon, he hoped, it would be joined by a wedding band. And then he kissed her, kissed her in a way that left her in no doubt that he loved her. Would always love her. That she was his, just as he was hers. At their feet, Mikey crowed in delight, putting his stamp of approval on the relationship.

When Lucius finally surfaced, he gazed down at her. The shadows were gone, the final barriers fallen. What remained, the love and certainty that solidified there, belonged to her and no one else. Well, except for their son, of course.

"You're wrong, you know. You're not the perfect woman for me," Lucius informed her. "You are, and always will be, more than perfect."

Epilogue

Lucius and Angie married as planned, taking their vows just as the sun set against the snowcapped peaks of the Olympic Mountains.

The bride looked like a princess in an ivory gown studded with Swarovski crystals over delicate undergarments held together with dainty bows the groom looked forward to untying later that evening. She also wore the bridal gift he'd surprised her with—a bracelet, earrings and necklace—and, of course, her engagement ring.

No one present doubted theirs was a love match. If the guests found it strange that the couple promised to love, honor and always be truthful with one another, they dismissed it as a mild and acceptable eccentricity of the very wealthy. Nor did they doubt how much the couple adored the baby the groom held in his arms throughout most of the ceremony, only relieved of his precious burden when the time came to kiss his bride.

And during that first kiss between husband and wife, the fire diamonds she wore seemed to capture the light of the fading sun, sending a blaze of fire shooting through the room, a magical flame filled with love's promise.

Everyone in attendance agreed.

It was all…Utter Perfection.

* * * * *

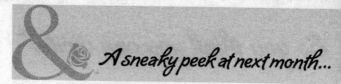

A sneaky peek at next month...

Desire™

PASSIONATE AND DRAMATIC LOVE STORIES

My wish list for next month's titles...

In stores from 19th October 2012:

2 stories in each book - only £5.49!

❏ To Kiss a King – Maureen Child

& The Paternity Promise – Merline Lovelace

❏ More Than He Expected – Andrea Laurence

& An Inconvenient Affair – Catherine Mann

❏ The Reluctant Heiress – Sara Orwig

& A Case of Kiss and Tell – Katherine Garbera

❏ Impossible to Resist & The Maid's Daughter

– Janice Maynard

Available at WHSmith, Tesco, Asda, Eason, Amazon and Apple

Just can't wait?

Visit us Online

You can buy our books online a month before they hit the shops! **www.millsandboon.co.uk**

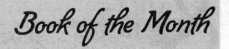

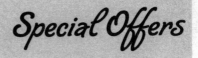
Special Offers

Every month we put together collections and longer reads written by your favourite authors.

Here are some of next month's highlights— and don't miss our fabulous discount online!

Paws, presents & proposals

A Puppy for Christmas

CAROLE MORTIMER · NINA HARRINGTON · MYRNA MACKENZIE

On sale 19th October

A Dance. A Desire. The Time of Her Life.

Strictly Seduction

Lisa Renee Jones

On sale 2nd November

PENNY JORDAN COLLECTION

Christmas nights

OVER 100 MILLION BOOKS SOLD WORLDWIDE

On sale 2nd November

The World of Mills & Boon®

There's a Mills & Boon® series that's perfect for you. We publish ten series and, with new titles every month, you never have to wait long for your favourite to come along.

Blaze®

Scorching hot, sexy reads
4 new stories every month

By Request

Relive the romance with the best of the best
9 new stories every month

Cherish™

Romance to melt the heart every time
12 new stories every month

Desire™

Passionate and dramatic love stories
8 new stories every month